Upper Darby Public Libraries

Sellers/Main
610-789-4440
76 S. State RD

Municipal Branch
610-734-7649
501 Bywood Ave.

Primos Branch
610-622-8091
409 Ashland Ave.

Online renewals:

www.udlibraries.org
my account

Connecting you to literacy,
entertainment, and life-long learning.

THE THREADS OF THE HEART

Carole Martinez

THE THREADS
OF THE HEART

*Translated from the French
by Howard Curtis*

Europa
editions

Europa Editions
214 West 29th Street
New York, N.Y. 10001
www.europaeditions.com
info@europaeditions.com

Copyright © 2007 by Éditions Gallimard, Paris
First Publication 2013 by Europa Editions

Translation by Howard Curtis
Original title: *Le cœur cousu*
Translation copyright © 2012 by Europa Editions

Library of Congress Cataloging in Publication Data is available
ISBN 978-1-60945-087-8

Martinez, Carole
The Threads of the Heart

Book design by Emanuele Ragnisco
www.mekkanografici.com
Cover photo © Caryn Drexl / Arcangel Images

Prepress by Grafica Punto Print—Rome

Printed in the USA

To Françoise Martinez and Laurent Amiot

CONTENTS

THE THREADS
OF THE HEART

PROLOGUE

My name is Soledad.

I was born in this land where bodies dry up, with dead arms incapable of embracing and large, useless hands.

Before my mother found a wall behind which to give birth to me, she swallowed so much sand that it got in my blood.

My skin conceals a long hourglass that can never run dry.

If you stood me naked in the sun and looked through me, you might see the sand endlessly crossing my body.

The crossing

One day, all this sand will have to return to the desert.

When I was born, my mother read my future solitude.

I cannot give, cannot take, never could, never will.

It was written in the palms of my hands, in my stubborn refusal to breathe, to open myself to the tainted air from outside, in my desire to withstand the world that was circling around me like a young dog, trying to enter through every cavity.

Despite my efforts, the air got in, and I screamed.

Up until that point, nothing had succeeded in slowing down my mother's walking. She was a stubborn woman, a woman who had been lost on a gamble, and nothing had been able to overcome her stubbornness. Nothing, not exhaustion, not the sea, not the sands.

Nobody will ever tell us how long our crossing lasted, how many nights these children had to sleep upright, walking behind their mother!

I grew without any attention on her part, clinging to her womb in order not to come out along with all the water she was losing on the road. I struggled to continue the journey, not to interrupt it.

The old Moorish woman who stopped my mother and touched her belly and murmured, "Ahabpsi!" as if raising a wall, and who, armed only with a hand and a word, stood up alone against my mother's fierce desire to continue on her way—heavy as she was with a child long overdue, she was determined to keep walking, even though she had already walked more than was possible and felt incapable of walking any more—the old Arab woman, her hennaed hands redder than the desert, the woman who became for us the end of the world, the end of the journey, our shelter, that woman also read my solitude in my palms, even though she could not read.

Her eyes at once entered my mother's womb and her hands searched for me. She gathered me from deep inside the body where I lay hidden, deep inside that flesh that had forgotten me in order to keep on walking, and, after freeing me of it, she sensed that my hands would be of no use to me, that it was as if I had given up on them at birth.

Without understanding each other, they gave me, each in her own language, the same first name. "Soledad" said my mother, without even looking at me. And, like an echo, the old woman answered, "Wahida."

And neither of these two women could read.

For a long time, my eldest sister, Anita, refused to accept what was written in my hands, written in my name. And she waited. She waited for a man to change my name and for my fingers to relent.

I remember a time when the young men of the Marabout district would linger outside our house in the hope of seeing me pass.

Nonchalantly leaning up against the housefronts, alone or sometimes in groups, they would lie in wait for me in the alleyways and fall silent at my approach.

I wasn't really beautiful, at least not like my sister Clara, but I had, apparently, an unusual grace that pinned them to the walls.

The young men would confide in my sisters, begging them to plead their case, and my sisters would repeat these confidences with a touch of derision, describing to me the ridiculous symptoms of their love, their stammering, their languid looks. And we would laugh.

But then I would think of their erect members straining at their pants, and I would be torn between laughter and disgust.

I had the choice, I had no father to force a marriage on me. Only Anita, the eldest, could have exerted her authority over me.

She never did.

She waited, constantly postponing her own wedding night.

Bound by a promise that had kept her husband from her bed for fifteen years: "We'll marry off all four of them first . . . "

One day, unable to make up my mind which of these unremarkable creatures I should belong to, I dropped the old black shawl bequeathed to me by my mother, and vowed that whoever picked it up I would take for my husband.

It was autumn.

For a time, I stared at that dark patch on the ocher ground, that pool of black fabric lying motionless at my feet.

Then they all came and swooped on it.

Motionless in the noon sun, I waited for the dust to settle again and for a hand to extricate itself from that tangle of suitors. But once the cloud had dispersed, all that remained of my sweethearts was a bit of hair, a few teeth, and long scraps of black cloth left behind in the battle.

The square was empty and the shawl torn to pieces.

With my hands, I scrabbled in the dust of the red desert, searching for the piece of material where my mother's name was embroidered.

Frasquita Carasco.

Mother never learned to write, except with the needle. Every piece of her handiwork bore a word of love embedded in the fabric.

The name was intact. I slipped the scrap of material under my skirt and joined my eldest sister Anita, who was sitting with the other women amid the wet linen.

In the shade of the wash house, the heat dozed.

I stood there for a moment behind my sister, watching her beautiful storyteller's hands waving against the wooden plank, cracking in the soapy water. Suddenly, doubtless sensing my gaze on her back, she turned and smiled at me mechanically, wiping the backs of her hands on the bright apron, dappled with water and light, that she had draped around her waist.

Her companions in the wash house pricked up their ears above their wooden basins. The thumping of the laundry bats became muted, and they even brought out the brushes that rubbed the linen in a long, stifled murmur, stirring the slightly dirty foam.

"I'll never marry," I confessed to her. "I sent my suitors packing."

"And how did you go about that?" she asked with a laugh.

"I dropped my shawl. They fought over it and tore it."

"Your terrible mourning shawl! They'll get you brighter ones. They'll all find the money to buy them or they'll steal them from their sisters."

"Did my son also trail after you?" María yelled as she wrung the collar of a man's shirt, its milky juice trickling down her thick forearms.

"I don't know. They were fighting so hard, all I saw was the dust."

My indifference had offended the women. The rhythmic thumping of the laundry bats resumed, the sheets were beaten more violently in the water, and the pace increased until their arms grew weary and the rhythm was broken.

"Look at her!" Manuela screamed hoarsely. "Another one who takes after her mother! Get your sister married off, Anita! She won't be wiggling her behind in front of anything in pants when she has a man in the house to stop her!"

"It certainly won't be your husband, Anita, who'll give that hussy the thrashing she deserves!" María went on. "A poor lad who's so little of a man, he hasn't even managed to give you a child in fifteen years of marriage!"

"The slut doesn't even have a father, so why is she so fussy?" came a third voice.

My sister laughed heartily. Nothing could mar the joy that had clung to her since her wedding.

The women lost their tempers and accused me of bewitching their sons, their brothers, their fathers, and so on.

Anita was amused at their jealousy. Among the husbands, she knew some who must surely have been involved in that fight. "Take a look at the bruises and marks on the bodies of your men! They'll come home after dark quite ashamed to have had a good thrashing, but clutching a piece of black cloth to their hearts!"

María, the hunchback, came and planted herself in front of my sister, hands on hips. She looked at her from deep within the dark wells that gouged her face. Far down in those depths, something lackluster was trying to shine.

"Your mother's dead, and that's a good thing! You still have the dresses, but one day they'll burn the dresses and shawls she bequeathed you, because they're full of evil spells! They'll tear them from your bodies and if they can't get them off, they'll burn you along with them! The devil won't protect you then!"

"Have you forgotten that wedding dress my mother made you to hide your hump, the dress you haven't even paid for?" my sister retorted. "Without that dress, you'd never have been able to have your son. Because your wedding night was the only time your husband ever mounted you, wasn't it?"

"The devil's dress! It was devoured by moths the day your witch of a mother died. Devoured! I had to throw it on the fire, it was full of worms!"

"Nonsense! Old wives' tales! And you, Manuela, you were heavily pregnant when Juan married you in church. Without my mother, you and he would never have managed to stop tongues wagging! You hadn't left your house for two months because you didn't want people to notice what was growing in your belly and only my mother could make it seem as if you were still a virgin! Without the beautiful wedding dress she'd worn out her eyes making you with pieces of cloth lying around your house, you wouldn't have been able to prevent a scandal!"

"I was concerned with my appearance in those days, I didn't pay attention. But it wasn't Christian to get something like that from little pieces of material. Four years later, when my little boy died, I cried a lot. And then I took out the dress to have a look . . . and took fright. It was all coming to pieces! And the shine on the material that could have been taken for satin had vanished! It was just a lot of soiled dishcloths stuck together!"

The women all started yelling at the same time.

In the midst of the swirling water, the shouting and scream-

ing, the thumping of the laundry bats and the flapping of the
sheets, at the heart of that echoing hysteria where Spanish with
touches of Arabic and Italian was mixed with French, I managed to murmur to my sister what I had been repeating endlessly to myself on the way to the wash house:

"Anita, I want to stay unmarried. You don't have to wait
anymore for the last of your sisters to marry. Go, make your
own children! My mother called me solitude, and I want to live
up to the name. I free you from your promise. I will never
marry."

Anita understood, and from then on I had no more sweethearts.

My youth perished that day, in a death rattle of torn fabric.
It was autumn.

The signs came all at once.

That very evening, I dried up. My skin became cracked and
furrowed. My features sagged, and I knew that I had nothing
more to fear from time.

My face was torn to shreds in one night by the shadow of ·
the years to come. My body shriveled like old paper left in the
sun. I went to sleep with the soft, smooth skin of a twenty-year-
old and awoke in an old woman's body. I became a mother to
my older sisters, a grandmother to my nephews and nieces.

It is almost touching, that ravaged face that comes to you
suddenly, that weary heaviness, those trenches under the eyes,
those traces of a fight lost in your absence, while you slept.

By the end of that night, I was exhausted. But I still recognized myself, recognized that little old lady looking at me in
the mirror and smiling.

I suppose I was also spared the long death agony of the tis-
sues, the little daily deaths, the radiance that gradually fades
away, the slow caress of time.

I mourned my extinguished beauty, I mourned the color

that had gone from my eyes. There was still water left in this great dry body. Tears rushed to fill my hollows. The salt and the season made all the folds red.

You can get used to living in an old woman's body.

If only there were no more trees!

Autumn here bathes whatever it can in blood.

The world has gone on without me. I have watched as all of Anita's children were born and grew up, and I still clutter up her house. I have lived alone, smiling, in the middle of a great crush of nephews and nieces, in a splendid uproar surrounded by desert.

I have waited patiently, knowing there was nothing more to wait for.

I am still afraid of this solitude that came to me at the same time as life, this emptiness that erodes me from within, that swells and spreads like the desert, echoing with dead voices.

My mother made me her living tomb. I contain her as she contained me, and nothing will ever bloom in my belly but her needle.

I will have to go down into the pit, where time twists and turns, where the severed threads are lying.

This morning, I at last opened the box that each of my sisters has opened before me, and in it found a big exercise book, some ink and a pen.

So I waited a while longer. I waited for night to fall and the house to be dark and empty. I waited for the hour when I could at last write.

I sat down in the gloom of the kitchen and lit the oil lamp above the big wooden table. It illumined the carcasses of pans and the old dishcloths and gradually revived the smells of food. I settled at this table and opened my exercise book, smoothing its large, white, slightly rough pages, and the words came.

Tonight the desire to write overwhelmed me.

So here I am, sitting at the table, looking at my nocturnal writing, and I know that this writing will blacken the time I have left, that I will eclipse this great paper sun with the scratching of my pen. I have ink even if I have no more tears. Nothing more to mourn. Nothing more to hope for, except the end of the exercise book. Nothing more to live for, except these nights filled with paper in a deserted kitchen.

Between two of the pages, I have slipped the piece of the shawl with which I used to adorn my shoulders in the days when I had lovers.

The embroidered name releases my mother's scent.

After all these years, it still lingers in the weave of the cloth.

That was all she kept of the crossing, that scar in the smell: the imprint of the fields she walked through, the olive trees at night, the orange trees in blossom, the narcissi carpeting the mountain like white sugar. Odors of stones, dry earth, salt, sand. My mother was made up of so many aromas, all mixed together. When I was a child, as soon as she let me approach, I would travel secretly in her hair, trying to imagine the places contained in those blue locks.

A scent and the flash of a needle in your fingers: that's what they have retained of you.

That smell imbued the fabrics that passed through your hands. The brides kept your perfume on their bodies until the morning after their wedding night.

The rumor soon spread that the dresses made by Frasquita Carasco from the Marabout district worked on men like love potions.

Every honeymoon in the area was filled with your scent. Hundreds of white dresses, as they fell, flooded the bridal chambers with blackbirds and brigands and caves and forests and sands and waves, all torn from our journey. In your time, the sea beat against the wooden beds, while the lovers, tossed about by the current, left knots in their sheets as their only wake.

It seems to me we all emerged from your body of wood. Branches born of you alone. Sometimes, I like to think that your long hands merely caught a few dandelion seeds in passing, and that my father was nothing but seed blowing in the wind, a faint breath in the hollow of your palm.

I must write to you so that you can disappear, so that everything can melt into the desert, so that we can sleep at last, motionless and serene, without fearing that we will lose sight of your figure torn by the wind, the sun and the stones of the road.

Oh, mother, I have to bring a buried world back up from the depths in order to put your name and face and smell on it, in order to lose the needle and forget that longed-for kiss you never gave me!

I must kill you so that I can die . . . at last.

My luminous exercise book will be the great window through which the monsters that haunt us will escape, one by one.

To the desert!

BOOK ONE

One Shore

THE FIRST BLOOD

O n the patio, old Francisca was scrubbing her daughter's shift and sheet in the wooden basin.

Frasquita Carasco, my mother, then a very young girl, stood waiting, naked, on that night at the height of summer, trying with a flannel to stem the blood that was streaking her thighs.

The red-stained water lapped around the old woman's words. "From now on, you will bleed every month. When Holy Week comes, I'll initiate you. Go back to bed now, and don't ruin your other shift!"

Frasquita covered her straw mattress with the hessian sheet her mother had given her and lay down in the silence of the night.

Even though the blood was flowing, she did not feel the slightest pain. Would she still be bleeding when she woke up? What if she emptied completely during her sleep like a cracked pitcher? Her thighs already looked so white . . . She preferred not to sleep, to feel herself die . . .

The dawn shook her. So, she was still alive!

Through her little window, she could already make out the other houses below in Santavela, slightly pink in the timid caress of a new sun that would gradually become more confident. Soon they would have to hold their breaths, live on their reserves of coolness, and remain hidden behind the white-washed stone until late afternoon. Only then would they be able to enjoy the light of the dying sun, to watch it impale itself on a horizon as sharp and dry as a blade and disappear slowly behind the great knife of the mountains, turned blood-red in an enormous death rattle of colors. Then the night would glide from east to west, black, almost moth-eaten in places, and a breath might perhaps come to stir the burning air, a breath laden with wet, salty aromas. The whole village would start to dream of that vast stretch of water, blue from all the skies reflected in it, whose outbursts, rages and beauty had been described to them by the few travelers who had strayed onto the winding lanes that led to Santavela.

Frasquita, my mother, looked at the forest of loose stones and dry trees that surrounded her world and thought how good it was to be alive, even here, and although her blood continued flowing, her only anxiety now was that she might stain herself.

"Don't eat figs or blackberries during your period, it'll show on your face." "Take care not to touch meat during that week, or hair will grow on your chin!" Don't drink this, don't touch that: there was no lack of advice.

Of course, it didn't kill you, but life had been simpler before.

During the eight months that preceded Lent, Frasquita was unable, despite all her efforts, to escape her mother's perceptive eye: her mother could sense the blood coming even before the first drop appeared, and she would immediately come running, brandishing the latest taboos gleaned in the past three weeks from every old hag in the village.

What Frasquita dreaded above all was the first night of her period. Then, without fail, her mother would come into her room in the dead of night, throw a blanket over her shoulders, and lead her to a field of stones where, whatever the season, she would wash her, muttering mysterious prayers as she did so.

And the next day she had to do her share as if everything was normal: wake up at dawn to milk the goats, take the milk to the neighbors, make the bread, do the housework, then set off through the hills with the animals and find them something to graze on in the middle of all those stones. All the while, of course, avoiding eating the best that nature could offer because everything that seemed good in normal times suddenly turned deadly when the blood flowed.

Unlike the other girls she talked to on the hills, who would announce to all and sundry that they were now women, Frasquita hated her new condition: all she could see in it was the inconvenience, and she would happily have stayed a child.

But nobody ever mentioned nightly prayers or initiations during Holy Week. Frasquita had not forgotten her mother's words on the night of the first blood and she sensed that she was to say nothing about it to anyone.

In whom could she have confided anyway?

She was an only daughter. Her mother's family had been decimated by a mysterious illness, along with half the village, and, at the age of forty-five, Francisca, her mother, who had become resigned to the idea that she would never have children, had suddenly, against all expectation, seen her belly swell.

Mother and daughter seemed inseparable, as if bound together by the miracle of that belated birth. For a long time, they had advanced side by side at the same pace along the lanes. At first, Francisca had adjusted her step to her daughter's, then Frasquita's strides had grown much longer until her mother could not keep up and the child had to submit to the limitations of the weary body walking beside her. Young as she was, Frasquita knew she was too frail to withstand the eyes of the village alone, and as for her mother, she had to keep her child by her side or she might have doubted her very existence.

Their bodies would move, driven by the same current, and it was impossible to say which of the two was imposing her movement on the other.

Frasquita did not betray her mother's eccentricities. The questions stayed with her, and accumulated.

From the first day of Lent, the future initiate was fed exclusively on unleavened bread, milk and fruit. She left the house only to attend Sunday mass. The tiny olivewood cross that she clutched in her right hand as soon as she walked out the door of her house and the small angular stones with which her mother decorated her shoes gave her the appearance of a saint.

Thanks to all this ritual and mystery, Frasquita finally got caught up in the game. It was of no consequence to her that the soles of her feet hurt, nor did she mind the closed shutters in her room, or the darkness, or the silence in which her mother shut her away, she was focused on that ultimate goal, that initiation that would make her a woman. She could almost touch it, and she prayed to God and the Virgin with a fervor increased tenfold by fasting and solitude. There were even days when she felt certain that Mary and her Son were present at her side. Overcome with a kind of ecstasy, she would throw herself to her knees, wild-eyed. In those blessed moments when it seemed to her that the room was suddenly filled with their presence, Frasquita would disappear into the prayers she offered up to them with the fervor of a twelve-year-old child who has been starved for several weeks. Entirely contained within those words she had learned, those poems recited and offered, she was nothing more than lips absorbed in something unfathomable.

Then her heart would beat at the same rhythm as the world that suddenly filled her dark little room. It entered in procession through the slits in the shutters, through the cracks in the walls. It spilled into the closed space of the bedroom, gathered in it, pressed in on her from all sides. She felt it beating in her ribcage, throbbing behind her eyelids. First came the sky, with its winds and clouds, then the mountains paraded past, one after the other, like the pearls of a necklace that had been thrown in under her door, then came the high sea, which made the walls warp like blotting paper. The whole of creation would gather around her, within her, and she would become the sky, the mountains and the sea. She would come to the world and the world would come to her.

But then her mother would open the door and everything would disappear.

On the night of Holy Tuesday, Frasquita is asleep, exhausted from too much waiting.

Her mother stands erect in the darkness by her daughter's bed. She throws cooking salt as she chants. There is a strong smell of garlic. Her bony hands move above the young face already swollen with sleep. The dreams flee. The white fingers move over her features. The voice squeals suddenly in the black dryness of the night.

A stillborn cry.

They must not wake father. Silence.

Her mother's gestures become more rapid.

Frasquita is torn between laughter and fear. But she does not laugh, and she follows her mother's small figure out into the night. Barefoot, steps weighed down by the silence. Their shadows follow lightly after them.

They both walk along the path leading to the cemetery. As soon as they are surrounded by graves, Francisca starts praying again. Her voice flows out of her like water, in great gushes. It rises to her mouth and overflows. There is always more to spit out.

A woman screams, and a half-undressed couple who have come there to be out of earshot of the living and enjoy the silence of the dead run off as fast as their legs will carry them. Frasquita shudders as her mother addresses her female ancestors, her voice and language no longer recognizable.

Two black headbands suddenly appear in her mother's empty hands.

"I have to blindfold you now. All the prayers you are about to hear, you will have to remember. They come from before the first book, and are passed down from mother to daughter. They can only be taught during Holy Week. You will have to learn them all, and, in your turn, you will bequeath them to those of your daughters who will show themselves worthy. These prayers cannot be written or thought. They are said aloud. That is the secret. You will accompany some of them with gestures I will teach you later."

Frasquita is blindfolded and her mother makes her turn around several times. She has lost her bearings. The ground falls away. She feels dizzy. Her eyes search for the light. She wants to run away.

Then a voice rises in the night. Not her mother's.

A voice that seems to come from the bowels of the earth, a voice from beyond the grave, a huge voice that whispers, at once close and distant, at once outside Frasquita and beneath her skin, at once clear and muted. She will have to repeat everything. Remember everything. She has only four nights to absorb a body of knowledge that goes back a thousand years.

Terrified, Frasquita does as she is told. In the darkness, she repeats what is whispered to her and the heavy words batter her, imprint themselves on her as she says them.

During that first night, my mother learned by heart prayers to shade the head from the sun, prayers for cut skin, for burned skin, for sick eyes, prayers for warts, prayers to get to sleep, and so on. For every small human misery, there was a prayer.

There were fewer prayers on the second night, and she found them harder to understand, utter and retain. They were prayers to cure people of the evil eye and protect them from spirits, from the white lady, from the creatures of the night.

On the third night, the voice taught her two prayers so complicated, so hermetic, that Frasquita could not even grasp who they were addressed to. She did what she could to utter these inarticulate, almost inexpressible sounds. A mysterious language filled her mouth like a thick substance that she had to chew for a long time. As she said the words, it seemed to her that there was a strange flavor flooding her palate and tickling her taste buds.

These were incantations to make the damned rise like cakes, to build bridges between the worlds, to open graves, to restart what is finished.

Finally, on the last night, the now-familiar voice emerging from the shadows gave her a gift.

"You now know how to cure the small ills of the body with the help of the saints, you know how to free souls with the help of the one who is called Mary here, but who has many other names, and I have taught you to hear the laments and lessons of the dead. But take care! You will have to employ your power sparingly. You will be able to use the prayers of the first night whenever you see fit, but those of the second night, if you do not want to lose them, you will have to use only when a stranger asks for your help and it will be of no advantage to your family. As for the invocations of the third night, those that summon spirits, they can only be used once every hundred years. As soon as you utter one, you will forget it. But beware, appealing to the other world is not without its dangers: the dead are not always benevolent and these last incantations have a will of their own. Remember that there are living words that burn the minds that they possess. I am entrusting you with this box. You must only open it in nine months' time, nine

months to the day, not before. If you do not resist the temptation, you will lose everything I have taught you until now, just
as your mother lost it before you. Farewell."

THE BOX

Even as a child, Frasquita had liked to sit in a corner and sew. It had not taken long for her mother to notice the girl's surprising speed and dexterity with the needle. She laughed to see the child replacing a button or mending a cuff with such extreme meticulousness.

Frasquita had started out by darning the seats of pants, and from one pair of pants to the next the trajectory of the thread had become more confident, the stitches finer, her hand movements faster, and her eye sharper.

During the Lent when she was initiated, she had been deprived of her sewing. That in itself had been a great sacrifice. So, immediately after Easter, she got back to work with renewed ardor.

In her mending, Frasquita had so far tried to imitate the weave of the material, to reconstruct it, and she succeeded so well in this that her work became invisible. Her father would search in vain for some trace of wear and tear on the knees or in the crotch of his pants: his clothes seemed to him brand-new. But after that Holy Week, weary of so much humility, she let her skill shine through increasingly often. Tiny white flowers started appearing on the sheets, and a few birds frolicked unobtrusively on the faultlines, closing the torn lips of the fabrics. White on white, black on black, her repairs were an initiation into embroidery, and little motifs multiplied on her mother's shawls.

Only her work helped Frasquita resist the terrible temptation represented by the box sitting on the ground in a corner of the room.

The massive black cube—made of rough wood but with a surface soft to the touch due to the patina of time—was waiting.

Of course, the centuries had smoothed its corners, but no worm had ever taken the liberty of eating into that dark flesh.

At first, Frasquita would sit down facing the box and look at it for hours on end, trying to melt into its black substance. She soon knew every knot. She would concentrate so hard on the object that she would feel dizzy.

But the box resisted. The box would not give up its secret.

Frasquita could now leave her room whenever she felt like it. She would roam the area with her little flock and, as soon as she returned, help her mother with the housework, then start darning, darning with passion, trying to forget the box.

She thought at first that she would never be able to resist for nine whole months that obsessive desire to open it. Several times, she was on the verge of lifting the lid, which had no lock to guard it. But then she remembered her mother, who had made that mistake before her, and the thought stayed her hand.

On the tenth Sunday after Easter, in the kitchen, Francisca began to teach her the gestures.

"You see, I know the music but I've forgotten the words: I can't recite the prayers, but each of those you have been taught must be accompanied by these gestures I am going to teach you. Today, we will do *carne cortada*. To treat cut flesh, all you will have to do is utter your incantations while performing these gestures you are about to see me perform."

She took two fine white eggs, cracked them against the edge of a bowl, scrambled them, then poured them into a cast-iron cooking pot.

"Take them out of the fire, they're going to burn!" Frasquita cried anxiously.

"They must burn, you see, and once they're quite black, you soak a cloth in olive oil and blacken it with what remains of the eggs. Then with it you draw three crosses on the injured person's cut so that it heals more rapidly."

At that moment, Frasquita, who was watching her mother with great attention, noticed how white her hair had become lately, how withered her hands. She realized that her mother had turned into an old woman.

"Mother, how did you lose the gift?"

"At your age, I received the same box you were given. But three months before the end of the trial, I opened it, thinking that nobody would ever know. The box was empty and I immediately forgot all the prayers I had been taught."

"But if you forgot them, who was it who taught them to me? Wasn't that your voice I heard among the graves?"

"No. When I opened the box, it was as if I was opening my own skull. All the words that had been locked in it a few months earlier escaped at once. I immediately closed the lid again. I only recalled one prayer, one of those from the third night. You heard me recite it in the cemetery. We've lost it for a hundred years."

"Who initiated you?"

"My mother. I'd like to ask you a favor. Hide the box in a safe place!"

"Where should I put it?"

"I have no idea, but hide it! I'm afraid, my child. Of myself. You must take your secret away from here, you must put it somewhere your mother can't get at it. And make sure I don't follow you!"

A man named Heredia ruled over the area. Everything belonged to him, even the smallest stone. Nobody knew how long ago, or in what circumstances, his family had taken possession of these lands so far from the roads of men and the light of heaven. Heredia had left God only the distant blue skies. Perched on their hill, the little white shell-like houses of Santavela were trapped between the sky and the stones. The sky belonged to God and the stones to Señor Heredia, who provided the villagers with their livelihood. Sometimes, people did not know to which of the two to address their prayers.

That very evening, Frasquita reluctantly went and buried her box in Heredia's olive grove.

For the first time, she found herself alone in the countryside at night. She did not recognize the very paths she had been treading forever. The most familiar objects took on unusual shapes in the darkness. She stumbled over every stone, tripped on steps, waved her big arms in the rough shadows. She lost her bearings, surprised by the size of the houses, the shape of the trees. Everything seemed to dissolve slowly in the night: the leaves merged into one another, the windows were holes in the shapeless mass of the housefronts, the outlines of things faded, melted into the gloom, the earth was eating the stones and the sky was eating the earth. The world had become covered in vague patches as dark as holes, and the fringes of a sky all spattered with light and torn by the blade of the mountains descended to the earth. Some fig trees already bristling with big green fruits as round as globes watched her passing in their shadows.

In one hand, she held her father's shovel; in the other, a wicker basket. She was afraid as she advanced along a narrow path that was half-engulfed by the darkness so that it seemed as if pieces had been bitten out of it. A huge moon rose and poured its beautiful, hazy white light over the olive trees, which snapped like fingers.

Frasquita was surprised that the night was so noisy. She

stopped under the biggest tree she could find and started digging. She buried the box quite deep, then closed up the hole
and made a fine heap of the dry earth with her hands. She was
beginning to tame the darkness. She made a careful note of
which olive tree she had entrusted her treasure to. Its trunk,
split in two at its base, merged into one higher up, like two
trees that had grown for a few years side by side before entwin-
ing.

Absorbed in the contemplation of that wooden couple, she
was gradually forgetting her fear when she heard a man's voice
saying a number behind her. She barely had time to hide
behind the trunk she had been looking at. A shadow was coming straight toward her.

The shadow had the face of a handsome young man.

He came to a halt in front of the twin olive trees at the exact
spot where Frasquita had just buried her box and cried at the
top of his voice, "One hundred and ninety-eight!"

Frasquita watched as the handsome young man with the
fine features who had scared her so much strode away. She saw
him stand to attention by the next tree, cry a resounding "One
hundred and ninety-nine!" then set off at full tilt to count the
other olive trees. As soon as he was out of sight, Frasquita
bolted with her shovel and her basket.

She ran to the village without turning around.

When she came level with the first houses, she met the shining eyes of some devil disguised as a cat to scare the field mice
and stopped dead, petrified. Those wild yellow eyes glittered
between heaven and earth, they stared at her for a few seconds,
pinned her to the nocturnal landscape like a common moth,
then turned away, and the supple form jumped from the tree
where it had been perched and vanished into the shadows.
Frasquita recovered her composure, although still not entirely
sure that what she had seen had been only a neighbor's cat, and
started running again. Panting, she opened the little door of

her house, groped her way across the main room, and threw herself on her bed.

The days and weeks passed. Frasquita, terrified by her nocturnal escapade, made no attempt to find again the twinned olive trees in the shadow of which she had buried her treasure.

Her mother, on the other hand, kept finding all kinds of excuses to turn the little house upside down or shift the old stones in the patio. Her curiosity would give her no rest. She was almost driven mad by her desire to solve the mystery of the box.

At last, she went to Frasquita. "That box was given to you in trust, I hope you haven't lost it, I hope you hid it in a safe place. If someone found that box and opened it before us, God alone knows what would happen. Is it still in the house?"

"No, it hasn't been here for a long time. We'll go to find it in three months in the place where it is and nobody will open it before us, have no fear!"

"Did you bury it in the courtyard?"

"Not in the yard and not in the village. It's too far for you ever to discover it without my help."

"Tell me where you put it! I'll go hide it in a place I know where nobody will ever be able to get it away from us."

"It's quite all right where it is."

"How can you mistrust your old mother like that?"

"Mother, whatever will be inside that box when the time fixed by the voice has run out isn't there yet, don't you see that? If you open it today, it will be as empty as it was forty years ago when you made the same mistake. The gift that was promised to me is growing there in the darkness. Give it the time it needs!"

Her mother burst into tears and apologized profusely, but, barely three days later, she resumed her questioning.

After the questions came the orders, and after the orders the blows.

Frasquita let herself be beaten for a whole month. She resisted: nothing could sway her, neither blackmail, nor little treats, nor physical abuse. She remained as silent and impenetrable as the box itself. She became the box, and every day her mother tried in vain to force her lid. Even her father, who rarely got involved in these women's matters, had to intervene several times to stop her mother from killing her.

After thirty days of violence, her mother completely changed attitude. She fell silent and spent her days twisting her long grey hair around her index finger. She stopped eating, stopped combing her hair, did not leave the house. She was letting herself die.

This second phase lasted as long as the first.

At last, one fine morning, having lost a great deal of weight, she had a sudden burst of energy and set off. Talking to herself in a low voice, she started digging holes at random all around the outside of the village.

At this point, the priest came to see young Frasquita.

A city dweller by origin, he was impervious to old wives' tales, and had no time for all the superstitious nonsense that some of his female parishioners, even though very pious, still practiced.

He was a strange priest, who did not care much for punishment, and did not believe in the devil.

"If my prayers run dry, it's because I ate badly at noon, or because it's cold in the church. I'll never hold some imp in clogs responsible for my human failings. Peter denied Jesus because he was afraid. The devil has nothing to do with it! If there is a devil, he's in the minds of men." That was how he liked to talk.

In the pulpit, he never read the passage about the possessed, and none of his sermons mentioned the devil, for what he feared above all was to unleash an epidemic of possessions. Even though his flock did not understand a word of Latin, there was no point adding fuel to the flames. In order not to awaken the devil, the best thing was not to speak about him at all.

He had long fought against these age-old occult beliefs that stirred the souls of which he had the cure, but he had not managed to bring his flock back onto the path of light. He had only silenced them: nobody spoke to him anymore about spells cast or bloody chickens' heads waved over the beds of sick children. He was a man of reason, and they did not say anything for fear of his anger.

When he had heard confessions from Frasquita and her mother after Easter, he had heaved a big sigh and made the two women kneel and pray at the back of the little church for two or three hours, which should have settled matters. But now, seeing that little old lady, all skin and bone, spending her days digging holes with her bare hands–her husband having confiscated his shovel from her–he guessed that this sudden madness was connected with the ridiculous story they had confessed to him a few months earlier, and he went to see Frasquita.

"Frasquita, what is your mother looking for?" he asked her.

"A box," she replied without hesitation.

"And what's in this box?" he insisted.

"We don't know."

"So your mother doesn't know what she's looking for with such determination that it's pitiful seeing her pulling up stones at all hours of the day, her old hands grazed from scratching at the earth?"

"Exactly, she's looking for something she doesn't know, something that doesn't even exist yet."

"You mean to say that, apart from anything else, this box she's obsessed with doesn't even exist?"

"Oh, the box exists, but for the moment it's empty. At least, I assume it is."

"Listen, I don't understand any of this. But you're going to look for that box and give it to your mother before she dies of exhaustion in the middle of a field of stones."

"No."

"I demand it in the name of God!"

Frasquita looked at him and slowly shook her head from side to side.

"You're stubborn, my daughter. Don't you see that your mother's not the only one at risk? If I know the people here, we won't have long to wait before another woman starts making holes everywhere in her turn, and then the men will stop calling your mother a crackpot and make up some good reason for her to be digging. They'll think she saw a treasure in a dream or something like that, work will stop in the olive grove, and they'll turn over that hill with their shovels until it crumbles."

"We don't have much longer to wait. In three weeks, we'll be able to open the box and then my mother will find peace again."

"But in a week, it'll already be too late! Those with vivid imaginations will have made up some cock and bull story, and all these people will have thrown themselves into a futile search. Within a week they'll be beyond help. Take care, Frasquita, you're too stubborn!"

Without another word, the priest walked out, in a rage.

He was proved right. By the very next day her mother was no longer the only person digging. The number of diggers increased day by day, and however often Frasquita told everyone that there was nothing in that box they were looking for, nobody listened to her. The shovels bit into the frozen ground, which was as hard as leathery meat.

Heredia tried in vain to stop this army of men, women and children crisscrossing his lands in search of a hypothetical treasure. Neither his authority, nor that of his sons, nor even their dogs, were capable of combating this dream. They were all in the grip of a fever, and the olives spoiled because nobody was there to harvest them.

Some bored so deep into the earth that they spent several days trapped at the bottom of the ditch they had dug before they were found and released from their prison of loose stones.

There were fallen rocks, fights, frostbite. The women and children pulled up thousands of baskets filled with earth, dust and stones.

After a week of hard labor, it was impossible to take a step without coming close to spraining your ankle or vanishing into a hole. And yet nothing had been found except a few broken pitchers, some fossils and a magnificent bronze mask, clearly very old, depicting a young man of unsettling beauty whose eyes had been angrily hammered out. This antique masterpiece aroused little interest. It was melted down, and the person who had discovered it turned it into jewelry for his wife and daughter. The beautiful young man was transformed into female adornment.

They then started wondering what they had been trying to find for more than a week. They realized that nobody had any idea, and they told each other that Francisca, who was still digging in silence, had a decidedly strange look in her eyes.

Gradually, the village returned to its senses and followed the priest's advice. Men and women went back to work, and only Frasquita's mother persevered.

At last, the time fixed by the voice fell due.

Frasquita waited for the dead of night to drag her mother to Heredia's olive grove, which was white with frost.

It was not difficult for her to locate the split olive tree. The ground had been dug up haphazardly, and these craters that nobody had yet filled in again gave the landscape a lunar appearance.

Frasquita, who had been unable to find her father's shovel, dug patiently with a stone. She soon hit the lid, and was able to extract the box from its straitjacket of cold earth.

Her mother was smiling broadly, as happy as a child, and her eyes ringed with lines shone like two black marbles.

"Go on, open it!"

Her fingers numb with cold, Frasquita lifted the lid.

The box was full of reels of thread of all colors and hundreds of pins stuck in one of those small cushions that seamstresses carry on their wrists instead of bracelets. Fixed to the lid with thin leather straps were a pair of finely worked scissors in a little red velvet casket, a simple thimble and, carefully lined up along a wide blue ribbon, needles of different sizes.

"It's just a sewing box," her mother murmured. "Nothing but a sewing box!"

"Look at these colors! How dull our world seems compared with these threads! Dust ruins everything here and the colors are swallowed by the glare of the sun. What a marvel! Even in the gray light the reels glitter! There must be places full of color, bright and gaudy lands as joyful as the contents of this box."

"I spent days on end digging in search of a common sewing box!"

Her old mother slipped off her woolen scarf, and her silver hair, which she had not brushed in so long, cascaded over her dark shawl. Then she laughed, with a hearty, liberating laugh, she laughed for a long time, glowing suddenly in the night like a second moon. She laughed and her daughter laughed and the two of them rolled on the ground, unconcerned about spoiling their clothes.

At last Francisca lifted herself and sat down beside the olive tree. Her eyes had lost their sickly veneer, the pupils no longer flooded the irises, the lashes no longer quivered around the whites of the eyes like the nostrils of some anxious animal. Her gaze had steadied. Frasquita recognized the calm, velvety gray of eyes no longer troubled by desire. She sensed that her mother was free again.

"It's late. Let's go home!"

THE BUTTERFLY

It was now that the time of colored threads began for my mother.

They had burst into her life, modifying the way she looked at the world.

Until then, there had been few elements of color in her daily life: the oleanders, the passion flowers, the flesh of figs, the oranges, the lemons, the ocher earth of the olive grove, the blue of the sky, the sunsets, the priest's stole, the Virgin's robe, the pious images, the dusty green of the local trees, and a few elusive butterflies. But now, there were so many colors in that box, she did not think it possible there could ever be enough words to describe them. Many shades were totally unknown to her, like that thread so brilliant it seemed to be made of light. She was surprised to see the blue turn green without her being aware, the orange turn red, the pink purple.

Blue, of course, but which blue? The blue of a summer sky at noon, the muted blue of that same sky a few hours later, the dark blue of night before it turns black, the pale, faded blue of the Virgin's robe, and all those unknown blues, strangers to the world, crossbred shades, with a greater or smaller admixture of green or red.

What was expected of her? What was she to do with this new palette the mysterious voice had given her in the night?

Bombard the winter-shrouded village with colors. Embroider multi-colored flowers on the frozen earth. Flood the empty sky with rainbow-hued birds. Daub the houses with color, turn her mother's sallow cheeks and weathered lips a bright shade of pink. She would never have enough thread, never live long enough, to see such a plan through.

She had to make do with the inside of the house.

No cloth on the table, no curtains on the windows, no carpets on the floor, no doilies. No material to embroider.

Sheets, and not even many of them.

"The sheets have to stay white," her mother said.

Two shawls and two mantillas.

"They have to stay black," her mother said.

Some underwear.

"White is cleaner," her mother said.

"What about my skirts and blouses?"

Two sets of clothing in all, which she took turns in wearing. Did she imagine they would let her do what she wanted, that she could trample on the habits of a whole region? They didn't go in for color here! Elsewhere, in other villages on feast days, the girls showed themselves off, so it was said, but not in Santavela! In this part of the world, the women had neither ribbons nor carnations!

"Because nobody ever comes to sell them any," Frasquita argued. "What if I only wore my colors inside our house?"

She would then have only one blouse to go out in, and she would wear it out twice as fast.

"I won't go out so often!"

And during all the time she spent embroidering, would she remain naked? Naked in her room, her needle in her hand?

"I'll wear a shift!"

The flowers and birds in black and white that she had multiplied lately in her darning were one thing. You could only see these fantasies if you looked closely, so closely that her father had not yet seen the fabulous bestiary that populated the seats of his pants. But what a whim it was, this desire of hers for color! They could live perfectly well without it!

"Not me!"

Her mother wept.

"Give me an old sack!" Frasquita insisted.

Her mother found one, so worn and damaged that the only thing Frasquita could get from it was a strip of material a few inches wide.

A spider hung from its thread in a corner of the room, spinning its web.

"Soon, I'll learn to spin and weave."

In the meantime, she looked obstinately at her little piece of hessian, which she had placed on her knees, wondering what she would be able to do with it.

She looked at it for a long time.

It was about this time that Heredia's niece arrived in the area. No elegant woman had been seen there since the death of the señora.

The following Sunday, she would be at mass.

There were more people there than usual, especially men. Spring had come early, it forced its way into the church.

Hungry for color, Frasquita was waiting to see the niece's dress.

But the dullness of everyone's clothes was relegated to the background, not by color, but by immaculate white silk. The white overwhelmed Frasquita as the dress moved forward, deep in the gloom of the nave.

White: my mother would come back to it later.

The wood of the front pew made wide folds in the material.

To understand white, you had first to master the colors, all the colors.

Suddenly, something moved between the fingers in their fine lace gloves, and a scarlet wing unfolded. The wing was beating rapidly, huge and red in that slender hand. Constantly shaking itself, unfolding then shrinking back like a turkey's gullet, the object fascinated Frasquita. Busy trying to grasp the motif embroidered on the red fabric, she did not catch a word of the sermon.

A fan! She would make a fan!

That very afternoon, she took out her piece of hessian and set to work. Cautiously, she first used a scrap of material to invent new stitches and try her hand at color. And as her thread whirled, a butterfly suddenly appeared as if from nowhere and impaled itself on the point of her needle.

There are times when we are out walking and we suddenly stop, forgetting what we are walking toward, and linger at the side of the road, totally absorbed by some detail. A speck on the landscape. A stain on the page. A trifle draws our attention and suddenly scatters us to the four winds, breaks us down before building us up again little by little. Then we continue on our way, and time resumes its course. But something has happened. A butterfly shakes us, makes us stagger, then flies off. Perhaps it takes away with it in its flight a tiny part of ourselves, our long gaze resting on its spread wings. Then, feeling both heavier and lighter, we set off once again.

A ray of sunlight came through the organic stained glass of its wings, warming the orange tones, intensifying the indigo. Frasquita studied these eye-shaped arabesques for a long time against the light. She delicately crucified the insect on the lid of her sewing box, taking great care not to spoil the thin layer of pigment with which the wings were covered.

When she was a child, her mother had explained the magic of their flight. "If you catch a butterfly by the wings, that which allows it to fly will remain on your fingers, and the butterfly will be pinned to the ground."

Perhaps one day she would gather enough of this powder to cover her own wings, the wings she would weave that would allow her to dive off these mountains. But how many butterflies would she have to kill and pin as a bouquet to her sewing box?

A fan was already a little wing. That same needle that had stopped the insect's movements, suspending its flight, now endeavored to reconstruct what it had brought down. Frasquita chose the colors of her threads and, for several weeks, labored to exactly reproduce her butterfly's arabesques.

When the wing was finished, she fixed it to some strips of white wood. Then she waved the fan and in that current of air and color, what had been merely a whim, a fleeting thought, returned to haunt her. Flight.

She decided then to make a second wing, identical to the first, and in that way create an entire butterfly, a butterfly made of fabric. It took her less time to embroider this second fan. She spread the two wings, sewed them side by side, opened the window of her room and waited. She waited for the huge butterfly, placed flat on the floor of the room, to move its colored limbs and fly away. With this aim in mind, she had sprinkled her work with flying powder. The butterfly that had served as her model had been reduced to dust thanks to her, but now what was left had to bring its copy to life.

For several days, the window remained open on the fields of stones. In her innocence, Frasquita did not lose hope. Her creature would go where she herself could not go!

Frasquita's mother never spoke to her about the magnificent thing that her daughter's imagination had pinned to the ground. She had told her that the color was too shameful to live in the light of day, and she could not go back now on what had been said. Yet the embroideries were so beautiful that she could not help taking advantage of Frasquita's absences to show the thing to a number of her neighbors. They went into ecstasies, but did not breathe a word. One old maid in particular, all stooped and wizened, with white hair and skin more furrowed than an old tree trunk, kept asking to see the object. Francisca could not refuse her that favor, and every day the old woman rushed to Frasquita's house as soon as she knew that she had gone out.

One Sunday, returning from mass, Frasquita found her room empty.

Her first creation was fluttering beyond the mountains.

THE NAKED VIRGIN

Frasquita was watching the lacemaker—as she called the spider that had set up home in her room—wondering if she would one day be capable of spinning her own web. "The beauty comes from those empty spaces defined by the threads! To reveal and to hide. To make the world thinner. What's magnificent is to see through it! Transparency . . . The thinness of the web puts a veil around a piece of the universe and in doing so reveals it . . . To display the beauty of a creature by covering it with lace . . . "

She was aware of all the things she still had to understand and master: color, white, fabrics, transparency. Time passed . . .

Holy Week was approaching. Soon, they would bring out the Christ of the Sorrows. Soon, too, the blue Virgen de las Penas would reappear in the streets of the village, soon she would climb on her flowery pedestal and advance above the small Santavela crowds. Her incredibly pale blue dress would make the villagers weep with love and affection, and they would accompany her on her long walk to her son's Calvary.

Every year, the same group of women took care of the blue Virgin, always with the greatest discretion. These women, of whom there were six, enjoyed great credit in the village and insisted on maintaining an air of deep mystery around their task.

Whenever one of them died, the remaining members, after much discussion, would elect her replacement.

The Virgin only appeared twice a year, for Assumption and during Holy Week. The rest of the time the huge figure was nowhere to be seen. Five days before Palm Sunday, the priest had to hand the keys of his church to the six women, who took it over for the duration of the festivities. Then the preparations would begin, and nobody else was allowed to enter the room adjoining the nave. The Six de las Penas, now fully in charge of the place, got down to work in the coolness of the little church, dressing Mary in preparation for the celebrations. The villagers attended mass and came to pray at certain hours of the day, but nobody would have dared go into that room without warning, for fear of seeing the Virgin naked.

The Six were not the only people actively preparing for Holy Week. The bearers of the Virgin, the *costaleros*, ten men chosen from among the sturdiest in Santavela, had resumed their training, accompanied by the penitents of their confraternity. Every night, at an hour when the village was supposed to be asleep, they would meet in the cobbler's workshop, then walk through the streets, practicing lifting the Virgin's empty *paso* and carrying it along as smoothly as possible. Blind beneath the thick curtain that hid them, advancing slowly, the *costaleros* would maneuver the *paso* through the narrow alleys, keeping it upright on the scattered flights of steps, obeying the voices of those who saw the obstacles, and remembering, every spring and every summer, the beating of the drums that set the rhythm for their long walks about the area.

At the other end of Santavela, some twenty men of all ages, the followers of the Christ of Sorrows, gathered in the workshop of a carpenter named Luis. For centuries, this confraternity had served the crucified wooden figure that sat enthroned throughout the year behind the altar and was also taken out into the open air during Holy Week. It took a great deal of courage and practice to hold the great cross steady as it swayed above people's heads in the narrow streets, threatening at any moment to collapse onto its bearers and those pressing noisily around it. To prepare for the festivities, these men, known to be loudmouths, also spent the nights preceding the processions walking through the alleyways in their normal clothes, supporting a huge, empty, crudely-carved cross, of the same weight and size as the one they would carry during Holy Week.

There had been an incomprehensible rivalry between these two confraternities since the dawn of time. The followers of the Virgin despised the bearers of the Christ and vice versa. Quarrels between the two groups were frequent throughout the year, and this tension became even stronger during the preparations for Easter, when the smallest thing could lead to open conflict.

To limit the points of contention, the village had insisted that the leaders of the two groups meet each morning to negotiate the itineraries of that night's practice processions. That way, they could all sleep easily—there was no danger that these men might meet by chance on the way and start breaking each other's heads with crosses. And every night, only the slow steps and heavy breathing of the bearers broke the silence of the streets of Santavela. Or almost every night . . .

In the village, Christ and his sorrow were admired, but everyone maintained a stronger intimacy with the blue Virgin. Her brief appearances made her more precious in the eyes of the faithful. The Virgin wept tears of glass beneath her embroidered canopy, suffering softly amid the flowers. As the *paso* swayed slightly, she seemed to be proceeding by herself above the women who whispered tender words, words of love, to her. As for the men, few of whom regularly attended Sunday mass, they suddenly demonstrated a rare devotion and praised her beauty. Her grief as a mother, her maidenly face and all the blue in which she was draped: these were the things that excited Santavela.

Frasquita's greatest wish was one day to assist the Six of the blue Virgin, but she did not know how to approach these women, walled up as they were in the silence of their devotion. At dawn and dusk, they would advance, radiant and noiseless, one behind the other, dressed in white until the first day of the processions, wreathed in holiness, as if separated, cut off from the prosaic world by that intimacy with the heavenly body of the Virgin. Throughout the preparations and festivities, these few women slept together in an old cave dwelling situated slightly back from the village. The villagers took turns bringing them their meals.

Frasquita was doubtless trying to force fate the night she let herself be locked in the empty church with her sewing box.

That was when she saw the Virgin naked, and she wept for a long time.

What exactly had she been expecting? Something tender, gentle, halfway between a virgin's body and a mother's. The only naked body Frasquita knew was her own: her smooth young skin, her budding breasts that she moistened every night with her fingertips to make them grow, the brown bushes gradually invading her armpits and pubis.

Seeing the Virgin naked should have been a dazzling sight.

Frasquita's parents had been invited to an Easter vigil at their neighbors' house, and she had taken advantage of this to escape. She slipped into the church before the Six left. Then she waited, heart thumping, hidden behind the altar. The women had long since quitted the premises before she dared emerge from her hiding place. She seized a candle the women had left to burn itself out and moved to the room where the Six had been busy for two days now. With the candle she lighted others, and there was soon enough light to allow her to gaze at Her.

It was already dark outside as Frasquita approached the Virgin's pedestal, eyes bowed, feeling both scared and impatient. Then she kneeled in prayer, and slowly raised her head toward Her.

At this point, she heard the rhythmical steps of the bearers of the *paso* as they came down from the upper village and prepared to turn onto the narrow street running along the right-hand side of the church.

Halted in her momentum, Frasquita lowered her head before she had seen anything, and concentrated once again on her prayer so that her gesture should be the purest, most beautiful possible. Nothing should be allowed to spoil this wonderful moment of intimacy. She was not a novice: she had carefully rehearsed her movements in her bedroom and, during each rehearsal, she had been dazzled as she raised her eyes to her imaginary Virgin.

But then a murmur came along the left-hand side of the church: the men carrying the Christ of the Sorrows. The two processions were about to meet on the narrow footpath that wound all the way to the cemetery. Frasquita waited for their encounter, the noises ceased, and in the silence she heard these words:

"Christ is behind schedule, He should have passed the church earlier."

"Not at all," Luis's voice replied immediately in the same tone. "You asked us to slow down when we left the square with the fountain, to let you get down the Santísima steps without problems. But you've got ahead. You must have rushed your genuflections to be here so soon!"

"That's it, go on, provoke us, but at least keep your distance, because you stink of wine! You must have had a good drink before you set off. Every year you upset the rehearsals. Now that we're face to face, the Son has to give way to his Mother!"

"Oh, really? Why? The Son gets to the cemetery before the Mother, everyone knows that. Isn't that so, boys?"

"You simply shouldn't have dawdled on the way here! Now it's too late, they're face to face and the Virgin has to pass!"

Things were gradually getting more heated. Another voice took over from Luis: "And where's your Virgin? Don't you have eyes behind those holes? Your *paso*'s empty and, without the Virgin on board, priority goes to the cross! So get out of here! We have more things to do than this. With all your filthy nonsense, people are going to be coming to their windows in a minute."

"We feel clean, the Virgin is in our hearts."

"Yes, and the cross is on our shoulders, so let us pass!"

"If you don't move back, we'll force our way through!"

Suddenly the cross and the *paso* were thrown to the ground, and Frasquita heard the men rush at each other.

Despite all the precautions, this scene was repeated every year. The two confraternities fought so hard before Holy Week that malicious tongues said this was why none of the penitents showed his face during the festivities and only the *costaleros'* espadrilles could be seen beneath the cloth that fell from the *paso*. Traditionally, the Virgin's men, with their candles and their book of rules, hid beneath high pointed red hoods with holes for the eyes, while the Christ's men had black hoods whose long points fell back over their broad white tunics. Only the musicians who accompanied the processions on brass and drums and the Six de las Penas, dressed in black for the occasion and with tall combs on their heads, advanced with their faces uncovered.

Frasquita knit her brows very hard in order not to hear all the hullaballoo.

Once the quarreling parties were quite exhausted, they set off again in different directions, dragging their feet. When the last curses had faded in the darkness, everything grew calm again.

Frasquita resumed her prayer and raised her large dark eyes.

No body! The Virgin had no body!

The Virgin had no flesh, below her beautiful white face there was a kind of empty shell, normally hidden by her blue robe.

Her chest, her trunk, the lower part of her body: all this was nothing but a vulgar tangle of wood and iron, a mere hollow frame.

For a moment, Frasquita kneeled there, looking up at the motionless skeleton of that pathetic Virgin, that face impaled on a structure of scrap iron, those white forearms attached to the rest of the body by a few steel wires.

So this was the secret so carefully guarded by the Six: the blue Virgin was nothing but a robe and a porcelain mask. Her mystery lay in emptiness and absence, not, as everyone thought, in the unbearable strength of the naked body of a virgin, mother and saint. For the inhabitants of Santavela, the blue Virgin was much more than just an image, she was flesh saved from decomposition by the power of both divine and filial love. That intact body came down every year from her heavenly throne to encourage the living, to give them the strength to worship a Father who had no face.

The Son did not have that power, his body of wood and bread and wine was subject to a thousand transformations and a thousand ills.

But the Virgin did not even have a heart to love her children: that was what Frasquita could not accept.

"There's nothing under her colored clothes," she said indignantly, demoralized by this revelation. "Just as Christ is made of bread, the Virgin is made of iron!"

Locked up in the church with the naked Virgin, Frasquita prayed until morning, refusing to let doubt overwhelm her and looking in her long night's vigil for an answer to this absurdity. When the women opened the door of the little church in the early sunlight, she ran out without any of them even noticing her presence.   •

She had decided to remedy the mistake, to give the Virgin a heart.

She managed to extract enough from that old hessian sack of hers to make a little heart-shaped cushion, and then, using the silkiest threads, embroidered both sides with little stitches. She worked for a long time on a bright red background, and, at the center of this bleeding heart—using that brilliant thread whose name she did not even know—tattooed a resplendent cross with her needle.

Praying all the while, she embroidered until the eve of Palm Sunday, when the Virgin was due to appear before her faithful for the first time that year, and then again let herself be locked in the church overnight.

But this time someone saw her enter and noticed that she did not come out.

The priest smiled as he thought how strong the girl's curiosity must be. Hoping that nobody else apart from him had noticed her, he went straight to bed because the week looked like being a long one.

He was torn when it came to these festivities. His heart swelled at the sight of all the preparations—he loved the pomp of the celebrations, the candles lighting up the night, the drums in the streets, the increased fervor of his parishioners, the wide eyes of the children, and all the prayers he heard rising in unison toward the sky. He even loved the cries of "*Guapa! guapa! guapa!*" that greeted the Virgin that everyone admired so much. At the same time, he dreaded the unreasonable wishes of those he saw dragging themselves on their knees along the stony paths to follow the procession of the Sorrows, he suffered when others flagellated themselves until the blood ran and the wounds they had already inflicted on themselves the day before reopened. Their suppurating backs and knees, their pierced hands and cries of pain struck him as pointless. He feared the clashes between the confraternities and the hysteria that overcame the village. For him, these few days were the longest of the year. These people's bodies, ready for any kind of violence, concerned him more than their souls, and he was constantly on the alert.

This year again, Holy Week unfolded with its usual share of madness and prayers and hopes and weeping and collective hysteria. Christ was led to his death, and the wood of the cross dried and cracked so loudly in the Friday sun that the faithful took fright and fled in all directions. Saturday, designated the day of silence, passed without anyone, even the biggest atheists in the village, uttering a word. And on Sunday, Christ and the Virgin reappeared in the streets, to general acclaim. The resurrection was accompanied with such joy that the whole of Santavela, that dead village, seemed to come alive again. Even nature appeared to revive, shaking itself one last time with some blustery wind as if to rid itself of the last dross of winter.

Having crisscrossed the surrounding area, the blue Virgin and her Son returned to the church when night had fallen and were led to their respective homes. The cross resumed its place behind the altar, and the priest, with a sigh, gave up his keys to the Six, who would undress the Virgin the following day and prepare her for her return to heaven.

The women entered the nave at dawn on Monday.

Eight hours later, a great clamor spread through the village.

A miracle had taken place.

The crowd pressed into the square in front of the church, from which one of the six women responsible for the blue Virgin had emerged a few minutes earlier, calling for the priest and proclaiming a miracle.

A heart had grown inside the Virgin during Holy Week, a heart of blood and light!

However, as nobody was allowed to see the Virgin naked, nobody was actually able to gaze at that heart. The priest himself had to negotiate for a long time before the women would allow him into the church.

He was led into the room where the carcass of the saint had pride of place and, from the doorway, saw with his own eyes, in the very center of that effigy of straw and metal, as if suspended in the air, a magnificent, throbbing red and gold heart.

Father Pablo was not inclined to believe in miracles, but for a moment, faced with that vision, he was speechless. Slowly and respectfully, as if fearing to dispel the mirage, he walked toward the Virgin. When the apparition was within reach, he realized that what throbbed there, sensitive to the least breath of air, was an embroidered heart, attached to the skeleton by a network of colored threads.

The Virgin's face seemed lit up with a new joy, it almost came to life in the glow of what was moving in her breast.

The women around him were chanting their prayers, and the little heart appeared to be beating to the same rhythm.

Then the priest remembered Frasquita. He swayed slightly and managed to tear himself away from the contemplation of that vibrant Virgin. He said nothing to the six women, who were praying flat on their stomachs on the cold stone, and walked outside. Ignoring the crowd of villagers he found kneeling around his church, bare-headed in the sun, he went straight to Frasquita's house.

The two of them walked side by side for a while on the path that led to Heredia's olive grove until the priest at last broke his silence.

"Frasquita," he said softly, "I saw you enter the church on the evening of Palm Sunday, but I didn't see you come out."

Caught out, Frasquita blushed, hesitated a moment, then confessed in a whisper, "I spent the night there."

"Did you see the Virgin naked?"

She raised her big black eyes and gave him such an innocent look that she suddenly appeared much younger. He needed to understand this mystery for himself, to know where this child had found the heart.

"Yes, I saw the Virgin naked, but not that night. The Six had already clothed her. It wasn't the first night I'd spent by her side."

"Do you have anything to do with what's been attached to the body?" he asked, as gently as he could.

"The heart? Yes, it's pretty, isn't it? Do you think it gives her pleasure that I embroidered it for her?"

"So it was you who made that heart?"

"Yes, I don't understand why nobody did it before. She was so empty. Was it men who tore out her heart?"

For a moment, the father was rendered speechless by Frasquita's innocence, as well as her talent, then, yielding to panic, he lost his temper. "But don't you realize the whole village is saying it's a miracle?"

Frasquita said nothing. She had lowered her eyes, and the priest became aware that she was weeping.

"Those six poor women," he nevertheless went on, "have almost fainted. They're lying flat on their stomachs around your handiwork. This is the second time you've driven the village mad. How do you manage to deceive people like that?"

"I didn't mean to deceive anybody," Frasquita sobbed. "I was only trying to give her a present."

The father regained his self-control, breathed in a few times, took a dozen steps along the path, then came back to the girl, who was still in tears.

"You've put me in a difficult position. I don't know whose side to take."

The embroidered heart came back into his mind, dazzling him. He looked at the girl with her reddened eyes, stroked her hair, and clasped her to him.

"Your gift to the Virgin is magnificent, how could we refuse her such a marvel?"

Frasquita sobbed even more as the priest cradled her gently to calm her. When the crisis was over, he ventured one last question. "Where did you get that golden thread?" And as she seemed not to understand, he specified, "That thread that's so shiny, where is it from?"

"From my sewing box, the one my mother was looking for, do you remember?"

"Do I remember? I still can't pray while walking without nearly twisting my ankle in one of those blasted holes. Well, we won't say anything, we'll let them believe what they want, but promise me to hold your tongue and never boast of your needlework!"

Frasquita promised, with a smile, and the priest walked away, confident that the little seamstress would not say a word to anyone about her work.

After all, there was something quite miraculous about the story. The villagers were not really wrong to believe in a miracle. The good father tried to see the Virgin's little heart one last time, but the six women slammed the door in his face.

How sweet it was to turn a blind eye for a moment and believe in miracles!

But this blindness could not long withstand the assaults of his reason! His faith—that faith that abandoned him sometimes and that he had to regain through prayer—was of another caliber! No, God's signs were not so simple, so easily decipherable! This was nothing but childishness, the whim of a particularly sensitive and talented young soul. Perhaps he would give her his threadbare old stole to mend. She would surely be capable of performing another little miracle and restoring its lost luster.

Last but not least, the priest vowed to bring back for Frasquita some of the worms that secreted that brilliant thread, which was called silk, the next time he went to the city.

*

The little embroidered heart haunted him his whole life, coming back to him in moments of anguish. Whenever his soul was gripped by doubt, the Virgin's transparent body veined with colored threads and her offered heart crossed his mind, and the obvious beauty of the image would reassure him.

The wedding dress

S oon my mother was of marrying age.
She must have been sixteen when they talked to her
about the wheelwright's son.

After the death of his father, he had taken over the business.
He was a hard worker who rarely left the house and was completely devoted to his mother. A good son often makes a good husband!

They told her his name: José Carasco.

Discreetly, he was pointed out to her in church: a handsome moon face burned by the fire of his forge.

They went to his house to meet his mother, who would be wearing mourning for her dead husband until her own dying day.

The Carasco residence was large and dark: the doors and windows had been walled up after the father's death. For almost ten years, the wind had not entered the building.

They made their way through the dense air that was stagnant with old sorrows and sat down in the gloom around the kitchen table. Gradually, daughter and mother managed to forget the stench of memories and the ten years of burned fat enclosed in the house.

José did not appear, but they spoke . . . or rather, Frasquita's mother spoke. Señora Carasco was almost mute, merely spitting out the occasional sound. As for Frasquita herself, she sat quietly like a good girl and said nothing: her marriage was of no concern to her . . .

But as she and her mother walked away after the meeting, their eyes hurt by the light outside, Frasquita could hear loud hammering.

It came from the forge adjoining the Carasco residence. She imagined the arm at the end of the hammer and the man at the end of the arm, and something drowned inside her.

From that point, her body urged her to marry.

The negotiations were lengthy. Of course the girl had no money, but she was an only child, and what little her parents owned would revert to her when they died. But until that happened, the dowry struck old Señora Carasco as quite meager.

In church, although José sat some way behind her, Frasquita could feel his breath on the back of her neck. Their eyes met a dozen times before the engagement, always as she returned to her pew to kneel, a half-dissolved Christ in her mouth.

One Sunday, her mother intercepted these glances and, when they got back home, slapped her, screaming, "You should have eyes only for the priest!"

"Why?" asked the future bride.

"Because he wears skirts," Francisca continued, in tears. "If anyone notices your little game, they'll say you're an easy girl, that you open your legs for money, and then nobody will want to have anything to do with you. Think of big Lucia and how all the men have her in the bushes, whether she wants it or not, and all because she was seen turning around during the mass to look at the man she'd been betrothed to. You may think he forgave her, and he certainly gives her a tumble whenever he meets her, but he married someone else."

Frasquita would have liked her mother to tell her more about the lovely Lucia whom the village had destroyed, and about what she did in the bushes with men, and about her own future wedding night. But she knew that her mother would not answer any of her questions.

As married women did not come back to the hills to tell true from false in the shepherdesses' stories, and as nobody spoke to the easy girls, a man's sexual organ took on all kinds of forms in the younger women's minds.

It was much talked about, and Frasquita would sit on her heels in a corner and listen in silence.

"I have something between my legs that I don't know and that only my husband will allow me to discover," she concluded. "Anyway, all you have to do is look at the animals."

When the south wind blew, the hammer blows would take her unawares in her room and strike her full in the chest. Then she would imagine that big male body she had been promised. She felt burning hands twisting the damp wood, pressing against her body, bending it beneath their yoke, forcing it to make itself a circle, to become a wheel so perfect it would not break on any stone. She struggled at first in the grip of those firm palms, then abandoned herself to their power and her damp flesh opened.

She had to take care not to disappear, not to be absorbed by her own desire. It was then that she was given the old dress her aunts on her father's side had worn on their wedding days.

One windless morning, one of those mornings when, even listening hard and holding her breath, Frasquita could not hear the man at work in his forge, she was wandering in the silence of the patio, trying to recreate within herself the hammering she now confused with her own heartbeat, when one of her cousins paid her a visit, carrying the little dress over her forearms, folded and motionless.

Frasquita would be the latest to wear it.

This tight dress had confined the bodies of all the women in her family at the very moment those bodies had ceased to belong to them.

Of course, it had symbolized virginity for so long that the

colors had faded and the material had become threadbare. But there was nothing else to give her. The dress was hers now. She could take her time: the date of the wedding had not yet been fixed. José wanted her, and if old Señora Carasco still resisted it was only to keep him under her thumb for a little while longer and get what she could from the girl's parents. She had already made them give up all they had. She would have to make up her mind soon. Frasquita would leave them in this dress.

That said, the cousin unfolded the dull little dress—not without that touch of solemnity that gives weight to things—and held it up against Frasquita's long body. The skirt was too short, creased and stiffened by the years. The visitor let out a slight sigh and, suddenly in a hurry to be rid of the gray thing, abruptly handed it over to Frasquita.

"Here, see what you can do with it, you'll look wonderful, I'm sure!"

The future bride thanked her cousin sincerely and immediately disappeared, taking the horrible little rag with her into her bedroom. From the main room, she could be heard yelling for joy.

"Is it her coming marriage that's making her so happy?" asked the visitor in surprise. "The Carascos are tough customers, though. True, the boy's a hard worker, but I've never seen him smile. As for his old bag of a mother, she gives me the shivers! Always wants to run the whole show. I'm not sure your poor little girl will carve out a place for herself in a family like that, at least not until the old girl croaks. And the bitch looks like she'll be hanging on for a while!"

"They have property and they want our daughter," replied Francisca sheepishly.

"Well, it's up to you, but I'm not convinced. Frasquita's too young and too soft-hearted to defend herself against an old dragon like that."

"We're getting old, her father's relieved to know she'll be married," concluded Francisca, embarrassed by this conversation.

As soon as the cousin had left, she went to her daughter's bedroom. Frasquita had spread the dress and was smoothing the creases with the flat of her hand, as if caressing a beloved body.

"You're very jolly," her mother observed.

"That's because I'll soon be getting married in the most beautiful dress that's ever been seen."

"We didn't give you any choice in the matter because we didn't have any choice ourselves. But we can wait a bit longer, put off the wedding till later, if you want."

"Oh, no, I'm in such a hurry! I feel ready to belong to José, ready to give him children!"

"Then my mind's at rest," said Francisca in a low voice and left the room.

Frasquita took her time. She carefuly examined that little dress soiled by the weddings of forgotten forebears, that dress that so many young women had lengthened or shortened or widened in order to get their virginal bodies into it.

After several days, she made up her mind to get going, to at last tackle this garment that had been yellowed by years locked in a chest. She took it outside and immersed it in baths of herbs and salt. She laid it out in the sun and left it to spend nights under the stars, soaking up the moonlight and the dew, until she had obtained a fabric of great softness, which she then worked on for days on end with her needle.

Nobody ever disovered how she went about it. Some said she managed, in defiance of biblical interdicts, in defiance of the laws of nature, to join together what the Almighty had separated; others, that she raised silkworms, which the priest had brought her back from Granada along with the plant they fed on.

Frasquita broke free of her mother like a ripe fruit falling from the tree. Alone, she scoured the lanes around the village in search of the beauties they might conceal, unearthing them in the most preposterous places and extracting them in order to incorporate them into her dress.

She tried to get thread from whatever she came across. If she had been able to wait longer for her wedding, the whole world would have unraveled beneath her fingers. She would have diluted everything in order to draw out the sap, the substance she could then spin. The landscape and its hills, that luminous springtime, the wings of the butterflies, all the flowers that lived between the stones, the stones themselves, the Heredias' olive grove: all would have been reduced to thread. God himself would have squirmed, impaled on the end of her spindle.

Everything would have gone into her dress: the roads, the towns she had never seen and the distant sea, all the sheep in Spain, all the books, all the words and the people who read them, the cats, the donkeys, all would have succumbed to her mania for weaving.

Nothing seemed to her too lowly, too absurd, too despicable, nothing in her eyes was unworthy to be spun. She picked nettles and fig leaves and olive tree branches and kept them at the bottom of a tub full of water, weighed down, until the fibres became detached from one another, then softened them by beating them wet against a stone. She explored every possible combination, mixing the threads of silk that she drew skillfully from its cocoons with more ordinary threads in order to enhance their brightness by way of contrast. She managed to extract the best from the material. Her spindle in her hand at all times, she created strange threads, more or less solid, more or less shiny, more or less fine, transforming her bedroom into a butterfly house, full of beating wings and leaves of white mulberry—she could not make up her mind to scald all the cocoons before the butterflies flew away. She soaked then baked everything that the area around the village offered her as vegetable life. She ended up creating fibers that gave off such a smell as they dried that the baker refused after a while to let her use his oven.

Her parents, busy with their own tasks, paid little attention to these marvels. They let her soak, dry, beat, spin, weave, cut, sew and embroider to her heart's content. They did not ask her any questions and refused her nothing, although they did weary a little of the butterflies and the lengths of cloth constantly flapping behind the house. They had decided that, as far as needles and clothes were concerned, she would have complete freedom from now on.

By the end of the process, Frasquita had mastered stitching and threading and webbing and lacework, discovered where to leave gaps, how to use openwork, how to layer, how to reveal the white satin lining beneath strips embroidered a different white.

From that little grey dress, Frasquita produced a gorgeous corolla of white material. The way it was cut and embroidered, the way other fabrics had been added to it, transcended the paltry garment that had witnessed a century of consummated marriages.

Her dress was ready, but her parents had not yet fixed the date of the wedding.

She was starting to find the waiting unbearable, and she made up her mind to ask her father, even though he was someone she never spoke to directly.

"You mustn't question me!" he roared, with all the gravity of a peasant who cannot utter the name of God without accompanying it with a solemn gesture. "And my God, when you're married, you won't be able to question your husband either. You'll only be able to speak if he wishes it and look at him if he looks at you."

But the question seemed to bear fruit, for a few days later her mother gave Frasquita five pieces of thread and said, "Make them into sheets with flaps!"

Her wedding was finally going to take place and she spent her remaining weeks as a girl embroidering her dreams on her meager trousseau.

On the day of the wedding, she set off before dawn in search of white flowers and plundered the Heredias' rose garden. There, she came across Lucia in her sequined dress, gaily dancing, with her hair loose, to the sound of her accordion. Frasquita greeted her with a sincerity that surprised her, then ran off bare-legged, her lifted skirts heavy with hundreds of still sleeping flowers, which, once in her room, she stitched onto her bodice.

Her mother was not allowed to help her get dressed.

She sat on a bench in the big room downstairs, waiting to see her daughter's dress, convinced in advance of its beauty, certain that she would once again be witnessing a miracle. Her metallic eyes sizzled as if they had been plunged white-hot into cold water. But, apart from her eyes and the red rooster embroidered on the fan that her daughter had given her for the occasion, the rest of her body was perfectly still.

Frasquita had never tried on her dress before today. Getting ready by herself, she slipped it on like a new skin. Then she looked at herself in a borrowed piece of mirror. All she could see in it were fragments of herself. But each of the fragments she discovered appeared to her more gorgeous than the last. She pulled up her dark hair, braided it with threads of white and ocher silk and hooked to the tall comb in her bun a magnificent veil of dazzling lace, as fine as a spider's web. The veil cascaded to the floor, flowing, alive, animated by the interplay of light and shade. In the mirror, every loop, every element of the masterpiece seemed to have its place. She saw her deep eyes, so black in all that white, she saw her full lips for the first time. She even surprised a delightful smile she did not know she had. She was afraid at first, so strange did the image seem to her, and it took her some time to familiarize herself with this woman who was about to get married. She walked around the room several times until she had accepted her own appearance.

When she opened her bedroom door, her mother was not surprised, but did not dare kiss her for fear of creasing the material. She let her eyes wander, trying to restrain their ardor in order not to spoil that magnificent white creation, calmly inspecting every flower, every stitch, every pleat, but keeping away from the silk veil or the embroidery around the neckline.

At last, Frasquita crossed the patio and appeared on the threshold, and the cortege of women waiting to escort her through the streets to the little church froze. The only sound was the wind in the veils. Frasquita outshone even the blue Virgen de las Penas.

The villagers immediately knew that a woman had taken shape amid these scrolls of white cloth. They sensed from her walk, the way she had of swaying in the light, the breadth of her movements, the unusual purity of her gestures, that her body was becoming conscious of its own capabilities. The village took offence at the sight of her advancing like that, as if straining at its limits, crying out within its walls.

What made her so striking was the way the dress perfectly matched her figure, so that all at once she was filling the emptiness in which up until then she had lain huddled.

At first, the looks they gave her were not enough to destroy this new creature appearing for the first time in the full light of day. Her confidence held out, she did not seem affected by all these eyes in orbit around her or by the movement of the crowd, which instinctively drew together to confront her. She cut through it without slowing down and the two halves of that vast mass shrank back in silence on either side of her, then reformed noisily behind her. In her wake, she left a trail of unrest and simmering violence.

The wake swelled like a wave.

She crossed the village, climbing and descending the stone steps, pushing the shadows back into the houses whenever the narrowness of the alleyways did not allow her dress to spread and show what it was capable of. The edges of it licked the walls, and the barriers melted, the stones buckled like blotting paper.

It was as if a raging tide was pouring onto the streets. And beneath the caress of that soft, perfectly white garment, the sun shimmered between her long bare thighs.

In a patch of shadow, a few sequins sparkled. The lovely Lucia, who never missed a wedding, had joined the party. She alone was delighted by the scene, nothing escaped her.

Frasquita's parents, walking behind the bride toward the little church, were gradually engulfed by the flood.

They were torn to pieces.

Everyone was looking for a way out, a way to put an end to this scandal, there was agonized speculation, there were grimaces of anger. Faces turned uglier, more on edge than ever. Arms and legs trembled. Bodies became agitated. Mouths twisted, bile was spewed. It was not right, seeing such a monstrous train behind the girl. As the fabric rustled, the down on her arms stood on end.

Her mother-in-law was drawn aside.

"I thought you said your son was gaining nothing by marrying young Frasquita? How can you not have a dowry when you wear a dress like that? You got a bad deal. You've ended up with a penniless princess, all their money has gone on her appearance. Her father must have been smuggling the

Heredias' wine for years to give her something like that to wear."

There was more wagging of tongues from the shadows. That gorgeous dress would soon be creased, they said. The family needed to be cut down to size.

And then suddenly, people emerged from doorways and spat in the bride's face. They refused to believe that this miracle had been achieved with needle and thread by the bride herself. The wedding was nearly spoiled.

At this point, Frasquita gave up.

She had not yet turned, intoxicated as she was by the movement of the fabric. For a while everyone had been overshadowed by that silken splendor, but now, as soon as the first person spat at her, she realized that all the beauty of this part of the world had flowed into her dress, that she had stripped the countryside of its small, scattered splendors and concentrated them all in this one piece of work. The balance of the world had been altered. Ugliness throbbed all around her, the village was sad and bare, the hill gray, there was not a trace of color on the women's cheeks, not a single eye glittered, the sun shone only on her.

The priest, who was waiting for her in the gloom of the nave, was equally stern-faced: hadn't she filched a piece of the stole he had entrusted to her?

She heard Señora Carasco demand a larger dowry, she realized that her old father was going to get into a fight on the steps of the church.

So she yielded to the looks of the crowd, she let them alter her beauty. Little by little, she held herself less erect, began to tarnish and flake.

Her whole being became concentrated in her closed fists. The turbulent beating of her heart withdrew into her fingers and she clenched her fists so hard that she thought at first that she would never be able to open them again. No more fingers, no more hands, no more needles, no more rings, never again. Hidden in the folds of her dress, her hands had closed once and for all after waiting for everything that was trembling inside her to take refuge there.

The lovely Lucia slipped away, there were no more smiles in the shadows.

Frasquita understood that day that her virtuosity could not serve her as an adornment, and the roses stitched to her bodice faded one by one, ruining the line of her dress.

As the blossoms died, the bride became less beautiful, the families were reconciled, and they were able to enter the church, to pray, to drink and to dance.

My mother did not try to pick the bowed little heads, the petals turned brown, she let them sadden her masterpiece.

Nobody knew, this time, that beneath each of the withered flowers was a magnificent embroidered rose.

The bride floated all day in a scent of dead flowers, midnight had sounded somewhere and the dress had wilted.

"Look!" cried a child. "The bride looks like a faded flower!"

They all turned toward the bride they had quickly forgotten in the midst of the party, and a huge laugh, a splendid powerful collective laugh, a laugh such as the village had never before known, broke over my mother's body.

No strong tide now, nothing but this roar, this big wave of dirty water.

My mother fell back, reeling.

To the sound of laughter, the young couple was accompanied to the wedding chamber, and then everyone staggered off to see the wine and the night through to the end.

The laughter took years to die. It would reappear from time to time like a fire that has not been completely extinguished. It was easily recognizable, it could arise at any moment in the throat of an old woman who suddenly, for no reason, uncovered her loose teeth. It always found an echo in neighboring throats. The laughter was as infectious as certain kinds of colic, the most serious kinds, the kinds where the contagion spreads by contact, and the faces burst open like grenades. There were always a few seeds of it in the air, ready to germinate in someone's mouth. Sporadically, the village was shaken by an outburst of it, and they all laughed heartily at the woman who had married in white and had faded on her wedding day.

They even made a song out of it.

Honeymoon

My mother watched the heavy white dress fall at her feet, then bent to gather it up from the floor.

On the other side of the screen, the man was waiting, his body languid in the nocturnal heat of the bedroom.

She shivered behind her thin rampart of wood and fabric. A long shudder stirred the painted flowers.

An accordion tune coming out of the darkness, a wedding present from an easy girl, shook her senses.

She appeared at last in her shift. Her thick supple hair framed her attentive face with ebony. The man lying on the bed motioned to her . . .

He entered her all at once, without saying a word, without waiting.

In anticipation of this first night, she had embroidered their initials on the sheet, but the material of the sheet was rough and now it irritated her skin as the man moved above her in a brusque in-and-out motion, crushing her. He clung angrily to her, brutally parted her thighs, squeezed her breasts so hard that she had to bite her tongue to stop herself crying out. He became more of a stranger to her than he had been before their engagement, when he had watched her during mass and she had stopped herself out of modesty from responding to his glances, feeling their weight hanging on her lips, her breasts, her hips.

He was sinking into her without even looking at her.

It did not take long. With a last squeal, he collapsed, then withdrew and moved away from the body he had just split down the middle.

Her legs spread, her shift pulled up to her shoulders, my mother lay motionless, exposed, waiting for something else to happen. She listened to her nerve ends and explored her flayed skin to see if she could detect in it any of the pleasure she had promised her body when she had agreed to the contract. The man, lively and talkative during the party, now lay silently by her side, with not a single inch of his skin touching her body. The heavy mass of my mother's hair, spread over the two bodies, covered a third of the bed in bluish shadows.

She did not dare free her long silky locks.

The accordion had fallen silent.

It struck her that she would have to learn to enjoy her husband's lovemaking, that, being a novice at such games, she was not entitled to expect more from this first night. So she gently pushed away his drowsy body, pulled her hair toward her, and braided it just as she did every night. After all, her husband had done his conjugal duty: the thin trickle of blood between her thighs bore witness to that.

She emptied the pitcher of cold water into the earthenware basin, savoring the sound of it falling in the silence of her wedding night, and washed herself more gently than she had ever done before.

The next day at dawn, her husband rose without seeing her. Frasquita was left alone.

She knew that she was a stranger in this wooden bed. The objects, the furniture, everything here stared at her. She gathered herself in the softness of the bed, searching for the imprint of her body. But all she found in the stained sheets was the hollow left by her husband's big body and the marks of other people's sleep, other people's lovemaking, stranger still.

The hole she had come to fill was not her size. Too small, too twisted. A wedding night does not have enough weight to leave a mark on things. The objects resisted her presence, refused to bend to her shape. Frasquita realized that in the long run it would be the bed that molded her.

José had already gone to his forge. His hammer marked the time in this place. The wind was of no consequence now, the whole building throbbed to the wheelwright's hammer blows as my mother took her first steps in the lair of the Carascos.

Her mother-in-law was waiting for her. Without a word, she showed her where everything was: the two big closets where the sheets were kept, the stock of candles, the table where they took the meals and where the body of her late father-in-law had been displayed, the chair where she could sit when her day allowed her the time, sit and darn, her chair, her place.

Little by little, the old woman's silence put an end to any tears there might have been on that first morning, and the women set to work.

Señora Carasco hardly, if ever, spoke.

Inaudible grunts, swallowed words, words torn to pieces, eviscerated, long chewed over, then spat out again like old tobacco. Black, full of saliva, half digested. The old woman spoke as if spitting. She tortured her tongue, twisted it like an old cloth to adapt it to her toothless mouth. There was a trickle of dirty dribble each time she uttered a sentences, the sounds were like gruel, and yet she never repeated anything. Frasquita obeyed these mangled words, accepted the authority of that shapeless tongue. As a daughter-in-law, it was up to her to grasp these fragments of speech.

The old woman spoke as if out of hatred.

The son, not much given to speaking himself, responded immediately to his mother's demands. He submitted to that empty mouth, those steely lips as thin as blades, sharpened by the years, that atrophied tongue. He never flinched, never questioned, never refused.

Señora Carasco's body matched her grunts. Ruined, twisted, and dry.

She still dressed in black, but the doors and windows of the house had been cleared to signify the end of mourning. The sunlight, entering the house once again, emphasized the traces left by ten years of gloom.

The two women whitewashed the walls of the main room to revive its faded sheen.

At noon, when the sun beat down, large areas of brightness entered the building through its open pores: the windows and doors. The whitewashed walls made the room seem rounder, the angles vanished in the glare of the whitewash, and Frasquita was swallowed by this house whose entrails she was lining while her own entrails were secretly being lined with the milky whiteness of my eldest sister, Anita.

At last refreshed, the house closed once more to protect itself from the heat and Frasquita again heard the wood echo to the wheelwright's blows.

She put her chair—those few inches of wood that the Carascos had allowed her—beneath the largest of the windows in the spotless room and sat down with a piece of cloth on her knees, the only unfinished piece from her trousseau.

She opened her sewing box. The reels with their shimmering colors made the white screen of the walls seem iridescent.

The threads were so numerous, their hues so bright and varied, that for a moment the old woman took that simple wooden case for a jewel box. Frasquita unfolded the cloth, stretched her long arms, and the fabric fell to the ground like wings in a current of hot air.

Surprisingly, Señora Carasco did not approach her. She

remained seated at the other end of the room, watching in silence as her daughter-in-law embroidered.

Frasquita worked carefuly, her fingers handled the rough material with a consideration, a deference, a grace that seam-stresses usually reserve for silk, satin, or brocade. Her hands caressed the linen, as if exploring a skin, enjoying the thickness of its texture. Then the thread traced its broad scrolls in the saturated late summer air, colored lines played over the white walls, the needle glittered for a moment in the sun before plunging into the thickness of the material, leaving nothing in its wake but a thin coloured stitch, a tiny patch that gradually spread and overcame the paleness of the cloth.

When her daughter-in-law embroidered, Señora Carasco withdrew into herself so that the shadow of the hand, the shadow of the needle should never break against her own dessicated shadow.

With a simple needle, my mother had breached the fortress.

Several times, dazzled by this marvel, the old woman—surreptitiously, without saying a word—gave Frasquita pieces of cloth. These gifts were the only ones that Señora Carasco ever gave her, for, against all expectation, her daughter-in-law was her one pride. Frasquita, her nose buried in her work, did not notice the overjoyed look on the old woman's face when a road beneath a twilit sky appeared on the linen, all in blue thread. Nor did she ever see that smile that revealed an empty mouth, a terrible toothless hole (who still thinks that only teeth can scare children?).

In contact with such beauty, Señora Carasco was softening day by day. If it had not been too late, she might have learned to speak again.

But Frasquita, whose eyes were constantly searching out the door, the window or the flat surface of her tirelessly embroidered flag, began to turn her gaze inward. When she felt the movements of the child growing in her belly, she abandoned her work, whose beauty had softened the old woman's heart, and spent her days listening out for this mystery within her, trying to capture its thoughts. From the first movement it made, she talked to the child, she used her voice as a needle, embroidering her inner space.

The women helpers

There was no doctor in the village. The "women helpers" handled both births and deaths.

There were two women in Santavela whose task it was to open the doors of the world.

They washed babies and corpses.

It sometimes happened that swaddling clothes became a shroud, that, called to the bedside of a woman in labor, they immediately closed the door that had just opened on life, that the baby's first bath would be its last, or that in being born the child would send its mother to her grave. But they were both considered the best midwives the village had had in centuries.

Each had her secrets. María, a thin old woman with lively but emphatic gestures, imposed her presence on the pregnant women several times before the onset of labor. She would follow the way their bellies were maturing as if studying ripening fruit. By touch, she was able to turn around those children who were in a bad position, or to feel those with little life in them, so little that in order to save the mother they would have to be left on the other side, the door slammed in their face.

In such cases, she would send for Blanca.

"It was María who told me to fetch you," the mother would tell her, weeping. "Apparently there's not much life in the child."

"Don't cry, he'll be back," Blanca would reply. "In three months, you'll have the good sickness again." And she would make a bitter concoction that would stop the mother from dying along with her child.

Whenever María saw that the child would soon be too big to get through the doors, too imposing to edge its way into a woman's pelvis, Blanca's herbs would speed up the labor. These two women knew the sizes of all the girls in the village.

Only a few women preferred, for fear of the evil eye, to give birth by themselves. They would shut themselves up and call their husbands, holding their child by one leg while he gave them something to cut the cord.

But, as often happens when two pieces share a single square on the chessboard of a village, rumour had given each a color. María was considered a holy woman, whereas, despite the respect that Blanca inspired, she had been given the role of the black piece, the witch.

María, who had lived in the village forever, had been sent to the other side of the mountains, to the city, to learn the science of helping girls in labor, while Blanca was only a solitary gypsy woman whose wanderings had led her to the village some years earlier. She had gradually established herself, but remained, and would always remain, a stranger.

María favored hygiene, Blanca magic. One represented the future, science; the other, the past and its dark and soon forgotten forces. Situated at either end of time, with the present in the middle, these two women respected each other, but never communicated verbally. Only one of the two was present while a woman was in labor. But if things looked as if they were going badly, she would send for the other. Then, without saying a word to each other, the two women acted in unison, and it was quite rare for them not to save the mother, for both, unlike many of those who had preceded them, put the woman's life before her child's, and it was no doubt on this tacit agreement that their understanding was based.

It was María who came to the Carasco house.

Accustomed to the task, she carefully prepared the bed, moving her long, thin but muscular arms, folding the worn but clean sheets in four, spreading them one on top of the other, making sure there were no bulges. She then laid Frasquita on the bed and started massaging her belly, exhorting her to cry out during the contractions.

"Go on!" she said, authoritatively. "The whole village has to hear you, my girl, you have to scream louder than your neighbor last month! The more noise you make, the quicker the baby will come and the stronger it'll be!"

Reassured by this thin little woman, with her precise movements, who knew her business, Frasquita obeyed, as if carried along by her. She let out cries more terrifying than those of a pig having its throat cut, while María massaged her belly and neighbors wiped her scarlet face.

After several hours of pain, when Frasquita had practically lost her voice, María said the time had come.

"The child doesn't want to come down, we'll have to get it out of there!"

She took a sheet, twisted it like a rope, and pointed at two of the women.

"You two, come here! You're strong women, make yourselves useful! Take one end of this sheet each and stand on either side of the bed. At my signal, hold the sheet, press with all your might on Frasquita's belly, and slide it up and down. You, my girl, as soon as you feel a contraction coming, make me a sign, breathe, stop and push! Do you understand? Don't shout anymore, your voice has gone anyway, just push! Go!"

For ten minutes, Frasquita pushed as much as she could, then stopped. "I can't do it anymore, I can't, I give up!"

"How can you give up, you big dummy?" María said, unsurprised but authoritative. "You have to get this little one out of your body, and nobody else can do it for you! Push a few more times and you'll soon have a lovely baby to cuddle! It'll be wonderful, you'll see . . . "

Frasquita pulled herself together and pushed so hard that

all the small blood vessels in her face burst, studding her skin with tiny red spots.

At last, the child appeared and all the women who had been watching ran off, screaming. María grabbed the head, turned it as if to unscrew it, asked for one last effort from Frasquita, and the whole body came free in one gush. She cut the silvery cord that still anchored the purple child to its mother, who lay drowned in the white and scarlet sheets.

"She's a bawler," María said out loud, "she'll never hold her tongue! I'm dipping the linen thread in brandy, I'm cutting the cord and tying it with a double knot. I'm tying it well inside of the doors, to make sure it stays! She's nice and clean, that's a good sign! What are you going to call her?"

"Ana, like old mother Carasco!" said Frasquita.

"Good. Well, Anita, I'm dipping you in a tub of hot water to wash away everything you've brought with you from the other world. That's you done! It's not everything, but as there's no one to help me, I have to take care of the two of you at the same time. Because it's not over, my girl, we have to take care of the afterbirth and wrap the child. Babies come from a warm place and catch cold just like that! No point going through all that for nothing, is there? Here, keep her against you inside the blanket while I finish you off. Lovely, isn't she?"

Again, María bustled at the foot of the bed. She asked Frasquita to push some more, and the placenta fell noisily into the bucket that had been prepared.

"Look at those women! Always the same! All whining during the labor, breaking my head with their chatter, and not one that stays by my side when the thing happens. As soon as the child enters the room, they all run away. They're scared, it still smells of the unknown, it comes from the other side, you understand. Girl's bellies are nothing but an antechamber!"

As she spoke, she carefully inspected the placenta, like someone reading an animals' entrails. Then she took the child back from its mother's arms and, after wrapping it and laying it in a cradle carved from a chest, she poured Frasquita a glass of brandy, sat down on a chair, and herself drank a few good swigs straight from the bottle.

"Hey, scaredy-cats!" she cried. "Come back here, I need you to call the father! Let him come to bury the afterbirth!"

"What did you see in there?" asked my mother, pointing to the bucket.

"What do you think I can see there? Your child's future? The date of her death? Stuff and nonsense! All I see is a nice afterbirth, perfectly intact. Not one piece is missing, and that means you pulled it off, my pretty one. Your little Anita isn't going to kill you."

Sitting on her chair, the skirts and the big apron she was wearing for the occasion pulled up to her knees, María seemed quite exhausted. She had been at my mother's side for more than six hours, and the effort had taken its toll. All the same, she found the strength to get up and pull the soiled sheets off the bed.

"I take care of the sheets because each time I leave them, it causes problems. The girls don't trust anyone to wash them. They're stupidly superstitious around here. Besides, I haven't seen your mother or old Señora Carasco by your bedside. Where are those two?"

"Señora Carasco's getting old, she can't climb the stairs any-more," murmured Frasquita, drowsily, "and my mother doesn't want to be in the way, she's too emotional, as you know!"

María made a bundle of the sheets and her own apron, which she had just taken off, threw a last satisfied glance at the child, who opened her big eyes, still blue and blind, and added, "I'll be here tomorrow to bathe her, pierce her ears and put her on the breast. Don't leave this bed before I get back."

Frasquita felt calm beside her sleeping child, who looked so small and fragile. Its delicacy did not worry her. She looked at her belly, which María had bandaged, and told herself that her life as a woman had really begun now. The best, the worst: the two extremes of marriage. Frasquita enjoyed neither of them with her husband. She listened to the noise of his hammer beating on the wood and iron with the regularity of a clock. The worst would not come: her children would grow to the rhythm of the hammer, and hundreds of wheels would leave José's hands and cross all the roads in the land.

The old woman dies

The Carasco house still smelled of milk when María returned.

This time, she closed the shutters, covered the mirror, that trap for souls, and stopped the clock . . . She had come for a death.

Señora Carasco had slowly and silently withdrawn from life. That feeble yet tyrannical body that had taken up so much space for so many years had gradually faded into oblivion.

She was found one morning, a naked little thing lying on the big wooden table in the kitchen. A child almost, a sickly child, with a thin, bony body, a human twig wrapped in Frasquita's flag. In a final patheic gesture, she had carefully pulled the twilight of blue thread all the way up to her chin, as if huddling beneath the blankets on a stormy night, a night of fear.

It was behind that thin rampart of colors, that linen suit of armour, protected by all that beauty, that Señora Carasco had chosen to leave. A lipless smile cut the bottom of her emaciated face in half.

How old was she? Nobody knew, and nobody had ever taken the trouble to ask her or to consult the parish records. José was thirty-five, she had looked three times as old.

She had been born twisted and hated. Her father, just before dying, had at last managed to get her off his hands by offering her to his apprentice. Carasco had taken her to settle his debts and everything had come to him together—the workshop, the house, the furniture—as if tied to that tiny woman.

No love, no desire, and in the absence of all that, a child had been born: José.

The husband had taken the bait, ignorant of how solid the hook—the woman—behind it was, and had struggled for a time, before submitting wearily to her will of iron. He had taken refuge in his forge, just as his son had done after him. The old woman never went in there, she merely pointed out the door to them when they did not get down to work quickly enough.

Señora Carasco had ruled over her house, crushing the people in it without any qualms, until the day her daughter-in-law had sat down on her little chair to sew. At that point, the iron had melted and the flesh hidden beneath it had returned to the surface, the tears had come, red with rust, and the old woman had opted for the sweetness of silence, repose and death. Her body had dissolved little by little and, by the time Anita was born, she was already so thin, so light, so transparent, that my mother could take her in her arms and tend to her as if she were a sick child.

For several months, Frasquita had warmed two creatures in her arms, a bawling little thing full of jerky gestures, a pretty round body, a beautiful energetic baby, and this old woman with a mouth as toothless as the child's, who did not cry, did not move, and asked for nothing.

Soon Frasquita had found that the only way to feed her mother-in-law was to draw her face to her breast and let the old woman, returning no doubt to childhood, gently suck her tasteless milk. Day by day, the child had become greedier, and day by day the old woman had become weaker. It did not take much to satisfy her, she was fading away.

Until the morning she was found lying dead on the kitchen table. She, who never left her armchair, had managed to drag herself to it and hoist herself up. It was on that table that her family traditionally displayed the remains of its dead.

The old woman had given up her place to the child who now enjoyed Frasquita's milk alone.

María gave this poor body its last bath to rid it of the things of this world, then threw the water out as a way of indicating an exit to the soul.

Dressed in black, her white baby in her arms, my mother received all the inhabitants of the village when they came to pay their last respects to Señora Carasco. But not a single one cast a glance at the empty shell lying there and nobody talked about the dead woman as they went out. They had eyes for nothing but the finely embroidered flag that served as her shroud, it was on everyone's tongue in the days that followed.

Frasquita vowed once again to give up sewing when the old woman's grave was desecrated, her shroud stolen, and the yellowing body that had been at its heart left lying on the ground.

José's sickness

At the time of his mother's death, José was spending most of his life in his forge. Nothing outside it seemed to interest him.

He had never let his house out of his sight, suffered whenever a procession or a broken axle forced him to move even a short distance from it, and had never looked at the sky or the horizon as he spent his days making wheels and carts that scoured the roads.

To everyone's surprise, he did not interrupt his work to pay his last respects to his mother, he did not attend her funeral or even the masses said for her. He seemed aware neither of her death nor of the arrival of his daughter and did not change his habits in any way, continuing to obey Señora Carasco's absent voice, still hearing her mangled phrases that had been so often drummed into him and remained so deeply etched that he could still feel the bite of them.

But after Anita was born, he gradually got into the habit of breaking off his labors toward the end of the afternoon, going into the backyard, sitting down on the bench in the henhouse, and contemplating the agitation of that little world of wings and feathers. After a few minutes, he would stand up and go back to work.

Frasquita wore mourning for a year, and not once did her husband notice her black clothes. But one morning, as he was getting ready to leave the kitchen and go to his forge, he suddenly realized that his mother's voice was no more, and was stunned by the silence. There was nobody to order him about, nothing that obliged him to get up from the table and go to work. Frasquita saw him freeze. She prepared the meal in the company of a man who had stopped moving, who ate nothing that day, either at midday or in the evening, and did not sleep beside her that night.

By the time she entered the kitchen the next morning, he had already gone. But the forge was empty and silent. She finally found him outside, sitting on the old bench, gazing rapt at the backyard.

My mother did not like her birds to be upset, but that did not stop José from abandoning his family and his trade and setting up home in the henhouse.

From this point, José left his bench only to walk several times a day around the backyard between the walls that enclosed it.

Nothing could budge him, neither my mother's entreaties, nor her orders, nor her threats, nor even the advice of the priest who paid him a visit in that unusual retreat. Not a single word seemed to get through to him any longer.

My mother would bring him his meals three times a day, wash him in a tub, dress him according to the season, and clean up the excrement he had left in a corner of the yard. Over his head, she built a wooden canopy to protect him from both bad weather and the sun.

At first, Frasquita strove to hide her husband's sudden madness from the village, and did what she could to persuade the customers to wait, reassuring them that all was well. Nor were her parents informed of their son-in-law's insanity.

But her female neighbors, intrigued by the silence from the forge, watched for the slightest opportunity to penetrate the mystery. They would come to the Carasco house on various pretexts and, without appearing to, carry out their little investigation, but they soon realised that they were unwanted and that the backyard was out of bounds.

Rumors were rife, some quite extravagant: it was said that José had left the village or that his witch of a wife, the very one who had married in white and faded on her wedding day, had beheaded him with an axe in a fit of anger. The women finally managed to convince their husbands that something was happening, and a small group of villagers was dispatched to the Carasco house.

The small delegation that demanded, in a very official manner, to speak with José was certainly not expecting to be led by his presumed murderess into a henhouse. Frasquita left them alone, surrounded by her alarmed poultry. They were unable to extract a single word from that carcass of a man, who seemed totally enervated, and left again, looking sheepish and apologizing for the disturbance. From that point, nobody mentioned José in the village, and nobody bought another egg from my mother.

During the two years he spent living in the backyard, José accomplished an incredible social odyssey.

The hens, scared at first by his presence, had gathered around the roosters in a flurry of feathers, droppings and dust. But soon the big, silent man had stopped worrying them. The master of the yard, an enormous rooster, had slowly approached this new object that had been set down in his court like an old treetrunk, and little by little, one after the other, all the other members of that small community had done the same, even the weakest of the hens had ventured, like the others, to peck at the soles of his leather shoes. José had made no move to stop them, and this familiarity had quickly become a habit, so much so that my mother had regularly to chase away the birds in order to try and save the leather.

In a farmyard, the roosters dominate the hens, but among both the males and the females, there exists an extremely strict hierarchy, an upright ladder going from the strongest to the weakest. The hen situated on the bottom rung submits to all the other members of the little community, while the rooster elevated to the highest level by age, strength and presence has absolute power over its subjects.

In less than a month of constant company, my father managed the feat of entering this world of poultry and becoming one of the members of the community, even though he did not have a single feather. He then went tumbling down the rungs one after the other until he was no longer considered anything other than the weakest of the hens in the group. Starting out with the status of a man, he was transformed, not into a rooster, but into the most wretched of pullets. My mother had to stay by his side as he pecked at his food, for fear that his dish would be plundered by the whole of the henhouse.

This spectacular decline lasted more than a year and a half. José let himself be humiliated by common domestic birds for so long that Frasquita finally despaired of ever seeing him recover his reason. Little by little, his eyes seemed to have become round and his head jutted forward. He would keep his arms folded against his body and constantly shrug his shoulders.

My mother watched this transformation, powerless to act.

She no longer made any attempt to keep the household afloat, no longer embroidered, no longer saw her parents, no longer left the house. What she did was speak.

She would speak to her husband as he sat, withdrawn, among the hens, she would tell him the details of her daily life, Anita's progress, trivial matters. She, who had never dared address more than two sentences to him, could now say whatever she wanted without embarrassment: her initiation, her pleasure in embroidering, what she felt for the materials, the threads, the things that needed mending. She even told him about the box and the desire she had felt for him before they were married.

Frasquita spoke to her daughter, too, as she had done from the first day. Even before her birth, Anita, my eldest sister, had been immersed in a universe of words. Frasquita recounted her own story, among many others. She developed stories about the most banal of everyday objects, seeming never to exhaust all the narrative possibilities.

As if hampered by the flow of words from her mother, Anita herself had still not started talking. Unlike her grandmother Francisca, who began to be worried by the little girl's silence, given that she was so alert in every other way, Frasquita was not concerned. She understood her child so well that she did not miss her words. A gesture, a look, a smile, and everything was clear.

It was about this time that the accordion was again played beneath her windows.

Señora Carasco having managed the household expertly, her daughter-in-law did not lack for money during all the time that her husband spent among the poultry. But big Lucia, whose trade was starting to prosper, was worried about the state of Frasquita's finances.

The young men had become wary of giving the pretty young whore a tumble for free in the bushes since she had adopted a stray dog so fierce that those who attempted to leave without paying would lose the seat of their pants.

Lucia had overheard conversations about the beautiful bride who had faded on her wedding day, and knew that nobody would come to her aid. Looking for a way to give her a little money, she had taken to eating eggs.

She came and bought dozens of them from Frasquita, who was more surprised every day by this gargantuan consumption. But neither of the two women ever asked the other a single question.

During these daily visits, they exchanged no more words

than were strictly necessary: the usual polite remarks, the number of eggs wanted, the amount of money due. Nothing more.

But they would stand there for a while in silence, listening to each other breathing.

Frasquita waited impatiently for these encounters, which gave rhythm to her life, and she could not get to sleep on the nights when, occupied elsewhere, the accordion did not come and cradle her.

One day, as she was feeding José, my mother felt a shiver go down his spine. Something was awakening in him. From that moment, José's eyes became less fixed and his arms began moving here and there to chase away the other hens. His first victim was the little red hen, mistreated by her colleagues, that so often came to bother him. He kicked her hindquarters and she bounded away with a cackle. She did not harass him again, but was content to avoid him and watch him from a distance out of the corner of her eye.

He had climbed the first step.

It took him six months to come back to the surface, regaining the upper hand over the hens one by one, confronting each of the roosters, from the weakest to the strongest. Having climbed the first rungs of the ladder, he had little effort to make to establish control over the poultry. Only the master of the henhouse made life difficult for him. The bird and the man both lost a few feathers in the struggle. Frasquita tended to both opponents: the handsome rooster with the multi-coloured plumage, quite stunned at no longer being king, and this silent man who was now at the head of a community of chickens and presumably still thought of himself as one of them.

From now on, no male was able to mount a hen without the man-rooster rushing forward and making the interloper pay dearly for its crime of lèse-majesty.

My mother, who had followed her husband's deeds of arms with increasing attention, panicked when she noticed that none of the eggs she left to hatch reached its full term. When she saw that there was no longer a single chick, she refused to cook the eggs that she collected, and savagely destroyed them.

Revolted by the way José was acting, she now fed him reluctantly, washed him roughly and, having been so persistent in speaking to him over the past two years, no longer said a word to him.

She was getting ready to twist the necks of all the hens in the backyard when her husband looked at her again.

He was naked, with his feet in his basin, and she was rubbing his belly and penis and thighs when all at once he turned his desire away from the hens' pretty feathers and focused instead on his wife's long brown hair. My mother immediately noticed the interest she was arousing. She raised her eyes to his face and saw that it was filled with desire, but he was still twitching like a bird and that made her run out as fast as she could and back inside the house.

He rushed after her, still naked, caught up with her on the staircase, pinned her down, and his penis foraged in her skirts for a moment before clumsily forcing its way into her. As the man-rooster moaned behind her back, she thought of Anita asleep and did not cry out.

Suddenly, José broke away, shook himself violently, and smoothed the feathers he did not have. He threw his chin out several times, then froze, his round eyes fixed on his wife's body. Frasquita waited, with her skirts pulled up, for this thing that had violated her to return to his henhouse. He made another few jerky movements as he looked with astonishment at the beautiful round buttocks wreathed in material, and gradually his body calmed down. He reached out his hand toward the white skin and attempted a caress. Frasquita let out a cry of surprise when she felt the tender touch of José's fingers. He quickly took his hand away as if he had been burned, and stammered that he wanted his clothes.

Frasquita leaped to her feet. Without even turning around, she ran into the bedroom, threw pants, shirt and jacket over her arms, and went back down to the kitchen where, somewhat embarrassed by his nakedness, José was sitting stiffly in what was definitely a human position.

He dressed, poured himself a large glass of wine, smiled at his wife and went into his forge.

Nine months later, María prepared a nice white bed, and Frasquita started to scream.

ANGELA

The workshop throbbed to the wheelwright's blows, the wooden bed squeaked, and Frasquita screamed, encouraged by her audience of neighbors. In the backyard, the hens cackled peacefully.

Everything was going wonderfully, surrounded by the requisite cacophony of the good sickness.

Suddenly, María turns pale and tells the youngest of the girls present to run and fetch Blanca. The girl rushes out. The older women look on, intrigued, and start to mutter among themselves. María silences them with a curt movement of her hand before their words can reach Frasquita's ears, although she is too busy screaming anyway.

"That's good, my girl, give it one last push!" María says encouragingly. "We're almost there, I can see its head!"

At these words, the neighbors all dash to the door in that wave of panic that greets the appearance of every baby, only to run straight into Blanca's massive body. This unnerves them even more and they push past the big woman to make good their escape. Behind them, the baby is already crying itself hoarse.

Muttering a few curses, Blanca approaches the sticky little thing, squealing like a duck, that her colleague is holding in her hands.

Frasquita becomes aware of this other presence in the room. The two women are standing between her and her child.

At the foot of the bed, a few feathers flutter.

Out of breath, her voice broken from all the screaming, the young mother cannot yet speak, cannot question.

Bending over the child, the two midwives cut the cord.

"You've made another girl!" cries María without turning toward the bed.

The neighbors knock at the door: the tub of hot water is ready!

Blanca goes to the door to take it, all the while chanting prayers in a language that reminds Frasquita of that used to raise the dead, those words she has learned but has never yet used, those words that lie dormant in her and terrify her.

"Why did you send for Blanca?" she manages to utter. "What's going on? Give me my child!"

"I was afraid it might go badly, Blanca came to the rescue. You'll have your little one after her bath."

The two women bustle around the tub, in a cloud of white down.

"But are these . . . feathers?" breathes my mother.

Blanca turns toward her, and gives her one of her huge smiles: she is a simple woman, a strong woman. "It's all right, it isn't your baby! It so happens I was plucking chickens when they came to fetch me, and I had to stop in the middle. I must have got a few feathers stuck on my dress. Don't worry, I'm not going to leave you in this state. We'll tidy up before we leave!"

María is busy with the placenta, looking at it from every angle, while Blanca continues bathing the baby they seem determined to hide from its mother.

"Show me my child!"

"She's coming, just let me wrap her," Blanca replies imperturbably.

After one last prayer, she at last gives up the child, a fat red-faced baby, to Frasquita, who welcomes it into her arms with delight.

"When you make a baby as big as this," says María after collecting the dirty sheets, "it's best to have two women like us at hand. Have you chosen a name for her?"

"No. I thought I was making a boy."

"Then we'll call her Angela," says Blanca, with a chuckle, while María quickly gathers the white down from the floor and stuffs it as best she can into her skirts. The two women throw each other a contented glance.

"We'll be back tomorrow to put her to the breast."

The soiled sheets under their arms, the midwives left the room, exhausted. They sat down side by side for a moment on the bench in the kitchen. Blanca rummaged in her skirts where she always kept a silver flask, and filled several little glasses with brandy, which they drank straight down, one after the other, without a word.

Standing around the table, the neighbors watched them, waiting for a sign.

"Tell the father he can come and that he has another little female," Blanca finally grunted, wiping her mouth with the back of her hand. "He can bury the placenta, it's in the bucket there!"

Returning to the bedroom, the neighbors noticed a few small wet bloodstained feathers lying here and there on the floor, and the rumor immediately circulated that the two midwives had washed, plucked and named little Angela before giving her to her mother and the world.

"It's the fault of the hens! José got too familiar with those damned creatures. Things that are against nature leave traces, believe me! The poor little thing will soon start cackling like a hen, you'll see. When that happens, María and Blanca will have to come clean."

"And that name! Angela! Who do the old girls think they're fooling? Angels don't hang around henhouses!"

Fortunately, Frasquita never overheard this gossip, nor did she see the smallest feather on her second daughter's body.

Blanca became so attached to this coarse-featured child that she got into the habit of spending several hours a day in the Carasco house. She would take her on her knees and press her between her huge breasts and rock her back and forth. The baby would open wide her excessively round eyes, huddle up against the woman's big, gentle body, and smile.

On the night after this second birth, the accordion, silent for nine months, had returned to play a little tune beneath Frasquita's windows.

So Lucia hadn't forgotten her!

Very gently, taking care not to wake her, the young mother had taken her baby in her arms and had gone to the window to show the sleeping child to her friend.

Pedro el rojo

Since his return to the world of men, José had not been idle. Nobody else in Santavela had his talents as a wheelwright and it was several days' walk to Pitra, the nearest village, where Heredia had sent his carriages to be maintained during José's long absence. As soon as the hammer blows had started resounding again through the forge, the customers had come running.

Dozens of clumsily patched-up wheels and rickety carts had trundled down the alleyways of Santavela to the Carasco establishment, and José had gotten down to work with a newfound pleasure.

Everything was back in place: the big rooster, once again master of the henhouse, crowed every morning, the neighbors had reappeared, and Lucia had at last been able to eat something other than tortillas, which had started to disgust her. Of course it had taken Frasquita a while to patch things up with her hens, but she had plucked a certain number of them to speed things up and, at last feeling at peace again, had for a time enjoyed a simple happiness she had not known before. Anita, who still could not speak, expressed herself with her body, hands and eyes, and her parents reveled in her mimes, which were full of subtlety and invention.

The birth of Angela upset this fragile balance.

When José learned that Frasquita had given him another daughter, he went to bury the placenta, then came back and sat down among the poultry. The old rooster, who recognized him despite his new clothes and all too human grimaces, looked at him surreptitiously, pecking away to keep up a brave face but expecting the worst.

Through one of the windows of Frasquita's bedroom, the neighbors saw the man sitting on his bench with his back to them, and hastened to tell his wife.

How long would her husband stay with the hens this time? A few hours, a month, a year? Would it ever end? How would she survive, alone with two children?

Even though Blanca had forbidden her, she got out of bed once the women had left and gazed at that sadly familiar picture: José surrounded by poultry. For a time, absorbed by the scene, she forgot Angela, who was whining, trying doubtless to remind her that time had passed.

So that was it!

José had another daughter when he was expecting a little boy! The remedy would be to give him a boy, but to do that he would have to get up from that damned bench!

Frasquita did not have long to wait this time: José's absence lasted only a few minutes. He pulled himself together and came to see his wife and child.

The next day, Frasquita consulted Blanca, who listened carefully, then said, "I don't help girls to choose their children's sex, that'd upset the order of the world."

"So you won't help me?"

"No."

"Then I'll find someone else to do it instead!"

"Who? Nobody here knows how. You have a belly for making girls, and there's nothing anybody can do about it. In some soil, hydrangeas grow pink and in others blue."

"Yes, I've heard about those strange flowers," replied Frasquita stubbornly, "but I've also been told that you just have to plant a few cloves for the pink earth to give blue."

"Do as you see fit, but you won't be able to do anything about it! Just don't trust old wives' recipes, there's a danger they'll make you ill or give you a little hunchback girl!"

Frasquita went her own sweet way: she set aside her discretion and shyness and went to see all the wives in the village.

She was advised to sleep on her stomach, or curled up, or with her legs in the air, to stay awake one night out of three, to eat only salty food, or sugary food, or stale food, or rotten food, to walk ten times around the outside of the church thinking of her son's future name, to find a round stone and put it in her mouth when her husband possessed her, to drink tea made with nettles, to speak only to women who made sons, to carry images of Christ around her belly in a garland, to dip her feet in pig's blood, to refuse to give herself to José for several weeks, and so on.

At last, she became pregnant, but some of the concoctions the old women gave her made her so ill that after six months of her pregnancy she lost the baby.

María had seen her through her miscarriage. Frasquita lay on her bed, silent. She had not wanted to see the unfinished little creature lying there, cold, in a piece of cloth. But she could not help asking what sex it was.

"Another daughter," María had replied.

While María prayed for the baby, Frasquita thought of the prayers she kept enclosed somewhere inside her, those prayers of which she was the receptacle, those terrifying prayers from the third night, the ones that raise the dead. But would the dead give her better advice than the living?

Her task complete, María left without a word, and Blanca slipped into the room.

"If you force fate to make a boy, then you will only ever have one," she said immediately, with fondness in her voice.

"One is all I need. If I have another daughter, José will

become a rooster again, God alone knows for how long. He must have a son! Just one!"

"I'll do what I can to make sure he has one," Blanca assured her, tenderly tucking her in. "Let me know when you next lose your blood. We must match your cycle to that of the moon, then when both it and you are impure, you will have to give yourself to José."

That night, the accordion played a tune so sweet that Frasquita was able to release all the tears she had been holding inside her.

If Blanca had not been there, nobody would have gotten to the Carasco house in time to help my mother bring Pedro el Rojo into the world.

The gypsy had been tending to Angela when the pains started, and she barely had time to lead Frasquita to the bed before the young woman's waters broke and she was wracked with unusually violent contractions. Barely ten minutes later, the baby was bawling in its mother's arms. Blanca went down to the forge as quickly as her massive body allowed her to inform José that he had a son and to ask him to bring up a bowl of water.

He immediately yelled his joy in the street and voices answered him from the nearby houses. There were blessings, congratulations, prayers. The whole neighborhood rushed into the kitchen while the water was boiling, and each person was given a nip of brandy. They waited until the baby had been bathed, then followed José into the bedroom.

His joy faded as soon as he saw his son's hair.

His red hair would exclude him from the village more surely than his sister's supposed feathers.

A whisper circulated, informing those who had not seen the child, and gradually everyone fell silent. The street itself fell silent, although crowds continued to gather outside the Carasco house.

"He's a strong boy, in a great hurry to enter life," joked Blanca, who had noticed José's disappointment. "He came to us by surprise: if your wife had been working with the animals, she would have made him on the hill, without anyone to help her."

The fact that her child had red hair did not in any way lessen Frasquita's joy. At first she was aware neither of the neighbors' curiosity and embarrassed silence nor of her husband's reticence.

José stayed with his son for only a few moments before forcing his way through the dense crowd standing motionless in the doorway of the room, on the stairs, and in the kitchen. He returned to his forge without even a glance at the henhouse.

Blanca chased away the onlookers.

She went back to Frasquita, who had been joined by her two daughters. Anita, still mute, was truly happy to greet her brother. Nearly seven now, she was a responsible, well-behaved child, already capable of helping her mother and watching over her little sister Angela, who was running about in all directions.

"You haven't given the boy a name," Blanca observed.

"Ask José to do it, I think he wanted the child to bear his name."

Blanca reluctantly went down, only to come trudging up the stairs again a few moments later.

"He's sulking because of the color of the boy's hair," she said, breathing heavily. "But he told me he'd think about it."

That night, Frasquita's mother slept with the girls, while José installed a bed in his forge, as he did with each new birth. As for Frasquita, she did not get to sleep until dawn. She waited all night in vain for the accordion to be played beneath her windows.

Since the miscarriage, Lucia had not shown her face. Thanks to the village gossips, Frasquita knew that she had become

Heredia's official mistress. She now had her own horse and no longer hired herself out to the young men of the village. My mother at last fell asleep, wondering if her friend still wore her sequined dress.

The next day, Blanca returned to put the baby to the breast.

"A boy doesn't drink the same way. Look at that, he really knows what he's doing! Does he have a name today?"

"Not yet, his father still hasn't given him his own. God alone knows what we're going to call him. All the men in our two families have my husband's name."

"You'll have to call him something, just give him his godfather's name."

Ten days later, the child still had neither a name nor a godfather. His hair frightened everyone and they all refused to make room for this boy they had already named among themselves "el Rojo."

The priest went to the Carasco house to try and put an end to the scandal.

A baby was a fragile thing and had to be christened as soon as possible before it was carried off by some fever or other.

"But to christen him, we still have to find a godfather for him, and a name!" said Blanca, who was cuddling Angela. "And nobody is willing to be his godfather, just because he doesn't have the same hair color as the other people around here."

"I talked too much about how I wanted a son," said Frasquita, looking down at the child clinging to her breast. "I shouldn't have opened myself up like that to all those women, I should have remembered my wedding day and kept quiet. According to them, I made a pact with some evil power to get my boy. José probably thinks the child isn't even his. I'm certainly not going to call him el Rojo just to please them!"

As he listened to this confession, the priest gazed at the

baby's gorgeous hair. How to get rid of that sign that marked him out in the eyes of the little community? He knew how superstitious these people were, and he wasn't sure he would be able to sway them, even in the name of God. Their terrors didn't go away so easily!

"It's possible he'll lose his first hair," he ventured.

Blanca looked at him in surprise. So even their priest, who was usually so sure of himself, could not see how to settle the matter.

"No," she said sternly, "unless it's shaved off, that hair will stay! That's its color, and I know what I'm talking about!"

The priest withdrew in confusion, although not without having first reassured Frasquita that he would do everything in his power to solve this conundrum and would talk about it in his sermon.

When he had left, Blanca pulled a face. "Our young priest is getting old, he doesn't stand up to the enemy the way he used to. He's a city boy who believes in reason. He's stuck here on the outskirts of civilisation and is starting to give up. He won't be able to do anything for us."

Frasquita did not notice that "us," but, without knowing why, Blanca's words did her good.

Time was passing and el Rojo still had no Christian name.

One evening, Frasquita was woken by an accordion tune. Instead of going to her window as she had gotten in the habit of doing, she went downstairs and opened the door to Lucia.

"You're a bit late to celebrate my baby's birth," Frasquita said after she had lighted a candle and the two women had sat down face to face across the kitchen table. "Do you also think this child with red hair comes from somewhere else?"

"No, but I've been traveling. Old Heredia has become besotted with me, and he's been taking me around the country. I've seen the world and now I'm not sure I can stay here much longer."

"Then don't!"

"I found out what happened to your son when I got back. Is he still not baptised?"

"Nobody in the village wants to have anything to do with him. He doesn't have a name or a godfather."

Their complicity, long silent, had suddenly become verbal. The words had come naturally. They two women were talking the way relatives talk, the way sisters talk, and it did not even occur to them that they had never done so before.

"I'd be happy to be the godmother, but I'm not sure it'll help your son much to be linked to a whore. María is more what you need. And as for a godfather, let me think . . . If my Pedro accepted, nobody would dare mention his godson's red hair."

"But why would Heredia do such a thing?"

"Out of gratitude for all the good advice your father gave him about growing wine! After all, it's thanks to him that the slopes yield so well in spite of the terrible climate here. Ask the boy's grandfather to go see Heredia, I'll take care of the rest . . . "

And that is how my brother inherited his name.

Lucia turned out to be right: nobody dared make the slightest comment in public while his godfather was still alive. But the village did not readily accept Pedro el Rojo and the women forbade their offspring from approaching a boy conceived during his mother's period.

"Don't play with the redhead, he's the spawn of the red moon, the most dangerous kind, the kind that makes everything rotten: if he bites you it won't heal!" That was what the women whispered in the ears of any child who ventured too close to the Carasco house.

The boy never had any playmates other than his sisters.

Anita, who was better integrated in spite of her muteness, could pass from one world to the other, but Angela and he were inseparable. He scared everyone so much, adults and children alike, that nobody came close to look for feathers on his round-eyed sister's back any longer. Everyone watched them from a distance as if they were strange animals and, with time, the two of them learned to make use of the fascination aroused by Pedro's red hair.

When Pedro was old enough to express his wishes, he asked that it should never be cut.

They both learned to live isolated from the rest of the world, and doubtless gradually became the unusual, unclassifiable beings, with special talents, that everyone wanted them to be.

Heredia was quite fond of this godson that his mistress had imposed on him, and invited him several times to his house.

Accompanied by his godmother María, the child would go there in his father's cart and spend the day with the old gentleman and the pretty, brilliantly dressed lady. What he loved above all in the big house were the tiled frescoes and paintings that adorned almost all the walls. He would sometimes stop for hours in front of one of these images and, when old Heredia told him the life story of this or that person in a portrait or explained the scene that the artist had tried to reproduce, the child seemed to understand.

On a wall in one of the drawing rooms, an ancestor of Heredia's had had a harbor scene painted: large sailing ships moored at the quay, hundreds of porters unloading brightly colored merchandise from the New World.

During one of his last visits, when the child could not have been much more than two, Lucia found him standing on a chair, his body right up against a fresco, as if trying to jump into the picture.

Figures

After Pedro was born, José did not sit down in the hen-house. On the contrary, he worked harder than ever. What fascinated him above all were his accounts.

While his parents had been alive, neither he nor his father had bothered much with figures: it was Señora Carasco who had held the purse strings in her little iron hand, she who had fixed the prices, negotiated for wood, and pursued bad payers. She loved figures with a love inherited from her father and had bought from the peddlers who passed every year to offer their merchandise to the people of Santavela two huge exercise books in which she had noted down every sum of money that had gone in or out for more than forty years. Unable to write anything other than numbers, she had invented a host of symbols to indicate at the beginning of the line what each of these numbers represented.

José spent an absurd amount of time deciphering these signs. He remembered as a child watching his mother's hand as she carefully drew her numbers. The only thing she had ever taught him, apart from silence and obedience, was how to count, but these additions and subtractions had been of no use to him before now, and he did not even remember that he was capable of such arithmetical feats.

In spite of the enormous number of eggs consumed by Lucia, José's long crisis had reduced the family's finances to nothing. Everything had to be started again from scratch.

Now that his accounts were accurate, just like his mother's, numbers no longer held any secrets for him. Soon he no longer needed to put his sums down on paper, or to note down the totals. He calculated with surprising speed and had found a remarkable partner in his daughter Anita, who had immediately absorbed the symbols. She would draw them on the ground, in the air, or on her father's hand.

Little by little, numbers took over José's mind.

At night, he would sometimes pursue that day's calculations in his sleep. Frasquita would hear him mutter sequences of figures, then see him smile, as if reassured by some solution. He soon asked himself more complex mathematical questions, and became interested in geometry. During his son's christening, he asked Heredia how to calculate the circumference of a wheel. Heredia had no idea, but promised José that he would find out, and unearthed for him a geometry book for beginners, with clearly laid-out illustrations. And so Carasco, who could not read, plunged into a world populated by the diameters of wheels, the figure *pi* and the metric system.

How many wheels had he made since he had started? What distance could they go before they broke? What distance had all the wheels he had made gone? How many leagues, how many miles from Santavela was Pitra? Or Jaén? Or Madrid? What was the circumference of the Earth? How many times would a wheel have to turn to go around the world? For, as he explained to his children and their mother, the Earth was round, as round as the moon or the sun, as round as all the wheels he made.

He had had never left Santavela, and these calculations made him dizzy.

His work was still his main precoccupation, of course, and he only allowed himself to indulge in such complex speculations when he took a break. Then, instead of sleeping, he would solve his arithmetical problems. Soon he was no longer only refraining from sleep in the afternoons, but was not sleeping at all, so engrossed in his calculations that he neglected the marriage bed. Intellectual excitement kept him awake for nights on end. He left the big accounts books to his daughter Anita, who was now aged eight: such commonplace sums no longer interested him—he needed time and space—and the girl accomplished her task with all the seriousness of a child.

Frasquita started to worry when she saw dark rings under her husband's eyes.

Was he going to sit down on his bench again?

"How long is it since your husband last slept?" Blanca asked her eventually.

"Two months," replied my mother with a smile. "He's been spending his nights with his figures and his days in the workshop."

"And what do you think of that?"

"I think it's like with the hens, and that it may last for years. But the henhouse I know something about, whereas figures . . . Why do all these men become mad? Look at my father: mother has to follow him everywhere for fear he'll get lost. Small as she is, she has to hold that big idiot by the hand and lecture him like a child when he tries to run away."

"We all have our moments of madness. Didn't your mother, who's usually so reasonable, spend some weeks of her life making holes all around the outside of the village? If the mind lets go more often here than in other places, it may be a question of climate, or of isolation. You live far from everything, turned in on yourselves, and none of you have the courage to leave and see the world. Your husband escapes in his own way, and your father tries to do today what he never imagined doing in his youth: get out of Santavela."

"What about you? You've traveled the country, why did you choose to stop here?"

"To flee the rest of the world. In Santavela, I get the impression that nothing can ever happen to me, that no ogre will ever find me. This land is the end of the Earth. I must have used up all my reserves of madness when I decided to live among you, even though I was a stranger here. You have to try and talk to José. He's not a bad fellow, maybe you'll manage to make him see reason."

Talk to her husband? My mother did not know how to go about it, she had only ever talked to him during his two years of exile among the poultry, when she had enjoyed confiding in that absent creature who seemed neither to listen to her nor to hear. Did he even remember her long monologues? Her voice? The moments they had spent side by side on the bench in the henhouse?

By the time Frasquita decided to speak, her exhausted husband was already unable to concentrate on his work, the numbers had even infiltrated the forge.

It had been an insidious process: at first a few simple calculations had wormed their way into his mind while the hammer continued its work, then the sums had grown more complicated without his noticing and the barrier had yielded, liberating great arithmetical journeys, miles of roads rolling around the world in every direction, and José had been unable to resist. He would have liked to sleep, but the figures that pursued him had seized the last bastion, they were massing around him in serried ranks and pressing in on him from all sides, right here in this forge where they had not been allowed to enter until now.

When Frasquita heard that the rhythm of the hammer had ceased, she knew it was time for her to intervene.

And so she too now entered the forbidden space, where José was sitting on the ground, muttering numbers to himself.

She talked to him as if cradling him, and recited, without even thinking about it, one of the prayers from the first night, a prayer to induce sleep. José gradually calmed down, the figures lost ground, deserting him little by little, and he sank into sleep.

José fell asleep on the ground, but the huge shadows that hollowed his face made it look as if his eyes were wide open, and in the gloom it took Frasquita a long time to notice that his eyelids were in fact lowered.

With the help of Blanca and Lucia, whom she had sent for, Frasquita carried her husband upstairs and laid him on the bed. Without mentioning the prayers, she told them he had fallen asleep as she was speaking to him and that she could not get him to wake up again.

"You can see from his eyes how tired he was," said Blanca. "Now that he's finally gotten to sleep, he may well be out for a long time."

"Provided he doesn't continue those damned sums while he sleeps!" murmured Frasquita, still astonished at how effective her prayer had been.

"And provided he wakes up one day," whispered Lucia. "I've never seen anyone sleeping like that before!"

One week later, Jose was still asleep. On Blanca's advice, Frasquita would wash him, give him something to drink while he slept, and frequently change the position of his limbs in order to avoid bedsores.

After thirty days and thirty nights of sleep, with the neighborhood thinking that José had gone back to his henhouse, Frasquita left her children with Blanca and paid her mother a visit.

It was extremely hard for Francisca to spare her the time: her husband claimed all her attention, as much as if he was a young child. He spent his days trying old keys in the locks of the house and wept when she tried to take them away from him. She managed to get him to sleep by placing his big head on her knees and tenderly cradling it.

"What are you complaining about?" the old woman said, amused. "They're so beautiful when they're asleep. Don't worry, those prayers from the first night can't bring bad luck. The one you recited will make José sleep for as long as he needs. Of course he will have lost a bit of weight when he wakes up, but better that than the hens or the numbers, don't you think?"

It was the last time Frasquita saw her parents alive.

They disappeared some time later, in autumn, without telling anyone. A search was organized in the surrounding countryside and their bodies were found lying entwined in a pothole a few miles from the village.

Frasquita's father must have managed to persuade his wife to leave, but Santavela did not let its prey get away so easily.

Frasquita was taken to see the corpses. Francisca's face was still turned toward her husband, and Frasquita saw on it the same expression of calm happiness it had had during their last conversation. The dead face seemed to be saying, "They're so beautiful when they're asleep!"

She demanded that her parents be buried where they had been found: they had not run away only to have their bodies brought back to the village. And so they would sleep side by side on the path that they had chosen. As the priest accepted this extravagance without flinching, nobody dared make the slightest comment: they reserved those for later.

Returning from the ceremony, Frasquita noticed that the rings around her husband's eyes were not as noticeable as before. So she hid the geometry book, lay down beside her husband and waited calmly for him to wake up, remembering her mother's last words.

Did she really find him beautiful, this man lying by her side?

She had moored herself to him like a boat to its dock and

now he, along with her children, was the only thing that still kept her tied to the village.

When José woke from his long sleep, he could barely sit up, and it took him a few days to recover his spirits. He had first to be convinced that he had slept for such a long time, and started counting the days on his fingers, which my mother considered a good sign.

Anita, who had carefully kept the accounts during her father's absence, presented him with the big book, which looked bigger still in her small hands. He smiled and told her that she, and she alone, would now be in charge of the family's finances.

He gradually got back to work. His customers had to wait some time before the orders already under way were completed, because the first piece of work to which he applied himself was a miniature red cart, a toy for his son. He constructed it with a great deal of care, making sure he got the smallest right, and on the canvas cover he had the words *Pedro el Rojo* written in bright red lettering.

Frasquita was struck dumb with surprise when Pedro received this first gift from the hands of a father who had previously ignored him.

A debt must have been paid, for life resumed at a calmer pace. It seemed to Frasquita that she had been through the worst, and that set her mind at rest. She no longer worried what other people thought.

It was in this peaceful climate that her third daughter, Martirio, came quite easily into the world.

THE YELLOW DOG

D uring this period of tranquil happiness, Lucia, who had put aside her sequined dress, came to the Carascos every day on horseback. Her friendship could no longer cause Frasquita any harm now that she was the official mistress of Señor Heredia, long a widower.

It was unlikely that she was trying to take her revenge on the people of Santavela, or even to show off: she went about on horseback because she had a horse and had learned to ride on the hacienda. It was convenient, that was all! She assumed that, even if they did not love her, at least the villagers would not despise her from now on.

She was mistaken.

At the time of her abortive wedding, the poor girl had been much pitied, the mothers used her story to strike fear into their daughters, the women saw in her nothing but a poor wretch, condemned to give herself to everyone, and the young men, those bastards, enjoyed laying her in the undergrowth for nothing. A little hussy who was paying dearly for her youthful error.

With the years, she had made herself a world of bushes and darkness and shady corners. An open-air world, full of well-trodden paths that wound across the countryside. She had learned to disappear into her sequined dress, to spread the bright tones of her accordion to attract her clients, to spring up in the very heart of the village through some hole. She had built doors that were hers alone. Thanks to her accomplice, the stray dog that had attached itself to her and did not hesitate to throw itself on cheapskates, she had managed to defend herself and to make those who took advantage of her pay. Her fierce protector had allowed her to grow her little business.

Everyone did well out of her until Heredia became besotted with her. Then the men had looked at her differently: her hair had taken on a golden hue, and they had started paying more to caress her lovely silky body and taste her dark red lips. They desired her now, not because she was in the vicinity and available, and better her than doing it alone, but because they had started to think of her even when she was out of sight, and to see her on every hill, behind every stone, in every bend in the road, everywhere where she was not. Lucia had become a rare pleasure, an expensive pleasure, the master's pleasure, and the wives noticed the glances their husbands threw her. This woman, who was supposed to belong to everyone, was getting away from them, and the farther away she got, the more evident, painful, hurtful even, her beauty became.

One day she had shut up shop and moved into the manor house with Heredia and his three grown-up sons who still lived there with their wives and children. The house was large enough to limit any conflict, and the long corridors gave everyone time to compose themselves.

The old man had not thought too much about what he was doing; Lucia had simply made her presence necessary to him in a way that could not be denied. Having been in decline for so long, he had experienced intense pleasure with her, he had felt as if he was being reassembled between her strong legs, and nothing and nobody could have made him give up his delight at being whole again.

For decades, the dust of the olive grove, which he had eaten and drunk and breathed, had settled on his aging skin, on his hair, on his eyes. It was a long time since anything had had any taste. Then one night, as he walked alone on this land that so resembled him, thinking about his fourth son, the youngest and most soft-hearted of them, the one who had chosen to leave for the North, he had seen her in her sequined dress and it had seemed to him as if a piece of the starry sky was advancing toward him.

She had come to him without a word, cleared the dust from him, and clasped him so hard in her long, muscular arms that he had thought he would die.

She had put him back together while the yellow dog looked on amid the olive trees. He still had a body, then, a body she had taken hold of that night, forever. He had forgotten how to love with his flesh, but she had made love to him, then she had left without asking for anything, and he had remained there for a long time, alone, listening to the merry song of the accordion in the distance.

He had come back every night to the olive grove and had finally found them all again, her, her star-spangled dress and the yellow dog.

Lucia, the eternal bride, had not acted out of self-interest. She had taken this man in the night in order to snatch something from life, something that would belong to her and her alone. She had plucked him like a fruit. And gradually those moments of love in the olive grove had become the only thing the two of them lived for. Their days were mere preludes to the moment when they would meet again.

One morning, Heredia had decided to move Lucia into his house, to make her part of his family, and nobody had opposed his will: his eyes were too full of the lovely Lucia's sequined dress. That dress—full of holes, dappled with light, beloved by everyone—she had ended up wearing only for him, in private.

That was how the whore had apparently escaped her fate.

But life in a manor house had done nothing to mellow the fearsome yellow dog, which followed the woman and her horse everywhere. He would stop at the entrance to the village and wait for its mistress in a shady corner. Nor did he enter the courtyard of the house. He would spend his nights, alone, in the olive grove, keeping watch. He did not like men: nothing could make it forget what some of them had done to him.

Heredia did not feel himself going. One morning, Lucia found him dead by her side. The village mourned ostentatiously, there was much noisy weeping, much dignified sweating beneath the black clothes, and the procession that accompanied the body to its last resting place was the finest seen in Santavela within living memory. The only bright patch in all that darkness was Lucia, who had dared to put on her sequined dress for the occasion.

She did not see the first stone coming.

Heredia's three sons did not lift a finger to defend her. They had so long feared that their father would remarry and have other children from a second marriage that this first stone, the source of which was unknown, may well have been ordered by them.

Lucia fell as she tried to run away, and the yellow dog, which had long been watching out for a moment like this, and had followed the ceremony at a distance, rushed forward as the stones rained down. It protected its mistress by laying itself flat on her body.

Frasquita cried out, a single cry that tore through the crowd and put an immediate end to the throwing of stones. Blanca, María and my mother advanced toward the entwined bodies of the dog and the woman.

The yellow coat and the sequined dress were both stained with blood.

Under pressure from the three women, the people dispersed, cursing. There were no more stones, no more cries, no more furious barking: the yellow dog was dead. While they bustled around the corpse of the animal and the body of the still dazed Lucia, the men watched them from a distance.

Lucia left Santavela that very evening, her sequined dress on her back and her accordion slung across her shoulder. She came and played one last tune beneath the windows of the Carasco house, and Frasquita opened the door to her and gave her a sack full of provisions for the road. They did not speak, but embraced tenderly. Singing a lively little tune, a party tune, Lucia set off on foot along the lanes, followed by the shadow of the yellow dog she had buried somewhere in the olive grove, in the spot where she had been that first night.

CLARA

No local woman came to help during the next birth. By living on the fringes of the village, refusing to let her dead be buried there, consorting with prostitutes, and giving birth to boys with red hair and girls with feathers, Frasquita had managed to put the neighbors and all the other respectable ladies to flight.

Solidarity, tradition, curiosity: none of these mattered compared with the general desire to keep the Carasco family at a distance. In compensation, Blanca and María were both present at the birth.

Clara arrived on a moonless night.

Frasquita had felt the first contractions at the end of the day, when the winter sun had just fled to other lands. The previous children, Pedro and Martirio, had been born so quickly that she did not fear this new delivery. The path had been laid, the latest child had only to follow the tracks left by the previous explorers. But apparently this baby did not see clearly, or perhaps it disliked well-charted paths.

Frasquita thought she would die during that night of labor, the longest of the year, the night of the winter solstice. Knives pierced her lower back at regular intervals, and these increasingly violent and increasingly frequent thrusts left her voiceless. She lost consciousness several times.

Through her swollen eyelids, she saw the two women bustling in the semi-darkness of the bedroom. Her brow was mopped, she was given something to drink, her belly and back were massaged. She was aware of her body being moved into different positions.

Sometimes, between two fainting fits, the shadowy figures made her sit up to help the child descend. From time to time, they checked the opening with their fingers, praying all the while.

She lay there in a moonless darkness made warm by the whispering of the midwives.

So Blanca and María were finally talking to each other! Unless all these words were addressed to her, but the pain was tearing her so violently from the world that she could do no longer understand a thing.

Where were her children? Who was looking after them? She must not cry out for fear of scaring them, but she heard herself screaming, she could not control the howls, the words, the moans emerging from her body, she spewed it all out with the water she was given to drink. Anita would take it upon herself to reassure her younger siblings: they understood her gestures like a second language. Anita, her big daughter, so strong, so reasonable! She had not been told anything, but she had understood. She knew that her mother's belly, huge again beneath her skirts, concealed some secret.

Why were such things hidden from children?

The intensity of the next contraction made her lose the thread of her thoughts, and, when she came to, it was her mother's gentle face that she imagined by her side. Old Francisca had never been present when she was giving birth, although she was often somewhere in the house, preferring to take care of those children who were already there and who huddled against her without understanding what was happening to their mother. Francisca was afraid to see her only daughter suffer. How beautiful her mother had been and how she had loved her, in spite of the gulf that her marriage had created between them!

Her belly suddenly contracted again, cutting off her breath.

The women ought to use thread to guide this child who could not find his way through her body. Tell them to give her a thread that she could grip . . .

Thread. Embroidery. Children like pearls cut from her flesh, embroidered smiles, so many colors on the fabrics to express her joy or pain. All these colors! Why, then, did white so fascinate her?

She had to understand, and in order to understand, she must embroider again, get back to work . . . Sew back the edges of the world, stop it fraying and coming apart. Mend her poor José before he was drained of himself.

Mend him, sew him to her flesh, otherwise they would soon be going their separate ways . . .

Sleep . . . No, she mustn't . . . Stay! Hold on! The child would soon be here . . . She must welcome her . . .

The butterfly fan was still flying beyond the mountains and the seas, that thing of cloth that had come to life, that she had extracted with her fingers, without any pain. A butterfly was less trouble than a baby.

My God, how violent life was!

There was a prayer she had learned, a prayer to be said aloud. But her lips were stuck together, the slightest whisper would tear her face . . .

If only she could go! Get out of this room of pain! Leave the child where it was! It was probably fine there, probably sleeping snug and warm. Why wake it? Why tear it from its mother's body? Why uproot it?

For a long time, the child remained in its mother's pelvis, between life and death. It was waiting for a sign: daybreak, a light . . .

It was Blanca's candle that guided it.

"Push, girl!" cried María, sitting on Frasquita's belly. "Push and above all don't let yourself go! Don't fall asleep again, or the child will go back. Here it comes . . . "

"Get down off your perch and cover the mirror!" Blanca yelled to her colleague when the baby appeared, still all tangled in its mother's entrails. "Cover the mirror, I tell you, or her soul will escape us! Look at the candle flame, my child! Look at that light! That was what guided you here, not its reflection! The reflection isn't the truth of the world, don't go getting confused!"

Then the first light of day entered the room and the child emitted its cry.

"She doesn't like the night, the little bitch, she's made that much clear!" breathed María, bathed in sweat. "You mustn't make children like this too often if you don't want to kill us. You know, I think we're getting too old for this profession, we need to think about training someone to take over. For several months now, the young Capilla girl has been assisting me when she can. She's good, that girl."

She was interrupted by cries from the street. One of the midwives was being called to the shoemaker's house.

"No sooner is it finished here than it starts somewhere else!" grunted María. "Aren't you people ever going to stop bringing children into the world? Please, Blanca, you go! If I do this next one, you'll be washing my corpse before nightfall!"

Blanca smiled. "So you're talking to the abortionist now?"

"When I see the village stoning a poor girl who's given herself before the priest could bless her, I tell myself you must have prevented lots of deaths by performing your abortions. So yes! Given the little time we still have left in this world of rocks and stones, I'd feel a bit stupid not to have told you that before you help me meet my maker scrubbed nice and clean! Never mind the abortions, I like you, Blanca, and I wanted to tell you while I still can."

"It might be better not to start all that chatter, you know.

After fifteen years of working together in silence, it's going to be hard to find anything to say to each other. We're a bit like an old couple: we've got our habits. You're going to have to use your last strength to help me bring up the tub of water. The next time you have a child, Frasquita, we'll deliver it downstairs, on the kitchen table."

María sighed and dragged herself to the window. In her big voice, she ordered the strapping fellow who had called up from the street to come into the Carasco house for two minutes and help them carry the tub. The young man did as he was told: the sooner he helped them, the sooner they would come and attend to his mother, for she it was who was in labor.

As the water was being brought up, Frasquita held, wrapped in a blanket, the little thing that had caused her so much pain. Its beauty fascinated her. In the first rays of the sun, the baby's skin had taken on an incomparable velvety smoothness. The eyes, of a rock-like clarity, were already lined with long dark lashes, the curly hair, although still bathed in darkness, stirred beneath her breath, and its bluish gleam became stronger with every passing minute.

The child was facing the window, and seemed to be diligently contemplating its first dawn.

Frasquita quivered with emotion, she was afraid of dropping this fine, transparent creature, breaking this life as fragile as glass, which she named Clara.

María never came back up to the bedroom. She was taken sick in the kitchen and was dead within the hour. Little Clara inherited a second Christian name: she became Clara María.

THE OLIVE GROVE MAN

At the time of Frasquita's birth, Heredia had four sons and no daughter and his wife was already in her grave. Two maids who lived on the estate took care of the meals and the housework and looked after the children.

The youngest of the boys suffered from a strange malady.

A bad fairy had cut the link between his will and his desire, condemning him to fight for what he did not desire and turn away from what he loved. The child was torn. The least of his desires would put him in a fever, unable to rise from his bed, but when nothing filled the murky spaces of his soul, his will would take over, and he was free to fight his brothers over something he considered worthless, or win a mountain of knucklebones from the children of the village without feeling any joy at the victory. He was unbeatable at games he did not enjoy and, weary of accumulating pointless trophies, would drop them on the roads. All the local boys walked with their heads down in the hope of finding the shiny little pieces of bone scattered by this strange Tom Thumb.

The boy often felt a strong urge to take refuge in the soft round arms of the older of the two maids. He would have liked his child's body to vanish between her heavy breasts, to melt in their warmth. In his mind, he savored the tender dampness that emanated from that velvety flesh. Everything about the woman was lullabies and sugar. This desire tormented him, twisted his insides, made him dizzy. But he never dared to approach that delightful body.

The day he turned eight, he made up his mind to fight this fever.

He observed the contradictory forces driving him, shook off the apathy he felt rising in him in waves and, in order to empty his head of female arms and the smells of milk and sleep, to resist heady lullabies without words, he took up a senseless occupation, and crisscrossed the family estate, bare-headed in the sun, counting the olive trees one by one. It was his way of trying to escape the living arms of a dead mother.

The olive grove man, as he was nicknamed later, found the antidote to his fevers in the counting of trees.

It was not that he had any great wish to know how many there were. That knowledge mattered to him so little that he was capable of withstanding the furnace-like heat of noon and the fatigue and concentrating for days on end on figures and trunks. In this endlessly restarted count, the child learned to live outside himself. The shadow of his desires frayed in the sun and finally dissolved amid the shadows of the olive grove.

Worried about his son's long absences, Heredia followed him one morning on the sly and observed his strange obsession. The land was bare, and it was not easy for old Heredia to hide. He would have to slip behind rocks or tree trunks. He even hoisted himself up into a big oak overlooking a plain of boulders and sat for a long time on a branch, watching his son between the leaves. He heard him counting the members of his scattered army out loud. He saw him stop beneath each of the trees, make an inventory of the olive trees lined up in their rows, catch up with the deserters on the side of the hill, the dead trees lying on the battlefield. The boy took care to say the figures very distinctly, in a loud, monotone voice, forgetting in this forest of numbers that he could have been doing something else: let himself be cradled by a woman's voice in the shade of the patio, kiss a young village girl or strike his father in the face. Sometimes, he broke off and screamed orders at his twisted soldiers. But none of the little general's threats could overcome their dusty immobility and nothing, not even the wind, responded to his voice. Not a single leaf trembled. The child would become irritated, complaining of the grotesque postures of his trees, the slovenly appearance of their branches, and criticizing their sickly air, their gray complexion, their knotted joints. Who on earth had put him in charge of such a battalion? Then he would let out a flood of curses and get back to work.

Sometimes, his will yielded and allowed him to look for shade under a tree. There, his fever, which had soon overcome him again, plunged him into a torpor filled with languid love affairs. Beneath the dusty, serene sky, he would give himself up body and soul to an intoxicating drowsiness.

It was in the olive grove, among these creatures of wood that he did not love, that he was to have his first experience of pleasure. His brown curly hair gradually took on the smell of the olive trees. According to Anita, my eldest sister, my mother gave him the name: he was the olive tree man.

At the age of thirty-five, when he met her, the only thing he had ever kissed was the bark of his trees.

Heredia never spoke to his son about his strange escapades, never questioned him. He would watch him set off on his pilgrimage, cry his sonorous "one" at the first of the olive trees, cross the avenue and yell a "two" to the tree opposite, and continue on his way, zigzagging to the gate. He was not tempted to follow him again: he knew that each time the crisis was on him, the boy repeated the same gestures, took the same paths.

The autumn his father's mare gave birth, the boy's fits of madness became more acute and he even started counting the fallen olives. Heredia realized that the arrival of the foal had made his son's state worse. Thinking to give him the animal, he proposed a wager that none of his children would be able to tell him, before the moon rose, the precise number of olive trees on the estate, and vowed to give the colt to whoever succeeded.

The three eldest immediately scattered across the stony ground, running at random from olive tree to olive tree. Without conferring with one another, they all three had the idea of marking the trees they had already counted with white crosses. When their trajectories met in the middle of the estate, they were quite surprised to find crosses in places they had not yet passed. They became discouraged, blamed one another, and fought until nightfall in the heart of the olive grove.

While his brothers were rolling in the dust and his father was watching out for his return, the little general had collapsed beneath the most luxuriant of the olive trees, the one that gave the most shade, and at the heart of a vegetable darkness marked with no white crosses, indulged in cruel daydreams. His desire for the colt overwhelmed him with images. He knew the number. But his fever held him, kept him in a tight grip.

The wall of his reason collapsed when the moon found him out between the leaves. He emerged from his hiding place and walked home on a clear night populated with routed soldiers whose number he no longer knew. He realized then that his trees would never be of any help to him, attached as they were, not to the earth, but to the rock, caught in the stone like ships in ice.

They were like ossified old men, condemned to grieve for their god, stumps bristling beneath a heavenly vault studded with holes. It seemed to the boy that this garden would never welcome anything but doubt and suffering and that he himself had no blood to weep. God was probably looking through a spy hole in the sky, trying to see him as he walked alone down the middle of the avenue to the veranda where his father was waiting for him. God had his ear to all the holes in heaven, but heard nothing.

The child reached home without an answer and without a voice.

Heredia shivered on seeing his son so pale in the thick shadows, he clutched that little moon-white, chalk-white face to his chest and wept without knowing why.

The boy did not speak again for years, except of course to his trees, which he never stopped counting.

The child put on a few inches, then a few lines on his face, and the curse became a habit. He lost his way even more as he grew older, always following paths opposite to those he wanted to take. He loved a young woman in secret, that cousin with the blood-red fan who had inspired Frasquita's butterfly. During the first months she spent in their house, he only went back there to sleep and met her on a mere three occasions. She eventually got engaged to his oldest brother, and after the banns were published it was thought that the youngest boy would die from the sun that had beaten down on him during all those days spent in the olive grove. From a nearby village, the maids sent for a bonesetter to get the sun out of his head. The old woman said her prayers and placed a plate filled with water and an upturned glass on the young man's hair. The water boiled and rose into the glass. But the woman, who was clever, asked to meet Heredia and advised him to send his son north, far from the olive trees and the stones, to the shade of a city.

The olive grove man left the village before his brother's wedding.

In Madrid, he read a great deal even though he did not like books, reluctantly obtained all his law diplomas, and became an efficient, punctilious clerk. He had found his tongue again but was bored for fourteen years, before his father remembered him on his deathbed and, thinking to please him, bequeathed him the olive grove. The clerk had to return home to obey Heredia's last wishes and take care of his trees.

All desire was dead in the man who returned from Madrid. No flesh, no water, no perfume troubled him now, or stirred his frozen, subterranean blood. His gaze moved over things without ever coming to rest. He managed the estate with a firm hand and nobody in the village recognized the powerless little general beneath the marble mask of the administrator. His fragility had taken refuge behind an unspeakable boredom.

Despite his angular good looks and deep-set eyes, he was not known to have had any love affairs. Since his return, he had not laughed, or cried, or even sweated in the sun. Nothing emerged from that stiff body.

For three or four months each year, he hired villagers to pick his olives and take care of his trees, and his only companions were an elderly maid, a donkey and a horse.

The people of Santavela assumed that he loved the solitude of his burned earth. They left him in his corner and forgot all about him.

He only ever went through the village at the hour of siesta, taking advantage of the silence that the sun imposes on men.

When they awoke, the villagers would sometimes find a few traces of his horse's passing.

At the hour when the sun occupies the center of the sky, bombarding the world with vertical rays, an hour without shade, the olive grove man would cross the space of men in a solitude unmitigated by any double. He had lost his shadow without anyone noticing, and it had been wandering alone, counting the olive trees, since that sad evening when the child had returned home without an answer.

Only the damned wander through the world in this way without company, only the damned know such solitude.

On one of these afternoons, at the height of summer, as he was walking with his horse's bridle in his hand through the narrow sundrenched streets, at that hour when even the deepest things give rise to light, his coat was snagged on a wrought iron grille.

The encounter

Ever since old Señora Carasco had watched over her son's work, José had fitted his windows with bars, in the shape of wrought iron roosters that spread their metal feathers at the entrance to the lair of the Carascos. The shadows they cast had long since stopped scaring off the children, although every child had hurt himself on a sharp beak or spur at one time or other.

It was the beak of one of these winged doorkeepers that had snagged the tail of the olive grove man's black coat.

My mother responded immediately to the cry of the fabric.

She appeared at the window, and all she saw at first was the damaged material. She paid no attention either to the body wrapped in the material, or the brown face atop the body, or even the absent shadow. She took a needle from the little cushion bristling with pins that she carried on her wrist like a bracelet, passed a length of black thread through the eye, took hold of the garment and attacked it with her needle.

Her right hand fluttered gracefully in the window frame.

The man submitted to the tranquil power of the hand and the thread. He looked at the woman's face as she mended his frayed being. The thread sank ever deeper into the thickness of the fabric.

But it was no longer just fabric, the needle went further. The point tickled the little boy sleeping inside him, retrieved his shadow, hidden at the foot of an olive tree, and bound them firmly one to the other. Frasquita put edge to edge, desire and will, and sewed it all back together. Then she made a knot at the end of the thread and with her teeth cut the bridge she had thrown between her and the man watching her. He suddenly felt like an orphan.

For a brief moment, he had seen her lips pressed to his coat as if leaving a kiss there. My mother's face had caressed the black wool and its lining of flesh. Then without a word, her lips, hand and needle had withdrawn behind the iron roosters and the curtains had been closed.

The street had recovered its ghostly immobility. Nothing seemed to move in the house. The vision had faded, leaving the mended man pinned to the furnace of a sky that was too big for him.

At his feet, a little shadow was starting to grow in the dust.

From that point on, the olive grove man had only one thought.

His will hitched itself to his desire and worked on it relentlessly.

THE RED ROOSTER

Clara was more than a year old the day my mother discovered the red egg.

Clara was a year old and the olive grove man had just snagged his coat on the window of the woman who had faded on her wedding day.

The hens were moving, intrigued, around the ridiculous object that one of them had just laid.

Alerted by his wife's cries, José came running into the henhouse. He tore the scarlet egg from her hands and forbade her to destroy it, which was what she had wanted to do, convinced as she was that nothing good could come out of such a shell.

"Look at the color of your son's hair before you open your mouth!" he grunted, and gave a dismissive shrug.

She ought to keep her mouth shut anyway, he would deal with this thing personally! He would build it a little box and keep it at the right temperature in his forge, close to the fire, until it hatched. My mother did not insist and watched with a sigh as her husband walked away.

During the days that followed, José never let the red egg out of his sight, and when the children brought him his meals he would tell them the same story repeatedly:

"You'll see, from this red egg a red chick will emerge, as red as fire, a scarlet chick, a chick I will make the finest fighting cock in Spain. This egg will change our lives. It's written that I won't die a wheelwright and that, however many of them there are, my daughters will all find good husbands."

He had never before spoken so much to them.

My mother was worried at this new fad of his, if the egg did not hatch, how long would her husband wait like this before he admitted that it was empty? As for the children, they feared that some dragon might emerge from the shell to devour them all. Didn't hens sometimes give birth to snakes?

While Clara took her first steps, arms stretched towards the sun, José sat on his egg.

One afternoon, José came out of his forge gesticulating wildly, so excited that he could not express himself normally. Blanca would have to come immediately, hot water needed to be got ready, the neighbors had to be informed: the red egg was hatching.

Making sure the news did not spread, Frasquita put on a little water to boil—she could always drown whatever was coming out, she thought—while all the children rushed after their father into the forge, where the blood-colored shell was starting to move. With a few thrusts of its beak, the little red thing destroyed its shelter and found itself in the open air, its down all sticky, with six pairs of eyes staring at it.

From the red egg, a red chick had emerged, a red chick José would make the finest fighting cock in Spain.

Struck dumb with emotion, he watched as his fortune got up on its legs and shook itself.

Should it or should it not be given a welcoming bath? Should it be introduced to its fellow birds? Was it hot? Was it cold? What would they call it?

When Blanca came as she did every day to see Angela, she immediately asked, jovially, for news of the egg and was told that José had given his own name to the red chick it had contained. My mother, exasperated, was making the soup for the next morning in silence, and Blanca burst into broad laughter that shook the house and made José come out of his lair.

"Blanca, come and take a look at my miracle! A magnificent

bird! A real marvel! Fierce and loud, a real dragon, the children are saying! No rooster will ever dare face this champion, we'll set off on the roads of Spain to make our fortune. You'll see, this rooster will be our goose that lays the golden egg!"

"Are you sure it really is a little rooster and not a common pullet?" asked Blanca.

José laughed. "Oh, yes, it's a male all right! I've spent enough time with hens to tell the difference! I'm going to finish the work I have in progress in the forge and then I'll devote myself to training him. Look! He follows me everywhere, he must think I'm his mother!"

"So this is him, is it? His feathers really are a strange color. You aren't having us on, are you? You haven't dipped them in blood?"

"Blood isn't that color! Red like that doesn't exist!" Then, directly addressing the tiny thing cheeping on the ground: "You and me, my chick, we're going to conquer the world."

The chick scurried after José as he wandered about the room, raving. On several occasions, the man narrowly missed the little beast, unaware of the danger his fortune was running as he walked up and down without looking where he was putting his feet. As she watched, Frasquita hoped with all her heart that he would crush it.

It was the time of the first swallows. Outside, the shadows of the birds flecked the white walls with brief dark patches then spurted off in all directions like sparks from a fire. José wanted his chick to live with its own kind and find its place among them. But he was unable to shake it off in the henhouse: the creature stayed right behind him, seeing nothing but the big shoes it kept following. Several times, José took his chick to the backyard and tried to leave it there, but the little red thing simply stuck to his heels. For the first time, Frasquita opposed her husband's wishes: she refused to let the chick sleep between José's shoes at the side of the marriage bed.

"How do you want this thing of yours to become a fighting cock if it has no idea what it looks like?" my mother said, unceremoniously throwing the tiny red ball out of the room. "You have to leave it out there with the others, then if it survives, it may know how to fight!"

My father followed his wife's advice and went down to sleep among the hens. He huddled on his bench while the chick curled up against his old leather shoes.

Early in the morning, Frasquita found her man lying full length beside the bench. She dislodged his champion from the shoe in which it had huddled and shoved under the half-asleep José's nose the droppings with which it had lined the inside of its nest.

"I'll walk barefoot if need be," José screamed, as red as his rooster. "Just don't come and provoke me with any more of your stupid remarks!"

My mother did not dare make the slightest comment. She watched in silence as the shoes died a death and her husband pampered his chick more than all his children put together. In a few weeks, the young animal had liberated itself from its two adoptive mothers—the mud-caked shoes—and begun to face its life as a fowl.

The sumptuous scarlet and crimson plumage that fascinated men did not impress its brothers—not until the massacre.

By the time the day came for it to conquer its territory, the young rooster's spurs, sharpened by its master, were already of a decent size and the wattles with which its head was adorned gave it the air of a wild beast.

Little Angela, then aged six, who already knew many things her parents did not, would wake up every morning with the crowing of the old rooster and, after making sure that nobody was watching, enter the world of the birds.

That morning, in the half-light of a gray dawn, she froze at the sight of the slaughter.

The old king of the backyard had doubtless crowed once too often. That peaceful daily song must have disturbed some delightful dream in the mind of the Red Dragon. Seized with a sudden rage, the young rooster found no opponent of its own caliber and sacrificed its male fellows one by one, beginning with its father, knocking him off his throne of loose stones and droppings from which he had just given his last cry.

Alerted by the hens' almighty racket, Frasquita and José came to see the aftermath of the massacre, which marked the beginning of a new era in the backyard. Nobody would ever again challenge the power of this fighter that had been born by chance in the midst of these harmless domestic animals. It had killed its brothers to make sure of this victory, attacking their carcasses over and over until the last breath had gone from them.

After the slaughter, when the backyard was carpeted with bloodstained feathers and the corpses of the defeated, it slowly walked through its territory and let out a long cry to announce itself to the living. The hens started at it with their round eyes. Now their sole master, it flung itself on them, its head and spurs still red with its father's blood, to satisfy that violent desire that had overwhelmed it in the morning, marking the dawn of the mating season.

"I absolutely must cut off your appendages," Jose said. "They're too easy to catch hold of and they put you at a disadvantage! Look at this! The blood is dripping down and half blinding you! Coxcomb, barbs, earlobes, everything has to go! They may look impressive, but they're too fragile and they don't serve any purpose. Any opponent that gets hold of you there would kill you easily. But what anger! No need to teach you to hate your fellows, you carry that hatred in you!" He turned to his wife and daughters. "Come on, girls, to work! We have to pluck them all! What we can't eat, we'll sell. As for you, my darling, no question of making you a common king of the backyard, your master has other plans for you!"

*

Some time later, the wheelwright turned cockfighter took the young prince from its kingdom and, armed with a simple pair of scissors, cut off its scarlet wattles. He did it clumsily, the amputated bird gave a brief cry of pain and José panicked at the sight of all the blood his hero was losing. He called for help, his hands, clothes and face all spattered with blood.

Without a word, Angela approached the man and his animal and stopped the bright red shower raining on both of them by applying a few downy feathers to the wounds. Then she went back to help her mother.

The young rooster was saved.

The warrior bird drew the men of the village to the Carasco house. They came back time and again to share José's enthusiasm and to witness the training of the phenomenon, the exercises, the massages, the rubbing, the cleaning, all the care and attention its master lavished on it. The bird would be made to sit for long periods on a trapeze, trying to maintain its balance, and the children took turns in running with it to develop its breathing, speed and resistance.

The house and yard echoed until late into the night with the voices of men. Jose was jubilant. He would engage in heated debate, his rooster sitting peacefully on his knees, and, as he spoke, he would distractedly smooth its feathers.

When his champion was ready and raring to go, no other bird capable of fighting him could be found in the village. Nobody in Santavela wanted to commit his own rooster to a battle that everyone considered lost in advance. Truly, the Red Dragon was a fine-looking bird: Jose had cut his feathers the way he had once seen a little nomad bird breeder do.

The day José decided to set off in search of an opponent for his rooster, Clara, his youngest daughter, was almost two.

Clara was almost two and the olive grove man had not forgotten the woman who had mended his soul.

THE FIRST FIGHT

The whole village accompanied José and his rooster to the muddy lane that led over one hill after another in the crumpled landscape before descending toward the world. He had tied his donkey to our handcart, which was filled with provisions and gifts for the road. The Red Dragon moved about in its cage as the villagers embraced this man, one of their own, who was setting off alone beyond the horizon to seek fame and fortune.

"I'm going to come back rich!" he cried excitedly. "From the red egg came a scarlet chick I've made into the finest fighting cock in Spain! And this rooster will be our goose that lays the golden egg!"

In the middle of the crowd, he could barely see his children, who were standing on the tips of their frozen little toes and waving to him.

He disappeared around a bend in the road.

But there, someone was waiting for him.

On the road a man was standing, stiff and dark in his fine mended coat. At his feet, beside his shadow—it was young still, his shadow, small and tender as a shoot, a child's shadow—a fearsome rooster, motionless and still gray with the dust of summer, was dozing in an openwork box.

The olive grove man had an opponent to propose: this wild rooster he had discovered on his lands, no doubt a runaway from some gypsy caravan that had come from the East.

"And who would bet on this ugly, plucked beast?" asked José with a sneer.

"Me!" replied the man, his voice oddly childish at times. "I'll gamble alone against everyone if need be. The match will take place in the village before you leave. That way we'll all be able to see your bird fight. You can go off on your journey afterwards . . . "

They came to an agreement: José would not bet money, Heredia did not want any, he preferred to leave money matters to others. Between the two of them, there had to be something more personal. They decided that the stake would be the Carasco house on one side and half of Heredia's olive grove on the other. The fight would take place in a week in the village square.

Halted in his travels a mere hundred yards from Santavela, José wrapped himself in a thick blanket, settled himself in a fold in the ground to have a bite to eat, and started daydreaming.

An olive grove! He who had never owned any land other than the backyard where he kept his poultry! An olive grove that employed the villagers during the winter! That olive grove for which their ancestors had built a village on the edges of the world, deciding to stop there and instead of hiring themselves out as day laborers and work only for the Heredias, their olives, their animals, their cornfield, their vines on the southern hills. That forest of loose stones concealed riches to which he had never had access, and now this young madman was offering it to him on a whim, just to keep him in the village and see his rooster fight! A few pieces of furniture against land planted with wild trees that brought in a good income!

Sated with bread and daydreams, José retraced his steps, full of confidence and happy to announce young Heredia's challenge to all and sundry.

The men of Santavela were delighted by what the young madman had promised. Heredia himself invited them that very day to the old mill in the olive grove, from which he had cut the sails long ago to make it his headquarters, and they were all able to watch the opponent in his enclosure. The pitiful beast, tied to a post by one foot, completely indifferent to their amused stares, was scratching at the icy ground in a vain search for insects.

"Where did you find this champion of yours?" the men asked.

"On the hills. I've been chasing him for a long time. I finally trapped him using another rooster that I'd hobbled as a bait. God alone knows where he's from, but I might as well warn any of you who might come along later and accuse me of deception, don't trust the way he looks, he's a nasty beast who doesn't like either his fellow roosters or men. He wounded me when I tried to free him from the trap."

"And have you given this chicken of yours a name?"

"No. Call him whatever you like."

"José has given his rooster his own name, but we all call him the Red Dragon. Your animal is black and lives among the olive trees. Why not just call him Olive?"

By the time they got back to the village, the men had all chosen the same champion, there being no doubt in their minds as to the victory of the Red Dragon. Young Heredia was clearly out of his mind to commit his fortune this way to a fight he was bound to lose. But of course, when you were rich . . .

For two days, olive picking was neglected so that the men could build a little arena in the fountain square, some ten feet in diameter, raised on a platform and surrounded by a wooden fence low enough to allow the spectators to watch the fight. The only villager who did not want to bet on either of the two roosters was appointed the referee. The priest had refused to take on this role. He would watch the fight out of curiosity, he said, but they shouldn't count on him for anything else. No, he wouldn't bless any rooster, not José's or any other! No, he wouldn't say a mass to boost anyone's chances! No, God would take no part in it!

The shoemaker, who could write, was given the task of noting down the bets, and he was kept busy.

José, on his side, was methodically preparing his bird for the flight. He loved that rooster: he had raised it since the first day, he knew every muscle in its body, had cut every one of its feathers. On the eve of the great day, he fed it raw meat and garlic, checked its spurs to make sure they were as sharp as bronze spikes, and rubbed it down for a long time.

The local men had started drinking to warm themselves up and had gathered around the little *plaza*. All these male voices raised quite a din. There was no doubt as to the outcome of the fight, but they placed bets on how long it would last. Olive would be killed in thirty seconds by a blow to the brain from the Dragon's spur! It was what they expected, but all the same, the fight had to last a little while, they had to have a bit of fun! They hadn't built all this for nothing! Oh, as long as they were fleecing Heredia, it was worth being here! It was certain that there was more to be plucked from the man than from his animal! What's more, his three brothers were also coming to play against their own blood. Would Heredia be able to reimburse everybody if his brothers got involved? Yes, to the village he had wagered money, but his brothers were only interested in his land. When the wild rooster lost, the little general would only have his coat, his horse and his donkey left with which to go back to the city forever! Everyone remembered the mountains of lost knucklebones . . .

Now they had their revenge.

Heredia arrived carrying his rooster in a solid hessian sack. He had great difficulty in extricating the bird, pulling it out roughly at the last moment, avoiding as best he could the vigorous thrusts of its beak. The animal and its master hated one another, that much was plain to see.

He remembered the iron grille that day she had first appeared to him. The window. The burning air. The hour without shade.

José was holding the Red Dragon by its body. In its master's hands, the rooster seemed perfectly calm.

The referee, who was standing on a box, gave the signal. They climbed on the platform and presented the opponents to each other, but without letting go of them. The birds tried to grab each other by the beak. Then the two men returned to their respective corners, and, at another signal from the referee, the olive grove man and the former wheelwright placed their champions in the arena.

An explosion of movement and color and tension. Two animals coming together in an indiscriminate tangle of wings, feathers and heads, becoming one new, fearsome monster. The spectators intoxicated by the battle, the blood, the cries, and the alcohol. And the woman somewhere, waiting, hidden in the mind of one man. The fight continues: lightning speed, chaos, savagery. In the crowd, he alone is silent. Absent. Far from the fray where men and birds merge together, swaying in front of his unseeing eyes.

In this apparent confusion of feathers, steam and blood, the roosters' movements are rapid, precise, well considered. They leap, arch their bodies, thrust their feet forward, strike with their tarsus bones, then regain their balance.

This close combat makes him dream of another embrace.

They crash into one another in mid air, some three feet above the ground.

He is lost amid the hullaballoo.

In the first phase of the fight, the black rooster proves less powerful but craftier and more clear-sighted than its rival. When the red bird leaps, Olive flattens itself, passes beneath its opponent, then swivels and leaps in its turn.

He is hungry for her.

After an uninterrupted succession of lightning-fast attacks and swerves, the two roosters pause, face to face, self-collected, watching each other.

He is hungry for her body.

The Red Dragon manages to catch its opponent by one of the few feathers on its head, thus ensuring its thrust reaches its target, pins Olive to the ground,

Hungry for her breasts,

and strikes home, hard.

her mouth,

One wing is broken. José's bird leaps forward again, one of Olive's feathers in its beak,

her vagina.

but this time the wounded rooster flattens itself, unbalancing its opponent and forcing it to let go.

He possesses her

The fight slows down, the two weary warriors keep their good wings well away from their bodies to keep cool, steam is coming off them, rising in the icy air, they push at each other with their chests,

body to body.

which stops them from leaping. Broken-winged but determined, Olive shows its courage:

He slips inside her,

although much weakened, it continues the struggle, withstanding its opponent's attacks.

she is open and soft.

The crowd is going wild. The Red Dragon, excited by its imminent victory and the taste of blood, speeds things up in order to have done with it, and in so doing drops its guard.

She writhes

Then, in a final bust of energy,

as his penis

Olive leaps,

goes in and
grabs hold of one of the the champion's gorgeous scarlet feathers and
out.
with a long thrust of its spur tears open the throat of the red rooster, which reacts to this mortal wound with surprise.
He goes further
Olive will not let its opponent go, it rips its flesh, opening wide gashes, and the red bird's guts gush out.
into her.
The Dragon has lost, gored by its rival's spurs.
More!

In the total silence that follows Olive's victory, Heredia was heard to murmur this one word: "More!" Then, still stunned by the outcome of the fight, the villagers saw him rush onto the platform to tear the remains of the defeated bird from the spurs of his wild rooster and, holding his own bloodstained beast by the feet like a common chicken, turn to José and cry, "Give it to your wife! Let her sew it back up! Maybe it can fight again!"

As Heredia stuffed the victorious rooster in his sack, José, aroused by this final hope, came back to his senses and, as he clutched the remains of his red bird to his chest, had the feeling it was still alive. He quickly put the guts back inside the stomach, took it in his arms and ran home, yelling his wife's name.

Heredia left, without joy, without a glance at its downcast brothers, without saying another word, carrying at arm's length, far from his body, apparently with disgust, the clear cloth sack, now stained with blood and shaken with violent convulsions. Olive, which had just doubled its master's fortune, giving him a share of his brothers' cornfields, animals and vineyard, Olive, so full of savagery and resentment, was still fighting an invisible opponent, in a fight to the death it had been waging forever and that it, too, would never win . . .

In the night, the men had children's nightmares . . . With a single gesture, Heredia was scattering their bones beneath an icy sky, spreading them through the village, on the red earth of the hills, abandoning them on lanes white with dust.

A mountain of white knucklebones shone in his dark pockets.

THE CARESS

L ike all the women in the village, Frasquita had followed
the fight from a distance, from her kitchen, relying on
the cries to imagine the scene. She had closed her eyes
and her body had opened to the men's commotion.

The exclamations, the roars of encouragement, the cries of
joy had suddenly disappeared, extinguished by a heavy silence.

Something touched her lightly on her taut belly, causing the
down on her arms to stand on end.

Had the others felt that caress?

And then a single call had broken the absolute calm that
had fallen over the area. Her name cried out in the streets,
knocking at all the doors, groping for her in the icy shadow.

The cold air had vibrated . . .

She had understood. She had gone upstairs to fetch her
sewing box and had waited for them, the man and the rooster.
And for the first time, her needle had entered living flesh.

Sitting by the stove, she had worked on the rooster while it
lay there as lifeless as a torn cloth. She had sewed it back
together with red thread, then had recited the prayers for *carne
cortada* and made the sign of the cross.

Once the rooster was saved, Angela, who had watched her
without intervening, had asked, "Why?"

Frasquita had not known what to reply.

Why?

She had no idea.

Because of that caress, perhaps . . .

The furniture

The day came when the first debt had to be paid: the olive grove man was going to take possession of their furniture.

Closets, beds, chests and chairs would go from their house to his. They would be left only with Clara's cradle, the cast iron stove, the kitchen utensils, the forge and José's tools, now silent and useless, and, of course, the handcart and the sewing box, both indispensable to the continuation of our story.

It is unfair to say that my mother was insensitive to the loss of her objects. I think that at first she resigned herself, feeling neither joy nor sadness, just a gentle indifference. Then, as she looked at her little world on the verge of departure, she felt something awake and touch her.

The caress . . .

Her cheeks turned crimson beneath a shower of red feathers and her hands got down to a task that absorbed her for two whole days: the objects that were leaving had to be more beautiful than they had ever been.

Frasquita left the younger children to Anita and began preparing the furniture.

Her gaze was drawn to a dented corner of the big table, and she discovered a forest of signs, the entry to which was usually concealed by habit. Her duster slowly followed the knots of the wood, blindly sensing the blows received, reading the oak as if it was a book. As her hand rubbed, my mother felt as though new sap was rising in the flesh of a dead tree.

She was repeating everyday gestures that had filled her life as a woman, but this time a hidden world came to the surface, revealing the tracks left by generations of dusters sacrificed on the altar of the Carasco inheritance.

It was on that scoured table that old Senora Carasco's tiny body had been displayed. That thin, shriveled body, which Frasquita had washed with María, that body so thin and light that she could carry it on her own without any effort. She remembered lifting that inert, naked little woman, that almost nothing, barely real. She remembered combing the hair for a long time, then draping the body in the *fantasía* of blue thread she had used as a shroud. She remembered all those who, coming for the wake, had kissed the end of the material—which she had embroidered sitting on that chair, her chair, her seat— rather than the thin, lifeless hands. She remembered how it had been stolen from her mother-in-law's grave and how, after that desecration, she had felt like throwing away her needles.

And now she had mended the rooster!

She would keep her chair! Frasquita weighed up each thing and jettisoned it, loosening invisible bonds, feeling an unknown intoxication as she stroked the door of a closet.

In that bed, she had dreamed unspeakable things. The sheets had kept their heady scent, a scent of olive trees, which José had complained about in the morning.

Frasquita rubbed the furniture until her arms hurt, sanded the feet of the rickety chairs, polished their wooden companions.

A madness took sudden hold of her, and she whispered words of love into the half-open chest, words of love that she then locked in it along with a bag filled with dry lavender cut out of the lining of one of her four skirts. She placed a kiss on the wooden lips of the gaping closet, cooled her cheeks against the cold hinges, kissed the lock, savoring it, and the iron seemed bloodstained.

The key was adorned with a tongue of red cloth that she treasured.

This detail made the massive closet seem tragically female.

Frasquita did not have to wait, he was already there in his fine dark woolen coat, the very one she had mended with her needle through the window, between the iron beaks and spurs.

Over her dark eyes passed the shadow of a caress.

She barely saw her house emptying.

THE EMPTY HOUSE

Frasquita was looking at her children in the flickering light of the oil lamps.

Martirio and Pedro were playing by the stove with the straw-filled rag dolls she had sewed for them and the toy cart, José's one gift for his son, while Angela, exhausted by her long day's work in the olive grove, had closed her excessively round eyes and fallen asleep with her head on Anita's knees. Anita herself was sitting on the floor, plunged in one of the priest's thick tomes. Their dresses, both stained with mud and dust, made a little ocher and gray heap, a little heap in the colors of the winter, which rose and fell to the gentle rhythm of their breathing.

The body of her eldest daughter would soon be transformed.

In memory of the women who had gone before her, Frasquita would have to initiate her.

Initiate her into what? Where was the magic in this empty house?

What had she herself done with her gift?

Life had passed so quickly . . .

And besides, no prayer could ever emerge from her daughter's mouth because she never spoke.

It was all doubly pointless. Absurd.

Anita said nothing, but her eternal smile drove the others to tell her their stories and she would listen to them all, young and old, with infinite patience. Nothing could ever stem the flow of words: whoever spoke to her lost all notion of duration. Time and finiteness disappeared, time was suspended on either side of this mute young girl's long attentive smile. Everyone confided their secrets in her, hiding nothing of their terrors, their impulses, their desires.

But what did she then do with all the words she had drunk in?

She would hold them close within her, she would never forget the slightest phrase, the smallest confidence. Everything had its place in her unfathomable memory.

And now, sitting beside the lamp, this silent young girl—whose body beneath her clothes, that little ocher and gray heap in the colours of winter, was beginning its silent trasformation—was reading as if reading was merely a harmless gesture and not a rare, solemn act reserved for a circle of initiates.

And Frasquita, looking at her, would feel her heart swell with joy and pride.

One day, the priest had called to Anita as she was passing the church. He knew that she was gentler, deeper and less severe than his confessional, which was why she was the guardian of everyone's secrets, old stories as well as the news of the day. Because of that, and in memory of another young girl and an embroidered little heart that he had never seen again but that he felt beating beneath his skin when it was cold in the church and his prayer dried up, he had asked her if she wanted to learn to read and write.

Writing anything other than figures did not interest her, but reading . . . That was like having other stories to listen to.

So several times a week she attended the lesson the priest gave to a few boys. Insatiable, driven by her hunger for stories, she learned very quickly to read. Lives of the saints, the Old and New Testaments in the common language, a storehouse of sad and edifying tales: she swallowed everything greedily, to the last drop.

Teaching a girl to read, a mute girl what's more, had been seen as yet another aberrant idea of the Carascos. That the priest should lend himself to such an absurdity beggared understanding!

Surprisingly, although she read in silence, for herself alone, nobody ever doubted her ability to decipher the words. The priest had seen by the way her eyes moved that she was going steadily through the text without making any mistakes. At first, she would fix her gaze on one finger in order not to lose balance, not to be thrown to the bottom of the page, not to jump from one word to the next or tumble several lines and catch herself up at the last moment on the crest of an initial letter, no matter which one. Later, she would use her finger, slightly moistened, only to turn the pages.

An infinite luxury, this reading, unknown to the others! All these words coming in and never going out again. A veritable stroll in a forbidden garden reserved for the rich, the well-read, the scholars, a garden where the pride of men flourished, concealed beneath an apparently innocent rosary of little black marks.

Was Anita not committing a sin, as her mother had done before her, by trying to brave convention in this way, by not contenting herself with being a wordless child who listened so well to them and their miseries? Would they still talk to her now that she could read?

Frasquita, proud to see her daughter engrossed in her reading as soon as her day's work was over, cared little about the gossip.

Although mute, her daughter was escaping, following a narrow trail toward a vast unknown world, a world entirely contained in that open object that absorbed her.

But which of the two was devouring the other, the book or its reader?

Frasquita made up her mind. At Easter, she would empty the box of her threads and needles.

At Easter, the box would no longer be hers. She would make herself a bag to put her gift in.

It was so long since she had last embroidered anything.

The bag would be gray-green on a red background, the colours of the olive grove where she worked now with Anita and Angela, since they had to earn a living and her husband was recovering at the same speed as that foolish scarred red bird to which he was now devoting all his time.

One evening, coming back from the hills, she had found the white walls of the kitchen all covered with drawings. Pedro had dispelled the emptiness of the house with clay and ashes. He had given the kitchen back its furniture. And as nobody had reprimanded him for it, he had continued, every day drawing more imaginary objects in the deserted rooms.

Gray-green on a red background.

For a moment, Frasquita was lost in thought. In the semi-darkness, her son's long hair was the same color as the ocher earth of the olive grove. By day, as she embraced the trees, slipping her hands between their branches so that the ripe fruit should fall on the sheets, or as she descended the hills with a basket filled to the brim with olives on her head, she would hear the horse's steps behind her, feel its close, hot breath on her back and her sight would grow blurred. At night, lying in the dark on the floor beside José, she could not always get to sleep, despite her fatigue, and she would wait determinedly for morning in an explosion of white flowers.

José entered the room along with the cold air from outside. Angela woke up, Frasquita emerged from her daydream, Anita put down her book, and they all sat down on the ground, beside the painted table, to have supper.

THE SUN CHILD

Curled up in a cradle that was too small for her, Clara would sink into sleep, whether she had eaten or not, as soon as the sun disappeared behind the hills. Blanca had to spend every day taking care of the child. Her mother did not see her these days: she would leave for the olive grove before dawn, and work there until the last light had faded and it was difficult to distinguish her hand from the barks of the trees. Men, women and children would then come down off the hills and walk in the darkness, their limbs like lead, along the paths that converged toward the village. At first, little Angela had sung at work or on the way home, and those with their hands free to clap in rhythm responded with *palmas flamencas*, but the recent cold weather had dried up her singing as it had those of the other *cantaores*, freezing the tears in their voices so that no modulated cry emerged now from their painful throats. They all walked at the same somnambulent pace, without any liberating sob to revive their great joy in feeling alive.

As nothing could overcome the sleep that engulfed Clara as soon as night had fallen, and as none of the two children remaining in the house were of an age to take complete care of her, she would have died of hunger if Blanca had not fed her.

Her magnificent clear straw-colored eyes, wide open on the sky all day long, would close abruptly, like doors being slammed, to escape the darkness.

Soon, there would be no more work in the olive grove and

Frasquita would again see her little girl's eyes. But my mother was not really pleased: something would be missing, a breath on her neck, that constantly renewed caress.

One day when an exceptionally clear sky had blinded the day laborers, drawing arabesques at the back of their eyes, as the afternoon was coming to its end and everyone was looking forward to the warm shade of their homes, Blanca came rushing into the olive grove, in a panic: Clara had disappeared. She had slipped away from her elders, and had been missing for several hours.

Frasquita abandoned her pole and called to Anita and Angela.

"She's always looking at the sun," said Blanca. "The weather has been wonderful today, she must have been drawn outside by the light."

My mother and her two daughters left the old woman—already out of breath, she would not be able to keep up with them—and hurried back to the village to try and follow the little fugitive's trail.

They walked westward, where the sun was already starting to sink in the limpid sky. Soon, it would be dark and whereas the light-filled day had been mild, the night would be icy. Frasquita was almost running, screaming her daughter's name. Her baby would die if she had to spend the night outside, especially as the cold would surprise her during her sleep. They had to go as fast as possible in the direction of the setting sun and catch up with her before nightfall.

Frasquita would have liked to hold back the dying sun, which was dropping on the other side of the world like the sand in a gigantic hourglass. She was weeping, and she could feel the cold of night fall on the stones and reduce them to sand.

From time to time, the echo of her broken voice would

answer her and mingle with the songlike cries coming from Angela, who was advancing in a parallel line a few hundred yards below her and could barely be made out in the gathering dark.

As for Anita, she did not cry out, condemned as she was to silence. But in spite of her anguish, she savored the strange polyphony of the other two as the echoes filled the countryside and, when the voices fell silent, she would listen in the silence for an answer, however weak, which was not that of the mountains.

All that remained now of the sun was its orange train. In the east, the darkness was gradually growing thicker. The stars came out one by one in an intensely dark sky untroubled by any moon.

Night. It was night and the child was lost.

Angela let out her last trills, and then there was silence.

"We must go home," said my mother, stifling her sense of helplessness and letting the little ones—yes, my God, still so little—think that it was only the icy wind that was making her eyes water. "I've already made you do a lot of running, you're going to catch your death of cold. Clara walks quickly but I don't think her legs could have carried her this far, we may have passed her. We'll find her on the way back."

Frasquita clutched her two daughters to her and, embracing them to give them more warmth and feel them alive against her—just as a piece of herself seemed to have been torn from her for good—she did an about-turn and set off in the opposite direction. They advanced in the thick darkness, trying to walk as steadily as they could in the driving wind.

As they went, they remembered Clara's pretty, round belly, her *why*s and *what is it*s, her wet, haphazard kisses, the way she placed her two chubby little hands on their cheeks to hold their faces still when she kissed them, and the way her laughter revealed miniature teeth ready to devour everything with love. And, well before all that, well before the laughter and the words, there had been that mouth turned indiscriminately toward the breast or the sun, trying somehow to escape the face in which it was set and catch, with a strange little sideways smile, the breasts of the world.

Then, as Frasquita recited the prayer to Saint Antony of Padua, one of the prayers from the first night, a prayer for lost things, Anita pointed to her left.

The following morning, the people of the village passed the word to each other.

The Carascos had found their youngest somewhere in the west.

On a hill something had been shining, a little flame that only the darkness of the moonless night made visible, a light that had no place in the black countryside. Nothing could explain its presence. It shone less brightly than a fire, it appeared totally motionless and could not be a lamp shaken by Blanca or José—who had set off after Frasquita—to show her that they were there or which road to take.

The people of Santavela recounted how my mother and her two daughters advanced toward the light without suspecting that on the other side of the hill they were slowly starting to climb, José, the priest and, far behind them, Blanca were just arriving, drawn by the same radiance.

According to the rumor that circulated, it was José who, having finally made up his mind to leave his rooster sleeping, had been the first to get there and take the luminous child in his arms. The words he was supposed to have said were repeated, with much adverse comment on their coarseness and blasphemy:

"Hey, padre! Come over here! This isn't normal! It's the child that's shining like this! Hold her a bit to see if she doesn't go out in your arms. Do you think it's right to light up the world when you're asleep? Unless she's dying. Go on, pray! Do something! Don't stand there with your mouth open! For once there's something strange that can be useful to us, more useful anyway than red hair or a stitched-up mouth, so we might as well keep this one alive! You talk to the man upstairs every day, tell him we want to keep her, he can have her later but right now she's too young to die. Pull yourself together, padre! Yes, she's shining, so what? We're not going to spend the night here!"

As soon as they got back from the olive grove, the men and women had spread out around Santavela in the darkness, turning over every stone, searching in the undergrowth for the lost child. When the Carascos returned home with her, the village echoed with cries.

But now the people once again turned against the family for being different. In this country where children dropped like flies, Frasquita had not yet lost any of hers.

They all accepted the fact that little Clara had shone in the dark.

And not only the malicious gossips, because even today my sister Anita tells the story of a child of light and says that something was burning so brightly inside her that her little two-year-old body could have been used to light a room.

Some nights during the last winter they spent in that empty house in Santavela, the light she gave off was so intense that Anita, who slept with her in her room, would creep to the side of her cradle and continue her reading.

It was as if Clara had kept on her skin all the luminescence accumulated during her days spent looking avidly at the thin bright patches cast by the windows on the floor of the house. Whenever she found a way out, Clara would escape and stand motionless in the yard, palms open, offering herself to the lukewarm rays of a sun held captive by the winter, a sun that lost more ground every day, that could only rise halfway up the sky, and even then only with a lot of difficulty, to be immediately driven back by the shadows on the other side of the world and drag down in its fall the long dark lashes of the solar child.

THE SECOND FIGHT

A nd the arena was rebuilt, while the birds squawked and the women muttered. But no protests, no warning could spoil the good mood of those laying bets: the resurrection of the Red Dragon was a sign from God. Having stayed out of the first fight, He would reward those who had not given up hope.

While the villagers had been picking olives, they had seen Heredia's wild rooster, whose broken bones had set in defiance of common sense, left unattended in its enclosure, surrounded by the furniture its ungrateful master had had to move from the old mill to make room for Frasquita's. Fine furniture, abandoned to the winter weather, much more valuable than my mother's, but which nobody would have dared to ask for, even to make firewood.

And for the first time that winter, working for Heredia had seemed to them not like an injustice, but like something that could have been different. The olive grove could easily have belonged to one of them and, with the arrival of that thought, the world had begun to shake. So, in spite of opposition from the women, who feared the Carascos, they decided to put their weight in the balance, hoping that the universe might tip in their direction with the thrust of a beak. José, cracked as he was, was like them, and the future of the village depended on him.

Nothing was unchangeable any more. For the second time, they would all bet on the red rooster.

Swollen with wine, hope and a sense of rebellion that was still quite new and unaware of itself, the villagers stamped the ground and yelled encouragement to the Dragon, which was more scarlet than ever. Not having to work the olive grove anymore, generation after generation, under the baleful eye of a Heredia: that was what the bird now represented. What was at stake was the end of all certainties. It was no longer only a matter of making a little money, but of actually upsetting the order of the world.

And yet, deep down in each of them, there were still mysterious feelings for Olive, a wild animal that was fighting even more against its ungrateful master than against its feathered brothers, even though it had already made it possible for him to increase his fortune. This time, nobody dared comment on its pitiful appearance, the way pieces of it held together as best they could, as if assembled by an age-old anger.

Heredia's brothers fought their own servants to get close to the arena. Having already lost so much land during the first fight, they had returned to regain what they had been dispossessed of and only that, for this time it was the whole olive grove that had been promised to Carasco.

An olive grove against what?

An olive grove against the house where my mother lived, that house with walls painted by a child, where only a few pieces of furniture had sprung up again. A house and its yard, a house and its window, adorned with iron beaks and spurs, behind which lurked the needle and the eyes of the woman who had pinned Heredia to the blue noon sky, the woman for whose scent he had lain in wait all winter long in his olive grove, hoping that the harvest would never end and that he could still keep seeing her long limbs through the branches of his countless trees. He would have gladly asked the whole village to continue its work, to pay them for an imaginary harvest, to suggest to them that they gather fruit that was not there, in order to watch her walking, carrying her empty baskets, for a while longer. He would have offered his income and his lands to have her embrace the flowering olive trees, to have the shadows of her skirt and the horse merge together, to keep touching the outline of her body cast on the ground by the sun, that huge dark figure enclosed beside him in a network of branches as if in a cage. But such madness had not been possible, he had not dared, he had not yet reached that point. In order for him to see her again, the roosters would have to fight once more, because he knew that this time the women would stir themselves.

And there they were, a few steps behind the noisy throng of men, silent and dignified, quite surprised to see that there were so many of them in this place where they were not expected, and the children were there too, having refused to stay away. And only a few seconds after the beginning of the fight, the women had thrown off their maidenly decorum, joined the men and the children—the latter whining that they wanted to see better—and without even realizing it, started shouting.

"Hey, Dragon, we'll let you drink brandy after your victory!"

"You can have all the hens in the village! Even mine!"

Heredia was not following the fight.

Standing on the bench beside the referee, he was looking for her on the edge of the dense mass of spectators. Starting to give up hope, he was coming down from his perch when he met her gaze. She did not turn away, but stood there motionless in the crowd, and for a long time they looked at each other, unblinkingly, from opposite sides of the platform. This look lasted so long Heredia thought he would die. The roosters were getting covered in blood, the feathers were flying, the cries growing louder, but their two bodies remained still, and neither thought of breaking that visual embrace.

Then they were jostled and lost sight of each other.

Olive had taken the advantage, and its savagery and resentment had unsettled the Red Dragon, which did not look as if it still had much hope of getting out alive. José, filled with pity for his champion and suffering at each new thrust of its opponent's spur, was yelling for them to stop the fight. He wanted to save his rooster, he was prepared to give up his house as long as he could save his rooster and care for it and win everything back at the next encounter.

But the spectators would not let him. A reversal in the situation was still possible! Who could have predicted Olive's victory in the last fight? Who could have imagined that that remnant of a rooster still had such reserves of violence and anger? They had to see it through to the end, they had all bet on the Dragon again and they were going to lose their shirts. They had nothing more to lose by letting the fight continue, they still had hope.

For José, it was all too much, he refused to stand by powerless as his bird died. Men threw themselves on him as he was getting ready to enter the arena and take out his bloodstained rooster, which was having difficulty keeping its balance but had not run away and was demonstrating astonishing courage. José was beaten black and blue in the process of being restrained. New bets were laid, some put ten to one on Olive in order to recover a little of their starting bet, others continued to believe that a lucky last-minute thrust of the Dragon's beak would kill the wild rooster. And that thrust came, covering Olive's head with so much blood that it now seemed to be striking out blindly.

Then the bets were reversed again, they let go of José, who, a little stunned by the blows, now also started believing again and yelled encouragement at his champion.

This was to underestimate the black rooster's survival instinct, its capacity to endure.

Accustomed to duels to the death, the black beast, reflecting and feeding on the violence of men, gathered itself, head, wings and spurs, and plunged into the scarlet torrent that flooded its eyes.

There was a brief sharp cry of pain.

The unusual fight had come to an end.

The red rooster lay on the ground, and Olive, blinded by its own blood, unable to find the remains of its opponent to savor its victory, continued blindly beating the mild late winter air that flowed over everyone's faces like a caress.

The wind of rebellion did not blow, and a woman's hands seized the heap of red feathers . . .

ANITA'S INITIATION

The following week, Heredia, abandoning his mill and his trees, rushed to the Carasco house and, as the lost furniture returned to its original dwelling, once again their eyes met.

The closet was bare, its red ribbon had been torn off.

Watching the man stroking the door frames, seeing the whitewash on the walls come off on his hands, my mother could no longer ignore what pierced her heart. He hesitated, then entered her house, clinging to her eyes, and his black coat caressed the hand that had held the needle. Frasquita knew why she had again stitched up the red rooster, and Angela asked her no questions.

"That rooster will never win!" was all the child said, with the man within their walls and her mother slowly walking toward the handcart laden with the few objects that remained to them. As this assertion did not gain her even the hint of a glance, she decided to tell her father as soon as he was in a state to hear her warning and perhaps take it seriously.

Those who were bringing in Heredia's furniture were surprised by the monumental childish frescoes that covered all the walls of the house. As the new owner of the premises remained silent and pensive, and did not even deign to answer their questions, they placed the furniture where Pedro had drawn it.

With Frasquita leading, harnessed to the handcart—filled with linen and objects, as well as the re-stitched Dragon, which

José had placed on it—Carasco and his children and poultry proceeded through the silent village, every look thrown at them a reproach.

The day after the fight, the arena had not been dismantled, but destroyed. Wrecked, torn to pieces, burned. The whole of the little community had taken part, with kicks and punches and blows of the ax. All that remained in the square was a little heap of ashes that everyone came and spat on when the desire took him. You had to understand them, these villagers whom José had led into the fight unwittingly, promising them not only a victory, but above all a better life. The dream that had carried them along with it was dead, destroyed by the defeat of the red rooster, and its corpse stank so much that it infested the world in which they had all lived until then without imagining they could change it. It would have been better not to dream at all, the corpse of their dead dream was making real life rotten.

The hope had died, but the beast was still alive.

Why was this family so determined to save the one thing that was to blame for their loss?

The Carascos settled in the old house that had belonged to Frasquita's parents and had been left abandoned since their deaths. A small dwelling place indeed for children accustomed to living in large bare rooms with painted walls.

Obeying Frasquita's softly spoken orders, all the children worked to make the place pleasant, to make it their own. Pedro was not allowed to decorate the inner walls, but with his elder sisters he whitewashed the front of the house, while little Clara stamped her feet with joy to see so much light.

A few days later, Angela was awaiting the return of the migrating birds, Martirio was luring Clara into the shade, using as bait the reflection from a fragment of mirror, Pedro was enjoying himself making colored arabesques—derived from the first flowers—around the windows, Anita was regularly emptying her shoes of olive stones and the pointed pebbles that her mother insisted on putting there, and the Seis de las Penas were dressing the blue Virgin. Life was somehow trundling on.

On the evening of Holy Tuesday, my mother wakes Anita in the night and drags her through the sleeping village to the cemetery.

After nearly twenty years, here she is on the same road, performing another woman's gestures, without knowing why: blindfolding Anita, turning her until she is dizzy, reciting the prayers, and giving her the box. But there is one difference. Anita does not repeat any of the words her mother's voice teaches her.

"It doesn't matter, they'll go in anyway!" Frasquita tells herself.

But as she is about to give up that cherished box, her one possession, she hesitates. Now she knows why her own mother found it so difficult to let go of it.

Frasquita is barely thirty and it is already time for her to give way.

She feels herself pushed toward the void by her own children.

Something brushes against her in the darkness, a caress that does not resemble the one in the olive grove man's eyes. Something brushes against her in the darkness as her feet sink slightly in the still cold earth. Suddenly her ankles are caught in an icy vise, she is really sinking now, she is being pulled down. In a panic, she hastens to give the box to the hands reaching out in front of her and to tear off the blindfold.

Everything is normal, no diabolical hand is holding her feet, no ghost brushes against her spine, the night is clear, the world is gentle and Anita is clutching the box in her arms. It is as if the girl is seeing it for the first time, and does not associate it with her mother's sewing box. Frasquita herself finds the object changed: the wood seems to her lighter in color and, against her daughter's chest, the cube is smaller.

"Could it be that in nine months this box that I emptied myself will again be full?" she wonders. "Could it be that hands gripped my feet and the dead ran over my back? Could it be that someone other than my daughter took my sewing box while this new box was given her by other hands than mine? Could it be that the voice I heard when I was a child wasn't really my mother's? Will I one day know all about the dead and their power?"

The ogre

The ogre came to the village during Sunday mass, right in the middle of spring, when half the women of child-bearing age had swollen bellies.

For several months now, Blanca had been training Rosa, the eldest daughter of the Capillas, so that there would be two of them to help on those nights of the full moon when the babies would all come out at once. But, according to Anita, Blanca already knew that she would not be able to remain in hiding for much longer. She could sense his presence, knew he was coming to her.

He dismounted in the square with the fountain. His hair, his clothes, his horse seemed to have been carved out of a moon-less, starless night. His donkey, trotting behind him, was loaded with a jumble of bags and boxes.

A stranger in Santavela was already an event in itself, but no stranger like him, no man of learning laden with plants, seeds and stones from the four corners of the world, had ever ventured so far down the lanes that led to the village.

Coming out of church, everyone saw him and immediately rushed home, carefully avoiding his gaze.

A smile on his lips, he watched them as they bolted. He hailed a woman whose joints were so painful that she could neither hurry nor make a detour in order to get home without having to pass close to the stranger.

"My name is Eugenio. I'm travelling in search of rare plants and I'm a past master in the art of using herbs and curing ills. I may be able to help you. Is it your joints that hurt?"

"The whole machine is jammed," the woman muttered without even looking at him or slowing down. "I don't go anywhere anymore except to mass on Sunday."

"Rheumatism . . . Do the pains sometimes change position? Leave one joint to attack others?"

"That's right!" she replied, still moving slowly forward. "And it's especially at night that these changes happen."

"You don't seem to me to be of a very sanguine temperament. The best thing to do would be to bleed you in the arm. But you must be treated because if your illness moves to the heart or brain, it might prove fatal."

"What should I do?" the woman asked, all at once less surly.

"Wait! I'm going to give you some plants to boil in water for half an hour. Just put your painful joints in it and leave them there until your skin wrinkles a little. You should keep the water, you can use it several times, you just have to reheat it."

Eugenio rummaged in the bags on his donkey's back and filled a paper cone, which he handed to the woman. As she seemed to hesitate, he burst into hearty laughter.

"It's all perfectly safe: rosemary, sage, hyssop, bay, wormwood, flowers of elder and ivy, and here's a good handful of sea salt to throw into the cooking water. It isn't the devil's brew! To be honest, I'm giving you all this for free as a bait for the others: when they see you running like a rabbit, they won't doubt my skill. And while we're about it, I advise you to treat your eyes too. They're running yellow—non-scrofulous ophthalmia. Poultices of soft cheese and whey will do the trick. Change them every three hours!"

The rheumatic woman seized the plants, muttered a formal thank you, and was getting ready to leave as quickly as her ills allowed when the man stopped her.

"Wait! At least tell me the name of this village before you go!"

"Santavela," she replied half-heartedly.

"Do you know a midwife named Blanca?" he asked her.

"Yes. She lives in a house over there, just outside the village."

"Now go home!" the man said, all smiles. "Go home and treat yourself! I'm going to need patients! Tell the others they can find me in the midwife's house!"

Everything about Eugenio was convincing: his grave, calm voice, his superior air, his intelligent eyes, his refined clothes, his magnificent black horse and, of course, the way he spoke, full of learned words, but always clear, always adapted to his audience.

The little woman did everything he had prescribed without further hesitation. And before long she felt better.

Eugenio moved in with Blanca, whom he knew, and in the days that followed the whole village visited him, surreptitiously at first, then in full view of everyone. There were soon so many people outside the midwife's house that it became necessary to make an appointment to see him.

He would cauterize wounds with a silver nitrate pencil he called an infernal stone, cure heartburn by diluting lime water in milk and ozena by making the patient sniff a highly concentrated concoction of bramble leaves. Wherever possible, he used plants and herbs from the hills to treat people.

"Nature grows remedies to cure ills," he would tell his patients. "But some afflictions come from a long way away, carried on the wings of migrating birds. They spread throughout the world, even to the most remote places. So it's very useful to know and possess exotic plants. And besides, I don't know the flora and fauna of the region well enough, I don't know all the things that can be found here. It's up to you to teach me the remedies you use and hand down from mother to daughter. I'm fond of them, that's where my knowledge partly comes from. But only partly . . . I've traveled a lot, met great men of science, read a large number of books and treatises. Right now, everything is happening in France: Monsieur Pasteur has made some amazing discoveries, about the rabies virus for example . . . "

They put their trust in him and paid him in kind: hens, oil, sacks of corn, bread, little services. He would fix his fees as he went along, according to the price and rarity of the medications he prescribed. He talked a lot, but was also good at asking questions, not only about their aches and pains, but also about their habits, their private lives, their dreams, their children, and so on.

If a young woman in the village struck him as pale and sad, he would immediately advise her to pay a visit to Blanca's, where he would examine her and prescribe something to revive her blood: water turned rusty by a sprinkling of cloves. And Blanca seemed to hate all this: the people he attracted, the power he was gaining day by day, the knowledge he was accumulating about everybody. Yes, she was giving him board and lodgings—although he was earning quite enough to do without her—but she did it reluctantly. Above all she appeared unwilling to leave him alone with his patients. She watched him constantly, somewhat neglecting her visits to women nearing the end of their pregnancy. Her irritation became very obvious when Eugenio offered amulets for good health or practiced bleeding—always with the patient having an empty stomach.

Often he applied the leeches he carried in his kit, making them release their grip with the help of a little pinch of salt, unless he let them gorge themselves until their thirst was quenched, even stimulating the bites after the animals had been taken off. In the cases of some women, who had soon started speaking to him unblushingly about their personal concerns, he would place some of these animals near their vulvas. "To get the blood flowing again," he would say.

But what he loved most was treating little children, to whom he frequently administered enemas. Enemas with cold water for constipation. Enemas with soot or salt against worms. Enemas with laudanum to soothe colic. He never failed to give the children gassy lemonade before they left to make them forget the enema and encourage them to come back and see him.

In less than a month, the villagers were so besotted with their doctor that they wondered how they could have lived without him for so long.

Blanca looked on anxiously as Eugenio's power and influence grew. Whenever anyone asked her why he had come to stay with her, she would invariably reply, "He's a relative," in a tone that discouraged them from asking any further questions.

Neither my mother nor Angela ever spoke to her about her guest. So far, no Carasco had yet paid him a visit.

The first to do so was José, who went about with his patched-up rooster in his arms. He was suffering so much, he could no longer mount a horse.

"Hemorrhoids!" cried Eugenio after examining him carefully. "Most of the time, it's better not to cure them. Treating them can expose sanguine people especially to congestions in the areas of the brain. However, in your case, we have to act! Your anus is forming a thick purplish roll of flesh and nothing can get through. Twelve to fifteen leeches applied to the roll itself will do the trick. Bend down and don't move, let me put them on. After that, we'll do a little enema with flax seeds, and we'll put your bottom on a bowl full of a strong brew of yarrow two or three times a day to receive the steam. In the future, avoid spicy dishes, do more walking, and remember that, as soon as you notice hemorrhoids, you have to try to get them back inside!"

As he talked, he introduced his leeches, one by one, head down, in a playing card he had previously rolled, then applied the little tube of paper to the exact spot where he wanted the leech to take root. As he repeated the operation for the tenth time, he was surprised to notice that José, even though he had his buttocks in the air, had not let go of his bird.

"That's a fine rooster you have there! Is it for me?"

"Oh, no! I always take it with me for fear of bad people."

"Bad people?"

"Many of those you treat would like to see him dead!"

"Really?"

"He lost them a lot of money. Haven't you ever heard of the Red Dragon?"

"No, never."

"That's because you haven't been in the village for very long. Barely a month, unless I'm mistaken. Nobody's talking about it now. But they haven't forgotten. He's quite a fighter, this bird!"

"I see! Now we just have to wait and make sure they don't bite elsewhere! Don't change position!" Eugenio went close to the rooster. "A fine bird indeed! But why the devil does he have so many feathers missing?"

"His opponent took quite a few and my wife tore out the rest to stitch him up again."

"She stitched him up? Where? I don't see any scars."

"That's because my wife has a gift for that! She used to only handle cloth. But now she's twice saved my rooster. All his guts were out in the open, and he had some really deep gashes! There's still a little line here. Look! Almost nothing. He wasn't a pretty sight, but now he's running again."

"Your wife's an artist! Tell her to come and see me, her talent interests me!"

"And my rooster?"

"Your rooster?"

"Do you think he's on his way to recovery? That he'll be able to fight again soon?"

"Frankly, he looks a lot better than you do."

"That goodness for that!"

José left feeling so pleased that he forgot what Eugenio had said to him about his wife. Frasquita did not meet the man until a few weeks later, when she came running in with Clara, who had just swallowed two needles that had glinted in the sun before she could do anything to stop her.

Seeing such a pretty child arrive in the arms of this panicking woman, Eugenio immediately dismissed the other patients who had appointments for that morning and were waiting outside the shack.

Highly agitated, my mother introduced herself and explained the reasons for her visit. Eugenio seemed enthralled by Clara's skin and big sparkling eyes.

When he got over his astonishment, he regained his composure and hastened to reassure Frasquita. "I wouldn't worry too much, it's quite unusual for such incidents to lead to complications. For now, just give her oil and some thick bread soup to get the thing out easier. Swallowed needles may come out through the arm, the leg or any other part of the body. But there's no danger. This question of needles reminds me of something . . . Aren't you the wife of the cockfighter? The woman who stitches up roosters more skilfully than the best of our surgeons?"

"Oh, you know how the people here like to gossip!"

"No, no, I know what I'm talking about! I was able to judge your work for myself the day your husband came to consult me. How do you manage to get such perfect scars?"

"I don't know, I just do what comes naturally."

"If you like, the next time I get a cut in here, I'll send for you so I can watch you operate."

"I doubt that anyone in the village would agree to be sewed back together by a Carasco. We're treated like pariahs."

"Yes, I know all about that . . . the rooster business . . . But I pride myself on having acquired a certain influence over the people here. It'll be easy for me to convince even the worst of your detracters. Isn't that the best way for you to rehabilitate yourself?"

As my mother did not reply, he turned his attention back to Clara, although he had really not taken his eyes off her throughout the discussion.

"Come back to see me in a week so that we can follow the progress of these needles. And you, little Clara, what would you say to a nice lemonade?"

Frasquita told Blanca about this conversation the next time the midwife paid her a visit.

"Don't go back," Blanca said curtly.

"But he's very clever. I've overheard lots of people saying he's cured them."

"He's a great doctor, but don't go back there! Not with your daughter anyway! It's best if he doesn't see her again."

They were both silent for a moment. My mother understood neither her friend's sudden vehemence nor the mystery she maintained around Eugenio. What exactly were they to each other? Why had he stopped in Santavela? And how long would a man of his caliber, a man who claimed to have treated princes, stay among them, far from everything?

Sensing Frasquita's curiosity, Blanca informed her that she was planning to leave. "I had to make up my mind to continue on my way one of these days," she said. "I've been living among you for so many years. Rosa Capilla will take over from me, I've taught her almost everything, she's gifted and, if the women let you, you can assist her if need be."

"You can't leave now, when so many girls are pregnant."

"A lot will give birth in the next few days. I'll wait until the rush has passed. I don't suppose I'll get much sleep over the next few nights. Don't let your children out of your sight."

"But what are you afraid of?"

"Ogres, I'm afraid of ogres! My heart won't allow me to say more. We see our children growing up but we never see them grow old. That's how it is. And since we're asking questions, tell me why you stitched up that damned rooster again. Angela says he'll never win, yet José is training him for a third fight and you say nothing, you're content to let your children be shepherds! What do you have left to lose?"

This remark put a stop to Frasquita's questions, and they talked of other things.

The births came in rapid succession during the following two weeks. It was now that the first child disappeared: a pretty little five-year-old boy named Santiago. The whole village searched for him in vain for several days. This time, Frasquita's prayers proved useless: the boy had not simply lost his way, and Blanca left discreetly so shortly after this disappearance that some put it down to her. But soon it was the turn of a little girl who did not come home from the hills, and they were unable to accuse the midwife of anything other than having abandoned them without a word at the beginning of summer.

That a child should lose its way, hurt itself, and die far from the village without anyone finding its body was quite possible. But how could they still believe this was all accidental now that two were missing?

Frasquita remembered Blanca's words. She was afraid of ogres, she had said, and had advised her not to let her children out of her sight, and not to go back to see Eugenio with Clara, whom he had not taken his eyes off during the consultation. Frasquita had since then forbidden the youngest to leave the patio, and had demanded that José install a latch sufficiently high to stop Clara from opening the front door.

"This door must be kept closed!" she had been screaming

for a month when leaving for the hills to keep Heredia's animals instead of Angela and Pedro.

After the disappearance of the second child, she ceased to be the only mother to take care of her young, and few children lingered in the streets without good reason. The young shepherds were replaced by their elders, and neighbor eyed neighbor suspiciously.

Frasquita did not try to speak to the villagers. Instead she went to confession, and repeated to the priest through the wooden grille what Blanca had told her before leaving.

"It's a serious thing, accusing a man of being a criminal. Before Eugenio arrived, children may not have disappeared, but more died. He relieves many pains and the whole village swears by him. For some days now, everyone has been blaming someone else and has been coming to tell me. And as I'm sure you know, your husband is in the firing line. I can barely calm people down."

"But José doesn't leave the house anymore, he's even given up taking his rooster for a run outside since the children started throwing stones at him!"

"That's precisely what I mean, little Santiago who disappeared was one of those who threw stones."

Frasquita fell silent. She knew her husband was innocent, but she also knew how long the villagers bore grudges.

"Don't accuse anyone, especially not Eugenio," the priest went on. "The village wants to keep its doctor and would be ready to lynch your husband to protect him. What's more, he told me he wouldn't be staying much longer in the area. Look after your children and I'll keep an eye on our man. Have you anything else to tell me?"

"No, nothing."

"No bad acts, no bad thoughts?"

"Nothing but love."

"Sometimes love itself can be guilty. If no other child disappears, and if José leaves his bird and goes back to his work in the forge, the rancor will pass in a few months. I'm praying hard for those poor children."

The priest kept his word: he dogged Eugenio's steps, giving as an excuse a sudden interest in science, an interest that was not at all feigned.

A week later, Eugenio, doubtless tired of the priest's eternal questions, took his leave of the little community, which was tear-stricken at his departure, and set off on his horse to find Blanca.

No other child disappeared that summer and the harvest was able to begin on the plateau.

The third fight

When, toward the beginning of September, José walked through the village with his scarred rooster under his arm, they all understood that he was heading for Heredia's new house, and they did not like the look of that. As he passed, the women called their children in from the streets and slammed the doors.

Deep down, the villagers knew that José was not the ogre they had imagined, and many were even starting to wonder if their good doctor, who had so calmly abandoned them to their rheumatisms and their injuries, had not filled their children with too much lemonade. But José was so passionate about his rooster! Nobody understood how he could devote his life to such an eternal loser. Above all, although they blamed themselves for having twice taken the red bait, they all feared being caught up again in the dream.

If there was going to be a third fight, Santavela did not want to hear about it.

José could go off the rails if he wanted, refuse to resume his work in the forge—which did not even belong to him anymore—gamble his life away, or the lives of his family, nobody would try to dissuade him. The priest had already tried, but in vain: the man was lost. As long as his witch of a wife was determined to save that damned animal, the animal would possess him.

As for Heredia, thanks to José he was now part of the village and would parade through the streets on horseback as if every inch of the ground belonged to him. The hills were not enough for him, or even the fields and vines of which he had dispossessed his brothers. There he was, at their very doors, several times a day, and they had to move aside and press themselves up against the walls as he and his horse passed.

The red rooster had increased their servitude by installing the lord of the manor among them.

Olive, the beggar bird, was not much better off. It was going round in circles in what had been the Dragon's backyard, from where it could no longer even smell the air of the hills, venting its anger on the walls that confined it, blunting its spurs and denting its beak in the process.

As soon as he had been in a fit condition, the Red Dragon had started answering Olive's call. And their crowing, echoing across Santavela, was becoming obsessive.

Something was brewing that everyone was trying to ignore. Two children had vanished a few months earlier, but the atmosphere had not been as tense in the days following their disappearance as it was now in those that preceded the last fight.

Because there was indeed going to be a new fight.

And Heredia agreed to it taking place in his yard. The man who prowled the streets every day in search of my mother's face, dying of desire for a woman whose voice he had never heard, agreed to gamble everything again in order to possess her.

It was a fight to the death, held behind closed doors, a silent, airborne fight. A sacrifice . . .

José did not return home that day, and nobody could stitch the prince of roosters up again for the third time. This time, the beggar had gored it beyond repair.

THE FINAL DEBT

Heredia reached Frasquita's house and stopped outside for a moment. Behind the window, the children gathered to spy on him through the slits in the shutters.

He was probably remembering the hand that had guided the needle to him, those eyes on his coat, that light kiss, that bond, that thread cut with the teeth.

He must often have become intoxicated with the smell of lavender with which she had impregnated his closet, the scent of that woman he was finally to be united with—forever, he thought.

He must have been remembering something else too. He hadn't been able to forget my father's face so quickly. His wide open eyes begging for his rooster to be allowed to battle on, begging for one last fight.

He could probably still hear that toneless voice betting his house—that bright little casket that contained as best it could the laughter and the games and the sleep of five children, but had no value except for them. He had almost turned away—why hadn't he run, why hadn't he fled the sway of that mad gaze sooner?—when my father's eyes had grown even bigger and in his excitement he had offered him his last possession: his wife's body.

My father had told him how her round breasts felt like soft, warm little animals in his palms. His hand had accompanied his opponent's fingers over the curve of her lower back, had guided them into the shadow of her dark, velvety vagina. Both men's nostril's had sniffed her armpits saturated with the scent of the hills.

Yes, Heredia must have been thinking of all that, and of the blood and the red feathers and that flaming rooster, as he stood in front of the little white house.

Two knocks on the door, and the children scattered. Tall and fluid, Frasquita crossed the room and opened.

Light flooded the almost empty room and the hostile little faces.

The dark figure of the man stood out against the luminous late summer dust. As black as his shadow, which was already stretching through the house. Heredia exuded a warm damp-ness, water oozed from every pore and the squashed handker-chief in his trouser pocket made a noticeable bulge. Angela glared at him, imagining that piece of material, all crumpled and hardened by his sweat and by his desire for our mother. She thought of the maid who had to wash it, to scrub it in a wooden tub, the one who, thinking only of her task, gave him each morning a smooth white handkerchief for him to pour forth his desire into it. This time, the handkerchief would be her mother, who looked so bright in this man's shadow.

"I've come to settle the debt incurred by your husband," he said in an almost childlike voice. "A gambling debt, a debt of honor."

"Is there still some object of value in this house?" Frasquita asked, looking deep into his eyes.

He sustained her gaze, without anything collapsing in him, without anything escaping.

My mother's body quivered, then slowly, very slowly, she turned to Anita and asked her to go outside and play in the street with the younger children so that this man who was sweating so much could come into the coolness of the house.

The children went out in silence into the dazzling dust. Only Angela protested a little for form's sake before agreeing to follow her elder sister. And the house closed up again.

Frasquita and Heredia found themselves alone, and the room filled with their scents.

Without saying a word, he took a step forward and entered the circle where her presence vibrated, the air she breathed. Closer to her than he had ever been, he lifted his hand and lightly touched her cheek.

She did not move beneath the caress.

She felt her body give way between the two big hands of the man who had won her. Then she saw his eyes roll and his gestures quicken. She knew he would have liked to say something, but that his desire did not give him time. She put up no resistance. She let him lay her on the floor. After a few clumsy moves and some brief wandering in the maze of fabrics, he realized that a skirt can be pulled up more easily than it can be taken off. She followed him, hands and lips moist, as he roamed wildly between the linen and the skin of her open thighs, then she saw his mauve penis spring up from his pants and his hand holding it like a dagger. He almost stopped at the edge of her flesh, and she felt his penis motionless for a moment against her silky brown hairs. But he continued on his way. He slipped deep into her, and it was sweet in spite of his impatience and strength. Then their bodies moved together at the same rhythm, and they sighed the same sighs, and then it was she who wanted more, stronger, further, it was she who wanted. She heard a thread break.

He wept when he came, he who had never wept. He did not want to leave her body and remained inside it as long as possible.

"Every day," he said to her. "I will come every day, I will take root in you."

And she remained silent, watching the shadow of this man who smelled of olive trees dancing alone on the bare walls.

She looked for the eyes she had so longed for, but the eyes had withdrawn, they were looking at the floor, where she no longer was. She stood there in front of him, naked and magnificent, and waited, but the frayed man no longer dared contemplate either her face or that body that he had possessed once and for all, perhaps.

Outside, the children wanted to know.

Angela started knocking on the door and the shutters, she wore out her fists on the white roughcast, small reddened fists, chalk white, the small bruised fists of a child of ten still powerless in the face of male desire. Exhausted, she turned to her great ally, her brother Pedro. The boy took a piece of wood with a burned end and drew.

He used the white housefront as a canvas and moored a huge ship to it, he who had never even seen a boat. A swelling mainsail, a magnificent hull and prow.

In the noon sun, heavy with indifferent brightness, the olive grove man left the house just as Pedro, held up by his older sisters, was finishing the top of the drawing.

He no longer cast any shadow.

His step was calm, and he did not turn around as he withdrew into the pallor of the village.

Leaving

Time blew on the scribbled wall with its drawing, on the bruised children, on the silent dust of the streets.

Time fled.

An eternity of dense sunlight.

And Frasquita Carasco emerged in her turn into the street, to face the children.

Her hair was neatly gathered in a low round bun. She looked as beautiful as a young corpse.

They did not recognize her at first. They saw only the sheen of the thousand cloth roses that adorned her bodice. Her neck, her shoulders, her face emerged from the flowers with their hard, silky petals. For a while, she stood there silent in her wedding splendor, as if carved out of some hybrid material: marble, skin and fabric, a merging of flower and woman.

Rooted to the spot, facing the street that was dying in front of her house.

Alone facing the village that was watching her, huddled behind its cold house fronts, muttering, its stone eyesockets surrounded by shadow, empty of pupils, of color, of irises, empty of all flowers.

She was alone facing the many eyes that stared at her beauty but were incapable of being dazzled even at this white hour.

Without a sound, without a breath, the shadows of the windows swarmed with invisible gazes. They were probably all sweating there in their holes, stinking, biting their tongues in the exhausted houses, hoping that a voice would rise, that a cry would come to break the enchantment or that a laugh would burst forth, one of those laughs like grenades.

But during all the time my mother took to make up her mind, nobody said anything and the street remained deserted. No laughter came to wither the new bride.

Then the children saw their mother turn toward those four walls from which she had extracted herself as if from a cocoon.

They saw the disemboweled housefront, and they realized that this passage, this door, was too narrow, that this shack was too small for our mother's wide corolla ever to have come from there, too dark to contain so much light. The tails of the dress must have opened once outside, the whiteness must have come from the glare of noon.

The children knew that their mother would never again be able to go back to her lair, that she had all at once become too big for it, too vast to live here in this black hole, in this street, in this village. It seemed to them that their mother's gaze, floating somewhere above a rose garden of cloth, would soon sink and drown in the bodice, in that splendid base. They dreaded the moment when their mother would vanish into the mirage of her wedding dress.

She turned away, her shoulders, her neck, her face turned slowly on their stem of cloth.

The flowers stirred.

And their mother stood there, intact, still floating in a myriad of roses.

Her dress became broader still, its whiteness appeared more intense until it hid the little door.

This woman-flower remained as a white patch on the children's retinas long after their mother had disappeared from in front of the house.

There was the black wound on the housefront. There was

that drawing that suddenly filled my mother's eyes, that house turned ship, that great sail of white roughcast, that clumsy trompe-l'oeil and the silence of the children, that blind street with its shuttered windows. Then, in that solar emptiness, there was nothing else anymore but the great ship, risen there all at once in front of her, like the only door open.

She saw it appear beyond the drawing. It was coming to find her, to take her away. So far from the sea, so far from any river, it had advanced along the roads, it had sailed up the dry streams. It had widened the dusty little street, in full sail, pushed by a constant wind, and run aground against her door.

A ship worthy of her, on which to load her pain and her joy, a ship to stop the horror of not belonging to herself, a boat where, at last, she could *be*!

Time to leave.

All the silence of the sea had flowed into the streets. So much water to come, so many roads to travel! And that red-headed child taking her on board his dream!

She could not resist the desire to believe in this way out, this drawn world.

According to some, a number of Jewish families persecuted by the Inquisition had one day set sail on such a ship, drawn by a rabbi on the wall of a dungeon in Seville. They had left the city, and Spain, and had come to the sea and crossed it and reached an oasis so remote that nobody had ever found them again.

She had to believe in this ship, she had to take her sewing bag and load all the children in the ark.

My mother stood there for a while longer with her eyes fixed on the drawing, on the wall, on the splendid caravel. At last the sail moved slightly, stirred by a tremor of the walls. The wind rose, swelling the huge white stretch of canvas, and my mother tore herself from the image. She turned toward the handcart, heaped onto it, in no particular order, the children, the blankets, the candles, the two remaining pieces of sheet, the previous day's loaves, oil, eggs, ham, bread, she took her chair too, I think, threw a last glance at the abandoned shadow that danced on the walls, and we left.

A rooster crowed in the hills.

BOOK TWO

The crossing

THE MIDDLE OF THE JOURNEY

W here to begin?
Despite all the words already laid down in this exercise book, the question of a beginning now arises.
We set off after our mother, aiming straight ahead.

It is said that I was already there, in her flesh, beneath the flowers of cloth. And then?

Then vast spaces, time like a circle, no beginning. A single stitch holding the infinity of worlds together. A stitch linking our fabrics of flesh and words. A stitch, a knot to unravel so that life could be.

Let us begin with the middle of the journey.

After three days' walking, the path that led out of the village forked infinitely across the hills. In the morning, Frasquita did not move.

All night, she had looked at her five children as they slept in the roots of a big solitary oak. Looking at that amorous intertwining of limbs and branches, she had been overcome with doubt. She had already been walking for a long time, impelled forward by the cart, without thinking of anything except not stumbling over these alien stones she was tramping for the first time.

She was about to move into a vast world.

Never again after that would the course of her thoughts slow down our flight. All her energy would pass into her legs.

But where was she going? Where would she find food for

these abandoned little bodies, their mouths open, in which the same sap circulated?

Not so far behind her, she knew every stone. But ahead of her, there were no limits to the horizon.

She was tempted to turn back, to retrace the steps toward what she had not yet ceased being, to rejoin that man to whom she no longer belonged and that other man caught up in his trees. Going back still seemed possible.

What was she doing here in the middle of nowhere, in her wedding dress, her heart still filled with the moment when the coat had snagged on her window, that high noon when for the first time the needle had pricked her finger?

And yet, as she knew, nothing could have prevented their encounter above the winged guardians, the iron birds, the backyard dragons. Nothing could have prevented that, no bars. A barred window is still a window and Frasquita had been keeping watch there, sitting on her chair, behind the shutters, since her arrival in the Carasco lair. Yes, if my mother pricked herself one day, it was that day, the day of their encounter. But who then had drunk the red drop that had sprung up on her finger? The coat, my mother, or Heredia, the man who smelled of olives, that I do not know.

To return. Not to have to choose from among these roads that presented themselves to her. These paths, drawn by unknown steps, that crisscrossed the world.

But along the one path that came from the village, nothing had caught up with her from her past.

Heredia was screaming to his wooden army to bring him back the woman who had mended him in the sun, but was doing nothing to rejoin her. His shadow, lost for the second time, was now haunting the house she had just left. As for Carasco, perhaps he was finally weeping over the corpse of the red rooster, and mourning also the death of his mother, the mistress of his sorrows.

No, nothing could hold her back any longer, except creeping death.

Angela and Clara, woken as always at dawn, the former by the birds, the latter by the light, were looking at their mother out of the corners of their eyes, fearing that she would run away and leave them alone amid these teeth of stone, as mothers sometimes do in fairy tales.

Why had she left?
The swallows were tirelessly embroidering invisible signs on the blue sky, signs that made sense only to Angela and spoke to her of the future.

Whatever the path chosen, it would have to stop somewhere, you just had to take it.
Frasquita woke the other children and headed south.

THE MILL

At the very end of the path that my mother had chosen, the mill appeared. Alone in the ocean of hills, waving its great arms as if inviting us to join it. My mother, hair wild, caparisoned in her flower-bedecked wedding dress, dragging her cart full of children, responded to the invitation. The miller, whose hair was white with age and dust, spotted her from a distance and, as if terrified at the thought of being alone in the world, ran toward us as we climbed his hill.

"Let me help you!" he cried. "My arms are stronger than they may seem! I'll go behind your cart and push! We'll be at the top in no time at all! How lucky that you were passing this way, and with all these children! My God, how many of them are there? They keep moving, it's impossible to count them! All the better, that means there are even more of them! I'll serve you water from the well, it's nice and cold! You'll see how good it is to sit under my arbor at the end of the day. With that water, I've grown a little oasis, a paradise . . . Look, take a seat! There are benches over there, you just have to dust them down a bit! Everything's white here. Sit down! I'll be right back . . . "

He brought them milk from his goats, still warm, and hard bread that they let soak in the milk to soften.

The children laughed in the shade of the climbing flowers, happy to have finally arrived somewhere. Only Martirio kept her distance, refusing to touch the bread and milk, and staring at the man impertinently.

"My mill is the oldest in the region, the people down there built it on this hill because of the wind. The wind blows stronger here than anywhere else, and my flour is the best. I'll give you some. You'll see, it's like nothing you've ever seen. All these children! How wonderful! That one's wilder than the others"—he pointed at Martirio—"and she doesn't talk any more than your eldest. Is she a mute too?"

"No," replied my mother, reassured by the mention of flour. "She'll get over it!"

With delight, the old miller told them his life story, he told them about all the people who came during the season. As he spoke, he laid straw mattresses in the little house adjoining the mill, one per child, all without asking my mother the least question about her journey or her strange attire. She was infinitely grateful to him for that.

When night fell, as Pedro was walking through the garden and filling his pockets with the big pieces of chalk that grew there like couch grass, the miller excused himself and slipped away.

"The wind's rising. It's been dead calm for days now. The wind is my one adversary, my one companion, I'm afraid of the silence on days when it doesn't blow. So when it does blow, I always answer its call. I'll leave you, I have work to do. Sleep well, a long road awaits you before you catch up with the men who've abandoned me lately."

They all lay down and, feeling sheltered by the wings of the mill, fell asleep immediately. The solitary old man's smile, his meager furniture seemingly white with flour, and the milk from his goats: all of these inspired trust.

But in the middle of the night Martirio slipped into the mill and watched the man at work. Instead of corn, he was busy feeding blocks of chalk to the millstone.

"Aren't you afraid of me anymore?" he asked her without turning.

"A little bit. It takes time to get used to your face."

"Have I become so ugly?"

"Do you grind stones?" she asked without answering his question.

"A tender white stone that doesn't damage my millstone, the whole west side of this hill is crumbly, that's where I find my stones."

"And the world?" the child asked.

"Before you arrived, I was afraid it didn't exist anymore. I've been alone so long. The night is clear, you see that ridge, on the right, just opposite my hill? Well, just behind, there was a plain rich in corn and men. That's where the world used to begin. If you turn left, along the mule track, you avoid the heights. It isn't so far. But nobody comes from down there anymore, and I don't have the strength to leave my garden and go see what has happened. I don't even know if they're still there. You have good legs, if you meet them, tell them I'm waiting for them, tell them the old mill is still standing and is hungry for corn to grind! Tell them about the wind here."

Martirio made no promises, but asked another question. "How long is it since men forgot you?"

"Nothing moves anymore but the wind," said the strange, chalk-white miller as he filled three sacks with powder. "Some days, when even the wind falls silent, I weep."

"Are these the sacks you promised my mother?"

"Let me work in peace, little girl," he murmured tenderly. "Go back to sleep. We'll see each other again soon enough and I'm sure we'll have time to talk then."

The next day, as my mother was getting ready to leave, the miller dragged three big, tightly fastened sacks to the cart. Frasquita hoisted them onto the bed of the cart with the help of the older children. It was a substantial gift: at least her children would have bread. She offered the man the remaining piece of ham, he refused it, smiling broadly to reveal the few teeth he had left. He kissed the children one by one, and said goodbye to Martirio, who glared at him but said nothing for fear of wiping too soon the expression of joy—joy at knowing her family would not go hungry—from her mother's face.

When, at noon, halfway through an ascent made even more difficult by the weight of the sacks, Frasquita and her children turned to look at the mill, it seemed to them that all they could see in the distance, under the sun, was a dismembered carcass of stones beaten by the winds, a ruin with torn sails and a roof on top of a mountain of chalk. As for the garden and the arbor, they saw no trace of it.

Martirio did not turn around. She knew.

Blanca, you're limping! Don't be silly, give me your bag, let me put it on my donkey!"

"Leave me alone, Eugenio!"

"It's easy to track you down now. Your legs betray you now that you're old. You see, I even give you a head start, I continue to enjoy myself for a while after you leave, and only then set off in pursuit of you. It's become too easy since Santavela. There, at least, you made life difficult for me. Sixteen years, it took me sixteen years to track you down in your mountains at the ends of the earth. Wherever you go, I will go. Will you break my legs again to get rid of me? This time, I'm prepared. You're my only tie. Do you remember that first time you abandoned me?"

"You didn't want to change. You promised, I forgave so much, forgot so much. Those little corpses . . . "

"I was young, with your help I might have fought it . . . Now it's too late, and it's your fault. I love their smell, their unshadowed faces, their curiosity, their life throbbing in my hands. I live, I walk, I breathe only for that, to touch those delicate little bodies."

"You weren't born an ogre. As a child, you were gentle, you wept in my arms."

"I loved you, I wanted to be what you desired. But I grew up."

"I won't listen to you anymore. You're nothing to me now."

"If I'm nothing to you now, why don't you hand me over to the authorities? Why do you run away every time without saying anything to them? If I'm nothing to you now, get rid of me! Take this knife and kill me! What are you waiting for? I won't do anything to stop you, I don't fear death if it comes from you! Think of all those children! Look, I'm coming within reach. The blade is on my neck. With a single move, you can erase me. Blanca, what are you doing? Come back! So you see, I do still count!"

Beaming, Eugenio picked up the big knife that Blanca had dropped before continuing on her way.

THE LAST RIDGE

At the foot of the last ridge stretched the plain, covered with fields, meadows, woods, black in places from the fires that had been lighted after the harvest, green with broad, shady trees, swarming with men moving about in every direction, passing from one house to the next, one road to the next, one hamlet to the next. So the world had not gone away: one day's walk from the old mill, it still throbbed with life.

"We'll have to tell them about the miller," said Angela.

"No, don't breathe a word," said Martirio with all the authority of her seven years. "Nobody would believe you anyway."

The vegetation was thicker on the side of the great embankment they were starting to descend, and the two younger girls forgot the mill and amused themselves flushing out the cicadas whose chirping stopped abruptly at their approach. Then they gathered so many flowers and leaves that the cart became a *paso*, with Clara sitting on the sacks playing the role of the Virgin.

Angela began singing a religious song, holding a big stick as a candle. The voice went on, trilling its hymn, intoxicated with freedom and joy. At this point, three men on foot, armed with muskets and pulling a donkey, and a bright-eyed horseman emerged from behind the stones. The song stopped dead, and the children huddled in their mother's still white skirts.

"Just married and already all these children!" said the youngest of the men. "You haven't wasted any time! What about the father?"

"He's right behind us," my mother lied.

"We've been watching you for a while and all we've seen is a woman alone in a big wedding dress pulling a cart laden with all her brats. Got anything nice in those sacks?"

"Flour to feed my children."

"Well, your flour can serve another cause."

As the men seized the sacks, my mother and Angela screamed and held onto them with all their strength. It took two men to contain Frasquita's anger, while the third tried to hold off the smaller of the two harpies, protecting himself as best he could from her teeth and claws.

The horseman dismounted. "Seeing that you're dressed like a princess," he said with a smile, "do you really only have this flour to survive on?"

"Nothing else," replied my mother, her hair all disheveled.

"Strange woman, don't you think, Salvador?" said the man who had spoken first, whose name was Manuel. "She doesn't look like the women from around here. Where do you come from, my dear?"

"From Santavela, on the other side of the sierra."

"And you want us to believe that you've come all this way pulling this stuff by youself?" the man said irritably, letting go of his donkey to try to immobilize Angela.

"Here!" said Salvador, holding out a purse. "This is for your pains. You can buy what you need in the village. Your daughter, the one who's defending herself tooth and nail, has a really nice voice."

Frasquita calmed down and Angela took refuge with the others against her mother's body. The whole family watched in silence as the men unloaded the sacks.

"Why don't you go to the village yourselves and buy your bread there?" cried Angela, the anger still in her throat.

"The civil guard are waiting for us there," said Salvador. "There more than anywhere. Anyone who feeds us is risking his life."

"Are you bandits?" asked Pedro, who was still protecting his two younger sisters behind his back.

"Bandits?" Salvador repeated the word as if to himself. "'We have to join the adventurous world of brigands, who are the only true revolutionaries in Russia,' said Bakunin. The three men you see beside me are local people, peasants. Along with others, we're fighting so that the earth they till should belong to everyone. The day laborers are with us, but many fear for their families. That's why they're married off, so that they can make children, and then the bosses have them by the throat. They're given barely enough to live on, many kids don't make it, but there's always one that survives, and that one prevents rebellion, that one stays their arms. Those who've seen their children die of starvation make wonderful fighters! It's their bread you've dragged all the way here. The bread of men hungry for revenge. Without your flour, we could all die in the mountains with our mouths open, waiting for the next uprising. Have a safe journey, and thanks for the bread."

Martirio was relieved to see them go. So the miller with the ravaged face knew what he was doing in deceiving her mother: the chalk had become bread.

She did not even wonder what would happen when the rebels opened the sacks.

IN THE MOUNTAINS

E ugenio!" said a man who had emerged from out of
nowhere in the solitude of the surroundings. "What ill
wind brings you to our mountains?"

"*Hola*, Juan, I thought you might need a good surgeon
around here!" said Eugenio, as armed rebels sprang up from
the bushes. "How are your plans going?"

"Nothing's moving. We steal what we eat, because the peasants are terrified at the thought of supporting us. You were
right: the revolution hasn't started yet. Poison some of the
landowners who bleed us dry! That'll speed things up."

"I'm not going to bite the hand that feeds me!" Eugenio
laughed, revealing his bone-white teeth.

"Two or three priests then, to help us put an end to divine
slavery," insisted Juan, who motioned to Eugenio to dismount
and follow him into the prickly bushes.

"I have enough problems with God, no point in adding to
them. The woman walking over there, refusing to stop, is
called Blanca, she's a midwife, she's traveling with me. She's a
bit of a rebel too. She may be useful to you. She won't listen to
me, but if you find her something to do, she'll stay as long as
necessary. She's skillful and devoted, and I can vouch for her
silence."

"She's come too late, Salvador lost his wife in childbirth six
months ago. The child didn't survive either. But if you think we
should, we'll catch up with her."

"So that crazy Catalan's still alive and kicking, is he? For ages he's been getting the country worked up, I'm quite surprised the civil guard haven't got hold of him yet."

After about thirty minutes' walk in the mountains through dense vegetation, the group reached a makeshift encampment where thin, ragged men, some of whom recognized Eugenio, were living in caves or under the trees.

"We set up camp here some time ago," Juan said. "It's a good hideout. We have a few wounded men who'll be pleased to see you, you and your medicine. Set yourself down there, in Salvador's area. He sleeps in that little cave. If I know the two of you, you're going to be spending your nights talking again."

Eugenio took the load off his donkey and unsaddled his horse. After leading them to the watering place where the rebels brought their animals to drink, he let them go free and made a little space for himself not far from Salvador's cave. He stretched a piece of cloth between three trees, and beneath it made a bed for himself out of his saddle and the blankets he always kept rolled up on his horse's back.

As he was preparing to go see the wounded men that Salvador's adjutant Juan had told him about, Blanca appeared, framed by two men.

"Who are these people?" she asked, when her guards had moved away.

"Anarchists, poor idealists who've thrown in their lot with Salvador, a northerner who was exiled to this hole by the authorities. By scattering the intellectuals, they're stoking the revolution instead of putting it down. It's a good example of a remedy that fails to cure the disease! When a limb is rotten, you cut it off and burn it, you don't graft it on another part of the body! He's a noble soul, this Salvador, but noble souls are the worst, they stir things up because they're intelligent and can talk. In other words, he's a dangerous man. Here's something to eat! Take it! You haven't eaten in so long, you can barely keep on your feet. It's stupid to refuse something just because it comes from me. Here, you can be sure you won't find anything else, just what I give you. Look at them, they are all dying of starvation!"

Blanca made no move to take the plate he was holding out.

"So you've already lived long enough, have you?" he said, mockingly. "It's true, though, you are old. Die, then!"

The world

The world was still calm the night my mother entered it. Of course, words had already been uttered, knives were being sharpened in the shadows, the silence was weeping. The belly of the world was humming with thousands of murmured prayers, the crowd of the desperate, held back by fear and tradition and centuries of servitude, could no longer pour forth its pain. The world was calm, but three sacks of chalk would suffice to set it alight. Three sacks that slowed Salvador and his men, three sacks that weighed them down enough for the civil guard to catch up with them as they tried to get back to their camp.

Three sacks: the miller's gift to a world that had forgotten his mill.

Yes, my mother arrived only a few hours before the world burst into flames.

Young people were running around our strange caravan, and the women came out of the houses to look at my mother and her children. Everyone wanted to touch Pedro's long red hair, everyone passed their fingers through it. "*Buena suerte. Buena suerte.*" Locks were torn out in passing. "*Buena suerte.*" Stories were already being invented. Some good souls offered them a barn where they could take shelter. Frasquita bought bread, fruit and almonds with the anarchists' money and the children feasted on it, sitting on the ground beside their cart, blithely ignoring all those who were staring at them. My brother and sisters licked their fingers and laughed. Fingers greasy with chorizo, sticky with sweet raisins.

Intrigued rather than hostile, the villagers stared at the strange picture we presented. A woman in a big wedding dress, without a man, pulling a cart filled with flowers and children, a boy with curly red hair, and a little girl who seemed to shine, yes, shine, in the midst of her flowers!

Strangers coming from God knows where, saying they had crossed the sierra without a donkey. What about the father? He was dead. Why, then, was his widow wearing that dress? The other side of the mountain was still Spain, people believed in God there, just as they did here, they wore mourning, just as they did here, they died of hunger, just as they did here! She must be mad! Poor woman, cast out alone on the roads like that!

"Maybe she's a whore! Someone who was run out of her native village. She wouldn't be the first to cross these mountains! The one with the accordion, do you remember her?"

"With all these children, that would be a first. Whores do everything they can not to have children, they know how to get rid of them or leave them behind somewhere."

"They're child killers, everybody knows that."

"All the same, when children disappeared around here, there wasn't any whore involved, but a learned man that everyone bowed and scraped to!"

"He was a good man, that Eugenio. He never asked more than what we could give him."

"Strangers, even with red hair, bring bad luck! Mustn't give this one the desire to stick around!"

"Instead of gossiping about this woman who's fleeing God knows what, we'd do better to rebel against those who are stripping us bare. We lick the bosses' asses, we beat our children to instill respect for their masters in them, tell them to be quiet in their presence, to keep their eyes down and cry out with hunger or pain. Not to mention Salvador and his boys dying in the mountains because none of us has the courage to take them bread."

"Salvador isn't one of us, he can read, he comes from the North, the rebellion he brings with him is none of our business."

"He says out loud what we're too scared to even think. He's seen that we peasants are just as poor as the workers in the North. We all have someone of our blood in the mountains, someone we pray for, someone we wait for at night, fearing all the while that if he comes he'll attract the civil guard to our homes. The roles ought to be reversed, the priest, the bosses and the big landowners should be shitting in their velvet breeches. That's what we should be doing: scaring them badly, so badly that they give us our land. There are more of us than there are of them."

At this point, a child came running through the village, screaming at the top of his voice, "They've captured Salvador, Quince and two other boys from here. The civil guard have caught them! They've captured Salvador!"

These few words made everyone forget my mother and her children. It was as if we had suddenly disappeared, or as if we had never been there. Nobody was interested anymore in Pedro's hair, or the wedding dress, or the rose garden of cloth, or even Clara's beauty. Everyone was hurrying toward the main square to see the horses of the civil guard pass, dragging behind them four rebels with their hands tied, their donkeys loaded with the sacks the miller had given Frasquita. Children were yelling the news on the roads, and the day laborers still in the fields or on the way home quickened their step to join the crowd that had massed opposite the barracks where Salvador and his men were being led.

As he was pushed inside the building, Salvador cried, "They want to know who among you gave us this corn, but we won't say a word!"

A rifle butt struck him violently in the jaw, but did not silence him: even with blood dripping from his mouth, he had time to cry "Long live Bakunin!" before receiving a new blow that knocked him bodily to the ground, where he lay silent and inert.

The guards' kicks made no difference, Salvador had stopped moving, and had to be dragged inside.

The peasants did not react. They did not notice immediately that they had come together for the first time, did not realize that they were forming a dense mass that was growing in size with every passing minute. They did not see the women who had joined them, nor that they were being pressed up against one another, sweaty, silent and motionless in front of the thick wooden door. All these round, sun-reddened eyes, all these arms dangling at the sides of thin bodies, had washed up here, borne on the current, and the gathering shadows of twilight did not disperse them. Some of Salvador's companions mingled with the weary crowd. They were the first to sense how they could turn this silent gathering to their advantage. It was with them that the murmur began, a murmur coming from deep inside their pain, a solemn murmur rising toward the walls of the barracks, hundreds of lips united in a soft expression of rebellion.

My mother and her children did not interrupt their meal. People were passing in front of them, all going in the same direction, and the words they spoke lingered in the air for a moment before melting into a distant murmur. They were talking about Salvador, and about the sacks of flour. Everyone was wondering who had had the courage to take food to the anarchists. They were all blaming themselves for not having done it earlier, for having condemned them to steal their food, to live by banditry.

Angela, who had been listening for some time to the lament being murmured outside the walls of the barracks, followed the last passers-by and their questions all the way to the square.

Inside the building, Salvador had regained consciousness. One of the guards was waving a knife in front of his face, as if to open it up and extract the answers to the questions they were asking. Where was their band hiding? Who was feeding them? Where had the sacks come from?

But Salvador and his three friends sensed that gathering force droning behind the walls and, above that deep rumble, they heard a voice spring up, poignant, unique, a child's voice that got in under their skin, made their senses bristle, ravaged their nerves like a knife. A voice that took up the murmured words and flung them violently against the walls. The people were roaring beneath the child's voice, and the captain was asking his questions, and the guard was cutting Salvador's face, gashing the cheeks, digging into the lines, attacking the muscle, widening the mouth, carving the features. But the Catalan was aware of nothing but that melody beneath the blood that streamed over his face. He would not have been able to talk now even if he had wanted to: he no longer had any lips, no longer had a nose, or eyelids, or face, just a wound. Then the man cut off his ears and the blood flowed into the song and drowned it.

Unnerved by the song, by the torturer's vigorous movements and by what he had drawn on Salvador's face, the heads of the garrison decided to make an absurd gesture, the kind that overturns worlds and provokes riots. They decided to take this man they had all thought could not be caught, this man who for so long had led them a merry dance through the region, this man who was stoking the rebellion of the dispossessed, and exhibit him to the very people who had the stench of rebellion on them.

"See what happens to an anarchist!" the captain yelled at the crowd, holding up the pale, flayed head by the hair. "Look at this man without a face! Look at his sign dripping with blood! And since most of you can't read, I'll tell you what's written on it. It says 'bread thief.' He took flour from you, this man, he took it from you because nobody gave him any. He had to steal it from somewhere. So you see, justice has been done!"

The murmur died down, and the song broke off. The little voice that had been chanting rebellion and hope sank to nothing. Silence descended on the square, a lull before the vast clamor that broke down the walls.

Although unarmed, the men rushed at the guards. The crowd lifted the unconscious Salvador, who was returned to his friends and swept off at a gallop in the arms of one of his companions, while the peasants launched themselves barehanded against the guards' rifles.

THE TORN FACE

E ugenio!" yelled Juan, his mouth still full of the bile he
had just brought up after being shown Salvador's
ruined face. "Eugenio!"

Shaken by this cry of horror, Blanca awoke Eugenio, whose
sleeping face she had been examining for more than an hour,
searching for the child she had loved.

"Get moving!" she said harshly, recovering her composure.
"Your friends need you!"

Eugenio went straight to the place where they had laid out
Salvador. He did not recognize him at first.

"What happened?" he asked Manuel, who had brought the
Catalan back on a borrowed horse.

"Things are hotting up down there. The revolution has
started. It happened all at once. The civil guard caught us,
Salvador, me and two others, with sacks of flour, and they tortured Salvador in front of us to find out where our camp was
and who had given him food."

"Then we have to get out of here straight away!" cried
Eugenio.

"No, they went too far . . . as you see. Salvador didn't say
anything. But the peasants got together and a child sang with
them the way canaries sing in a cage. Her voice drove the soldiers mad, I think that's why they did this to his face. My own
eyes filled with tears when I heard that singing, I couldn't see
anything, it was so beautiful. We'd had all that inside us for so
long, and now it was coming out loud and clear through the

mouth of a little girl. From inside the building, we could hear the people proclaiming its sorrows. After they were done with Salvador they brought us all out. They'd stuck a sign on him. 'Bread thief.' it said. That was when the crowd rushed at them. It happened all at once, like I said."

"It must be a fine mess down there by now!" Eugenio said. "A real massacre! And what about the two others who were with you, are you sure they won't talk?" he insisted, mainly thinking of his own skin.

"The day laborers freed them at the same time as me. They're fighting beside them."

"All our men have gone down to support the peasants," said Juan, roused by young Manuel's story. "It really is all as sudden as a storm. I'm off to join them. You stay here with Manuel and Salvador, I entrust him to you. It looks like you've come just in time. Farewell, comrade."

Blanca had followed Eugenio and, while Manuel was light-ing torches and oil lamps in the little cave that served as Salvador's bedroom, she was already bustling around this man whose face had been ravaged and redrawn by human hatred.

"I'm surprised the town got worked up over so little," said Eugenio ironically. "I know it's not a pretty sight, but for these good people to fling themselves at armed men, that's a bit much! When you think of how long they've been dying in silence! Mind you, from a distance, he'd make a good Christ of the Sorrows, a pity the blood has drowned his features. Their torturer should become a sculptor. He's talented, not many works of art can stir crowds. What can we do for you, my poor Salvador? There's a lot to sew back together."

"He's coming to," murmured Blanca.

"Better to put him back to sleep, just so we don't hear him moan. I have all I need in my bag."

"Wait! He's trying to say something."

"The human will never ceases to surprise me. How can anyone expect to utter a word with a mouth like that? Be quiet! You're tiring yourself out for nothing. The only thing they didn't cut off you was your tongue."

Through the gaping wound, words emerged, painful and bloody. Articulated not by lips but by the open flesh. He knew who had been singing. That voice, the voice of rebellion: he had recognised it.

Angela had started singing in the middle of the crowd. Her lament had risen above the gathered throng and the people around her had quickly hoisted her on their shoulders so that her song should carry further, so that everybody should see the face of this unknown child, this little girl with excessively round eyes, who was extoling their sorrows with such force and freshness. Her voice amplified their words, she took them into her own throat and projected them against the walls, against the studded door, through the streets, and onto the sky, which was already darkening in the east. A lament of the poor, beauty extracted from the horror of being dispossessed of their own identities, being turned by their masters sometimes into hunting dogs, forced to search, nose to the ground, hands stuck in the mud, and sometimes into mules, never allowed to hold themselves erect. A song torn apart by the thorn of mute suffering . . .

And then that carved face had appeared—Angela had not recognised it—that mask of agony, still breathing, a living masterpiece, and she had been unable to continue singing.

To make sure that everybody could admire the torturer's handiwork in spite of the fading light, the guards had brought their torches so close to the open flesh that it had sizzled slightly in the silence that had fallen.

At this point, Angela was sitting on the shoulders of a man who was robust despite his age, an innocent who had not let go of her when he had rushed forward toward the soldiers. How did he hope to fight with a child on his shoulders? Panicked by the rifle shots and the sudden violence of this human wave, she kicked the man's ribcage, hoping he would let her down, not thinking that a girl of her size would not have been able to survive in the bloody confusion that reigned a few feet below her. Raised above the rebellion in this way, she became its standard. Everyone was convinced she had not stopped singing, because her voice still echoed in their chests, and it seemed to them that it always would. But Angela now screamed something quite different, and the idiot who had become the standard bearer cut through the battlefield in all directions so that everyone could see her and keep courage, so that the song of near-victory that had come to her when she heard them murmur could float ove their heads.

My sister could not bear being waved about like that above the human fray, she could feel the bullets whistling around her head, and she dug her nails into the man's cheeks and pulled out his hair in handfuls. From the walls of the barracks, now stained with red, some of the soldiers were aiming at her, she was sure of that: they probably saw her as the leader of the uprising. She had to get back to her mother, they had to continue their journey! But the idiot was laughing like a drain in the midst of the dying, wading through blood, clambering over the bodies, ducking and swerving, and in this way he managed to enter the barracks behind his comrades, who were still screaming out, as if with one voice, that song that had carried them away.

It was pitch black by the time Angela was torn from the arms of the grinning old madman, covered in blood, shivering in every limb and weary of the slaughter. She did not have a scratch on her, but from that first experience of war she was to keep a slight tensing of the lower lip, a permanent expression of sadness that only her huge bursts of laughter would ever be able to dispel.

Some women carried her back to her mother, who had been shouting her name in the rebellion-swept streets.

Fires were being lighted on all sides, and the autumn air was filled with the smell of blood. While the wounded screamed, the church was torn apart, as was its priest. Intoxicated by slaughter, men armed with rifles and torches marched in procession toward the haciendas. Most of the envoys dispatched onto the roads to call for help and bring reinforcements were killed like rabbits. It was the general feeling that all the harm possible had to be done before dawn, that all accounts had to be settled, all old ills avenged, because there would not be another night. The very next morning, the army would come running, and they would have to fight again and die.

"I too recognized the voice that sang," Manuel said, trying to silence Salvador. "The child is with a woman from Santavela, on the other side of the sierra. She says she dragged her cart all the way here."

"This woman you're talking about," Blanca said, "did you notice if she had a son with red hair?"

"Yes, she did, and behind him there was a radiant little girl with straw-colored eyes."

"But that's Frasquita, the seamstress! She's the one who could mend his face. You must send for her . . . Manuel! If you want Salvador to live, go back and find that stranger. She alone will be able to patch him up for you the way you want. But be quick about it, he's coming apart before our eyes!"

Frasquita did not like the world. It was not as she had imagined it, up there in her mountains. She did not wait for the sun to rise before setting off again. In the middle of the night, she pulled her cart southward. They had to get away from the slaughter as quickly as possible.

Despite the fatigue of the journey and the late hour, only Clara was asleep in the cart, dazzling in the midst of flowers that had closed for the night. None of the other children could get what they had seen out of their minds: the corpses on both sides abandoned on the square, trampled by those still fighting, the priest who had been dragged from his church, guts spewing from him, leaving a bloody trail behind, the little boy, hit in the head by a bullet, bobbing up and down on the shoulder of the woman who must have been his mother and who did not seem to have noticed yet that the child she was carrying was dead, the cries of the old woman recognizing the wide-open eyes of her youngest brother in the middle of a pile of corpses.

The fires consuming the presbytery, the barracks and the public buildings lit up the night sky, making the town look suddenly imposing, sending free men out from it and through the countryside. Free, that is, to make a class that had starved, terrified and used them pay them back for centuries of humiliation, free to smash, to kill, to rob, to scream.

Free to die.

Manuel passed columns of fire raisers intoning Angela's song, and he asked everyone where the woman was, the stranger who had arrived wearing a big wedding dress, the mother of the child who had sung in the main square.

Everyone remembered the child, she was part of their story now, she was the heart of it. Who could have called her a stranger? She had been born in the region, of course, this girl whose birdlike voice had carried their cause. She had died in the main square bombarding the civil guard with her song. A heroine! One person had seen her fall from Jesús' shoulders after a bullet had hit her full in the chest, another said that the captain himself had rushed to her and cut her throat, but that for a long time the melody had continued to emerge through the long gash in her young neck. The astonished captain was said to have been stabbed in his turn by one of the comrades as he was shaking the dead girl to silence her. According to others, the child was still alive, and had rejoined Salvador in his camp.

"She'll be here tomorrow when the army comes. Unless she escapes in time to lead other men into battle in other towns. Long live the revolution!"

Manuel could not get any reliable information from these hysterical people caught up in slaughter and unmoved by anything but fire and blood and the beauty of that ink-black sky lapped by the flames of rebellion. He finally came across one of the women, spared by the collective madness, who had taken Angela to her mother before seeing to the dead and wounded. She pointed out to him the route the cart had taken. In a column of beggars, he recognized Juan and managed to tear him from his revolution by reminding him of Salvador's importance to their cause. Their leader's life depended on Frasquita, and both of them set off in pursuit of her, spurring their horses mercilessly.

She had gotten farther than they would have believed, and at first categorically refused to retrace her steps. But when they mentioned Blanca, she calmed down and agreed to let Manuel take over pulling the cart so that they could get back to the encampment. But there was no question of her mounting behind on one of the horses in order to get there more quickly. She would not abandon her children to a stranger, especially not on such a night! Pedro and Angela were mounted on Juan's horse and Martirio and her mother on Manuel's, while Manuel himself walked between the two animals, holding their bridles. As for Anita, she had taken her place on the cart with her box in her arms, next to Clara, a small light barely visible in the firelit darkness.

On the way, Frasquita tried to remember the face of the man who had given her his purse a few hours earlier. She recalled each of his features with a precision that surprised her. Perhaps she was reinventing them as she wanted. The two rebels insisted that she sleep: she would need all her strength to sew Salvador back together.

The night was quieter now. Of course, fires were still burning, but only a few shots still echoed in the distance. The presence of the men, the breathing of the foam-flecked horses, their tranquil pace all reassured the children. They had never before ridden such animals. Angela had fallen asleep against her brother's back, her face buried in his red curls.

"Why are all these people fighting?" Pedro finally asked the man who was leading them.

"To invent a new world," replied Juan. "'The joy of destruction is at the same time a creative joy.' They've suffered too much and accepted too much for too long."

"They smashed everything!" the child went on.

"Don't believe that. The old world is tough, it has every chance of being born again from its ashes. The peasants are far from having won. Tomorrow we'll probably all be hanged or garroted. But it hardly matters, we're already dead."

It was still pitch black when the little group reached the camp. Blanca hugged Frasquita and told her that there was nothing to fear for the moment and that she would take care of the children. While waiting for them, she had made them a bed out of moss and leaves in a cave not far from there. They would be fine. She would make sure they got to sleep.

Her sewing bag in the colors of the olive grove across her shoulder, my mother entered the little cave where Salvador lay. She barely greeted Eugenio. For a long time, she examined the torn face by the light of the oil lamps.

From among the reels she had inherited, she chose a very fine but very solid thread, inserted it in one of her needles, and set to work. In spite of the blood, she stitched away as calmly as if the skin were fabric.

The half-light was a strain on her eyes, and she started to feel her sight become blurred. As it did so, the olive grove man and the cry of his coat as it was torn by the iron spurs came back into her mind. That was the first time she had mended a man, giving him back his shadow and his desire, but the stitches had not been solid enough: he had left her house once the debt was paid, he had not followed her on her journey, she had seen his shadow moving alone on the walls for some time after his body had abandoned the place. Perhaps she would make this face that had been entrusted to her into something other than was being asked of her. As she darned, as she said the prayers for cuts, for pains, for sleep, as she called age-old powers to the bedside of this revolutionary and gave him a face, she realized what she was doing. After all, she was free now, nobody could force her to be what she didn't want to be, to keep quiet, to hide her work, to hate or love. She was free, as free as the tor-turer had been when he had given Salvador this nightmare face. Others pillaged, slaughtered, burned, why couldn't she mend this man the way she wanted? And even if he looked like some-one else, nobody would be able to take his blue eyes from him.

She remembered what he had said the previous day, the passion with which he had spoken of his cause as his compan-ions tried to load the miller's sacks on their donkeys. In this man, desire was immovable. She smiled at him and stroked his right cheek, having just given him the last piece of it.

"Your work is astonishing!" cried a delighted Eugenio, who had been regularly dipping his dark little pen into scarlet ink, taking notes and making sketches. "How do you know where the muscles are?"

"I don't even know what a muscle is," replied my mother, jolted out of her daydream.

"The muscles make the different parts of the body move. They shrank, but you managed to find them anyway in all that mess."

"It's like a thread, you pull it and see what happens. I try it and then I understand."

"And those prayers you say, what's the point of them?"

"Things like that can't be explained. I have custody of them. Find me some eggs and something to boil them in."

"Are you hungry?"

"No. Stir the embers too!"

Eugenio knew he would not be able to find out more this time. He put down his pen, went to look for the two eggs he still had in his basket of provisions and a little cast iron casserole, then watched Frasquita as she treated the *carne cortada* and tried to note down the words of her prayer.

As his pen flowed over the paper, he felt dizzy and collapsed on the floor of the cave.

Day was breaking, the combined effect of Frasquita's prayers and Eugenio's drugs was slowly wearing off and Salvador started moaning. Frasquita was making one last stitch near the upper lip when he half opened a huge purple eyelid. Frasquita smiled at him as she put away her needles and, stepping over Eugenio, who was still lying on the ground, she left the cave to rejoin her children.

She went and lay down beside her children in the cave where Blanca had chosen to put them. She noticed with amusement that Pedro had already daubed the stone walls with chalk, drawing a big welcoming face, beneath which he and his sister were curled up. A toothless angel to guard their sleep.

A few hours later, she was wakened abruptly by Eugenio, who was looking everywhere for his notebook.

"Give it back!" he implored. "Tear out the pages about yourself if you like, but give me back that notebook. You can't read, so it's no use to you anyway!"

"I haven't touched your notebook."

"When I lost consciousness, I saw ghostly figures working with you on Salvador's face. Later, you stepped over me and something grabbed the notebook I still had in my hand. Did I dream that?"

"All I saw was my sewing. No ghosts, no demons, no notebook. Nobody but a man to be sewed back together."

"Go on, get out of here, you!" cried Blanca, who had fallen asleep while keeping guard outside the cave and had been wakened by Eugenio's shouting.

Eugenio obeyed reluctantly, his hands reddened by the ink that had spilled when he fell. He walked past Clara, who was trying to plant back in the ground the flowers she had gathered the previous night, glanced into the little cave where Salvador lay, his face swollen, and went and collapsed on his bed a few yards away.

The balcony

In the town, the rebellious peasants woke up from their night of killing as if from a night of drinking, their heads throbbing, their hearts heavy. In broad daylight, their revolution looked very different. It was impossible now to be blind to the previous night's slaughter. Now that they could count the victims, many realized the cost of their rioting. So many corpses, so much blood, so many ashes! The embers were still dying down. Yesterday's murderous and sacrificial unity had disappeared. They looked for their dead in the streets, screaming their names.

They lamented, cursing the anarchists and the civil guard, cursing Bakunin and that child who had sung their sorrows. Of course the shops and the haciendas had been plundered, but once their bellies had been filled, the pain seemed stronger still.

The uprising would not bring back those whom poverty had killed in the past. The barracks had yielded, but how many had fallen in order to enter it? A hundred, perhaps more.

Some even wondered what was to become of them now that they had no more masters. Others, including the anarchists, felt an immense relief, which they tried to communicate to the weeping widows and mothers. The most persuasive took turns on the balcony of the still smoking remains of the town hall, a balcony that threatened to collapse at any moment and on which the flag had been torn to pieces. They harangued the crowds, exhorting them not to let their passion run out of steam. Hope would spring up again, despite the horror of the early morning, despite the taste of tears. Now that the abscess had been lanced in the necessary savagery of a spontaneous uprising, the future presented all kinds of possibilities! The State, the Church, the army, the king, the scheming of politicians in the pay of the landowners: the whole repressive apparatus was now obsolete. They were pioneers, builders, they took turns in proclaiming from the height of their unsteady perch, facing the bitter street.

What a victory! They declared the municipality of P. a free commune. The peasants had not died in vain. They would now have to hold fast and organize the defense of the sanctuary!

In one of the rooms in the town hall that had been more or less spared by the flames, what remained of Salvador's group had established its headquarters. Here, they pondered what to do next. It was obvious that, even though Sagasta's falsely liberal government had just established universal male suffrage and authorized all parties, it would not let them take over a municipality like this. The army was sure to march on the town! The authorities would not flinch, they would send a captain at the head of at least five hundred men to put down the uprising before it spread throughout the region, passing from town to town all the way to Granada, from where it would set all the south of the country alight.

It would take more than a song to overcome a regiment. The rebels had collected a good deal of paraphernalia: hunting weapons from the landowners, rifles from the civil guard, ammunition, powder. Everyone had to learn to use them. This time, anger, knives and pitchforks would not be enough.

How much time did they have left to organize their defense? They had no idea. Children would be given the task of keeping watch, they would be posted in trees or behind bushes and would sound the alarm immediately anything moved on the roads.

Another question arose: what to do about those few men

who had already installed themselves in the haciendas, enjoying the luxury that had belonged to the dead, sleeping in their silk sheets, caressing the still warm bodies of their women? How to bring such people, led astray by the previous night's violence, back to the path of reason?

Juan organized the clean-up operations in the town. The streets had to be cleared and the dead buried.

When it came to sewing the shrouds, they missed the priest and the church. The meager words of these ragged anarchists could not match the eloquence of Catholic ritual, they could not promise these men who had fallen for the cause any kind of afterlife! The farewells took on a permanent and derisory character. Bodies rolled in flags, tablecloths or the curtains of those public buildings still standing were shoved into hurriedly dug trenches. What a price they were paying for this freedom! For reasons of hygiene, they also buried the men of the civil guard, the priest, a dozen bourgeois and nobles, and a few local worthies, and to erase the bloodstains already partly imbibed by the sun and earth they stirred the dust in the streets and the main square, which had been renamed Plaza de la Esperanza as a tribute to the events of Jerez de la Frontera.

The balcony creaked when Juan spoke in his turn of that good red rich earth that the wealthy had fed with the corpses of starving children for generations, that charnel house forever watered with the sweat and blood of the peasants and which was now everybody's. Each person would be entitled to his share, but there would be nourishment for the soul too, he insisted: a school would be opened where children and adults could learn to read and write . . .

Juan moved about, facing the deserted street, crying his hope in the future to a few passers-by with dead eyes and dangling arms who watched him as he gesticulated, alone, perched on his rickety promontory.

It was then that the balcony gave way.

FEAR

U ntransportable!" declared Eugenio. "Your Salvador can't be moved, nor can many of the others! We'll stay in the mountains as long as is necessary. The wounded need me down there, you say? But I have enough work here with those they've brought back to the camp. I have more men to tend to than I need! Not to mention the place where you put them! A cave with a worse echo than the refectory of a monastery! I'm alone with two women and a whole lot of kids, dealing with some fifteen poor fellows who've been badly messed up. Take Blanca with you, she knows a lot of things! Or Frasquita, she's a miracle worker! Take them to town! I'm not going to set foot there. And, while we're about it, I prefer the people down there not to know I'm here. They're going to blame me for the disappearance of those three children a year ago . . . They're hungry for justice and blood, your peasants, and I know there have been rumors about me . . . So I'm staying here! Of course, I'll need fresh supplies. In the countess's house, there was a fantastic collection of plant extracts of all kinds. I'd like to take a look at that. I hope that old hag is dead, at least?"

"Her body hasn't been found," replied Manuel, Juan's go-between now that he had settled in the village. "Some say she escaped with the help of her servants."

"What?" Eugenio said, all smiles. "Your rebels let the greatest enemy of the people slip through their fingers? Do you want my opinion? Your revolution is a failure! A tiny garrison of civil guard, a common captain with no prospects and a few bourgeois who weren't too bad: the big fish got through the net! Anyway, for the moment, I'm not moving! The army will soon take back your damned commune and I prefer to keep out of the fighting. But at any rate, you can tell Juan that Salvador has been saved. As soon as Frasquita has finished her prayers, you can go talk to him. He's got his own little cave. Don't you think it takes the cake that a follower of Bakunin should be put back on his feet by saints and ghosts from another world? Not to mention that those damned creatures stole my notebook! One way or another, your revolution will have to pay me for all that! And the sooner the better!"

Apart from Salvador, the rebels wounded in the previous day's fighting had been laid on the ground in the largest of the caves in the side of the mountain. As he approached the huge cave, it seemed to Manuel that the stone itself was groaning, but it was the laments of the wounded echoing around the rocky walls.

He felt as if he was entering the mouth of hell when he crossed the threshold: what filtered through to the outside was as nothing compared with the din in the vast cave. Beneath the roof of this natural cathedral, the sounds of pain were like a deep lugubrious pedal note on the organ: the weeping of the wounded and the howling of the wind merged with Blanca's steps in a terrifying symphony, in which every drop of water secreted by the monumental stalactites also had its place. A few torches, their flames flickering in the icy breath from the stones, emphasized the sinister, desolate aspect of this place where his companions lay dying.

Manuel stood there for a few moments, stunned, contemplating this antechamber of Gehenna, this nightmare of shadow and stone where doomed wretches waited for the great gate of the dead to open to them. To tear himself from the morbid thoughts inspired by this Dantesque spectacle, he had to concentrate on his breathing and feel his heart beating in his chest, he had to convince himself that he was still alive. Only then could he overcome the anguish that had caught him by the throat.

He went from one friend to another, whispered in their ears, listened to their confidences, caressed the sweat-plastered hair of a dying man, and thanked Blanca. She was doing her best to clean, bandage, relieve and comfort all these men who only the previous day had been perfect strangers to her. The months she had spent walking had made her terribly thin, but she kept the emphatic gestures and heavy gait of the strong woman she had been. This persistent memory of a body incapable of being thought of as thin gave her a deceptively robust look.

"You can't see anything," she muttered in a low voice as she came and went amid the bodies lying on the ground or resting against the damp walls. "You've put them here and now we have to grope about in all this noise to tend to them. It's amazing how the slightest whisper becomes a roar in this hole. And these poor lads are even stopping themselves crying out as much as they can. So you can imagine the screams of pain! This morning, we ourselves had to bellow to bear the din. Even those who are suffering the most have understood, and they bite their shirts. And then there's that wind that comes from the back of the cave and chills the blood. It would have been better to leave them outside in the shade of the trees, the weather's mild. What an idea to pile them up here! Move them! We've been doing what we can. We've pulled them into the light on blankets, but in order to get them properly settled they'd have to be lifted, and most of them are too heavy for Frasquita and me. As for Eugenio, he refuses to move them, he says we'll kill them by carting them about like that. It'd take two people like you to lug them about without making them scream too much."

"I'd gladly send you a few of the boys to help you," replied Manuel, shaken by the spectacle of the dying, "but, to tell the truth, it isn't easy down there either."

"Are you still fighting?" Blanca asked, walking back with him into the open air and the silence of the trees.

"No. But there are so many bodies, so many wounded! We have to restore order, calm everyone down, stop the looting, reassure those who are starting to regret yesterday's events. Things aren't over yet. I'm going to talk about all this with Juan. But would you be willing to come down tomorrow to help? There are women and children down there who need care, and Eugenio's refusing to go."

"That doesn't surprise me! I'll come on one condition: that you bring me back here before nightfall."

"I promise. Tell me, do you think I can go see Salvador?"

"Why not?"

"Because of the ghosts and the saints. I wouldn't like to be in the way."

"So you're scared too! You know, these stories of ghosts are just rumors, you mustn't believe everything you hear! Look at these poor boys, half of them are having hallucinations because of Eugenio's drugs, the others are in pain and almost dead, is it any surprise we see strange things in this gloom? When fear becomes tangible, when it mixes with the air we breathe, we try to find a face for it."

"Eugenio says that ghosts stole his notebook."

"Eugenio's the king of liars! And unfortunately, that's the least of his vices. Come on! Frasquita's no witch, she knows things that have been forgotten and she has a gift, that's all! Your rifles and knives are much more dangerous than the powers she summons."

"If you're talking about powers, that means you believe in them!"

"I believe in everything. But I believe without fear."

Suddenly, Frasquita's daughters ran past, pursued by their brother Pedro. Manuel gave a start and Blanca yelled at them to calm down, not to go into the woods, and above all to remain together. Manuel caught the hint of anxiety in the old woman's voice, and that made all the confidence she had managed to instill in him fade abruptly. His fears, which had briefly vanished, returned with a vengeance, and he had to force himself to enter the cave where Frasquita was taking care of Salvador.

It was much brighter than the big cave that was being used as a field hospital, the sunlight poured in through the wide opening, and only the far end kept its secrets. Manuel noticed for the first time that there was a narrow passageway there, which seemed to lead into the belly of the mountain, and it struck him that you would have to be very thin to slip into that crevice. He had never thought about it before, but it was very dark at the back of all these caves where he and his friends had found refuge. The generalized sense of dread that pervaded the camp had put him in a state of alert, even though it did not feel quite the same in the woods as it did in the town. It seemed to him now just as unlikely that you could get to sleep in one of these caves, even though he had already spent several nights here, as in the town hall surrounded by traces of blood and remembering the previous evening's screams.

He really would have liked to sleep, though!

Frasquita was finishing her prayer at Salvador's bedside. His face was swollen and only one eye seemed alive, buried there and forgotten as if in dough that has been left to rise for too long. That blue gleam ringed with purple told Manuel that his friend wanted to know.

Out of respect for Frasquita's mysterious work—his entrance had not distracted her from her prayers—he waited, turning his broad-brimmed black hat in his hands, then took a few steps forward. The look that Salvador had given him as he stood there in the mouth of the cave had been enough to get the ghosts and other infernal creatures out of his head.

When Frasquita had finished at last, she greeted Manuel.

"Are you leaving his face uncovered?" he asked her in a low voice. "Aren't you going to protect him from the flies?"

"No insect will come to rest on his wounds."

"How can you be so sure? There are lots of bluebottles in these caves."

"I very much doubt you'll see a single insect on his face."

"Did you tell him everything that happened down there?"

"No."

He had stopped thinking about it, but as he watched her go out he saw her silhouetted against the light and thought he could make out some bright figures with her. Again, he shivered. He decided not to turn his back on the far end of the cave and placed himself in such a way that he could see, on the left, the opening that looked out on the sky and the trees and, on the right, the shadowy depths of the little cave.

More or less reassured, he recounted yesterday's and today's events to Salvador's half-open eye. As he spoke, the rest of the face withdrew into the background. In that one blue eye, the pupil was throbbing and all the words he uttered plunged into it, as if translated into images. Even silent, unrecognizable and in pain, Salvador remained the best antidote to Manuel's fear. He would so much have liked to hear his velvety voice, at once gentle and authoritarian, which always swept away doubts and urged to action. To see him so diminished, unable to lead the town into battle at this crucial moment, seemed the worst of injustices. Manuel owed him so much: two years earlier, the exiled Catalan had formed an affection for this boy who had just lost his mother and had not yet finished growing, and had taught him to read, write and fight.

With a gesture of his hand, Salvador indicated that he

240 · CAROLE MARTINEZ

wanted to write. Manuel knew where he kept his writing case; he took out his materials for him, dipped the pen in the ink and presented it to him along with a blank page. But writing while lying down proved to be a complicated operation: the black ink trickled in rivulets down the wounded man's fingers, staining his forearms and his shirt, which was already covered in dried blood. A single sentence sufficed to exhaust him. All the more so as, in order to read and write, Salvador usually rested his little spectacles on his nose, spectacles he had had to do without this time.

"In order to survive we must spread the revolution."

Manuel read the one sentence aloud.

Spread the revolution. He developed the idea to make sure that he had quite understood: rouse the surrounding towns, announce the good word, unite the other little groups and secret societies active in the region, not remain isolated in the face of the response that was being prepared. Shout from the rooftops the victory of a few pitchforks over the rifles of the civil guard. But which way to go? Salvador was becoming agitated, pointing in all directions at once.

His donkey's bridle in his hand, Manuel was getting ready to go back down to the place where he had left his horse when he noticed the cart. Frasquita was trying with the help of her children to get it through the woods and back onto the path.

"What are you doing?" Manuel said, surprised.

"I'm going on my way," replied my mother.

"You can't leave now, you're too useful to us. And besides, you'd get lost, alone in these woods."

"And who's going to keep me here against my will?"

"Nobody. You aren't our prisoner! You and your children will want for nothing. Even the villagers don't know where we're hiding. They won't come looking for you here. Blanca!" He yelled at the figure he had just noticed between the trees.

"Come quickly! I can trust you with your friend. Keep a close eye on her, make sure she doesn't go and get herself killed on the road!"

"Frasquita!" Blanca said in surprise as Manuel went on his way. "You're leaving just as the sun is going down! Where were you planning to go at this hour, with your youngest about to close her eyes and the others not much more awake?"

"You know perfectly well I can't stay any longer. You yourself warned me in Santavela. The ogres . . . Do you remember? . . . "

"Did that vermin try something?" Blanca said indignantly, drawing her friend aside from the children.

"No, but I sense a threat, there's something lurking here."

"Wait until tomorrow! He doesn't act hastily, and I think he's afraid of you. Come! Manuel didn't arrive empty-handed, he brought us some flour and two goats. We'll put the children to bed between us tonight in the same cave where we slept yesterday. Nothing will happen, they'll rest with their bellies full. Just wait, girl! Tonight, the roads are no safer than our holes in the rocks. Let the world calm down. After that, you can walk as much as you want."

Frasquita yielded to Blanca's persuasion.

In the cave that served as their shelter, bats were whirling in all directions and they felt cold tongues licking their bodies at regular intervals. From the first night, Pedro's drawings had appeared on the smoothest walls of their new dwelling. In their frames of stone, waves of chalk broke over the white face of the miller, who seemed to be offering his empty smile to the darkness. A toothlessly smiling Neptune in a sea of rock. Before falling asleep, my brother pursued that inner sea of his, and one of its opaline waves moved against the current of cold air and the rumble that came with it until it died at the far end of the cave. Standing facing the great fresco with a candle in her hand, swept along by the tide, Angela was following the long movement of the water with her eyes. Her gaze came to rest where Pedro's gesture broke.

A passage. The wind was emerging from the mountain through a passage. The two children shoved their heads inside. They could not see the end of it, although they could hear what sounded like distant sobbing. Suddenly, the mountain exhaled and spat its icy breath in their faces.

They would set off the next day for the centre of the earth. For tonight, it was best to block that opening.

A few large stones were enough to silence the noise.

After making sure the children were asleep, Frasquita and Blanca stood together at the mouth of the cave and talked. Frasquita was still wearing her wedding dress, stained now with the blood of the wounded.

"Don't you have anything else to put on?" Blanca asked.

"No, it's all I brought with me," Frasquita replied, showing her the bag in the colors of the olive grove that she carried across her shoulder. "José gambled me away and Heredia took me. They all stood behind their windows watching the humiliated woman, the one her husband had sold like a donkey. So I put on this dress, did my hair, and left. I thought about Lucia and her sequined dress."

"I remember your wedding day. You were very beautiful before they withered you. Where do you want to go now?"

"Wherever my feet take me."

"You always had that whiff of departure about you. Like me, you'll be a stranger everywhere. But in my case I know what drove me onto the roads."

"What?"

"My blood first of all—my mother was a gypsy and my father was always off somewhere—and then Eugenio. Eugenio's crimes. Do you think it's possible to forget your own child? I did everything I could to leave him far behind, and now he's caught up with me for good. I'm his mother, you understand that, don't you? He's pursuing me, me, the only person he can't deceive, the only person who knows everything, and I can't stop him, I can't save these children who aren't mine by denouncing the one creature who ever came out of my belly."

Frasquita could find nothing to say to console her friend, who was not weeping. They stood for a long time, side by side, in the silence of the night.

"Three men will die tonight in the cathedral cave," my mother said after a while. "Eugenio pointed them out to me and I said a prayer over them to make them sleep. They'll go without even noticing. What's going to happen now?"

"If you leave tomorrow, Eugenio will go after you. In pursuit of your little Clara who attracts him as light attracts a moth. Don't be fooled, he's only tending to these poor men because your children are here! He's waiting for his opportunity. If you stay, it'll come in the end, that's for sure. But here, there are two of us to keep an eye on him. If you leave, you'll be alone on the roads, because I shan't abandon these poor suffering boys. And besides, the whole region may well go up in flames, the town may only be the beginning. In these caves, we're a long way from the coming battle."

"So Eugenio will follow me everywhere, just as he followed you here! And why wouldn't he choose to remain with you?"

"He's not afraid of losing me anymore, I walk too slowly for his liking."

There was a cracking sound in the shadows, and Frasquita turned abruptly toward the wood and peered into the pitch darkness.

"The horror lurking here, I sense it," she murmured, her eyes still fixed on the dark mass of the trees. "I've never felt that before. Something is breathing in these caves, that wind that comes from elsewhere . . . "

"It's the wind of war, rising from the plain," replied Blanca, looking at her friend's tense, still face.

"It's not just that. The memory of the slaughter and the fear of dying, the pain of the wounded and this monster lying in wait, all of that is mixed up with my memories of Santavela. And these prayers exhaust me! Last night, I saw the afterlife over our heads and the dead caressing the living. I'm afraid of sleeping, Blanca, I'm afraid of dreaming again. My dreams are full of that face I just sewed up. It seems that in mending him I brought the borders of two worlds closer together. Death is prowling around us."

THE SCREAMS OF THE MOUNTAIN

S alvador's wounds did not become infected, not a single fly ventured onto them, and the very next morning the swelling began to subside.

After saying her prayers at his bedside, Frasquita bent over the motionless face she had reshaped. The eyes were closed, he must be sleeping. It pleased her to look at her work. She loved to see the wounds dry, the crusts form, the edema diminish. His features were already taking on a way of moving that she recognized.

"They're so beautiful when they're asleep," she thought as she joined Blanca outside the big cave.

"It stinks so much of men in there, we could almost forget to be afraid!" said Blanca, who was carrying soiled blankets. "They've been doing it in their underwear since yesterday. I've looked in every corner for old clothes to change them, but they all wash fully dressed and I couldn't find anything, so I wash what I can. Good news: there are two of them who can stand. But they aren't yet strong enough to transport their friends. As for the corpses, they aren't here anymore, Eugenio has taken care of them. As he couldn't get them on his horse, he borrowed your cart to transport them. But the bodies smell less bad than the living, and the stench even withstands the wind coming from the back of the cave."

"I have no prayer that would stop them stinking," my mother said, smiling without realising it. "We'll just have to put up with it."

"Are you smiling? Well, don't go in there or you'll soon

become disillusioned! Deal first of all with the two who've set themselves up outside! Maybe some of your surprising gaiety will rub off on them. As far as I'm concerned, it makes me retch just to think of going back in that hole. I hope Manuel comes quickly!"

It had been decided that Blanca would go down into the town with Clara, despite Eugenio's protests that it was risky for the child. In his opinion, diseases would reach the village before the army did, they followed slaughter like vultures and made them worse, piling mass death on mass death, carrying off the young especially. It was to avoid disease that he had already got rid of that night's three corpses.

"Impossible to bury them in those loose stones!" he complained. "I just piled them up! I almost collapsed making a funeral pyre for them! I'm waiting for them all to be dead before I set it alight."

"A big bonfire that'll attract the army here after they've retaken the village," Blanca observed with sudden cynicism. "You've found a way for the dead to betray the survivors!"

"Now I'm being blamed for my humanity!" simpered Eugenio.

Frasquita merely stared at him and waved her hands about to scare him. He immediately stopped his showing off and left to get on with his task. Maybe he wasn't so dangerous after all, if her two hands could put him to flight! He hated war, prayers and ghosts, he killed the weakest and always stayed on the winning side.

Manuel was alone when he got back to the camp. Nobody had been able to come with him. Juan had broken his leg when the town hall balcony had collapsed, the others had set off on the roads to announce the victory of the people over the oppressor, and he had thought it best not to indicate the position of their camp to any of the villagers.

"They're not exactly brimming over with courage at the moment," he complained. "They lower their heads and wait for the blows like dogs that have bitten their masters out of fright. When we put rifles in their hands, they look disgusted and don't really want to learn how to use them. A song would stir them up. You wouldn't like to give us your little girl, the one who sings?"

But Angela had stopped singing since the slaughter. And a whole battalion would not have been enough to take her back down there. If anyone had suggested to her that she go back to the town, she would have bitten them on the mouth. It was best to leave her free to hang about the camp with her brother.

Manuel paid a brief visit to Salvador's cave, was informed of the deaths of his three comrades, then, sadly, set Blanca and Clara on his donkey.

While Frasquita was busy in the big cave, blessing the wind that periodically renewed the pestilential air, Angela and Pedro cleared the entrance to the gallery they had discovered the previous day. They could hear the murmurs of the wounded distorted by distance and the interplay of stone, water and wind.

Angela now entered the bowels of the earth. She preferred to hurl herself into that stone mouth that was breathing its icy breath in their faces rather than think again of the slaughter that had occurred two days earlier. She had spent her last two nights trying to erase that horrible night, to bury it as deep as she could inside herself, and to stop up the passage that led to it with a thick layer of insignificant images. She needed the excitement of these underground depths and their whiff of adventure to stifle the memory of the bullets whistling past her ears, the loud laughter of her mad bearer and the trampled bodies drowning in their own blood.

And so they crawled, one behind the other, into the passage. Pedro had stolen a lamp, which he pushed in front of him. The gallery opened out, and soon they were able to stand side by side. Angela plunged with delight into this winding tunnel that would surely lead them somewhere where memory had no place.

"What if the lamp goes out?" asked Pedro, who had slowed down.

"Are you afraid?"

"Of what?"

"Of getting lost, of animals, ghosts, dying."

"A bit, what about you?"

"I'm not afraid of anything anymore," said Angela, and her voice was like a flare lighting her brother's darkness. "I'm immortal, even bullets can't touch me!"

"Come on!" said Pedro, spurred on by his elder sister's self-confidence.

The gallery branched out until it formed a veritable maze of underground cells that were infinitely terrifying and infinitely delightful in the light of their little lamp. On several occasions, they had to retrace their steps because the passages became too narrow. They advanced cautiously, sometimes keeping flat against the limestone walls, or making their way over unsteady heaps of fallen rocks. At each intersection, Pedro would take out one of the big pieces of chalk from the mill that he always kept in his pocket and marked the route they would have to take on the way back. At last they came to a gigantic underground cave where their cries were amplified.

"Now we're in the dragon's den," said Angela, shivering but delighted.

They screamed until they reduced their memories to silence and, at last free of all anxiety, they decided, in spite of the cold, not to go back straight away. Skirting a chasm at the bottom of which flowed some kind of subterranean river, they continued their wandering in the maze of limestone rocks. Sometimes, when the wind stopped blowing, the air became difficult to breathe and they both felt faint. It seemed to them that they could then hear murmuring, and that it was very close. They listened to the whispering of the stones without understanding it, and felt like partners in crime.

They plunged ever further into the depths of the earth, sometimes climbing, sometimes descending, because of the uneven ground, until the current of air became stronger and indicated the way out.

At the bottom of a shaft, they could see daylight, within reach.

Pedro, slipping his hands and feet into cracks swarming with insects, descended against the wind into the blinding light of day, then helped his sister to extricate herself in her turn from her prison of stone.

They had come out into a cave a long way from the ones occupied by the anarchists. They hid the lamp they had stolen, and once their eyes had again become accustomed to the brightness, they pulled aside the wall of vegetation, scorched by the heat and the wind, that concealed the opening and went outside.

A wonderful warmth caressed their skin. They closed their eyes and breathed in the warm scented air of the forest as deeply as they could, submitting delightedly to the sun. But then, in its fierce light, they saw, just in front of them, three corpses heaped one on top of the other on a bed of dry wood. One of the faces, thrown back, stared at them, its big, pain-filled eyes covered with swarms of bluebottles.

Horrified by this scene, the children ran away along the side of the mountain, and luckily, got back to the camp a bit higher up.

Their screams from the heart of the maze had been heard even in the cathedral cave, where Frasquita and the wounded men had held their breaths in order not to attract whatever thing it was that had doubtless been awakened by the smell of blood and their importunate moans. The huge roar coming from the depths of the mountain had finished off one of the dying. Two poor devils, galvanized by their fear, had managed to drag themselves outside, while seven others, still unable to crawl into the sunlight, had continued to stare at the far end of their cave, where the shadows looked like monsters ready to devour them, long after the roaring had ceased.

When Frasquita saw Angela and Pedro, their clothes even dirtier than usual, she was horrified and beat them. They lied and said that they had been running in the woods. They revealed nothing of their unusual underground adventure but, realizing that they were the ones who had struck fear into the grown-ups, they smiled as they were beaten.

After the meal, Anita, quick and silent as ever, continued to help her mother, taking food and drink to the wounded men. My eldest sister had been somewhat forgotten in the commotion of events. In that vast world, she always kept herself barely a few paces from the wooden box where her gift was germinating. She had not let it out of her sight since the beginning of the journey,

As for Martirio, she sat motionless and withdrawn in a rocky recess not far from the big cave.

Pedro and Angela decided to creep up on her and take her by surprise. In the event, she did not even jump, but they saw what she was holding in her hands: a notebook full of sketches and red ink.

"What's that?" asked Pedro.

"I found it, it's mine!" replied Martirio curtly, trying to hide the notebook beneath her skirts.

"Show it to us and we'll take you into our maze," said Angela.

Martirio shrugged. "The tunnel through the mountain? Do you think you're the only ones who've been that way!"

"You walked in our tunnel on your own?" Pedro said, surprised.

"Where do you think I found this notebook? You always think you're the only ones to know everything. But you don't know anything! You don't see anything!"

"Is that right?" said Angela, hurt. "And what do you see more than we do?"

"Death. I see death."

"Don't think you can scare us!"

"I'm going to die soon," Martirio went on.

"How do you know that?" her brother said, astonished.

"The miller told me."

"According to Juan, we'll all end up hanged or garroted!" said Pedro, suddenly serious.

"*I'll* never die," Angela boasted. "I'm eternal!"

"You're stupid, you'll die like everyone else!" said her brother.

"You'll all die, but me first," said Martirio, vacant-eyed.

"Do you belive that old madman on his hill?" said Angela. "He was just trying to scare you!"

"No, on the contrary, he did everything not to scare us. But he couldn't fool me. Talk to the people here about your miller! You'll see!"

And Martirio walked away.

"But up on the ridge," said Angela, going after him, "she told us we shouldn't talk to them about him."

"Why not? Come on!" said Pedro. He walked toward the two wounded men who were lying in the open air.

He engaged them in conversation. He was soon joined by his sister, who listened without speaking.

"I recognize you," said Quince, turning respectfully to Angela. "You're the kid who sang in the square. That was a lovely song of yours! You wouldn't like to sing us something?"

"I recognize you too!" she replied harshly. "You were one of the men who took our sacks from us. I don't want to sing for you."

"But Salvador bought those sacks!" replied Quince.

"They weren't for sale!" she retorted with a grimace, her throat knotted with anger.

"The miller on the mountain would have given you flour too," said Pedro.

"What miller, son?" said Quince, his features twisted from the pain in his bandaged back. "There's nothing left up there in the mountains but a ruined windmill. The old man who was in charge of it died a long time ago. You remember when old Julián died, don't you?"

"I was a boy," replied another young man, whose name was Luis. "It's been at least fifteen years since he kicked the bucket."

"No, we're not talking about the same person," Pedro insisted. "Our one was alive, we talked to him, he was hard at work."

"We can't be wrong," said Quince. "Julián's was the only windmill around here. I remember when we used to go up there in the season. He'd sit us down in his arbor and give us bread as hard as wood. We'd have to leave it in a bowl of milk to get soft. We were fine there in his paradise, he used to say, and it was true that we felt fine, sitting on his benches in the shade after all those hours of walking."

"He gave us milk from his goats, too," said Angela, still as bad-tempered as before. "He even gave us the three sacks of flour you took from us. If he's a ghost, he can't be very pleased that you stole them. Maybe he's the one who's yelling under the mountain. We're not afraid of anything, he likes us. But you, well, that's another story."

"Stop taking the mickey, you brats!" said Pablo, who was in the worst state of the four anarchists, and who was already sufficiently shaken by the screams heard from the cave. "Go back to running about in the woods! And don't come back here, banging on about this nonsense of yours!"

"You abandoned your Julián alive on his bare mountain, that's the truth!" insisted Angela, not scared of anything now.

And with that, the children ran off to look for Martirio, leaving the four adults dumbfounded.

Frasquita had slipped into Salvador's lair.

There was no reason for her to have come. All the prayers had already been said. She only wanted to watch him sleep.

Part of her wandered over his new face.

What had she done this time? What had she bound to her by mending his flesh? She had stopped thinking to escape, she had even stopped being afraid of the ogre, or the war, or the roaring of the mountain. What she had really been trying to flee the night before was the feeling that now took violent hold of her.

To stay where this face was! It was obvious! Everything was tipping over, becoming muddied.

She could fool herself no longer, she recognized her desire. Of course, finishing off her work and finding out what was to become of the patched-up face seemed to her a sufficient reason to wait. But there was also that desire to be embraced by arms that would not let go of her. She was in love with this man, this stranger she had partly created, there was no doubt about it. And since she could no longer run away, since her children would run even greater risks on the roads than in these terrible caves, she would stay, and perhaps he would look at her in spite of the fight he still had to wage. This was where she wanted to read her destiny, here on the stitched-up lips of this man obsessed with his revolution. A man who had paid for those sacks of flour, when he could quite simply have taken them, without any concern for her or her children. An exile like her, whose only home was wherever there was a battle. She would have liked to stay in the little cave for a long time, waiting for his blue eye to half open and look at her. What a sight she must look, with her wedding dress all spattered with mud and blood!

She went even closer to that damaged flesh until she could feel the warmth of it on her own skin, her own moist lips. She breathed gently on the wounds, passed her hand through his curly hair, then kissed him lightly on his thick mouth. With a rapid gesture, he caught her hand without even opening his eyes, and the contact was painful.

Frasquita was so surprised that she was barely aware of the moan that escaped at that moment from the back of the little cave.

Martirio could not read, but she kept leafing through Eugenio's notebook, following those long, sinuous red lines with her finger. Besides the words, there were all those anatomical drawings, those bodies turned inside out like socks, exposing their mysterious organs. Angela and Pedro tried to get the notebook away from her several times as the afternoon wore on, but in vain. She defended herself so well that they gave up and contented themselves with begging her to show them what it contained. She refused, but ended up telling them the whole story.

That first night—she said in a monotone voice—as they were sleeping with Blanca and their mother was sewing the Catalan's face back together, she had seen the miller in a dream. He was standing motionless in the cave where she lay, in front of that white fresco that Pedro had already sketched, showing her the entrance to the tunnel.

She had crawled into the pitch black space without a lamp, following her strange guide with the chalky white face. For a long time, she had moved forward blindly, wondering when this strange dream would end, until the moment when, in the windswept darkness, she had felt an icy hand slip this notebook between her fingers.

The contact had wakened her. She was no longer lying with her family in the cave, but actually standing in the cold and the dark, her right hand clutching the little notebook. So she really had been sleepwalking in the darkness!

Without panicking, she had groped her way through the narrow gallery in the icy blackness until she was back in the cave. She had lain down on her bed again, buried the little notebook in her skirts, and gone back to sleep.

In the morning, she was convinced that nothing had happened, that it had been a dream within a dream, one of those night terrors so common in childhood but which sometimes persist in adulthood, when our minds play tricks on us, making us think we have escaped our nightmare and are opening our eyes on the real world, until we discover with terror that the monster, the apparition or whatever, is still there in front of us, as if it has stepped straight out of our dream.

But as Martirio was getting up, something had fallen from under her skirts: a little notebook with a flesh-colored leather cover stained red in places.

That was when she had known that the miller really had come. The whole cave was smiling with the same empty, benevolent smile as his ghost.

There indeed, at the far end of the cave, was the passage, with the cold wind blowing through it.

At the end of their little sister's story, Angela and Pedro were silent for a moment before bursting into laughter. Martirio was a great storyteller!

As promised, Manuel brought back Blanca and Clara as the sun was sending out its last oblique rays and the shadows on the stone were lengthening. He did not linger. Juan needed him. But it had been agreed that he would come back for Blanca the next day at dawn. The poor boy had deep shadows under his eyes.

Blanca watched him tenderly as he left.

She had come back deeply upset by what she had seen below. She told them how the villagers were looking for someone to blame, how the anarchists were gradually losing their remaining credibility, how everyone was shirking responsibility for the uprising.

Eugenio, who had listened attentively to his mother's story, followed her to the watering place. The shadows were gaining ground. Night was coming. They were alone and Eugenio took advantage of this to launch into one of those tirades that had become his specialty.

"It's like in all wars," he began. "Human horror gradually reasserts itself: everyone blames everyone else, you get used to the smell of corpses, you accept any humiliation to survive. Human bonds are cut. The child who dies before our eyes isn't ours, so why should we give it what our children need? Let a stranger's child, our neighbor's child, our friend's child, our sister's child die instead. Only our closest circle matters to us and that circle shrinks until, with a scream from some, and not even a tear from others, that circle, that last bastion of humanity collapses before the survival instinct, and then we give up our relatives, we sell our children, our companions, because they hurt too much, all those ties. I'm not talking about will, but that powerful impulse that forces us to live. How do some manage to resist? Where do they find the strength to fight their instincts? That's the real question! Cowardice, horror, laughter, massacres don't surprise me. I'm only surprised by those heroic moments when, in a chaotic world, a being as naturally imperfect as man lets himself be swayed by pity and love. Could it be an unconsidered gesture? When so many others have already died around us, when we've become fully aware how vulnerable we are, how absurd our little lives, when we know with certainty that we will die, and that those we love will die with us, of hunger or thirst, or that they'll be tortured—to then give the little bread we have left to a person dying in front of our eyes, or give shelter to a person everyone calls a traitor or an enemy, could a sacrifice like that be only a whim? Do you think, mother, that I'll have my sublime gesture? That I could risk my own life, without even hope of redemption, for some wretch I don't even know? A gratuitous gesture that would make me feel important? It's possible. In fact, I'd be quite happy to leave this absurd world in a spontaneous and heroic about-turn. After all, why shouldn't the peacetime monster become a hero of the revolution?"

Blanca said nothing. She would have liked to talk to him about all the broken people, all the people who give up and let themselves die, and who, without any sublime gesture, simply do not bother to defend their own little selves in a world deserted by love. But she knew that her son would see nothing heroic in that, and that his long speech did not require a response.

THE DAY MANUEL DID NOT COME

The next morning, Salvador felt well enough to get up, but Frasquita insisted on his lying down for a few hours more.

He was getting impatient: Manuel was late. While waiting, Blanca had gotten Anita to help out, and the girl was standing on her box, kneading dough on a large smooth stone.

The morning passed and nobody came to the camp.

By early afternoon, it was obvious that Manuel would not be coming. The adults all suspected that something had happened in the town. But nobody was saying anything. Even Eugenio, who was usually so talkative, remained silent, listening for the slightest suspicious sound. Only Angela, Pedro and Clara laughed constantly, unaware of the threat hovering over the camp, spared the fear that ate away at the grown-ups.

The roaring of the mountain resumed in the afternoon and the final five occupants of the cathedral cave were at last taken out and laid under the trees. Frasquita noticed that her cart had gone. Eugenio had borrowed it again to transport the latest corpses.

He had dragged the cart to the place, some distance from the camp, where he had started erecting his funeral pyre, and had spent part of the day piling up wood. The place was particularly dry, a spark would be enough to set it alight. His bonfire would probably be seen for miles around.

After some hours of effort, he heard children's voices. They came from behind the curtain of dry plants that covered the side of the mountain at this spot. The cart was concealed by the funeral pyre, so he slipped behind it and waited for something to happen.

It was then that he saw Angela and Pedro.

Beaming, they were coming out of their hidden little cave where they had yelled to their heart's content.

How many adults would they kill this time?

Still shaking with cold, they were delighted to see that pile of wood, and walked toward it, but a stiff gray hand that stuck out reminded them that there were corpses here, and they ran away, laughing.

Eugenio abandoned his hiding place as soon as their voices had faded and went in through the curtain of plants.

At first, he saw nothing. But after several minutes his eyes grew accustomed to the gloom and he discovered a large white feather and two lamps that the children had left on the ground. He lighted one of the lamps, looked at the feather and the walls of the cave, made shiny by some animal rubbing its geasy fur on them, then raised his head and saw the shaft. With a laugh, he hoisted himself up into it.

Eugenio had stopped fearing ghosts. It was becoming obvious that, in this upside-down world where everything was going to the dogs, the children were deceiving the grown-ups. They had found a way to create chaos, and those screams heard in the cathedral cave had come from their little sparrow throats. The mountain had become a megaphone. They may even have been playing at being spirits that first night. Those shadowy figures he thought he had seen as he lost consciousness could easily have been them.

It was like a fairy tale and these Tom Thumbs had stolen his property!

If his notebook hadn't vanished into thin air after all, he might be able to get it back from them!

Plunging into the windswept galleries, he thought of how he could turn this unlikely maze to his advantage. Whatever he decided, he had to act fast.

The army had already reached the town, he was sure of it. Fleeing now would get him nowhere. As for Salvador, seeing the turn that events were taking, his friendship would not be useful to him in the future.

If he wanted to save his skin and profit from all this mess, he had to indicate the position of the camp to the enemy by setting fire to his funeral pyre and the surrounding woods tomorrow morning. As for what happened after that, he had his plans worked out. He could be a traitor if he wanted, this wouldn't be the first time.

He would strike tonight, while the sun child was fast asleep.

But then another idea came to him, borne on the wind that swept the limestone galleries, a very different idea, an absurd idea, a grandiose idea. Large amounts of air circulated in these underground caves. The strength of the gusts varied, but their direction remained constant . . .

A hint of a smile hovered over his lips. In the end the wind alone would decide.

The ogre, death and the little light

Manuel did not come that day, and with good reason! The army had indeed entered the town just before dawn.

The street fighting had not lasted. The peasants, so brave a few days earlier, had surrendered without firing a shot. Only the anarchists had attempted something, but there were not enough of them: many had set off on the roads to stir up the region. Juan, with his game leg, blew in vain on the embers, but the fire was out.

The soldiers were looking for the leader, that Catalan.

Manuel, Juan and a few others were taken prisoner. The army could not execute the whole village, culprits would have to be chosen, they had to drive individual villagers to denounce their fellows, especially if they were going to silence that hysterical countess with her shrill voice, who was demanding mass hangings and a general garroting, as well as the cleaning up of her house and the restitution of everything that belonged to her!

At the very moment Eugenio was plunging into the maze, Manuel, his hands tied behind his back, was entering a windowless room in the town hall to face torture.

A sharp smell hung in the confined, rarefied air, an infinitely nauseous, human smell.

Facing him, two men with inscrutable faces, in their shirtsleeves.

His legs suddenly gave way beneath him. The lower part of his body had stopped responding. A stench of fear and suffering.

On the floor, fresh blood. The blood of his comrade Juan, whom he had heard screaming for two hours. Screaming, then falling silent.

He had savored that silence, that painful silence.

Exploring the galleries, Eugenio saw the chalk marks that Pedro had made at every intersection. A mill, a smile, a boat, a bird, dozens of white sails. Following the trail of these drawings, he reached the dragon's den, where he admired the folds in the vault, from which drops had oozed to create huge concretions, then, following the chalk wave, he finally came to the tattooed cave where Frasquita and her children slept.

The cave was empty and nobody saw him come out, apart from the miller, swimming up there on the wall in a tumult of hypnotic white curves.

As he was passing Salvador's cell, the Catalan hailed him. Salvador had gotten up by himself, but Eugenio saw immediately that he was only able to remain standing by leaning on the rocky walls.

The brightness of Salvador's eyes struck Eugenio with such intensity that it was only later that he saw the purple shadows around them. The face, although crisscrossed by dark crusts, was no longer in any way repulsive. The wounds had stopped suppurating, and each part had found its place, probably not exactly the one it had had before the torturer had gotten to work, but a place sufficiently harmonious to give the whole a coherent appearance that was already almost aesthetically pleasing. His face was no longer as swollen as it had been the day before, nor was it that morning's impassive mask. The features were coming alive.

But he was not yet smiling: either because he did not consider a smile the appropriate expression, or because the grimace he sometimes made was the only smile remaining to him.

"They won't hold out!" he said in his fine soft voice.

"So you're on your feet again, looking quite handsome and endowed with the power of speech!" cried Eugenio with genuine enthusiasm. "Forgive me, but I don't know what you're talking about."

"My comrades," Salvador said, taking care to enunciate clearly. "They're probably being tortured at this very moment, and they won't hold out. We'll have to get out of here!"

"What about your last five men? They can't move yet. Are you planning to abandon them to the army? You won't be able to transport them, that'd finish them off."

"I have no choice. The rule is that after forty-eight hours without news, we move."

"You have some strange customs."

"Knowing that your suffering is limited in time helps you bear torture!"

"Do some hold out longer?"

"Forty-eight hours of silence is already heroic, believe me! And Manuel is so young!"

"He'll give us away, is that it?" cried Eugenio, indignantly. "I was sure of it!"

"The words you use! You really make a poor revolutionary. My dear old Eugenio! I wonder what you're doing among us this time. Why haven't you run away yet?"

"What makes you think I won't do precisely that tonight?"

"Whatever you decide, I thank you for staying beside us for so long. As for us, we're leaving these caves tomorrow morning!"

"And where will you go?"

"Frasquita said you regularly borrow her cart to transport the dead. Have you brought it back to the camp?"

"No, I left it next to the corpses and came back a different way. I'll go and get it at dawn."

"We'll put the wounded men on it. I feel dizzy, I've been lying down too long. Help me to take a few steps, will you? I have to recover as quickly as I can if I want to be on that journey tomorrow."

"I'll lend you my horse."

"If you're still here," said Salvador, with a grin that could really have passed for a smile this time.

That evening, Frasquita and Blanca lay down across the entrance to the cave where the children slept, Frasquita's head by Blanca's feet, and fell asleep confident that the ogre would not dare step over their bodies. Anita was sleeping curled up around her box, while Clara's slight luminescence cast a faint light on the face of her sister Martirio, who lay huddled beside her, her eyes closed and her mouth open. As for Angela and Pedro, they had settled down somewhat apart from the rest of the litter and lay holding hands, both smiling the same smile in their sleep.

It was on that deep, peaceful night that Martirio again heard the voice of the miller.

"Get up, my girl!" the voice murmurs. "Take your little sister who is sleeping by your side and follow me to where the wind blows through the mountain."

Martirio wedges her precious notebook in her belt, looks at Clara's beautiful, luminous face, and takes her noiselessly in her arms. She seems so light that Martirio again doubts the reality of what is happening.

The stones concealing the entrance to the tunnel have been cleared.

She plunges into the windswept gallery, clasping Clara's warm, luminous body to her.

"My girl," the old man says, with infinite gentleness, "you will have to die. But have no fear, I am here."

"Why?" asked the child in a sad, limpid little voice.

"Your death will save them all."

Martirio feels a sense of dread rising inside her. No, she isn't dreaming. Her little sister is breathing against her shoulder. Her warm breath caresses the down on her neck. Where is he taking her? Who will take Clara back to the sun, if she herself is to die down here? Clara feeds on light. She will die of cold and dark, buried alive, and it will all be Martirio's fault.

The little notebook crushed against her belly flaps in rhythm with her heartbeat.

In the biggest of the underground caves, the one that Angela and Pedro have named the dragon's den, the voice urges her to enter a shaft with narrow, sloping sides that she has not yet explored. Martirio stops, tears off the first page from the notebook, rolls it into a ball, and drops it on the ground. Angela and Pedro will understand, they will save Clara. Scattering the pages as she goes, she advances slowly after that invisible ghost, who watches her without saying a word, merely hailing her at each intersection, to indicate which way to go.

Clara feels increasingly heavy in her arms. In spite of the prevailing cold in this maze, big salty drops trickle down her temples and cheeks. Tears and sweat mingle. She is bathed in sweat. She feels dizzy. Seeing that she cannot go on, her strange companion lets her breathe for a moment. Then, as she is shivering in every limb, he exhorts her to start walking again. She obeys meekly.

Martirio walks in this way for a long time, in the sometimes rarefied air of the depths, without suspecting that an ogre is striding toward her somewhere in this same maze beneath the mountain. An ogre who is coming to find the fragile, luminous little life she is clasping in her arms. And each of these balls of paper swollen with red ink she leaves behind her is his.

*

Borne on the winds, Eugenio slips into that sea of chalk where the children are asleep. The lamp he has left inside the gallery casts a dim light on the cave and its drawings. The miller's face smiles in the backwash. The two women are sleeping peacefully on the threshold as Eugenio creeps through the cave.

Clara is nowhere to be seen. The other little girl, the one with the cold eyes, has disappeared too.

An enormous sense of frustration sweeps over him.

What has Blanca done with her? The bitch is again trying to thwart his desires! What business is it of hers?

He is on the verge of tears as he moves about amid the waves, turning in circles like a caged animal. He can barely control himself. He needs to assuage his desire in order to regain control of himself. His gaze moves over the other sleeping children and comes to rest on Pedro's long red curls. The boy is snoring a little, mouth open, wedged in the arms of his savage of a sister. His pink lips are thick with sleep. He approaches the boy, lightly touches his chalk-whitened hands, then takes a cloth and a little bottle from the bag he is carrying across his shoulder. But his gestures are unsteady, clumsy. His body contracts, he would like to scream. He takes a deep breath and opens the bottle.

As he gets ready to pour the mysterious contents of the opaque little bottle onto the piece of cloth, a long harsh moan is heard.

Eugenio stops dead.

A gentle smile on his lips, he puts the cork back in the bottle, stuffs the bottle and the cloth roughly back in his bag, and plunges again into the gallery.

He will find Clara, he will caress her solar body, she won't escape him!

His oil lamp in his hand, he retraces his steps, and in the big cave he has already crossed on the way here, and which seems to have been carved out of the rock to serve as a lair for some monster, he notices a bright little shape on the ground. Yes, next to a crack, there is something there.

He approaches, bends down.

A crumpled paper.

Unfolding the sheet, he is overcome with rage. He flings down the crumpled page, a page he himself wrote several years before, addressed to his mother, and rushes into the stone gully. He advances quickly, his huge back stooped, along the narrow gallery that begins at the bottom of the shaft.

Another page rolled into a ball. Then yet another. His whole notebook is here, torn to pieces by those silly bitches!

He becomes heated, he is full of desire and anger as he follows the traces of the two little girls.

Martirio has stumbled on the rock she was trying to climb and has fallen backwards, screaming in terror but without letting go of her sleeping sister. Invisible hands have caught her before she can break her head on the rock.

"We've arrived," the voice says at last.

"Where are we?" Martirio asks, cautiously putting her precious burden down on the ground.

"Behind this mass of fallen rocks is the back of the cave where the wounded were being kept. See, it isn't so dark!"

"And why have you brought me here?"

"I have time to waste. I know some things, but there are areas of shadow in your destinies. Dark areas where even death cannot stick its nose. Now, you're going to leave your sister sleeping in this recess. She has to be quite visible from the cave. Like a little light in the dark."

"Isn't she at risk here?"

"Don't worry, you've saved her. They'll find her. The forest isn't far. If you listen carefully, you can hear the trilling of a nightingale and Quince snoring."

"Can I get out that way?"

"No, you're going to have to retrace your steps and face the monster alone, and you must be quick about it. Let's go to meet him!"

"A monster?"

"A man! I don't know any other monster. Let's hurry!"

So Martirio reluctantly abandons her sleeping sister and plunges back into the dark tunnel.

She turns one last time toward Clara, a dim light so reassuring in all this gloom. Dying was nothing as long as she held this soft, serene little body against her. From now on, she is alone.

Eugenio stops for a moment in the underground chamber where Martirio caught her breath a few moments ago. He sniffs, listens, looks around, and finally hears little steps approaching. They're coming! He extinguishes his lamp, unconcerned that he is now completely in the dark. After all, what could he possibly have to fear? He is the predator! The darkness and the cold wind that reign in this nightmarish world do not frighten him. Why on earth should they?

He waits for his prey, which is groping toward its preordained death.

Blindly, Eugenio soaks a piece of cloth with the liquid from the bottle. The smell of it catches him slightly by the throat.

The noise of footseteps gets louder. He tenses, ready to pounce.

The child is there in the dark, he senses her by his side, she has stopped, but he can hear her rapid breathing. She is alone, motionless and terrified, within reach. He senses her fear, feels it in his flesh. Delighted, he soaks it in. She risks a step forward and brushes against him. It's all too much!

He throws himself on the girl, and she screams at the top of her voice.

He must silence her!

The screaming spreads in all directions. The cry hits the walls, bounces off, looks for a way out, rushes into the galleries, swells, is distorted, amplified, reaches the cave at the entrance to which the two women are posted, enters their dreams, shakes them, breaks them.

They wake with a start.

They light a lamp. The children are already on their feet, terrified. Anita clutches her box in her arms. Martirio and Clara have disappeared, and the huge cry that freezes their blood is coming from the back of the cave. Without conferring, Pedro and Angela rush immediately toward the source of the cry. The opening to their tunnel is clear. They plunge into it, with the others at their heels.

"Shut up, you bitch!" mutters Eugenio through his teeth as he tries to press the piece of cloth he has prepared over Martirio's mouth.

The child struggles in the total darkness against the big hands that have seized her. Small as she is, she defends herself with all her might, screaming all the while. But the ogre immobilizes her and presses the cloth over her nose, stuffs it in her mouth. She stops crying out, she can't breathe, the strange smell of the cloth is stifling her. Her arms and legs move in all directions. She really can't breathe anymore! She goes limp and faints.

The cry has ceased abruptly. Giving way to a silence even heavier than before.

Frasquita, her bag in the colors of the olive grove across her shoulder, stops in the dragon's den, looking for a sign. They all hold their breaths. Pedro lowers his eyes and discovers the piece of crumpled and reddened paper at the side of the shaft. He shows it to Angela. They both enter the passage. Blanca cannot keep up, she picks up the paper, red with words intended for her. Words of love, the first page.

In spite of his excitement, Eugenio has noticed that the child he is holding, the child he has at his mercy, is not Clara. But the blood is beating in his temples, that warm little body is against him, he can smell it. He ought to go, he knows he has to escape, he knows that Martirio's screams have doubtless alerted the camp. He knows his trail will be easy to follow, that the pages torn from the book of his life will lead them to him.

But he cannot stop caressing and licking the body in his arms. From his bag, he has taken out his big knife, the very one he held out to his mother on the road a few days earlier. The one she refused.

"So you hid your sister and now you can't tell me where you put her, eh, girl?" he whispers into the deaf little ear. "You nearly spoiled my pleasure, you dirty bitch. But you see, I'm happy with you too! There . . . Gently now . . . Can you feel my spear? It's you, my fresh bread, my burning little sun, you bad girl!"

It is as if he has been split in two, caught in the snare of his dizzying desire. He'll be caught if he stays! But no: time, they'll need time to get to him through the underground tunnels. He can enjoy his prey a little before moving. He'll find a way out, straight ahead of him. He's always found one. As he lifts the child's skirts in the pitch darkness, kneading the tender flesh of her thighs, edging toward her hairless genital region, he suddenly feels icy hands encircling his neck.

A second cry stops Frasquita as she runs. A deep cry, an adult cry. She has almost reached her target. No more than a few dozen yards at most.

Eugenio has let go of Martirio to protect his neck. But the hands that were strangling him have gone. He gropes for his lamp without interrupting his long cry. The lamp has disappeared. As he tries to catch his breath in the rarefied air, it seems to him that fingers as cold as death are drumming on his neck, his back, his penis. With his knife, he lunges blindly at the empty air. He takes the little girl in his arms again, feels her warmth escaping, and clasps her to him, weeping, as if to protect himself behind that delicate rampart of flesh, protect himself from the ghostly hand that is playing with him. By slashing the air in all directions, he ends up cutting himself in the arm. The blood gushes out.

There is suddenly a stampede of feet, and at last a bit of light. He is going to get out of this hellish darkness! He is going to escape these hands without a face and their icy horror.

Frasquita and the children come out into the cave where Eugenio is huddled with his breeches down and his big knife in his hand. Martirio is covered in blood. With a roar, Angela rushes to her lifeless sister, but Eugenio, his eyes rolled upwards, keeps her at a distance with his knife.

Blanca appears on the scene, out of breath, her arms laden with crumpled pieces of paper. She looks at her son's face. He is weeping, calling her in a small, almost childish voice.

"Mother, I'm scared! Help me!" he breathes, curling up behind the limp, bloodstained doll he is holding in his arms.

Blanca slowly approaches her terrified son. She tenderly strokes his cheek, sits down beside him, and embraces him. He calms down, gradually loosens his grip, and finally lets go of the little girl, who rolls on her side, skirt lifted. Then he abandons himself in Blanca's flaccid arms and buries his big head between her breasts.

Frasquita throws herself on her daughter's lifeless body, kisses it, lifts it, all without uttering a cry.

"What about Clara?" she finally asks in a low voice, without taking her eyes off Martirio's pale little face. Everyone looks around.

No trace of the little marvel.

The trap

Martirio's screaming had awakened Salvador.

Her cry was nothing like the howling that had so terrified his comrades the day before. Someone needed help. It had taken him a few minutes to come back to his senses and stand on his still weak legs. As soon as he felt capable of it, he had lighted his lamp and tried to inch his way into the crevice at the back of his little cave that led to the underground galleries. The cries were coming from in there, he was certain of it. But the passage was much too narrow for an adult to slip into.

He had rushed outside and had seen Quince coming toward him.

"Salvador! There's something in the stones at the back of the cathedral cave! Something shining in the darkness!"

The group of anarchists sleeping outside the huge cave had heard those horrible cries, and the bravest of them had stood up and seen that luminous little figure in a slightly raised recess in the middle of a mass of fallen rock right at the back of the cave. None of them had yet dared to go and see what it was. But now that the voice had fallen silent . . .

Without hesitation, Salvador entered the monumental cave and advanced toward the little light.

From the threshold, all his comrades looked on, holding their breaths.

There they were, in the silence of the night, their senses alert, trying to make out something, anything, when they suddenly became aware of creaking behind them. Quince turned and signaled to his comrades to keep quiet.

Many footsteps, leaves trampled underfoot, broken twigs.

A troop of soldiers was approaching through the dark forest, making as little noise as possible.

The men standing there gradually withdrew into the cave. Then another scream escaped from the bowels of the earth and shadowy figures started appearing between the trees.

The army! It was the army!

The anarchists were caught in the crossfire. Their comrades, lying on the ground near the cave, in too bad a state to stand, had stopped moving. They were within range of the rifles, which were doubtlessly already trained on them. Those who had just slipped back into the shadow of the great cave could not come out again for fear of being shot down like rabbits. They had to choose: the garrote or the monster.

Despite the screaming of the beast, all of them, except Pablo, edged slowly into the cave, at the far end of which Salvador's lamp was twinkling. Salvador was calling to them, but his voice was covered by the terrible howl that filled the space.

Quince and his companions rushed toward their leader. They had to escape, to hide. They were caught in a trap. Outside, the wounded were screaming and lights had been lit. Pablo stayed where he was, in front of the cave. He had raised his hand and the army's oil lamps cast his wavering shadow inside the cave and multiplied it.

Salvador was holding Clara in his arms. He was getting ready to climb back down the section of rocky wall he had just clambered up in order to gather the sleeping child when he saw his comrades rushing toward him.

"The army's outside the cave," said Quince. "If the girl got in here, then there must be a way out. It's too late to save the others. We can get between these stones!"

As Eugenio's terrible screams had stopped, Quince's last words echoed in the silence and Pablo, hearing his comrades fleeing, turned abruptly and rushed in his turn to the far end of the cave. Shots rang out, but Pablo still ran, preceded by his oversize shadow. The first soldiers took up position on either side of the entrance to the monumental cave. They saw Quince and Salvador in the little recess, holding their hands out toward Pablo to help him clamber over the fallen rocks. A few shots whistled by their ears and Pablo collapsed, hit in the head. Quince took Clara in his arms and they rushed into the opening at the back of the recess.

They were running straight ahead, guided by the lamp that Salvador was holding at arm's length. They noticed the pieces of paper on the ground and guessed that they indicated the way to follow. After a few minutes, they thought to pick them up. No point making their pursuers' task any easier. In this maze of stone where feet left no prints, they would not be easy to track. If there was a way out, they had a chance. They had all stopped thinking about the beast they had imagined lurking in the rocks.

Soon, they reached the little cave where Frasquita and her children were, along with Eugenio, who was still huddled against his mother's chest.

"What happened here?" asked Salvador, his eyes bulging.

The faces were frozen in surprise and horror, and shadows danced over them, emphasising the features, turning them into terrifying masks.

Anita was standing a little back, weeping tears that fell on the wooden box she clutched to her chest and formed a little puddle. She was the first to see what Quince held clutched to him. A limp, slightly luminescent little body. She stroked her mother's arm to rouse her from her torpor.

Frasquita looked in the direction indicated by Anita. "Is she alive?" she asked, her face impassive.

"She's asleep," Quince replied. "We found her at the back of the cathedral cave. The strange thing is, she was shining. But what happened to the child you're holding? Why is she covered in blood?"

"He killed her," my mother said, pointing to Eugenio, who looked shrunken in Blanca's arms, and was still hugging his big bloodstained knife to his chest.

"We have no time to lose," said Salvador. "The army has flushed us out! Which way did you get in?"

"Through the cave where we were sleeping," replied Pedro.

"They must be there already. We can't get out that way. We're trapped!"

"If we hurry," said Angela, "we can get to the galleries that lead to the heap of branches and dead men. Come!"

"Salvador, my friend," muttered Eugenio, "set fire to it!"

Salvador did not reply: he had already set off, overtaking Angela and Pedro. Anita had to shake her mother to force her to follow the group. Frasquita threw a glance at Blanca, who was still sitting on the ground with her son in her arms.

"He won't come after you. I promise," Blanca said. "Go, and forgive me if you can!"

Frasquita disappeared into the gallery, carrying Martirio's body.

Everything was calm again. Blanca had managed to light Eugenio's lamp and was cradling him tenderly. He looked up at her with a smile and handed her his knife, that knife that was too big for him.

"You know, mother," he murmured affectionately, "the child isn't dead yet. And if they observe the direction of the wind, they may yet win their revolution. Everything is ready. Salvador will understand. My sublime gesture—"

With a kiss, she stabbed him.

Outside, surrounded by soldiers, his hands tied, young Manuel was weeping.

Carried away by excitement, the officers had sent most of their troops after the fugitives. Their men had discovered the two entrances to the tunnel. The anarchists were trapped like rats! Salvador, being wounded, would not be able to escape them. A hundred soldiers ran into the rocky maze, one after the other. They spread out, piled into the galleries, massed in the caves. This mountain was a real Swiss cheese. It had swallowed all the soldiers! Only a few men had been sent to the forest to look for other exits.

Thanks to Pedro and Angela, the fugitives made their way through the mountain, against the wind. They came out on the lower level, where the funeral pyre and the cart were waiting.

No noise came from the galleries: the wind that swept through this side of the mountain caught the sound and muted it. Nothing could get through against the current. Not a whisper. And yet, even if he could not hear the noise of their steps, Salvador had a strong suspicion that the soldiers had entered the galleries after them, although he had no idea how many of them there were.

"Salvador, we have to go," whispered Quince, who was still carrying Clara in his arms. "But Frasquita doesn't answer when we speak to her and she's hugging the body of her dead child so hard that we can't tear it away from her to put it on the funeral pyre with the others!"

"Put both of them on the cart," replied Salvador. "As for this one who's sleeping in your arms, put her there, too. She's weighing you down! We'll take them as far as the path, it isn't far. There! Look! We can go through the trees." He turned to Pedro. "You, boy, go take a look and come back and tell us if you see any soldiers!"

While Quince reluctantly let go of the little marvel, whose

serenity, as she had lain calmly in his arms, was so contagious that he would have liked to keep her for a long time, still asleep, against his heart, Salvador was looking at the heap of dry wood and corpses and thinking about Eugenio's last words.

"Set fire to it!" he had said.

He was presumably talking about this funeral pyre. Why did it matter so much to him? A blaze in the forest in the middle of the night would immediately inform the army of their presence . . .

He had to try! He had to trust the friendship of that old madman!

He ordered his companions to leave. He would join them in Brisca, where a friend of his led a similar group to theirs.

Quince and the comrade named Luis, both exhausted and barely recovered from their wounds, set off, one pulling, the other pushing the cart, where Frasquita sat, vacant-eyed. The last of the anarchists preferred to escape in another direction.

Salvador waited for them all to be out of sight before he set fire to the funeral pyre.

Then the miracle happened.

The cave functioned as a chimney, a huge draft of air swallowed the smoke, which spread at great speed through the entrails of the mountain. The black and grey wreaths were caught in the maze.

The trap had closed over the army. Salvador could imagine the panic, the crush, all those choking men trying desperately to retrace their steps, capable only of trampling one another. The battle for any available pocket of air. And the officers who had stayed in the cathedral cave, by the entrance to the maze, listening aghast to the amplified screams of the dozens of men trapped in that charnel house.

"As long as Manuel wasn't dragged into that trap, as long as he isn't in there!" Salvador thought, looking at the huge flames of that inferno without smoke, before escaping in the direction Quince had taken.

Behind him, the forest was ablaze, raising a curtain of fire between the fugitives and their pursuers.

The prayer of the last night

My mother was still sitting in the cart, drained of herself, heedless of the outside world, her lifeless child on her knees. Although jolted in all directions, she had stopped reacting and her dead eyes terrified Quince, who, despite all his efforts, kept turning around to look at the beautiful, impassive face of the woman to whom he considered he owed his life.

A debt. They had a debt toward the woman who had taken care of them with a mother's tenderness over the last few days, even though she did not know them. He would save her come what may. Especially as Quince felt something else. That magnificent exile, in her wedding dress, weighed down with children and cast into an adventure that was bigger than her, had moved them all, from the first encounter.

But the spirit had deserted Frasquita's body, no breath animated her, she was an empty, motionless shell clinging to the corpse of her child.

As the sun rose, the desire came over Quince to weep the tears that she herself was not weeping.

Salvador managed to catch up with the cart hurtling through the trees just as Clara, touched by the first rays of the sun, was opening her eyes. Quite surprised not to be in the cave with its walls of foam where she had fallen asleep the previous night, she stared at her mother, tried to stroke her wooden cheek, then touched her sister's cold body. Despite the early hour, Clara let out such a scream, it gave the impression that it could never be extinguished. Salvador took her in his arms and tried to calm her without slowing their progress. But it was no good: she struggled and screamed even more. Angela moved close to her, took her little hand in her own, and softly sang a sweet sad tune to her, playing with her fingers. From under her dress, she took a long white feather and gave it to her. At last, Clara calmed down.

They reached the road.

It was then that Frasquita's mouth began to speak.

Do some words have a life of their own?

Those that took hold of my mother's mouth that morning seemed to obey their own will. They resembled nothing else.

An unknown tongue possessed this woman who had been torn from herself by grief. One of the prayers from the last night. One of those that make the damned rise like dough passed between Frasquita's dry lips. And these murmured words echoed, vibrated all around the cart, entered each of the fugitives, contaminated the air they breathed, the space they were crossing. The prayer formed a kind of circle around my mother, a circle encompassing the anarchists, the children and the small patch of ground over which they were advancing. A piece of landscape redrawn, removed from life, silent. A piece of the world where the incomprehensible words of the prayer swallowed the song of the birds, muffled the noise of footsteps, stifled the squeaking of the cart and silenced the stones on the road.

They reached the main road thinking that they would find roadblocks, but they saw nothing. Not the slightest trace of soldiers. Nothing. The road was deserted.

The children broke away from the prayer to ask for water at a farmhouse.

Just a few paces from the cart, the world was reasserting itself, the world was singing, a warm wind was blowing, insects were buzzing peacefully, and the colors regained all their intensity.

The good people who opened their doors to Angela and Pedro looked from a distance at the cart and the broken figures who had taken turns pulling it all this way. They saw the woman sitting in profile, erect, as if planted in her cart, only her lips moving.

Something was happening on the road. Death hovered over the ragged, exhausted group, under that sky laden with motionless violence.

They did not suggest that the children come inside, but gave them more than they would have dared ask for. Large goatskins filled with cold water, bread and even almonds and a little gourd of brandy. Then the peasants quickly closed their doors again, anxious at the thought of letting in whatever it was that was roaming the roads like that.

Behind their windows, they watched as the cart went on its way again, its motion jerky and unreal. It was as if a painting had stopped in front of their houses, figures had stepped out of the canvas, then the painting had set off again. Without giving it time to dry, the painter had passed his hand over his canvas, sweeping away the lines, blurring the shapes, erasing the colors. The sun itself seemed unable to enter the frame.

These people were not walking, they were floating in a partial eclipse somewhere above the road. In their wake, a storm of words, of phrases, rumbled.

Everything was getting dark. A real storm was looming, but Frasquita did not flinch. The road, the silence and the broken thread of time were as nothing compared with the visions of her grief-stricken mind.

The incantation summoned her ancestors into the pentacle drawn by her voice.

All those women who had been bequeathed the box and

the prayers before her came running, carrying their deaths like new bodies. Violent death, painful death, gentle death, helpful death, hoped-for death, death accepted, rejected, terrifying. Each death came and caressed the warm body of the woman who had called them. A crowd of ghosts pressed about her, drinking her life like nectar, and each kiss offered my mother a different death. She visited all the terrible facets of it, lived the agonies, the surprises, the terrors. The panic-stricken hands of those who had died by surprise, forever astonished that they no longer existed, demanded their stolen lives from her, tore from her a piece of her own life and devoured it in a shadowy corner. Her life fell to pieces, flayed, swallowed, worn out by icy caresses and kisses. She was struggling in a magma of grief and fear, begging to be given back this child caught in the folds of the afterlife.

But what could they do for her, these dead who pressed in on her from all sides, these women doomed to eternal agony, frozen forever in the torment of their last breaths?

Then, on the edge of the circle that had formed, Frasquita glimpsed other, more distant figures looking at her. A luminous gathering.

Death still had secrets, lights concealed in the kingdom of shadows. Perhaps these specters had to mourn for the living before finding peace.

She could no longer resist and offered herself up to every torment. Perhaps that was the price to pay! Martirio's little corpse lay huddled against her chest. Pale, her eyes open on the hosts of the dead. And in the whirl of figures brushing against her, Frasquita saw the child smile.

Suddenly, the door open on the afterlife closed again and everything disappeared.

Frasquita came back to consciousness as if coming up to the surface of a well.

She was lying in a ruined tower. Anita was sitting on her box, mopping her fevered brow. Frasquita still had her arms around Martirio's body. But, despite the fever, she realized that her daughter's flesh was hot and that beneath her hand her little heart was throbbing.

The child was sleeping peacefully on her mother's belly. She had succeeded. The prayer she had spoken was now lost for a hundred years, but her daughter was alive. Death had released its prey, death had yielded.

Frasquita learned that her lethargy had lasted several days. And that Salvador, Quince and Luis had taken care of her children during all that time. The fugitives had finally managed to rejoin their comrades in the Sierra Nevada. Presumably nobody had dared to stop that ghost cart wrapped in shadows, mystery and wind as it advanced southward.

Salvador bent over her.

Only a few thin scars still streaked his face. His friends in the Sierra Nevada had not recognized him at first, and had doubted the whole story. Especially as the two men sent by Juan to inform them of the town's victory over the civil guard had themselves hesitated when they saw the Catalan's new face. Fortunately, Quince and Luis had not changed, and the legend that had followed in the wake of the cart had finally weighed the scales in their favor. It was rumored that a whole battalion had chased Salvador into the caves and never come out again.

So Salvador, the man with the new face, would become a hero, a mythical figure of the revolution. His name would cut through the land like a sword.

"Now tell me where you're going like this with your children and your cart," he asked Frasquita tenderly.

"I'm going south," replied my mother, laying Martirio, still asleep, in the bed the anarchists had made ready for her.

"I need a flag," Salvador whispered in her ear.

"I must continue on my way," replied my mother, distractedly.

"Make me a flag," Salvador insisted, taking her hand.

At this point, Martirio gave a little cry, very similar to the one that Frasquita had heard in the cave that had served as Salvador's bedroom. She was waking up.

The flag

What exactly happened between my mother and her creation, that Catalan anarchist she had sewed back together, that man with the embroidered face to whom, apparently on a whim, she had given the features of a lover abandoned amid his olive trees on the other side of the mountains?

Anita, the storyteller, never revealed more. My other sisters said they knew nothing, and I have no desire to make things up. Many stories have been told about my mother, but on this subject everyone has been silent. We like this silence. This silence and the mystery that goes with it.

Frasquita spent two months by Salvador's side, time enough to make him his flag. She would probably have stayed longer if the revolution had not interfered. And we would probably not be on this side of the world if Salvador had not had that other love.

He had left everything behind in his little cave. His writing case and his guitar, the only objects he had managed to preserve since his adolescence, objects he had inherited from his father, were lost forever. But above all, he often thought tenderly about young Manuel, who had, according to rumor, bought his freedom at the expense of his mentor's head.

My mother, though, had left nothing in the caves. Endless reels of thread, needles, pins and finely carved little scissors: all were crammed together in that bag in the colors of the olive grove that she carried across her shoulder day and night. The purse that Salvador had given her and that she had immediately tied beneath her skirts continued to beat against her leg as she walked, sometimes jingling slightly when the knot came loose. Her cart was there too, the cart in which the anarchists had placed her and where she had sat straight-backed, dressed in her eternal wedding gown dappled with cloth flowers, mud and blood.

She agreed to follow Salvador for as long as it took her to make him his flag. A symbol of the cause he had espoused. A flag intended to serve as a sheet on his wedding night. Without knowing it, she was making a trousseau for this naked man.

She took her time. On the fabric that Salvador had given her—a stolen linen sheet on which, according to legend, a crowned head passing through the region had slept—she applied pieces of other fabrics torn off during the looting in the haciendas or recovered from the corpses of the anarchists. Each of their operations carried off one or two comrades, and Salvador had gotten into the habit of giving her little pieces of the fallen men's clothes, relics on which Frasquita worked her embroideries before adding them to her flag.

The anarchists had made her a loom that they took it upon themselves to take apart and put together again every time the group had to move.

Salvador's flag and the woman who worked at it ceaselessly inspired a religious respect in everyone.

She never undid the work done the previous day in order to stay with him longer. She took her time because the work needed to be perfect, commensurate with Salvador's love for his revolution, commensurate with the man's face and his hopes.

Patched up, but perfect.

She savored this period of tranquility, but knew that it would not last long, and that a mysterious hand was working with hers on the enchanted flag.

As for the children, they got on with their lives in the

makeshift camps. Eugenio's death had freed them from their mother's constant attention, and her anxieties. They came and went as they pleased and had all developed a taste for this new-found freedom. Pedro and Angela were learning to fight, Anita was reading Bakunin and listening to the rebels' stories, Clara was enjoying the autumn light, and Martirio tended to the graves. Her sojourn among the dead had made them even more familiar to her.

There was no more talk of continuing southwards.

One morning, though, Frasquita brought the flag, carefully folded, to the man who had asked her for it.

"Your flag is finished," she said, handing over her work.

With the help of Quince, Salvador unfolded it on the ground.

The mysterious pattern gave a sensation of harmony and plenitude. Nothing figurative, but the mosaic of cloth, assembled by an artist's hand, created a new and absolutely complete universe.

The enthusiasm aroused by the flag was contagious. It made you want to breathe in the world deeply, to greet it with open arms, to enjoy it with all your senses, to live every moment of it more intensely. The flag swarmed with strength, desire, joy, passion, and idealism. Its colors vibrated fiercely in the autumn sun. Everything had been sewed onto it—hope, the future, war, peace, the world, men and women—and it all held together, as if these things had always been in harmony. The revolution that found its expression here was leading to a new golden age.

There were, though, in the middle of the flag, a number of large clear areas containing only a few enigmatic symbols to which Frasquita herself did not hold the key.

"Those who see your flag will never again doubt the future," Salvador said, with his gentle smile and bright eyes.

"This will be our banner, as of today. Manuel's alive, he's informed us that the officer who led the troops to our caves will pass through the La Cruz gorge this afternoon with a small group of soldiers. We'll wait for him in the mountains. Will you postpone your departure until I return? I'd like to talk to you about us before you go on your way."

"I'll wait for you," replied my mother as she went out.

Quince overtook her and, once outside, whispered to her in a shaky voice, "Tell him not to trust that bastard who already betrayed him once! Tell him, he may listen to you!"

"He believes in his love. Manuel is like his son. Why would he betray him?"

"Because he's already done it once. Because he's hated by everyone now and he knows he'll never again have a place among us."

"How can you blame a tortured man for talking? Even Salvador knew the poor boy wouldn't hold out."

"But Manuel wasn't tortured! Salvador may have thought of him as a son, but he gave him away from the first minute, he pissed in his pants and gave him away. Manuel was never even touched, do you understand? And now he knows he's a coward."

"Who told you all that?"

"It's what they're saying. Manuel is young, he can read, and write, and fight. He knows our faces, our habits. He's quite a catch for them. They've promised him the moon."

"Quince, look at me! If everyone said your son was a coward, wouldn't you try to prove them wrong?"

"I don't have a son, and neither does Salvador," he concluded, stubbornly, and turned his back on my mother.

A group of armed men left for the gorge toward noon. Quince was among them: he had not wanted to let Salvador fly his flag alone.

Frasquita watched them as they set off, some on horseback, the others on foot. The flag, which had been unfurled for the occasion, waved colorfully above the smiling face that she loved. She had lifted her large right hand to shield her eyes from the dazzling autumn sun and watch him as he moved into the distance.

But, once the small band had disappeared, when it was no longer even a tiny dot beneath the blue immensity of the sky, Martirio drew her out of her daydream by gently stroking her left hand, which she had left hanging by her thigh.

"Mother," she whispered, "the beautiful young girl who was sewing beside you has just said farewell to me."

"What young girl?" asked Frasquita in surprise.

"The one who guided your hand on the loom. She told me you wouldn't be able to do anything for him. That you had to be prepared."

"I don't understand."

"Salvador is going to die, mother."

Frasquita did not doubt her daughter's words for a moment. She ran and begged for a man to be sent to catch up with Salvador and warn him. The anarchists who had remained in the camp yielded to her wishes—they were not insensitive to premonitions—but the only remaining horse rolled its huge eyes when someone tried to mount it and struggled fiercely, kicking wildly in all directions. The emissary had to set off on foot. He arrived too late. The army had been planning this ambush for a long time, and only Quince had escaped with his life.

He managed to bring Salvador's body back to the camp, riddled with bullets and rolled in his flag.

He was laid on the ground, with the embroidered banner beneath him.

Death presided in a corner of the flag, invisible to all, but emphasized suddenly by the open wounds. Salvador's blood had flowed into those clear spaces that seemed to have been left blank by Frasquita, revealing a new motif: a beautiful young girl with a scythe in her hand and, at her feet, a man's head, a severed head with its features intact, bright-eyed and with an engaging smile. Salvador's face before the torturer's knife and my mother's needles had gotten to work on it. The face that death loved.

"You knew he would die, and you said nothing," murmured Quince, turning toward my mother.

"I embroidered blindly, obeying his desire to find the right image," replied Frasquita, stunned to see again the old face that she had forgotten. "I knew nothing. His blood has drawn the rest."

"Today, death has proved its talents as an embroiderer!" Quince said with an ironic laugh. "You and death made that banner together. Death inspired you, gave you the setting it wanted to be filled with blood. A picture created with a needle and a knife."

Frasquita said nothing. Her arms hanging limp as she stared at the bloodstained body of the man who had represented her future only a few minutes earlier.

"What are you waiting for?" Quince cried in a sudden rage, shaking my mother. "Why don't you pray for him as you prayed for your dead daughter? Go on, perform your miracle!"

Frasquita kneeled by Salvador's corpse. Without praying, without any word coming to her lips. Quince waited, motionless.

Nothing happened. Death was resisting.

Frasquita stayed there in silence beside the body for so long that she saw it gradually change color. She was brought food and drink. The sun drew its circles in the blue of the sky, the moon grew a little rounder every night, the wind turned colder.

But no word sprang from this woman pinned motionless to the earth.

The others came to bid her farewell. Even Quince had stopped believing. He tried to lift her. Tenderly at first, as if consoling a widow, an abandoned mistress, then he lost his temper, grabbed her, begged her. At last, in desperation, he too left, although not without first promising the children that he would be back.

Left to themselves in the abandoned camp, the children tried to survive. As the cold grew stronger in spite of the blue sky, they covered their mother with one of the blankets the anarchists had given them.

Soon, what had veiled Salvador's eyes turned green. Soon, he no longer had eyes.

Then my mother started digging. Her nails bled. The children all helped. Frasquita tipped everything—flag, corpse, revolution and hope—into the hole. She ate and drank what the children offered her. She tried to stand, but her legs, unsteady and covered in sores, could not even bend. As her body no longer responded to her, she silently entrusted her purse to Anita, who took care of her and her hungry sisters and brother. And when she felt capable of it, without even telling the children, Frasquita harnessed herself to the cart and resumed her journey to the south.

The children caught up with her. They had made ponchos for themelves out of the blankets, cutting holes in the wool with a knife.

Going south

S ince Frasquita had resumed her walk, she had stopped looking at her children. Stopped naming them. Stopped counting them.

We met gypsies who tried to understand my mother. This woman insulted, then mortally wounded by fate. This woman who was powerless despite her gifts, harnessed to her cart like a beast of burden. This woman who had buried all her hopes in a hole.

The oldest of the gypsies spent most time with her.

"It is we gypsies who make the world go round by walking," he told her. "That's why we keep going without ever stopping longer than we need to. But you, my dear, why are you walking, why are you going south like the storks in winter, with your brood behind you, their little feet bleeding? Why force them to make such a journey?"

My mother did not reply. Her belly was getting rounder.

She advanced faster than them and they disappeared.

At last, the cart reached the sea and the children breathed, convinced that their mother could not go any further.

ANITA'S LONG POEM

On the beach, the children played with their huge, incredible shadows, cast on the sand and the waves by the low winter sun.

Once past the surprise they had all felt, faced with that immensity, each of them forged his or her own private bond with the sea. Each retained a color, a noise, a movement, a rhythm, a smell. Each experienced the sea in his or her own way.

But my mother saw nothing but an expanse of water to be crossed.

Facing the sea, Anita put down the box she had carried throughout the journey.

Nine months had passed since the day it had been handed over to her. It was time.

Frasquita no longer worried what her daughter might find in it. Magic had ceased to have any attraction for her. Nothing mattered to her now: food, drink, fatigue, her bleeding feet, the children's frostbite. Only the walk seemed to keep her alive. Something had been started that she could no longer stop, she had to pursue her route now that she had one.

Intrigued, the younger children jostled Anita as she slowly lifted the lid.

The box was empty.

For a moment, disappointment showed on their little faces, even though they knew nothing of the prayers or the gift, all they knew was that this forbidden object, which had been moored, so to speak, to their eldest sister's body since the beginning of the journey, fascinated them.

Then the children froze. In the silence of that winter night, the words came. For something spoke, all my sisters have testified to that, a whisper escaped from the open cube, and that voice entered my eldest sister's throat. Anita was astonished to hear herself speak for the first time, in the soft, warm, powerful tones that nothing has ever diminished since, not even age. The open box had become silent again and the words flowed now from my sister's mouth, simple, clear and alive, while her hands moved as if to guide them or knead them. The words came to us, supported us, cradled us, embraced us, warmed us. And the words did not dry up.

The voice began telling our story, it whispered in the night with the sea in front of us and that woman, our mother, with her back to us, trying to find a way to get across the obstacle, to continue her southward course, to reach the other shore, and not even hearing the breath with which our souls were swelling.

Anita, my eldest sister, dreamed us with the tips of her fingers, with the tips of her lips. In her voice, our doubles grew like bamboo. We died every day, without slowing down. The little bodies, whipped by our mother's madness, drew their strength from the well of Anita's dry lips, her velvety voice, her tranquil prayer.

So many words, so much sand, so many steps, countless steps.

Through Anita's odyssey, through the infinite poem that flowed from her, we walked.

Words as the only thing we left in our wake, strange stones!

The voice preceded us into the towns and *ksars* and tents, and everyone heard our story. Anita told it in her language, sitting on her box, to all those we met, she invented it anew on each occasion, and the voice sounded for a long time after we had passed on.

The storytellers of the lands we crossed still speak of the woman who had been gambled away and her caravan of exhausted children.

When the sun beat down on the children's faces, when their bodies gave way beneath them, when the sand got into their espadrilles and slowed them down, the voice set the pace, the voice told our story.

Subject to Anita's breath, we became great sail boats and glided on, our story whispered to the stones, to the sea, to starless, dreamless nights.

And her hands, have I ever told you about her hands?

The hands of storytellers are flowers waving in the warm wind of dream, they sway at the top of their long supple stems, wither, rise up, bloom again in the sand at the first shower, at the first tear, and project their giant shadows into even darker skies, so that they seem to light up, torn apart by those hands, those flowers, those words.

Anita cannot read anymore, she has forgotten how to, she has rejected written words.

She says that writing will bury the storytellers' hands and there will be no more voices to guide us through the darkness of myth. Written letters, those curves, that ink, those separated words, will rot on the page, a dead memory. The stories will be forgotten. For her, any book is a charnel house. Nothing must be written anywhere other than in our heads.

She has stories tattooed on her lips, and a kiss from her mouth, a caress from her hand, imprints them on our brows.

Anita's hands started dancing in front of the sea when we thought we had reached the ends of the earth and that our mother would be unable to go any farther.

When we had to abandon the cart, when the ferryman took us on board, when we had to row in the storm, when my mother faced the waves alone like a great mast, then Anita's voice rose.

Her vast whisper spread over the sea.

She told our story like a lullaby, the weight of the words and the gentleness of her voice flattened the mountains of water, and we crossed.

From that point on, nothing real happened, time withdrew into itself, into the sea, into the stony deserts, time made knots even in our veins and our bellies and, for a long time, I forgot to be born.

I was waiting for the last line, the one that would announce me:

"That night Soledad was born and mother stopped."

I am that last line, that red, hennaed hand that put an end to our headlong flight, I am the one who forced my mother to lie down. I am the end of the journey. I am the anchor, and all I can do is write, so that the story that cradles us and walls us in and makes us different creatures, untranslatable and alien to everyone, can die at last.

Because something took hold of all of us then, something that held us tightly against one another, and bound us together so strongly that we thought we would never again be able to free ourselves from the arms and legs of those who were not us but had become one indivisible mass.

Limbs and hearts and thoughts braided tightly together, like ropes drenched and knotted in the breakers, then dried and whitened in the sands, the children, large and small, advanced at the same pace, at the rhythm of their mother, their leader. They felt the curve of the earth beneath their bare feet. They saw the shape of their mother walking toward that ever more distant place where the horizon was slightly round, like a belly.

I am not talking about love, I am not talking about the ties that bind mother to child or sister to sister, or even about what makes some lovers inseparable. I am talking about other, tighter knots. Tied solidly like the rope at the end of which the hanged man swings, as strong as that knot. It is pointless to take down the body swinging in the wind, the knot has passed into his throat!

The crossing bound us all, almost to the point of choking us, so that none of us was able any longer to think separately from the others, none of us could breathe through her own mouth, for herself alone, because the burning air that entered her lungs blew in all the others, burned all our mouths with the same fire—mine too, even though it had never yet known the air.

So it was that we advanced on this other continent, without a cart to rest in, advanced until we slept with our eyes open, until we slept even as we walked, without ever getting lost in the dust, without ever slowing down, night or day, in the white dazzle of noon, in the sky loud with stars, in the shade of towns, in the fields, in the rain that twice made the stones of the desert bloom, covering it with flowers that were immediately swallowed by the sun. We walked in gentle green valleys, sometimes following mule tracks, sometimes inventing new ones, passing donkeys with their backs broken by years of burdens and which, like us, were walking, chained to their masters, to their tasks, walking toward a constantly receding horizon, without any hope that another sea would rise to stop us, without even waiting, without even imagining the end.

Only Anita managed to tear herself away. She begged in all the houses in all the villages we went through, she watched for nomads and their camelhair tents. Everywhere, she told our story. And the women gave us biscuits of millet baked under ash, bowls of sour milk, baskets of dry fruit, goatskins swollen with water, slippers—although none were small enough to stay on Clara's wounded feet. Women ran to wipe our faces, to moisten our mouths, weeping beneath their veils the tears we did not weep, shouting words we did not understand, insulting our mother for imposing this madness on us. One of them even offered us a donkey, which allowed our sister Anita to replenish our stocks of food and drink and freed the arms of the three elder siblings of little Clara, whose bruised feet had changed color and whose cries had finally fallen silent.

And the donkey became part of our hearts, our arms, our legs, until it too slept on the rocky paths, until it shared our thoughts and our water. We now knew the pain of a broken back, and it understood our mother's madness. And we drank its blood to survive.

No, it was not love. There had been love before, there had been hearts that beat separately and that could love, weep, lament, but since the boat, there had been only one heart, too exhausted to love, to remember what it was to love or to have its own feet, its own arms, its own breath.

It was much stonger than love.

Much too strong to live with!

"Ahabpsi!"

BOOK THREE

The other shore

I was born here after my mother had moved in a great circle through the steppes of esparto grass, the stony deserts and the *djebels* of this vast land. I have known nothing but Anita's stories and this hot wind bearing with it the sands of the Sahara.

My life was decided before I came into the world.

My space is reduced to a few scraps: some fifteen dusty streets I have walked up and down since childhood, always the same ones, worn smooth by my steps; the red earth of the waste grounds, as vast as deserts, at the far end of which, in the distance, glitter the roads that lead to the heart of the city; the dead-end street and its gate, that gaping hole leading to the square courtyard we share with our neighbors and where our poultry peck the ground. Do they peck the crumbs that remain to me, those useless hens incapable of laying anything but eggs with insipid shells?

I saw nothing of the journey that made me a foreigner. And yet it haunts me.

I was born here and I have few memories of my mother.
Almost none.
Did she ever speak to me?

Did she ever kiss me even once, me, the child of the journey, condemned to live in an area no wider than the palm of that hennaed hand that extracted me from her body? Did my mother ever caress me before abandoning me between these four walls, beneath her deathbed? Did she ever take the needle from her mouth and put down her threads and dare to caress the little body that looked enviously at the fabrics sitting enthroned on her knees?

I would have loved to be the rag doll I cradled gently as my mother lay dying on her esparto mattress, just above my head, and agitated words filled the room. If I had been made of cloth, she might have mended me too, as Anita said she had once mended a man, the anarchist who may have been my father.

But I was nothing but skin, flesh and bone screaming with love at a time when my mother had stopped caressing anything but her thread, when only her sewing kept her alive. I was nothing but a solitary little girl, listening, singing to herself and dreaming, invisible beneath the bed springs. A four-year-old child, quiet and cheerful, hidden under a bed, playing pretend tea parties, and what I ate in those chipped little plates were the stories, murmurs and moans of pain with which the walls were heavy.

Imprisoned in these few blank pages, I have dreamed more of her life than of my own. I know that, but it doesn't matter. What had to be dreamed has been.

The box opened only last month no longer belongs to me.

Tomorrow, Martirio will hand it over to her eldest daughter, Françoise, to perpetuate the tradition.

There is only one prayer from the last night remaining to us, the others have been lost. One last prayer, a tenuous link between us and the other world.

I sometimes feel the desire to waste that prayer, to shout it out to the four winds and stop the dead ever again coming and devouring our lives. No more inheritance. No more pain. No more echoes in our souls. Nothing but the present, flat and uneventful.

Isn't it the pain of our mothers that we have been bequeathing to each other since the dawn of time in that wooden box?

The pale box is beside me, filled with written words, with a disjointed story.

I will go soon into the rocky desert that stretches beyond the fields. I will go beyond the mountains, I will go and offer all this to the wind. And I will call to you.

The carpet

Of that long journey—the imposing landscapes, the mountains, the villages and the dried *oueds*, the caravans of camels, the tents of the nomads, the vast expanses of red earth that we crossed—my mother had seen nothing but her rage. And now she woke up naked, her womb empty, lying in a room devoid of furniture, a strangely-proportioned room, as long and narrow as a corridor, the floor covered in mats and small threadbare rugs.

Now she was naked and she was screaming.

Taking advantage of the respite that had followed my birth, Nour, the old Arab woman with the hennaed hands, had stripped that exhausted woman whom a wound had cast upon the world. She had divested her of the wedding dress donned like a second skin at the beginning of the journey, that dress my mother had doubtless never taken off since then, except perhaps to conceive me. Of the magnificent embroidered dress strewn with cloth flowers, all that remained were a few scraps of material that clung to my mother's gaunt body like climbing plants to a stone wall.

The dress had fallen for the second time, in a cloud of brown dust. My mother, standing thin and naked in the big zinc basin, had accepted the violent caress of the massage glove and the shock of cold water. Nour had cut her dirty, tangled long hair and slowly trimmed her almost looped nails and removed the mask of grime and sand that covered her face.

Once this long, meticulous process was over, Nour had admitted my mother to the room with the carpet.

The old stone and adobe house, of which Nour was, as we realized later, the keeper rather than the owner, consisted of two rooms: the smaller one, smelling of spices and coffee, where objects were heaped up—the *kanun*, the coke for heating, the zinc basin—and this second space where she slept, with three large barred windows through which the light streamed in: a surprising architectural feature in a land where shade is a commodity as rare as it is precious!

We were there too, by her side. A woman and her children, as naked as worms, in the wretched dwelling of that old Arab woman with the hennaed hands, asleep at last, lying on the floor of a world they did not know, although they had already crossed it from one end to the other.

It took several days of care and tenderness and rest, several days too of combing and tears, before Nour would let us go out and walk in the narrow streets of the medina. But only us, the children! My mother had to stay confined in the room with the carpet for a while longer.

Very quickly, her rage had regained the upper hand and she had wanted to continue on her way. But Nour, fearing that she would again drag us around in circles, had blocked the door with the help of a wooden lintel, and, from outside, the passers-by could hear my mother beating against the walls and screaming that she wanted to be let out and continue walking. Despite her cries and entreaties, none of the children freed her. Not even Angela, even though she hated cages. They all trusted Nour and her whispered word that had put an end to their forced march, and, terrified at the thought of having to go back into the desert, they preferred our mad mother's screams to yet more infinite wandering. For every night we walked again, we walked as we slept, incapable of really stopping. Every night, bodies and minds set off and our legs moved even though we were lying on the ground. At dawn, we would wake with dry lips, cracked in places, burst open by our burning dreams.

One morning, though, my mother fell silent.

Nour had taken advantage of her having a dizzy spell to empty the room of its little rugs, which she had taken outside and vigorously beaten. And from that point on, my mother had stopped her screaming.

The children thought she had perhaps lost consciousness from throwing herself at the walls so much, and they became anxious. But when, a few hours later, Nour decided that it was time to open the door again and put back the threadbare mats, they discovered their mother awake and calm, gazing rapt at the floor on which she was sitting. None of them had noticed until then that, beneath the worn rugs, a woolen treasure was hidden. That was what had absorbed my mother's attention.

Nour doubtless knew what she was doing when she opened that window on the world for my mother. The crossing had to continue here, in this room built around and for the work of art that it had housed for centuries. A unique carpet, forgotten by men, a painting in wool, spun for a king, in which the cosmos had been enclosed, just as a distant, starry sky is reflected in the water of a pool.

In the center, against a midnight blue background, shone a huge fire-red medallion, filled with endless veins of foliage and colossal flowers, all symmetrically arranged. The crenelated perimeter of this central motif, this woolen sun with its shifting outline, made the whole work vibrate like a drum or a heartbeat. Yes, something was throbbing—an enigma, a fiery star—in the vastness of the night sky enclosed within a carpet made by an ornamentalist of genius!

For a long time, my mother continued her journey between the lines of the carpet's red woolen weave. She let her mind wander over the peonies studding its velvet sky. Her eyes, her hands, her arms, her feet, her naked body—for she had so far refused to get dressed—meandered over the plantlike arabesques, searched the darkness of the background, traveled through the fragments of blue stars, cut off by the edge but reconstructed in her mind with such force that the walls of the room disappeared, fragmented by this shower of stars, by the force of this colossal work of which Nour was the last keeper: she who had not had children to whom she could entrust her task, she, the sterile woman with the hollow face and flaccid belly, repudiated by the man to whom she had been given in order for the tradition of the carpet to be perpetuated, for the cosmic knowledge engraved on the wool to be saved and for the central star with its hypnotic power to continue vibrating in the most secret place in the world. That central star was doomed to disappear and be replaced by another, whose first branches appeared in the lower portion of the carpet, just as the last rays of a first, absolutely symmetrical star still lingered at the top, the reflection of a power now gone. It was just a carpet, a few square feet of threads bound together, but it recorded the infinite movement of worlds and the transience of all creation. Its colored threads were the threads of fate.

In the evening, when everyone gathered in the big courtyard where I grew up, when the time for stories came and Anita told this story, she would claim in a whisper that the carpet made whoever looked at it feel so dizzy that it was almost impossible to step on it. To cross it, the children would keep to the walls or look away.

My mother went all over that infinite space in search of the one thread, the initial stitch, that would unravel all the others, without even understanding that this labyrinthine carpet was a mirror and that, in looking into it and questioning it, she was looking into herself and seaching for a way out, searching for the road to take when the carpet disappeared.

And the carpet did indeed disappear.

One morning, we woke up in a room emptied of its treasure. Nour did not give us any explanation. She dressed my mother, meek now, in a long tunic cut from a striped cloth and led us to the very edge of the native quarter, to this courtyard facing the waste ground of red dust.

We approached the big half-broken gate, hearing snatches of Spanish emerging from it, familiar words being screamed on all sides. Dozens of children came to greet us, speaking a mixture of languages. We were installed in one of the modest houses that lined this big courtyard where some fifteen families lived, most of them Andalusian. In this border territory, my mother would be able to rebuild her life.

We never found out how Nour had managed to get us this accommodation, but for whatever reason we were not asked to pay anything for a year. By the time the owner at last put in an appearance, my mother's reputation had reached the coast and we were in a position to settle the rent.

We never saw either Nour or her carpet again. The old woman's dilapidated house, her hennaed hands, the incredible masterpiece of which she was the keeper: it was as if all that had disappeared around the bend of one of the medina's winding alleyways. But my mother was launched, like a shuttle on the loom: for the first time she had been in the presence of a work of art, and she had understood what to do with the time she still had left.

THE MATING SEASON

Pirouli Caramelo qué rico y qué bueno!"

As it did every week, the peddler's cry came across the waste ground and stirred up the courtyard. Children pestered their mothers, demanding coins, rolling in the dust, weeping, begging. Some huddled in the shade of the walls, their hands over their ears in order not to hear. Others returned triumphant, their pockets full of salted squash seeds or brandishing colored cones on a stick, the true object of envy, which they proceeded to lick slowly in the sun.

In the arms of one of my sisters, I listened to the lucky ones sucking their candy.

And my mother watched, looking for a way to survive in this new land.

As she looked at the bodies of the young girls in the courtyard, watching them walking about in the closed space, a neighbor came up to her.

"You're a dressmaker and you don't talk much, so they say. I'd like you to come to our house, my daughter needs your services and your discretion."

"I can sew and embroider and keep my mouth shut. I'll be there."

This neighbor's daughter, Manuela, had a belly so round that no dress could hide what was growing in there for much longer. One night, she had let herself be led into the desert of red earth, where young Juan had put his hands on her.

"He barely spoke to me, and now I'm getting big!" sniveled

the girl, who had not left home in nearly three weeks. "I had no idea a few tender words would do that to me."

"Stop it, you!" fumed her mother, slapping the girl with metronomic regularity. "Words don't get girls pregnant. Everyone knows that, even the priest! You should have behaved yourself, that's all! Or at least told me before now, instead of acting as if butter wouldn't melt in your mouth. You're lucky your Juan still wants you and that he's managed to bring forward the wedding! After the ceremony, you'll leave and live with your aunts until your sin emerges from your belly. In the meantime, we're going to have to hide it. The wedding is in two weeks, and God alone knows how much bigger you're going to get between now and then."

"Come here, let me feel you!" my mother ordered calmly.

The girl moved close to the dressmaker's hands and abandoned her belly to them. Frasquita felt the taut flesh beneath the material, and said, without any change in her tone of voice, "You're seven months gone."

The girl began sobbing. "I could feel something moving about in there, but I did all I could to forget it!"

"About time you started crying!" said the neighbor, slapping her daughter's face again. "Will you be able to make a dress that can hide this slut's sin?"

"Yes, but I have no material, you'll have to provide it."

"We aren't rolling in money, you know."

"Give me all the pieces of cloth you can find, I'll do the rest. You can come to my house at night for the fittings, once everyone's taken their chairs inside."

"And how much you will charge us?"

"Just find work for my older daughters and give me food for my children."

"They'll be able to do cleaning work for the Cardinale family in the Villa Paradis, it's a bit further down on the main road.

I know they're hiring. But the lady of the house is quite strict, I should warn you. My daughter worked there for a while."

"She's a bitch!" Manuela burst out, her tears forgotten for a moment. "And she only speaks French! Your daughters will have a hard time satisfying her!"

"As for you, break a small crust of bread tonight between your nails and shape it into a cross," Frasquita ordered her young customer. "Bring it to me in three days with a thread stolen from your fiancé's coat."

"Why?" asked Manuela.

"Because, on the day of your wedding, they'll tell you you're beautiful, and if they don't say it, they'll be thinking it," said Frasquita Carasco as she walked out.

Two days later, at dawn, in order to leave Anita and Angela free for work, I was entrusted, wrapped in my mother's black shawl, to Martirio, who was not even nine. My two older sisters crossed the waste ground to the main road and vanished from my days. The horizon had taken them from me, it had swallowed their kisses. For a long time, they ceased to exist. They had abandoned me on this side of the world to polish window panes, flagstones, wooden floors and silverware for a mistrustful lady who still preferred Spanish women to Arab women, although when you came down to it they were all thieves.

My mother had taken up her needle again and, in two weeks, had created a gorgeous dress the cut of which totally concealed Manuela's sin. On the wedding day, the whole court-yard went into raptures.

Captivated by what Frasquita had produced, the girls dreamed of getting married in their turn and parading about in a dress fit for a princess, and the boys were well pleased. There was a profusion of kisses and slaps. The flowers were gladly picked, and there followed a wonderful season of hurried weddings and shameful secrets. Every young girl of childbearing age found herself a beau and, as all the families could afford the dressmaker's talents, the church was constantly full. The elderly parish priest married so many couples and baptized so many babies in the months that followed Manuela's wedding that he died of exhaustion.

A few pieces of cloth, a little flour, oil and bacon, a little crust of bread carved in the shape of a cross, and Frasquita Carasco would get to work.

Day and night, she would convert pieces of cloth.

My mother even made a dress for María the hunchback, a girl with a twisted body that the fabric somehow managed to straighten so that, for the first and last time in her life, she actually looked beautiful.

When all the girls in the courtyard had married, others came, from the neighboring courtyards. Soon the dressmaker of the Marabout quarter had so much work, she was able to increase her prices. Little by little, her clientele changed.

My sisters returned. I did not recognize them, but Anita tamed me by buying me one of Pirouli Caramelo's candies and Angela, whose features had grown terribly coarse, laughed and gave me some big white feathers she said she had plucked from her rather stooped back.

THE DRESSMAKER

Within a year, my mother's reputation had spread across the desert of the waste ground, leaped from quarter to quarter, and reached the whole city. Daughters of colonists came in their dozens to order their wedding dresses. Every day would bring us its share of future brides to be dressed. Every morning, young girls would appear at our door, hoping to find the shell that would house their virginal bodies, or at least bear their colors. My mother was expert at probling their bellies, and equally expert at hiding the shape of those bellies.

They would arrive escorted by a noisy herd of aunts and sisters and friends, all laden with magnificent fabrics. Like wise queens, they went into ecstasies in French around my cradle . . . out of politeness. Our "stable" echoed with laughter, the chorus of fine ladies sang the praises of my mother's talents, the words rained down, the expressions of gratitude accumulated, the air was saturated with powder and perfume and the poorly-lit room was carpeted with acres of white cloth. The straw dummies multiplied, a faceless little army on the way to their pre-ordained weddings. The betrothed girls would follow my mother into my sisters' bedroom and come out again looking drained of blood, reduced to a few measurements, as pale as their future dresses.

The wave of full, colored petticoats would ebb at noon, leaving the house to its ghosts, its white calm, and my sisters would cleverly create a draft to purge the room of the remains of gossip and perfume.

Then the dresses would start to come alive on the motionless dummies.

In the courtyard, little businesses sprang up. The neighbors set up tiny stalls selling candies, *mantecaos*, shortbread, lemon pancakes and sugared fritters, for the mothers and aunts of the rich young fiancées to feast on as they waited for the fittings to be over.

After the girls came the French merchants. Alerted by Frasquita's success, they came in large numbers to sing the praises of their products and bury her in samples. Little by little, the main room had become draped in white, just as in the early days of Frasquita's marriage, but now it was the clean, supple whiteness of cotton, then of satin, and, finally the whiteness of silk and ermine edged with gold and silver thread.

Our mother was never to know that we would get up at night to watch her embroider, sitting on the floor, huddled up against one another, dazzled as much by the concentration and gestures of the artist as by the magnificence of the fabrics with which she concealed our poverty.

Before long, she was spending all day and all night in her cocoon of white thread.

She would examine the girls for a long time before choosing the fabrics they would wear. She had stopped taking the mother's tastes or the daughters' preferences into account, and did not even look at the sumptuous fabrics their entourages brought with them. She would send everything back, impose her own materials, demand such and such a shade of blue in the white. She did whatever she wanted and the women would fall silent at her approach as if at the approach of a prophetess. The rumor had become a legend: Frasquita Carasco sewed people together. In the lining, she would incorporate a little crust of bread in the shape of a cross that supposedly protected the couple from the evil eye and made sure they would never separate.

The merchants came in ever greater numbers to fight over her favors. They jostled and insulted one another, and constantly besieged the house. We agreed on a day to receive them, and soon my mother did not even deign to look up from her sewing to listen tolerantly to their gallant remarks in bad Spanish, she preferred to delegate this task to Anita, who was no longer working for the Cardinales.

From that point on, my eldest sister dealt with the suppliers. She would serve them *anisette*, offer them *mantecaos*, pretend to listen to them distractedly and maintain order in French with the air of benign authority she had gradually acquired.

Knowing that the person who chose the fabrics of the greatest dressmaker in Africa was not even fifteen, the merchants sent her their most charming sons and the handsomest boys they could find in their entourage. But it was no use, Anita remained stony-faced. She had no qualms in dismissing those whose prices seemed to her prohibitive, or whose merchandise was second-rate. No word, no compliment, no glance, no smile, even the most seductive, could distract her from her task or make her change her mind and accept a price which was not the one she herself had fixed.

Very soon Anita was able to detect other people's intentions behind their smiles, she learned to negotiate and became a master in the art of making deals. She knew the correct price of every fabric and, although she did not understand why the sellers of cloth had suddenly grown so much younger, she took great advantage of this time when she was only being sent inexperienced young men to learn French, to test her talents as a negotiator and to find out the upper limits to prices. She was able to get the prices reduced to such an extent that the exasperated fathers dismissed these young dandies and decided to go themselves. Sons and nephews were left in the back shops, but age had no more influence on Anita than youth. The old men were powerless.

Nothing surprised her anymore. The merchants struck her as a race apart, very expressive, and fascinating to observe. They were her teachers: in their desire to get one over on their competitors, they gradually revealed to her the tricks of a trade of which she had previously known nothing.

And while Anita juggled with figures, while she counted and recounted, and while my mother caressed her fabrics, Angela waited until it was time to open the box that her elder sister had bequeathed to her at Easter.

The big mirror

Take care, there'll be seven years of bad luck to anyone who breaks it!" the remote, tragic old women sitting on their chairs in the shade of the walls kept saying as the marvel was unwrapped in the dusty courtyard so that the whole of the little community could take advantage of it for a few moments.

"My God, how big it is! It'll never get through the dressmaker's door!"

"You'll see, she'll have to leave it in the middle of the courtyard!"

"In your dreams! It's made to measure. They've worked it all out."

"Look, old girls, it's your reflection! There you are in a gilded frame, like a painting!"

"They're really giving themselves airs. Sitting on their doorsteps like that, all in black, they might as well be dead!"

"Not yet! The dead don't like mirrors!"

And the old women blinked, dazzled by the reflection of the sky cast in their faces by the big mirror. At the slightest movement of those carrying the thing, the whole courtyard, as framed within the mirror, tipped over. As it moved, it caught everything indiscriminately—the blue sky, the hens, the windows, the children standing about, the old women in their tight clothes—and set it dancing on the silvery surface. The faces flew past, trying to catch themselves in flight. Everyone felt dizzy and euphoric.

When the object was at last still, the gathering stopped shifting about, and even the old women moved their chairs closer.

"Don't push! Get in line! If everybody rushes forward, you won't see anything! For once we can see ourselves full-length."
"But I don't look so hollow! This mirror isn't right!"
"Oh, yes, it is. You really are thin!"
"Look how I'm moving, I look like a reed that's dancing."
"That's it, you've seen enough of yourself. Stop twirling your skirt. It's my turn now. And you, Ricardo, come here! Let's see what we look like when we're side by side! What a pretty couple we make! Hold me by the waist! And you behind, calm down! You're moving so much, you're blurring our reflection!"

The little community looked deep into the mirror, eager to see itself. In their Sunday best for the occasion, they struck grave poses, threw each other emphatic glances, tried to tame their gestures and features. Even the children did not dare pull faces. Everyone became stiff, straightening their limbs in order to see themselves full-length. In the meantime, Clara laughed as she chased patches of light.

Then they were told that the sun would tarnish the mirror if it stayed too long in the courtyard, and it was taken into the dressmaker's house. But in the days that followed, my mother had to put it on the upper floor to stop people coming into her house unannounced to catch their own reflections.

The day the big mirror arrived, Angela did not take part in the celebrations. She had gone up to the terrace, where the washing was hung out to dry, in order to open her box. For a few moments she stood there among the wet sheets, silent, contemplating the wooden box, before bending to examine its contents. When she raised her head again, a crow, perched on the lid, was looking at her, its eyes wide with questions, like someone observing his reflection in a mirror and, in its eye, the world took on its full meaning. The bird flew up and landed on my sister's shoulder. She felt its wings beating behind her back and, when it flew off, part of Angela fluttered after it, so that she saw the rectangular courtyard gradually shrink and the desert of red earth become tiny beside it. She saw the main road all the way to the city, the smart neighborhoods, the parade ground, the sea, the harbor and, as it was a clear day, she saw distant fields, snowcapped mountains, she saw the great circle traced by Frasquita Carasco in the stony desert and the figure of the traveler who had been following their traces for months now.

She was able to see the other shore through the eyes of this bird that was never to leave her again and would lead her one morning to the great aviary.

THE BALL GOWN

Nothing had gotten the better of Frasquita Carasco so far, not the sea, not her sorrow, not the sands, yet she collapsed in a few weeks like a house of cards because of one small thing, one wrong pleat, one red thread.

The lovely Adélaïde, who entered our house one day without knocking, had no need of my mother's talents to look beautiful. Her splendor was a challenge to Frasquita, which was probably what Adélaïde wanted.

The door was pushed open, without creaking, and Angela quivered at the sight of that gorgeous creature, so slender and white. The light of the most beautiful fabrics was nothing compared to the texture of her skin. Angela told herself that her mother would have to spin mother-of-pearl for a dress not to seem bland in comparison with the glowing sunlight of her complexion.

Adélaïde came in. Astonishingly, she was without an escort, without any laughing companions, without the cumbersome entourage that usually accompanied a young girl of her station. Her power was clear in her manner: she knew how to make herself obeyed, and it occurred to Angela that this was all she knew. She was so confident that she had crossed the waste ground on foot, alone, dressed like a princess, to come to our house, in this courtyard on the edge of the medina, a quarter considered one of the most wretched in the city and one of whose existence she ought to have been unaware.

But who would have dared force her to come accompanied?

Even though she was standing against the light, she cast no shadow in the morning sun.

"Is this the house of Frasquita Carasco the dressmaker?" she asked my sister, who was tidying the room in preparation for that morning's fine ladies.

"Yes, it is!" Angela replied, as calmly as she could.

Adélaïde smiled, and the pearls that appeared in her mouth wounded Angela. The lovely Adélaïde's smile was like a bite, as the crimson casket of her full, velvety lips parted for a moment to reveal her teeth. Angela immediately dreamed of breaking them one by one, then sewing the red lips together, sealing up forever that perfect smile that had offended her, that had hit her like a slap.

"I'd like to order a red dress from her, a ball gown!"

Until then, my mother had made only wedding dresses. The stories that circulated about her spoke of her aversion to color, her passion for weaving, for what could be bound together. For sewing, for solemn vows . . .

And now here was this strange, disturbingly beautiful young girl forcing color on her.

Martirio entered the room and looked coldly at the visitor, who greeted her like an old acquaintance before going upstairs to see my mother and have her beauty reduced to a few measurements.

"She hasn't gotten any older!" Martirio murmured in surprise.

When Adélaïde came back down, she had lost none of her haughtiness. But my mother had turned pale.

And from that point, red invaded the downstairs room. The merchants brought all kinds for Frasquita Carasco to make her choice. Fabrics of amaranth, cerise and poppy. Lacework of madder and vermillion and beads of garnet. Crimson velvet and purple taffeta. Porphyry buttons and tears of blood in their gilded casket. Ruby gleams in the dressmaker's dark eyes. Corals of wild silk and fiery geraniums. The few remnants left over exploded in the cottony whiteness of the wedding dresses. The red gown, in all its mysterious ferment, eclipsed its cloth sisters. It drew the eye relentlessly and little by little Frasquita devoted all her attention to it.

In two weeks, the gown was ready and Adélaïde returned for a fitting.

In our mother's room, where the big mirror acquired thanks to her success stood enthroned, Adélaïde's reflection vacillated for a moment. Unsettled by the breath of the red gown that she had just put on, she lost some of her arrogance, and for a brief, imperceptible moment time stood still. A sense of peace settled on the world and all the agonies were suspended while Adélaïde looked in the mirror. She felt at home in that silky satin with its vivid colors in the midst of which only a complexion as exceptional as hers could survive. But the truce did not last. She immediately recovered from her astonishment and, with a gesture of her arm, broke the harmony that had been established despite herself between her skin and the fabric. Then a battle began between the girl and her blood-red gown: each wanted its place, each wanted to be the only thing visible. The balance was lost, the garment stifled the girl, who, in struggling, crushed the garment. The red casket turned vulgar. And Adélaïde discovered the mistake. That thread that protruded only slightly, like a hair on a chin, but that irritated the flesh of her forearm before she caught it between her nails and crushed it. And, as there was always an element of mystery in my mother's work, that one thread, in breaking, broke the architecture of the fabric, and a whole section of the skirt collapsed at the girl's feet.

"No, this won't do!" said the lovely Adélaïde, amused, smiling her perfect smile. "My gown was only hanging on by a thread! It has to be redone! One waltz, and it would have wilted competely!"

My mother was surprised by the fragility of what she had produced. She got back to work. She had never failed before now. She could not understand it.

My mother knew her business.

From one detail to the next, we watched, powerless, as our mother came unstitched. Obsessed by the tiny adjustments demanded by Adélaïde, she forgot to eat, she lost sleep, she scattered threads and buttons and needles and pins.

Frasquita Carasco was coming to pieces. The more she mended the dress, the more her own being came apart. With each new fitting, the invisible defects in the blood-red ball gown increased, and Adélaïde's perfect smile would underline them with casual cruelty, while my mother's gaze increasingly lost its way in the red cloth reflected in the mirror.

Her hands began to tremble, her gestures became jerky, her eyes tarnished. With its fingertips, death had pulled on the red thread and our mother was fraying.

"We must get ready," Martirio said one night, stroking my forehead in the dark toom where we all slept together.

"Get ready for what?" Angela asked.

"Didn't you recognise it?"

"Recognize what?" asked another voice in the shadows.

"That face painted by Salvador's blood on his flag, the beautiful lady embroidering beside our mother," Martirio whispered. "Death is having a ball gown made."

"Adélaïde!"

"I hate her smile. When I see her, I feel as if I want to kill her."

"That's what she tries to inspire in some. Others are more docile."

"We must destroy that poisoned dress!"

"Our mother wouldn't survive."

"It's too late, her soul is hanging on by a thread," Martirio concluded. "Soon we'll be alone. Let's sleep."

UNDER THE BED

I am barely four years old and I am listening to the last words of my mother with her mind unstitched. Sentences of colored wool, words linked by chain stitch, pain reduced to a thread. I listen to the stories she weaves like heavy cloaks, like coats of arms, like colourful banners. I listen to the cries, the tears, the pearls, the gemstone cabochons, the sequins of precious metal. I listen to the long silences like openwork stitches lightening the air in the room, which is dense with fabulous patterns. White suddenly in the long agony, *punto in aria*. I listen to my mother's breathing, the threaded needles, the silken webbing, the lace, the decorations embroidered by her white lips on the pockets, the colors, the buttonholes and buttons of imaginary waistcoats of scarlet cashmere.

Sometimes, the silken words are layered flat and do not penetrate my mind, engrossed as it is in its games, but they are bound to it forever with invisible stitches. My soul is embroidered with the past, covered in meticulously assembled layers of bird feathers. Both embroidery and mirror, my mother's words add pieces of silvered glass or mica to my inner landscape. The long monologues she pours out into the room dot my childish games with memories that are not mine. Her dreams are sewed on me one by one with the help of invisible needles, so fine that they barely wound my delicate material. I make myself a fabric for her, I lie back on the wooden loom, I who am nothing but flesh, bone and blood. I secretly gather all that escapes from that body creased by spasms, all that moves in the damp cocoon of sheets and words, I amass all that emerges from my mother.

And so the line crosses me, fills me with a complicated network of looped and twisted stitches succeeding one another row by row.

I hold my breath. I do not want her to feel my presence in the privacy of her death agony. I lack air, I am drowning in the heady perfume given off by her last breath. I choke sometimes in the rustling of the esparto grass with which the mattress is filled and, at other times, I forget and I sing to myself, nursery rhymes learned in the courtyard, learned outside, in the bright air suffused with sun. But my voice does not reach my mother as she lies on the other slope of the world, beyond the springs, the mattress, and the soaked sheets. I wait for an answer that does not come, the knot that will make me complete, the crumb of tenderness, the kiss. I wait for her to utter my name in the middle of her weave of words and threads. But nothing comes except thousands of bohemian crystals, pieces of string and wooden beads, nothing comes except the blood- red satin spat out into the chamber pot next to me. What she is giving me before dying is nothing like a kiss, and I hug the torn, half-empty body of my doll, trying to hold back the flow of sand spilling from its belly.

That was what I had come there for—it comes back to me now—I had wanted her to mend my toy. I had slipped noiselessly into the dark velvety room and had not dared tell her that my doll was leaking.

The kiss of death

If I stand in the middle of this courtyard, in the spot where the sun beats most strongly, where no shade can penetrate, in the very same place where my sister Clara stood motionless for days on end lapping up the daylight; if I stop on the marks left by her feet, I hear the distant echo of all the stories with which Anita filled our being for fifteen years. They ooze from the cracks in the walls, and come streaming toward me. They are alive and they possess me. Nothing happened in the night except those stories. The chairs fought for a place in the front row, and the walls themselves vibrated, imagining themselves made of flesh. The stone would come alive to dream with us in the darkness, to be part of the journey, the earth felt legs growing painfully on it, and we followed Anita's voice. Martirio would listen to the story of her life to come, Angela would watch her face turn plain, and Clara never heard anything but the beginnings of stories, her sickly sleep robbing her of half her real life and three quarters of her narrated life.

I grew up surrounded by stories, without ever trying to untangle the threads of time or distinguish the real from the dreamed, my body from my mother's. I swallowed everything and what I am now vomiting up onto paper is that knot, filled with blood and words echoing from the walls of the courtyard.

Martirio was getting ready to open the wooden box in her turn when the lovely Adélaïde came to Frasquita Carasco's house for the last time. The other children were watching over their mother upstairs. The door did not creak and Martirio did not feel any presence behind her as she lifted the lid. But all at once she dropped the box: with supreme gentleness, Adélaïde was stroking the back of her neck with her hot hands, stroking her throat, her shoulder, slipping inside her bodice.

"Do you know why God became bread?" breathed the voice of death. "It's because I bit him so hard that he fled from all flesh!"

My sister managed to turn, but she could not resist that perfect smile. Her visitor kissed her and slid her tongue into her mouth.

"I offer you my kiss," the red lips murmured, biting her ear lobe, and a hot breath went through her body. My sister sank into a deep sleep. She did not see death taking away her ball gown.

That same night, in the darkness where we slept, Martirio told us how Adélaïde had come and taken back her red gown.

"Did she at least pay you?" asked the most rebellious of us.

"She gave me a passionate kiss and sniffed at my soul," replied Martirio. "Her lips tasted like honey. I'm afraid. I've inherited the terrible gift of death. It was so pleasant to be licked by that bitch. Now I know the paths that lead to her lair. She throws herself on the world as if on a stone, and tonight I hear her howling around our mother's bed. We must kiss Frasquita Carasco for the last time."

I was taken out of my warm bed. Somebody held my hand. I entered my mother's room behind the others, barely touching the icy floor with my bare feet, and silently waited my turn, clutching my half-empty doll to my shift.

But my turn did not come. Before I could get to her, Martirio leaned over my mother's burning forehead and swallowed her soul.

DRAWINGS IN THE SAND

Our mother was dead.

The fabrics were taken back, the merchants deserted our courtyard. The pretty girls wept for their unfinished dresses, the neighbors mourned their flourishing trade in sweetmeats, and we were alone, orphaned.

Martirio continued to take care of the house, and of me and Clara. Pedro found work with an Arab maker of ironwear in the medina. Angela and Anita again became maids of all work in French houses and the big mirror was sold. We ate our fill, trying not to spend too much of the money that Anita had managed to save during our three years of luxury. But Anita was still a minor. If anybody had reported us to the authorities, we would certainly have been separated. The little courtyard fell silent. And in spite of the silence, our father found us again.

When he was not working on wrought iron, Pedro would sit down in a corner of the courtyard and draw brightly-colored frescoes on the ground. He would fill his pockets with colors, squeezing his universe of pigments into little cloth bags. Stones and roots reduced to powder, ocher earths, brown earths, sands, chalks, dried petals.

For some months now, however, Pedro had been unable to complete his drawings. My brother had become a strong, thickset adolescent with huge hands. He was not yet fifteen and all the boys of fifteen or over dreamed of confronting him. But Pedro turned out to be much more peaceable than his brutish physique might suggest. As nobody here mocked the color of his hair or his sister's supposed feathers, Pedro no longer looked for a fight. Neverthless, the word had spread among the local youths. There was an infallible way to get him to fight, a provocation he never failed to respond to. You just had to wait for him to draw one of his images in the dust of the courtyard or outside, in the alleyways, in the red desert, and when the picture was quite far advanced, walk into the circle of colors and wipe your shoes on it. That never failed: the young artist would flare up and that colored space became a boxing ring.

After which, whoever had provoked him had to suffer the consequences.

Pedro, absorbed in his drawings and his adolescent fights, was unaware that a man was coming to get him, not an ogre this time, no, but a man whose only baggage was a little red wooden cart, a toy he had carved for him with his own hands years earlier. The man was following the trail of the woman who had been gambled away and her caravan of children, he was following the stories scattered in the desert under the stones, questioning the nomads and advancing step by step toward this son with red hair, as red as the feathers of the rooster he had loved so much. And as the world is smaller than it may seem, as the roads going south are not so numerous, as beautiful stories are not forgotten but are transformed by time and region and the various storytellers who recount them, and as everyone remembered the stories that young Anita, sitting on her box, told in her language in order to survive, he had managed to track us down in this vast land. But José listened to nothing except the direction he had to take.

Our father came to the courtyard only a few days after our mother's death. He threw a glance at the poultry and knocked at our door.

Martirio led him to the empty bedroom, and he stretched himself on the esparto mattress and lay there with his eyes open. He said nothing when his children, all big now, returned after nightfall. They all ate their soup in silence. Then, at the end of the meal, José took the pieces of the little cart from his pockets and, as we watched him assembling them, I at last realized who this man was that Martirio had put in my mother's empty bed and who did not seem to have seen me yet.

"Tomorrow I'll look for work!" he said, handing the little red cart to Pedro. "I'm sure they need good strong hands in this new country."

"Tomorrow is Sunday!" replied his son, in that new deep voice that José was unfamiliar with.

"I see my boy is talking like a man now! I'll wait till Monday, then. I won't let it be said that I sponge off my children. My madness died along with my rooster. I'll never abandon you again!"

On waking up the next morning, our father peered out through the window of his room and saw the winter sun already high in the sky, then looked at the courtyard and the poor people who lived there. His gaze moved to Clara, motionless in the light, before coming to rest on his son, that young giant with red hair, huddled in the center of a circle of colors surrounded by other boys older than him who stood there waiting. The three oldest looked at each other, hesitated for a moment, then entered the circle together. Pedro leaped to his feet and swooped on the intruders.

No doubt José only discerned one dimension of the scene, he saw only the fight and was blind to the reasons. He was aware only of his son's anger and his bare fists, the violence of his blows, the blood at the corner of his lips. He concentrated on Pedro's three opponents lying in the dust, and paid no attention to the work of art the fight had erased, reduced to nothing.

He had come all this way for this fierce boy with his red hair, and he would make this red child the greatest fighter on this side of the world. Then he would cross the sea again and go back to his country, to show everyone his champion, his new Red Dragon.

He felt like a new man, and ran down the steps four at a time to embrace his son.

On Monday, our father did not look for work as he had promised, but talked to us for a long time about his plans, the great hopes he was pinning on Pedro.

"I'll go tell your boss that you won't be coming back. I'll take care of your training. You look older than your age, adults won't hesitate to confront you. Your mother earned a lot, we'll invest the money in you, my son. I came with a toy in my pockets, but we'll travel the world with that same cart life size, a cart as red as your hair with your name written on it in big letters. We'll find you opponents in every town. We'll pitch our tent everywhere and the crowds will come to watch you fight and cheer you on!"

We listened open-mouthed to our father's prophesies.

"As for you girls, you'll have to work hard to make sure your household wants for nothing and your brother fulfils his destiny! But you can be sure he'll pay you back a hundredfold for whatever you do for him! Anita, give me your mother's purse and your account books."

"Here they are!" said my sister, and my father threw himself on the figures without even noticing that his eldest daughter was speaking.

Pedro did not want to fight, but he liked the loving way that José looked at him. It was a look he had missed. So he did everything his father had decided, he became a fighting cock to please him. His muscles developed as he trained, he made the palms of his hands harder by hitting wood, let himself be kneaded, massaged, molded by his father, who never let him out of his sight. He had put away his colors, but would get up at night to look at them in their little linen bags and, each time he slept, he would draw scenes and faces under his eyelids.

One night, my father took him down to the waterfront, filled with men in their undershirts, and said, "Now fight!"

Pedro looked at him without understanding.

"Choose an opponent from among these men and fight!"

"Why?"

"Your apprenticeship is over, now you have to come up against real opponents, fight somewhere else, not just in the courtyard, hit flesh and blood instead of stone and wood."

"And how will I get one of them to agree to fight me?"

"I'll provoke them, and then you take over! This one coming now looks quite strong, but not too aggressive. He's perfect."

The man was whistling as he came toward them. José stepped out to block his path and cried, "Your mother's a whore!"

Surpised, the man stopped, unable to get past José. "Are you talking to me?"

"Yes, I *am* talking to you, you bastard—"

José was unable to finish his sentence: the stevedore's huge hands had already closed over his cheeks, squeezing them like a vise, and José's feet were lifted off the ground. Pedro stood there, watching the scene with a smile. The offended party flung his father to the ground with a single movement of his arm and continued on his way, again whistling.

Pedro approached José, who was still on the ground, and held out his hand to help him up.

"But you didn't do a thing!" José spluttered indignantly. "You didn't fight! Look, my jaw is half torn off thanks to you!"

"He was a good man, you insulted his mother, he reacted. I didn't feel any need to intervene. I might as well tell you: I don't like taking blows, and I don't like dishing them out."

"But I saw you leap on three boys twice your size! You hit them really hard for someone who doesn't like fighting!"

"They stepped into my picture. They were wiping their feet on my mother's face."

"Your mother's face?"

"On the ground. I'd finally managed to get her eyes right."

"But you don't mind if someone mangles *my* face! Let's go home, I think I'm going to die! We'll find a way."

The chalk cockfight

Anita did not like our father's plans, she could see the family's finances being frittered away and bitterly regretted having scattered so many stories in the desert.

"If my words had been eaten by the birds, he'd probably never have found us again," she liked to tell Angela. "The French instructor who comes every morning to teach Pedro French boxing and kickboxing is costing us too much. God knows how long we'll be able to keep going like this! And then there's that strange character with the broken face who eats here every night, that man named Smith. He comes for free, but your father's determined there should always be wine, so he costs us even more than the boxing instructor."

Smith was an American who had traveled a lot and had a smattering of many languages. In Spanish, he would tell my father about his clandestine matches. In his day, they fought without gloves in makeshift rings, he said, and the blood poured.

"You could really get badly beat up, as my face testifies, and people bet a lot on those fights. But when these Frenchmen climb in a ring, they're so polite, they hardly touch each other. The public likes seeing men falling, though, it likes seeing lips split open and hearing bones breaking. Your son should go to America, that's where they still hold real fights."

"You can do anything here," José would reply. "It's a new country, the authorities won't interfere in a few bare-knuckle contests. We'll start on this side of the sea and when we've made enough, we'll cross to America with the mules, the cart and the girls and buy an olive grove."

"After they put gloves on us, it was even worse," Smith went on, as if talking to himself. "The gloves only protected the hands, not the face. You could hit even harder without breaking your fingers. Now they have cushions on their hands."

"Have you ever killed a man?" Martirio finally asked, after listening in silence to the old man's drunken ramblings for more than two weeks.

"Sometimes you hit too hard, it's one of the risks of the trade. But I swear I didn't do it out of hate. Me, you know, I've lost most of my teeth, I can only see through one eye, and my fingers are so busted, I couldn't write even if I'd ever learned. There are days when it hurts just holding my glass, and plenty of mornings when I feel so dizzy I can't even get up. But believe it or not, I don't bear any grudge against those guys who beat the hell out of me while the punters yelled and smoked, it was the rule! So I assume that those I sent to their maker don't bear me a grudge either and I sleep well at night. Oh, yes, I sleep well!"

"There's one thing that bothers me," José said one evening. "It's that my son only fights when he's angry,"

"Oh, that's the big worry. Controlling your anger. That and the fear of being hit too hard. The biggest worry!"

"He isn't afraid of anything!" my father said indignantly. "He just needs a good reason to fight. He does these drawings, you see, and when anyone touches them nothing can hold him back. I thought maybe he could do a drawing on the floor of the ring before the beginning of the fight and when his opponent steps on it, the match would start."

"And what about the rounds? What about the bell, the referee? José, your wine is good and I like your company! And I don't mind telling you that I've never seen a fifteen-year-old as strong as your son, so I'm not here just to eat and drink, more than anything else I'm here because I'm curious to see what'll become of your boy. But believe me, if he doesn't learn to control his anger, the only thing you'll be able to make of him is a fairground attraction. Even on the other side of the Atlantic, they won't want to have anything to do with him!"

"You've drunk too much tonight," my father snarled, after a long silence. "Pedro will see you home."

And old Smith, who was not even fifty but had taken so many blows that he seemed twenty years older, old Smith who lived in the medina because he didn't have enough money to live anywhere else, old Smith went out on Pedro's arm, singing tunes from his home country, and my father never invited him again.

So now Pedro had somewhere else to draw other than on his imaginary canvases. José even gave him a set of multicolored chalks thanks to our mother's money, and he wept for joy. Then our father again took him to the waterfront and asked him to do a drawing.

Immediately, the boy sat down and started making a picture for his father, he remembered the Red Dragon's second fight, he remembered the roosters' movements, the savagery of their thrusts, he tried to render all of that with his few chalks and became totally engrossed in his picture. He wanted his father to admire him for something other than his fists, he wanted to show him what his fingers were capable of. The magnificent drawing surrounded him, overcame him. José waited until the work was almost finished, then provoked a man twice as big as his son into stepping on the image. Pedro leaped up, and a fight ensued over the picture. The Red Dragon, prince of roosters, was gradually erased, as was Olive, its eternal opponent, the memories went up in dust, and the stevedore collapsed in a cloud of colors.

Pedro, his fingers and nose bleeding, was mourning his picture. "Did you see it?" he screamed at his father. "Tell me, did you see my drawing before it was trampled?"

Delighted, José replied, "Not very well. I was waiting for it to be finished before I took a proper look at it, but you just have to do it again, I have all the time I need! Look! Here are more chalks!"

The same scene was repeated so often that everyone on the waterfront soon became aware that they could see a young man fighting, an exceptionally strong young man, and that if anyone beat him they would make quite a packet.

So the toughest characters came and wiped their feet on the chalk picture the son was trying to make for his father. It was unusual for him to lose, but it did happen. Twice, he was left for dead and his elder sisters said prayers for him and watched over him. His gentle face became dented and swollen, his body was covered with bruises, his hands grew warped, but he would not give up, he wanted to please his father, he wanted to finish his picture.

The bets were coming in thick and fast until the day the police interfered. The fine was a big one, and Pedro had to leave and finish his picture somewhere else. But he did not leave us so quickly, there were other neighborhoods.

One Sunday morning, Angela watched her brother as he held his spoon clumsily in his wounded fingers.

"He came back for our sins, and you welcomed him the way the father in the parable welcomes the prodigal son," she finally said to him in a toneless voice. "The man is your father, not your son, and no father should make his child endure what he's making you endure."

"Don't talk about him like that," replied Pedro gently. "He trusts me, he loves me. And a son must obey his father."

"So now he's dragging you into his madness. Look at your hands, soon you won't be able to draw."

"My pictures are gaining in color and force what they're losing in delicacy. I see now that my pain is part of my work. My last picture was so beautiful, I almost killed the brute who trampled it. Come and watch my next fight and you'll understand."

Angela and her bird attended the last fight Pedro gave in the city. And both were moved by the drawing of the cockfight, the suffering of the two roosters, the violence of the men around, that eternal repetition, that circle, that wheel, that ring around the fighters. That day, Pedro took a few blows, but felled two men, knocked them out flat.

On the ground, blood and chalk merged.

The morning he was due to leave, Pedro limped down the stairs.

"I dreamed that a man entered my circle," he told Angela with a smile. "I fought till dawn without seeing his face, and now that I'm awake, I'm limping like Jacob."

"I saw you fight yesterday and your picture moved me," she replied, in tears. "I don't know when you'll be back, but we'll wait for you, you can be sure of that."

"When my picture is perfect, nobody will dare trample it. That day, my father will understand and I'll be back."

With the remaining money, José had bought two mules and the famous fairground cart, painted red. On the canvas cover, he had had written in big flaming red letters: *José Carasco, the Red Dragon*. And there he stood in the courtyard, flashing his victor's smile, ready to set off on the roads with his champion, this son he had found again and who he was going to make the greatest fighter of all time.

"I always dreamed you would bear my name: the eldest son of the Carascos has always been called José! What do you think, girls?"

The girls did not think anything. We watched in silence as our brother limped through the gate. Martirio clasped Clara to her as if to stop her from following him.

Thanks to her black bird, Angela hovered for a long time above the red cart and was able to follow our brother until he disappeared over the horizon. Then the crow cawed a curt farewell and returned to perch on the shoulder of its weeping mistress.

The wounds on the walls whisper our brother's story to me, that story so often told in the night by Anita before my choice of eternal solitude freed her from her promise. Pedro was our favorite and, at night, in the courtyard, surrounded by chairs, she would bring him back to life for us for a few moments.

She would always start like this, telling us about Smith, telling us she had seen him again in town, drunk and staggering as usual, and that he had recognized her. She would say that he had rushed up to her to give her news of Pedro, that great artist who was her brother. Then he had told her the end of the story of the Red Dragon and how he had crossed the path of the scarlet cart.

It was in winter, he had ended up in a garrison town somewhere, a town full to bursting with legionnaires and women of easy virtue. He was penniless, telling his life story for a few drinks, getting himself invited to eat by men he amused, when he came across the tent of the Red Dragon. Following the legionnaires who had adopted him for the evening, he had gone in, as if entering a circus, and, despite his drunkenness, had recognized our brother. Pedro had aged, the fights had made a terrible mess of him, Smith had seen in him a brother in suffering, and the desire to urinate that had been growing in the American for a while had abruptly passed. Dressed in a ridiculous coat of scarlet feathers, Pedro was in the center of the ring, intent on finishing a sublime fresco: two roosters in motion, surrounded by colorful faces with vague outlines, faces distorted by grimaces as they cried out and, in the midst of that crowd, two pairs of eyes stood out, two pairs of eyes staring at one another through that blur of colors and sorrows, in that decaying world, two pairs of eyes placed there by that fighter with broken fingers and puffy eyes: our brother. Two loving gazes, like a bridge thrown above the frenzy of the spectators.

A huge man with empty eyes was waiting in silence on the edge of that chalk-red arena, getting ready to enter the circle, while our father, a megaphone stuck to his mouth, provoked him, screaming at him that he would never dare face his son, his scarlet champion, wounded certainly, but unbeaten. And Pedro, tiny and alone in the centre of his great work, Pedro devoured by chalk, Pedro huddled in his wretched fairground costume, imperturbably continued his drawing.

Then a last cloud of color, blown there by the bruised artist, tore the drawing in half, opened it liked a belly, and the picture came to life. The opponent looked at the vibrant image at his feet and his empty eyes filled with tears. He retreated. In the audience, nobody spoke, all eyes were on the drawing, spell-bound. Breaking the silence, the opponent murmured that the picture was a pentacle and he refused to set foot on it, he would lose his soul if he did. Our father stamped his feet, desperate to find another challenger for his son.

"Come in, three or four against one," he roared while his son stood in the middle of the picture, looking down at it and smiling. "Come in and fight! If you win, you'll share the prize money! I'll stake everything we've won so far, everything we've accumulated in seven years of fights! What are you afraid of, you bunch of cowards? Are you afraid of spoiling it? Spoiling what? Look, it's just chalk, it's not meant to last! Look, I'm going into this picture, with both feet, and I'm stamping on it! Look, it's easily rubbed out, it's nothing but colored powder! What on earth are you afraid of?"

*

At this point, every time she told the story of Pedro el Rojo, Anita would stop to catch her breath. Something was breaking in her voice. She would stop, as if trying to hold back her tears, then continue in a slightly different tone.

She would go on to describe the way her brother looked at his father destroying his masterpiece, the father he had followed for years in the hope of one day offering him that miracle he had just achieved at last after so many blows received, the miracle he had just achieved with his broken hands. He had looked at his own father destroying the vast fresco, that space of color and combat that had somehow annihilated all violence, that had put an end to all fighting and changed his destiny. He had looked at him for a few moments, that man whose love, respect and gratitude he had so longed for, he had looked at him tenderly then flung himself at his throat and twisted his neck with an abrupt movement, like someone killing a chicken.

THE ENGINE DRIVER

Damned! Our line is damned! Teeming with absurd stories that stifle us, teeming with ghosts and prayers and gifts that are so many wounds.

Here we are, advancing on the edge of our lives, on the edge of the world, incapable of existing for ourselves, bearing sins we have not committed, bending beneath a leaden fate, beneath the burden of centuries of sorrows and beliefs that have preceded us! The courtyard encircles me, my sisters surround me, whispers pursue me, poison my space: echoes, prayers, my dead mother's moans as she embroiders her madness on the back of my skin, Angela's somgs, driving men to crime, the cawing of her crow, the low voice of Anita the storyteller constantly repeating the scene of our father's death, or that of Clara's departure, each time adding an unexpected detail, inventing a line of dialogue, a new character.

Wasn't my story told to me before I lived it? Wasn't my solitude invented for me?

I begin to have doubts about the reality of my memories. Did I really choose to be alone? Or was solitude imposed on me, dictated by a mother, a sister, a story told over and over in the courtyard? Was I even born here, behind a wall, after that superhuman crossing? Did I really stay so long in my mother's womb?

In Anita's stories, I remember, my father was always different: sometimes a man who smelled of olives, sometimes a crazy cockfighter, sometimes an anarchist with his face sewed back together, sometimes my father was merely one of those poor anonymous devils we encountered on the road, wandering with bundles over their shoulders, one of those nice fellows who pulled my mother's cart for a while in return for a little affection.

I don't know anymore, the stories gush from the walls, contradicting one another, submerging me. There are voices all around me, talking about me and the mother who never loved me.

I was five when the red cart disappeared through the big gate, I was five when we were orphaned for the second time. Without even a brother to protect us. And penniless.

The evening Pedro left, Anita opened the false bottom of the big chest and showed us the only things that remained to us of our mother: the wedding dresses she had made for her daughters. Marvels that Anita had hidden from our father and had hesitated to sell. Anita's dress was the simplest, Angela's sported dozens of white feathers, while Martirio inherited a garment much too large for her slender little body. For Clara, Frasquita had made three wedding dresses.

There was nothing for me: she probably hadn't had time, said my sisters.

In the weeks that followed, Pirouli Carameli sang only for the others now, and the only things I was given were some of Angela's eternal white feathers. Until that Sunday afternoon when a train crossed the desert of red earth and stopped in our courtyard. A train whose carriages we sensed and which was to lead us, irrevocably, into that world of stories and fantasies endlessly woven by our big sister Anita, woven every night in the open air for the fifteen years that preceded her honeymoon.

Juan arrived in our lives with a whistle in his mouth, a fob watch in his hand and a stream of beaming kids clinging to him. The Oran-Algiers express braked noisily beneath our windows and dropped off one of its little passengers. It was getting ready to leave again when a dozen travelers, all under the age of twelve, rushed into the station, demanded their tickets and clambered screaming onto the carriages.

Anita came out of the house behind us to watch the spectacle. Bathed in sweat, Juan was pulling a hundred wild children who clung to each other in single file and, although the game had been going on for a long time and he had already gone through half the town on foot dragging ever more numerous carriages without even finding the time to quench his thirst, he was smiling.

"My lips are dry from the dust, you couldn't let me have a little water?" he said gaily to Anita, who was hiding her apron behind her back: she had hurriedly taken it off when she saw him. "I've never pulled such a long train before, but—engine driver's honour—I really don't mind. These children are insatiable but when I see how happy they are, jumping up and down behind me, I don't have the heart to stop the game and leave them on the platform."

My sister rushed into the house and filled a large glass with water. I saw her tidy her hair a little and smooth the folds in her dress before joining him outside among the cheerfully noisy children. He drank the whole glass in one go, eyes fixed on his good Samaritan, and when he asked for another the travelers grew impatient and booed. Anita and Juan both laughed heartily, staring at each other's lips.

"Thanks," he said at last, taking a breath. "What an idea to spend my day off pretending to be a train for these damned kids! They won't catch me out again! Anyway, my day won't have been wasted, because I've met you and you're laughing! Careful, you lot, the train's about to leave, keep off the tracks!"

The whistle blew, and from the back of Juan's throat came the shrill cries of a huge steam machine setting off slowly in a cloud of dust, before gradually gathering speed, dragging behind it its collection of children's feet and faces. Juan turned one last time to blow a kiss to Anita, and the train went on its way toward the medina. The cries of joy behind him took an eternity to fade.

Invisible sleepers were laid on the waste ground and Anita's laughter became the heart of a network of truant tracks. All the switches in the country led only to her. As soon as he could, Juan dropped by the courtyard again. He noted the days and hours when she was there and soon his itinerary became a regular one. Always punctual, he would knock at our door and, with one bound, Anita would come out and join him on the doorstep. They would stay outside, standing, leaving the space of one or two imaginary bodies between them, laughing and chasing away the children buzzing around them like flies.

After a month, she finally dared to offer him a chair, and they sat down side by side against the wall of the house. As it was clear that things were becoming serious, the mothers scolded the children who went too close to them. The neighbors were keeping their eyes open, talking in low voices about this burgeoning romance between the dressmaker's eldest daughter and the young engine driver. He was a good boy, polite and helpful, who made a fuss of them as if they were all his future mothers-in-law. Everybody in the courtyard liked Juan, not only the children: he was always kind and attentive to everyone. He carried with him a kind of simple, straightforward joy, which he offered to everyone: you just had to look at him and smile to be entitled to your little share of happiness.

Several times a week, he would bring vegetables and poultry, which was a great improvement on the Carasco children's daily fare. Now that he lived alone, he had nobody else to spoil.

His father, a stonecutter, had come to this side of the Mediterranean fifteen years earlier with all his family, looking for work. But he had fallen so seriously ill that he had had to go back where he came from. An illness nobody spoke about, a shameful illness. He was a good man, but a great lover of women. Juan had not gone back to Spain.

"Until the day you smiled at me, I'd never wished to caress anything but the steel of my locomotive. Now, I want you so badly that being by your side without touching you burns me up. I want you for my wife!" He said all this in one go, without daring to look her in the face.

"But I'm already a mother," replied Anita after a long silence, "a mother to all my sisters, and I have to bring them up before making my own children. If we marry, you'll suffer even more, because we won't be able to touch each other until the last of my sisters is married. When you look at me, I feel as if a needle is going through me and I want to touch you. Soledad is only five. How will we be able to resist?"

"If that's your decision, we'll cuddle up and love each other in words."

"What if I touch you here, just above your lips? What would you like?"

"I'd like more."

"More caresses, more kisses?"

"I'd like you naked beside me."

"And when you imagine me naked beside you?"

"I want to be inside you."

"You see, we won't be able to help ourselves if we sleep together, if we kiss, I'll give myself to you and we'll make lots of children. And I can't make any more children, I can't do that. I haven't your strength, I couldn't drag more children around with me. I was a mother too early."

"But I'll be there to help you!"

"Men don't understand what a burden a child is."

"You have such a complicated family!" Juan sighed, still smiling.

"I want you so much I feel like peeing," she whispered to him as she waved to a neighbor who was coming out for a breath of fresh air on the other side of the courtyard.

"What are you talking about, silly?"

"It's true," she said with a laugh. "It hits me in the pit of my stomach, it makes me squirm, my breasts feel as if they're bursting."

He also laughed. "Well, if you really want to know, I don't dare move, for fear the effect you're having on me will be all too visible through the material of my pants. I'd happily give you a tumble behind a bush right now, even if you are a mother!"

"Imagine we're behind that bush, where would you like my hands?"

"These things can't be said."

"Say it!"

"On my penis."

"That's where they are, they're stroking you. Close your eyes!"

"Stop or I'll do the same thing to you!"

"What's stopping you? I've lifted my dress. And your fingers are already between my thighs."

"Not only my fingers. Can't you feel?"

"You're certainly not wasting any time! But then I have nothing else to kiss but your mouth."

"Your words are caresses."

"Do you think the neighbors can see us?"

"What would they see except two well-behaved young people sitting side by side? Nobody's depraved enough to notice the little stain the pleasure you've given me has just made on my pants! Now we'll have to wait for it to dry. No, please, don't look."

"Why not? Are you ashamed, Juan Martínez?

"Marry me, I shan't touch you, I give you my word. I shan't touch you properly until the last of your sisters is married."

"In the Carasco house, nothing is said lightly. Words are magic."

"Your sisters will be my daughters and your voice my only pleasure. I swear it solemnly. Engine driver's honor!"

A WHITE FRONTIER

Anita put on the wedding dress her mother had made for her, a straight, serious-looking dress, without the slightest adornment, but one that followed the curves of her body with surprising accuracy. No adjustment was necessary. The dress seemed to have been made to measure. A line of fabric, a clean line emphasizing her contours, marking the territory of her body without constraining it or confining it. A white frontier.

Juan entered the church on the arm of the oldest of the female neighbors and Anita was walked to the altar by François, one of the two friends her future husband had invited to the ceremony. Their union was blessed and, when bride and groom joined their lips, it looked as though, in spite of the white edge of the material, their bodies would not be able to break free of each other, as though the flesh of their lips was intimately joined forever. Father André had to clear his throat and take gentle hold of the bridegroom's chin to put an end to that indecent kiss. The two bodies separated and the bride and groom forgot what they had to say. It took a few crude words, whispered to each other on the way out of the church, to quench their desire.

In the big courtyard, tables had been laid out on trestles and the whole of the little community took part in the celebration until late at night. Guitars and brass instruments had been hired by the groom for the occasion. There was singing and dancing, and Juan had laid on enough wine to get the whole quarter drunk. Contrary to the custom, the young couple did not leave their guests. Amid the din of the party, they whispered in each other's ears throughout the night. The glasses were never empty, the children themselves fell asleep drunk on wine, laughter and singing. Only Hassan, one of the two friends and colleagues Juan had invited to the party, noticed that the young engine driver was in no hurry to consummate his marriage. But Hassan was as discreet as he was sober.

"Do you drive an engine too?" I asked him before he left.

"No, I'd have to be French for that."

"But Juan is Spanish!"

"Not any more! He's French now."

"Not you?"

"No, not me. I'm still an Arab."

"What about me, then? What am I?"

Hassan took his leave and helped his friend François to get home. All the other guests lived around the courtyard.

By the end of the night, Juan and Anita had fallen asleep on their chairs and none of those who were still there felt sufficiently strong to carry them to the bridal chamber.

When the rooster crowed in the ravaged courtyard, stones were thrown at it. After such a night, everyone wanted peace and quiet.

As was her habit in summer, Clara was the first to get up. She dressed quickly to enjoy the sun's rays as soon as possible. She saw her big sister sitting in her straight, serious dress amid the remains of the party, her eyes closed, her head tilted to the side, her open mouth up against the ear of her husband Juan, who was also asleep on his chair, smiling and filling the courtyard with his regular snoring. Clara gently stroked her sister's cheek, not knowing that she would have to repeat the same gesture for years, and that that touch would for a long time allow the lovers to keep their secret. Every morning, at dawn, she would shake the couple as they sat there exhausted with desire, until she herself left this courtyard to live through her first wedding night, asleep.

It was that very night that Anita became a storyteller.

After dinner, the whole family came out to enjoy the fresh air, and our eldest sister began to tell us the stories that were to become our daily bread.

She would tell them until Clara closed her eyes, then carry on until the neighbors took their chairs back inside, and carry on even longer into the night until Juan fell asleep in his turn, cradled by the sound of her voice. Only then would she ask Martirio to put Clara and me to bed, while she herself tenderly wrapped her husband's body in a thick woolen blanket before settling down in a deckchair for the night. The few times it rained or was too cold, the gathering took place in the downstairs room, but every other evening, the couple slept outside under the stars for fear of being unable to respect that terrible promise they had made each other, for fear of no longer being content with words and of giving in to the desire that overcame them in waves every time they went too close to one another or found themselves alone in a room.

For fifteen years, Anita and Juan fed on words to keep their word.

The first night, Anita told us the story of Frasquita Carasco and the olive grove man, the man whose desire had been sewed back together, and who might have been my father. It was the first time I heard the story of the woman who had been gambled and lost.

And so, night after night, the stories unfolded, and I would be the last to stay awake, resisting sleep to find out what was to become of Salvador, or of Lucia, the beautiful accordion player. I would shiver, terrified by the ogre, amused by the description of the man-locomotive entering our courtyard by chance with his long train of children, revolted by the perversity of Clara's second husband, surprised by my mother's talents, moved by the fate of my patricide brother. As I grew up, I understood each of these stories better, without being able to separate fact from fiction, without worrying about the veracity of the events. Nevertheless, even if everything has become blurred in my memories, it seems to me that Martirio was not yet fifteen and still held me on her knees when Anita told me about my murderous sister's repeated pregnancies, that the luminous Clara still shared our room when the sad story of her second mariage was recounted, and that I was only a child when I heard for the first time about my future solitude.

Yes, the more I think about it, the more certain am I that there was some kind of magic in all of that. Unless we are made of words.

AT NIGHT, IN THE COURTYARD

Listen, my sisters!
Listen to this sound that fills the night!
Listen . . . to the sound of mothers!
Listen to it flow into you and stagnate in your bellies, listen to it as it lies dormant in that darkness where worlds grow!

Since the first evening and the first morning, since Genesis and the beginning of books, men have slept with History. But there are other stories. Subterranean stories conveyed in the secrets of women, tales buried in the ears of daughters, sucked in with mothers' milk, words drunk from mothers' lips. Nothing is more fascinating than this magic learned with our blood, learned with our periods.

Sacred things are whispered in the gloom of kitchens.

Deep in the old pots, in the smells of spices, magic and recipes rub shoulders. The culinary art of women abounds in mystery and poetry.

Everything is taught us at once: the intensity of fire, the water from the well, the heat of iron, the whiteness of sheets, fragrances, proportions, prayers, the dead, the needle and the thread . . . and the thread.

Sometimes, from the depths of a cast-iron cooking pot, some dried-up figure emerges. An anonymous ancestor looks at me, an ancestor who has known so much, seen so much, endured so much.

Our mothers' silent sorrows have muzzled their hearts.

Their laments have passed into their soups: tears of milk, of blood, spicy tears, salty and sweet flavors.

Smooth tears in the palates of men!

Beyond the restricted world of their homes, women have glimpsed another world.

The little doors of the ovens, the wooden bowls, the wells, the old lemon trees have led to a fabulous universe that they alone have explored.

Mounting a stubborn resistance against reality, our mothers have managed to bend the surface of the world from deep inside their kitchens. What has never been written is female.

THE GOLD BUTTONS

When Clara's turn came, when she stained her dress for the first time, my sisters conferred and decided that nothing would be able to enter her at night, nothing would ever penetrate her leaden sleep. No word, no prayer.

The initiation was supposed to take place during the nights of Holy Week, and night itself was becoming an obstacle.

And besides, Clara did not care about the world around her. Clara would stand for hours letting the sun go through her. Clara would listen to stories without waiting for the ending. Clara would laugh uproariously at reflections and stroke the few blonde heads of hair that came within reach. Clara loved the silvery surface of mirrors without seeing the lovely face reflected in them. What need had she of these prayers that had already been of such little use to her sisters?

Our luminous Clara did not completely live in our world even though she held the center of it and her beauty drew everyone's gaze. She spent most of her time alone in the sun, doing nothing. When its rays no longer passed over our houses and shadows began to fill the courtyard, she would sometimes go outside to pursue it in the red desert and the men watched her, always surprised by her beauty. None of them dared approach her, the fascination she exerted kept them at a distance.

Clara would walk through the city like a luminous ghost, without recognizing the route she took, even though it was always the same one. We no longer had to track her down, her walk inevitably led her to the same place, the parade ground in front of the town hall, where we knew we would find her at dusk. Then those of us with the task of bringing her back would take her by the hand and, although the crossing had taught her to walk while asleep, her legs sometimes gave way beneath her. When that happened, we had to carry her like a dead girl.

It was during one of these walks that she met the young officer who was to become her first husband. He had carefully polished gold buttons. Buttons that drew the attention of our beautiful heliotrope. It seemed to her that the sun had fallen in a shower on this tall young man and when, in his bright voice, he asked her name, she replied.

He was a Parisian and did not understand a single word of Spanish. She herself had never bothered to learn either French or Arabic. In fact, she had never bothered to learn anything at all. Like me, she had gone to the nuns to learn reading and writing, but the windows of the classroom were not large enough for her taste, the corridors were too dark, and there were too many black letters in the books! Only the whiteness of the pages fascinated her and it seemed unseemly to blacken them so assiduously with all these fly specks. While pens scratched on paper, or the other snotty-nosed brats stared at the blackboard, Clara would follow with her eyes the reflections cast by the spectacles of the nun taking the class, or worse still, she would turn away ostentatiously from the platform where the teacher sat and look at the sun through the grimy windows. Such behavior was quite unacceptable! In point of fact, Clara learned no more by day than she did by night. And slapping her with a ruler proved useless. Her teachers choked with rage, but in vain. Very soon, to spare their nerves, she was not forced to do anything at all. My sisters let her do as she pleased, fill herself with as much heat and light as she wished.

So Clara grew up in the courtyard, standing motionless in the sun, while the boys turned around her solar beauty, at once attracted and repelled by her brilliance, like so many small planets in orbit. They all feared the stern Martirio, who watched jealously over her little light.

As Clara got older, her limbs grew unusually long, like shadows in the setting sun, and her features became more refined. Her thick eyebrows enchanced the strange golden clarity of her straw-colored eyes and the satiny red of her lips. Yet the light she gave off, which, it seemed, she had somehow accumulated during all those years spent in the sun, dazzled everyone who looked at her, so that her face appeared always a little vague and she left on the retina a large bright star-shaped patch that followed men even in their sleep.

Clara disturbed the dreams of the boys in the courtyard, and lit up their bedrooms even more than this room where we slept beside her. The men would utter her name as they slept and their furious wives, using their snoring as a pretext, would shake them, hoping to tear them from the irresistible warmth of her arms.

The hostility of the women increased gradually as male desire bloomed, and reached its height when Clara was seventeen. They could no longer stand always seeing her there, right in the middle of the courtyard, motionless, as straight as a post, paying no attention to the compliments of those young men who occasionally grew so bold as to say a few words to her, words to which she merely replied with a smile or a nod of the head. She was called silly, scatterbrained, useless, and some mothers even added that she was cruel.

With time, the halo of light that she gave off at night had lost its brilliance, but I remember a slight glimmer. Around her, the darkness was never total. And I never saw her naked, it was always Martirio who put her to bed after the gatherings in the courtyard.

In summer, Clara would wash and dress before we were up; in winter, she would wait until I had left for school. Around the solstice and on rainy days, when there was sometimes not enough sunlight to draw her outside, she would play for hours with the little pocket mirror Martirio had given her. Her own reflection did not interest her, she may not even have noticed it. No, what she loved was the light she managed to concentrate in that silver circle and then project back onto the walls of the room.

It may be that all she saw of Pierre was his gold buttons.

At the bend in the street that led her to the parade ground, they were there, wonderfuly lined up, at regular intervals, shattering the sun into many suns. There were so many that she was spellbound by them and forgot her perpetual westward course. Her hand stroked the little suns one by one and the young officer, overcome by this luminescent apparition, did not move, for fear she might vanish. He savored the moment intensely. Never before had he seen a young woman so close in broad daylight. At last, she raised her straw-colored eyes to the handsome face above all those glittering little discs and the young officer's fair hair made her smile. Encouraged by this smile, Pierre ventured a question. She told him her name, as if revealing a password, then stroked his hair and took his arm with a spontaneity that added to her charm. In silence, he let himself be taken to the parade ground from where she liked to watch the sun go down.

Martirio and Angela could not get over seeing their sister on the arm of a stranger. As the sun was already skimming the surface of the horizon and Clara refused to let go of her beau, he walked back with the three of them. They had walked for a long time before Pierre noticed that Clara had fallen asleep. It was he who picked her up and carried her when she collapsed at the entrance to the red desert.

The courtyard where we lived struck him as quite wretched,

Martirio as quite hostile, and his feelings for this sleeping young girl as quite powerful. He felt as though he was in a fairy story and remembered those his mother had read to him. Then, standing quite erect, he introduced himself politely to Anita and kissed her hand before taking his leave.

Within a few days, all the men in the courtyard were in mourning. Pierre had asked for the hand of the girl around whom all their dreams revolved, and had not been rejected. We never discovered which of them tried to immolate Clara, but just before the engagement someone set fire to the bottom of her dress as she was standing motionless as usual in the middle of the courtyard, her eyes filled with sunlight. An unexpected gust of wind from the south-east suddenly brought so much sand from the desert that the fire was extinguished before she even noticed a thing. Her legs half covered in sand and the fine particles that had stuck to her face and arms made her look rather like an unfinished statue.

The order of things had been upset. Angela and Martirio should have left before her. Angela, who was married to her black bird and had accepted her own unprepossessing face and excessively round eyes, did not fret at still being unwed, but Martirio rebelled against this hurried marriage to a young stranger. It was true that she had never been interested in the world of men, but to tear her sister away from her was to doom her to struggling in the dark. She opposed the wedding with a violence they had not known she possessed, and when she realized that she could do nothing to stop it, that Clara was getting away from her, and that the reasons she gave for breaking off the engagement did not stand up and merely made her two older sisters smile, she waylaid Pierre as he was crossing the red desert, determined to have a heart to heart talk with him.

"So you're marrying a silly girl who loves only what glitters?" she scoffed. "The day you take off your uniform with its gold buttons, she'll lose interest in you. How do you plan to live with a fool who falls asleep as soon as night falls?"

"I've known about your sister's peculiarities since we first met. As for the buttons, I'll have them sewed on my skin if need be, I'm prepared to do anything to keep her and outshine the sun that fascinates her. But a few buttons wouldn't have sufficed. Have you seen the way she looks at me? She loves me as nobody has ever loved me. Clara isn't a fool. She's a poem. I also hate the night. It's always scared me. I don't care if I never see the moon and stars again in my life! I'll live at my wife's rhythm, and rise at dawn so I can enjoy her straw-colored eyes for longer."

"I already died for her once."

"As long as I live in the city, you can see her every day if you like. I have no desire to cut her off from her family."

"You don't even speak Spanish!"

"I'm a quick learner. Listen! I'm going to talk to you like a brother. Do you know that you could also be beautiful? You'd only have to smile and your face would be enchanting. With all those dark clothes you wear and your cold eyes, you're like a negative of Clara. Find yourself a husband who loves darkness and leave your sister alone!"

"I don't know how to smile and my lips are poison!" cried Martirio, and she ran back to the big gate.

The wedding was held, with great pomp, at the barracks. The family was in its Sunday best. Juan wore the same suit as on his own wedding day, but he had put on so much weight since then that he had found it difficult to button his shirt and pants and now felt cramped. We sisters each had a pretty new dress. Clara was wearing one of her three wedding dresses. Anita had chosen for her little sister the one that corresponded best to the season and the groom's station in life. Frasquita Carasco had managed to guess her solar child's future measurements. Anita assumed that her mother had made her three dresses so that at least one might fit perfectly.

The party took place one summer afternoon. The neighbors did not come, having unanimously declined the invitation with the excuse that they had nothing to put on and that this young man was not one of them. In fact, the rumor was already circulating that only the breath of the devil could have saved our sister: the flames that had consumed the bottom of Clara's dress when she announced her wedding could not have spared her otherwise.

Everything in the elegant gathering was intimidating: the women's richly-colored dresses and voluminous hats, the electric lights, the whiteness of the huge tablecloths, the posture of the butlers, the braid on the men's uniforms, and even those crystal glasses that were so fine, you hardly dared touch them with your lips for fear of breaking them. The white wine they contained, whose tiny bubbles seemed to get up your nostrils, was treacherous. It demanded to be drunk with discrimination.

Clara's eyes went wild: several hundred luminous little buttons moving in all directions, waltzing, laughing, coming undone. The women were wearing glittering jewelry, the men had silvery hair, the walls were covered with huge mirrors in gold frames. Dozens of spectacle lenses and crystal chandeliers glittered with a thousand lights. Enough to drive her insane! Where was her husband amid all these buttons? How to distinguish him in the midst of all this brilliance?

At last, he came toward her and she recognized that light in his eyes that made him unique.

Martirio was watching the scene from a distance. She saw the young bridegroom reach out his arm to her flickering little light, and the awestruck look Clara gave him made it clear to her how her sister felt. So Pierre was right, it wasn't only the uniform, a few buttons would never have sufficed.

Martirio was wearing a garish red dress that seemed out of place amid the discreet elegance of the other guests, but her eyes were so fearsome that nobody dared make the slightest comment. She was looking at the world from such a height, it seemed, that they preferred not to take any notice of her. Pierre saw her watching them from a French door and, as his wife danced with his father, who had made the journey from Paris to be at his youngest son's wedding, and as Clara whirled about, staring all the while at the chandelier that hung just above their heads, he headed in the direction of the red dress.

"Don't worry," he said. "I shan't blow out your little light. You feel hurt because she's getting away from you, but have you ever seen her as happy as she is today?"

Making it clear that she wanted to speak to him, Martirio drew him behind the red velvet curtains. When they were alone, hidden from the rest of the ballroom, she attempted a smile. Then, before Pierre had time to make a single gesture, she pressed her icy lips to his mouth. He did not free himself from this unexpected embrace.

Shrouded by the red curtains, they were invisible.

MARTIRIO THE MURDERESS

The first light of dawn wormed its way beneath the curtains protecting the bridal chamber, found out their weak points, the areas least well defended by the material, and filtered into the room where the lovers were sleeping. It crept as far as the bed and tenderly caressed Clara's closed eyelids to wake her. My sister opened her eyes and, even before rushing to the window to enjoy the new day, she remembered Pierre, Pierre's bright eyes, and looked for him. But the man lying there beside her was gray and pallid, and his wide-open eyes were colorless. A red patch on the pillow and sheets framed his sad bloodless face. Disappointed, Clara had to make do with the window. She pulled back the curtains, delivering the room to the sun, which kept its promise every morning. Pierre had given her several bright dresses, which were very much to her taste. She donned a golden yellow one and ran downstairs, in a hurry to join her loving sun in the barracks gardens.

But what had happened to her husband with his bright voice? He had already abandoned her. And who was this feeble-looking man who had been slipped into the bed beside her while she slept? Yet she rememberd falling asleep in Pierre's warm arms, she had even tried to resist the coming of night in order to enjoy his caresses for longer. There had been so many hurried kisses before the sun had gone down . . . And now her luminous lover had disappeared and been replaced by this cold gray fellow bathing in his red pool.

Not that she cared all that much, because the sun was vibrant and faithful, and the clear sky promised a radiant day. She smiled, thinking about nothing now but the pleasure offered her by the reborn sun.

Pierre had died on his wedding night, in the midst of his honeymoon. He had been drained of his blood through his left ear as he slept. A cerebral hemorrhage, said the experts. He had not sustained any blows. The autopsy cleared his half-mad young bride, who refused to understand, to make the connection between the young officer with his bright voice and sparkling eyes whom she had just married and this corpse found by her side the morning after the wedding. Although she did not show any grief or shed any tears, she was judged too upset to be disturbed more than was necessary. The poor woman, mad with sorrow no doubt, had withdrawn into a terrible silence. She spent every day in the sun, doing nothing, spoke only to her family and was unable to answer the investigators' questions except with smiles or simple nods of the head. But what had most struck everyone was her beauty. The case was considered a very sad one, and the city's newspaper devoted an article to it.

Clara inherited a small income, to which she was indifferent. She refused to wear mourning, and even her father-in-law was not offended to see her wearing the luminous dresses his son had given her. Realizing that Pierre's death had no place in her disturbed mind, he offered to take her with him to Paris and have her treated there. As Anita opposed the idea, Clara took root again in the middle of the courtyard, in the sun, and for a long time Martirio hid in the shadows and wept.

One autumn and one winter passed, during which Martirio kissed only dying old people, thus putting an end to their sufferings. She offered death in a kiss to whoever asked for it and used our secrets to relieve the living. Of all of us, it was she who most often said those prayers of which we are the unfortunate guardians.

I myself had at last become a woman, I had had to walk in shoes adorned with olive stones and hold the little wooden cross, I had had to fast and repeat obscure words. I had been initiated. I had been given this box in which today I put away my big exercise book and my mother's embroidered name, and had slipped it under my bed, waiting for the time to come to open it.

Why did I put off that moment for all those years?

I was in no hurry to penetrate the secret of the box. Every day I saw Martirio mourning the death of her brother-in-law. I knew she was incapable of kissing us, terrified by the idea of the death she claimed to carry within her, the poison on her lips, and I feared the gift contained in the box, the poisoned gift, the black bird cawing at my side, the voice putting the lover to sleep every night, the fatal kiss, the colored threads and the needle tearing my mother apart. I was so afraid of that thing lurking in its wooden prison under my bed, imposed on me by the maternal line! The box was like the promise of a great sorrow to come, a weight to be borne, which I refused to share with my sisters. It seemed to me that if I stopped thinking about it, the wooden cube would disappear or at the very least be emptied of its deadly contents. The most effective thing would doubtless have been to force it open before the gift matured, but I had been incapable of that too.

And so, imagining the amount of solitude that might be confined in that banal case, I put off opening it, just as I had already, according to Anita, delayed my own birth.

GLAZIER!

"Glazier, glazier!" yelled the bearer of light.

Clara laughed uproariously as she followed the man and his shrill cries through the city.

"*Vidriero, vidriero!*"

For the second time, she had turned away from the sun to trail a stranger.

Concentrating on the windows of houses, he did not immediately notice the pretty creature, dressed in yellow satin, who was following him so joyfully. The day was drawing to its end and pickings had been slim. His face streaming with sweat, his back broken by his burden of glass, he stopped at last and cautiously unfastened his dazzling armor. He rested the big rectangles of light against his long thin legs, took a dirty handkerchief from his pocket, and mopped his brow with it. Facing in the direction of the setting sun, he closed his eyes and wiped away all the sweat that had dripped down into them. When he was able to see clearly again, he gave such a start that he almost broke the sheets of shimmering glass covering the lower part of his body. Clara was standing in front of him, motionless, smiling, her straw-colored eyes fixed on him with disquieting intensity. Caught in a vise between the setting sun and the indirect light reflected off the panes, my sister seemed unreal.

"Have you been deliberately trying to give me the jitters? You think that's funny, do you? It's a bad joke to play on a glazier! If I break my merchandise because of you, who's going to pay? *I* will, I'll have to pay an arm and a leg! This stuff is fragile, you know, and it's my bread and butter!"

He was reprimanding her in French. She continued staring at him without replying.

"Why are you grinning at me like that without saying a word? Cat got your tongue or what?"

Although he had not asked her name, my sister told him she was called Clara, from which the glazier deduced that she was Spanish and might not understand much French.

He found it somewhat reassuring to hear the sound of her voice. How could he ever have imagined he was dealing with a ghost? He was definitely too sensitive. He bent down and hoisted his burden of light back onto his bony shoulders. Clara had not moved and was watching every one of his gestures with great attention.

"Why are you staring at me like that with those honey-colored peepers of yours?" he asked.

She liked this lanky man's carapace of glass and bright eyes. The panes, which his shoulders could not conceal, stuck out on either side, wreathing his angular body and face in light. She had already been following him for a long time and had got lost. He would have to help her find her way again. She lived in the Gambetta courtyard of the Marabout neighbourhood.

"Well, you're a long way from there!" he exclaimed. "And I don't much feel like going out of my way before getting home and putting my stuff down. Not even for you! You just have to carry straight on in that direction, you're bound to run into some other sucker who'll return you to the fold! Bye for now, my darling, I'll be seeing you!"

The sun was starting to disappear behind the horizon and Clara could feel her strength fading. She caught up with the glazier as he walked away, whistling, and placed herself in front of him.

"You really stick like a leech, kid! What do you want of me? The nighttime, when the town's asleep, is when I mess with silly girls like you, but by day I slave away and don't think too much about women. Mind you, you don't look as if you're the kind of girl who hangs about at night. Are you afraid of the dark, is that it? You mustn't be, you know, the night is still the best time of day, and not only for crooks. All right, then, if you promise me a big sloppy kiss, I'll walk you home! But otherwise, it's nothing doing!"

Clara promised, without really understanding the glazier's extravagant way of speaking. She took his arm and, reassured by his warmth, fell asleep without slowing her pace.

He continued talking without noticing that her eyes were closed and that she had not heard a word of his long monologue.

He was nicknamed Lunes because he had been born on Monday and that day had always brought him luck. He knew the city like the palm of his hand and had been going up and down its streets ever since he was a child.

Fortunately for him, my sister's legs did not give way. When they were bang in the middle of the red desert, he stopped and demanded his kiss.

"We're almost there, so you can pay me now, I don't think you could call it an advance, seeing how far we've walked already."

He let go of my sister's arm, unfastened the felt-covered wooden frame in which he carried his panes of glass, and wiped his face again before turning back to Clara.

The almost full moon cast its soft white light down on them, but he had the impression that it was not the only thing shining in the night, that the diaphanous young girl motionless by his side was also glowing slightly. Surprised, he looked at her for a moment and realized, from her closed eyes and regular breathing, that she was asleep.

"Is it the moon that makes you shine like that? I can't see myself kissing you while you're sleeping, even though you promised me that kiss. It wouldn't be right. And the fact that you're giving off that light gives me goose flesh! You're one strange kid, but my God, how pretty you are! You'll pay me back for falling asleep while I'm talking to you and not paying your debts. You won't get out of it so easily, believe me!"

Far from abandoning the sleeping beauty, he entered the courtyard, and the neighbors who were taking the air pointed out our house to him.

"You should have left that slut where you found her!" he was told.

"Not much milk of human kindness around here, is there?" replied Lunes.

"That's none of your business. You can knock at the dressmaker's house, it's the door just opposite."

"Thanks anyway."

Martirio opened the door and looked at him so coldly that he had to lower his eyes.

"She asked me to walk her home. Well, she's home now, as far as I know! It's strange all the same that she sleeps as she walks. Don't you think you should take her to see a doctor?"

"She's been like that since she was born, there's nothing to be done," replied Martirio. "My eldest sister and her husband went to look for her. Didn't you pass them on your way back from the parade ground?"

"That's not where I found her. She was following me like a puppy dog and laughing to see me slaving away."

"Thank you for bringing her home, but now go, and make sure you don't come back!"

"Why not?" replied Lunes, who hated restrictions. "Especially as she has a debt to me. She made me a promise."

"A promise?"

"If you're her sister, I can tell you: she promised me a kiss. And, believe me, I didn't have to insist too much, she was looking at me with those huge peepers of hers as if I was the most beautiful thing she'd ever clapped eyes on. I think she's crazy about me. She was that stuck on me, I didn't even ask to be paid in advance."

Martirio felt a wave of hatred come over her, but she hesitated. There were people outside, they might see her. "What if I pay the debt in her place?" she suggested in a low voice.

"It's a deal!" replied Lunes, daring now to look her in the eyes.

"Wait for me behind the biggest bush on the waste ground. I'll be there as soon I can get away."

And she slammed the door in his face.

Feeling quite perky, the glazier went and laid his tall, thin body down on the red earth. His panes carefully placed on a blanket beside him, he waited, thinking of the two sisters.

Shadow and light living under the same roof!

His lips would have their due, but his hands might get their share too. He would only need to say that the younger sister had promised. No, he would content himself with a kiss, that was enough to be getting on with, and he'd be back to see if he could get more another day. He didn't much like the idea of a girl who fell asleep without warning and sweated light! But he'd only have to get her promise and then make the other one pay, the one who looked down on you and gave herself in the dark. She certainly couldn't be as cold as she liked to make you think. Well, every day had its pains and every night its pleasures!

With his back on the dry earth and his nose in the stars, he let his nocturnal daydreams wash over him. What if she didn't come?

Several times, he heard footsetps, but none of the dark figures walking on the paths that crossed the waste ground approached his bush.

His thin muscles relaxed little by little, and his body sank into the ground, heavy with fatigue and desire. He mustn't fall asleep, just close his eyes for a moment or two to rest them. Just for a moment. But how heavy his eyelids were! He would never be able to open them again! He felt as if he was surrounded by empty air, as if he was going to tip backwards and fall . . .

Then a shudder ran through his body and he pulled himself together, digging his nails into the earth to slow his fall. His heart was thumping in his chest. In a panic, he looked about him. Martirio was sitting by his side, darker than the night. Leaning on his elbows, he raised himself to a sitting position and rubbed his almost hairless face with his long thin hands to chase away both his sleep and his fear. His heart became light again.

"Have you been here long?" he asked my sister, with a yawn.

"For a while," she replied coldly. "I was about to leave."

"You should have shaken me. The days are deadly long. There shouldn't be something like summer. The sun is too heavy to bear. And your sister really made me walk! Come on, get close to me so we can smooch! Don't be afraid, I'm not going to eat you! Here, in my arms! That's it! But you're cold, you're shivering! I'll warm you up, don't worry!"

"Are you quite sure you want your kiss?"

"And how! You smell so strongly of night, I'm dying with desire. And besides, it's still Monday, things are always better for me on Monday. It's my lucky day. So I won't let go of you until you've stuck your lips to mine. You'll see, you'll ask for more: my kisses are like sugar."

"It's what you wanted all along!"

"Oh, yes, you can say that again! I've been waiting long enough for it! At the rate we're going, it'll soon be Tuesday."

And so Martirio moved her mouth closer and Lunes caught it greedily. The glazier's long feminine hands with their dirty nails tenderly enclosed my sister's icy face, then went farther down and inched their way into her dark cleavage. Martirio abruptly tossed the night in all directions to free herself and, once out of Lunes's arms, she ran until she was out of breath, weeping, across the shadowy moonlike desert.

She went in through the big gate and, when she got to our room, sank onto Clara's bed, and looked at her luminous smile for a long time.

For the second time, she had given death to a man who did not desire her.

Despite her tears, she could still feel the trail of the glazier's hot hands on her face and breasts. Thin, soft hands. Almost a woman's hands . . .

Late the following afternoon, Clara ran off in pursuit of the sun and stopped running in the place where she had met Lunes the previous day. But she waited in vain, the man with the glass carapace did not appear.

Martirio was given the task of finding her sister before nightfall.

Clara stood on the parade ground, radiant, her back to the sun.

And there he was beside her, wreathed in his panes of glass, laughing and making her promise hundreds of kisses and caresses, all the while waiting for night to come.

"Your damned kiss stirred my senses," he whispered to Martirio when she joined them. "I was in such a fever, I scoured the low dives all night."

"What are you doing here?" she asked, pale-faced.

"You're looking at me as if I was a ghost," he said, surprised. "Don't get me wrong, I have feelings, I'm not just after a quick one. But I'd really like to have another go, tonight. Your cool body against mine . . . I'm always too hot, I sweat so much I'm afraid of melting on those days when the world shimmers in the overheated air. So before your pretty sister falls asleep, tell me if you'll take her place again tonight and give me all the good things she promised me. Because otherwise I'll demand payment right now from this strumpet with the straw-colored eyes, she's dying for it."

"Come back to the bush at midnight and I'll pay. But now take your dirty window panes and go!"

"See you soon then, my little night!"

Death had no hold over Lunes. Martirio's poison became honey in his mouth. All summer, he sank into the night, caressed its shadows, wept with pleasure, caught fire against the cold body of my sister the murderess, whose nocturnal scent he loved so much. And Clara kept promising more, until the fall day when Martirio felt a warm throbbing in her belly. There was a new breath deep inside her and she smiled alone in her corner, she smiled for the first time.

She did not say anything to Lunes, but he eventually noticed the transformation that was taking place: his night was full, she was becoming as round as the moon. His first thought was to run away, to leave the red desert and never again see this young woman, her cold eyes encircled with shadows, who smelled of the night. But he could not escape his desire. The woman's cold body, surrendered every night in the bushes, had become indispensable to him. For just one day, he disappeared and went elsewhere to quench his desire. Martirio assumed he had died at last, leaving her that life deep in her body.

But the following night, Lunes was back.

"You're my night," he confessed. "I might as well come clean: I'm not interested in your sister. She blows heat on my tired eyes. It's your shadow I long for all day, that cool shadow that springs up from the depths and caresses my burning limbs. You're pregnant, I can see. I didn't want a family to feed, I didn't want brats on my back as well as those damned window panes. But now, there's only you in my dreams, you've chased away the others, the floozies, the whores. And without you, my nights are so empty I could scream. Yes, you're my night. So look, I think maybe we ought to think about just loving each other and living together in a place of our own. If you want me, I'll go see your eldest sister tomorrow."

"I love you," Martirio whispered to him in the night.

They were married as quickly as possible, without much ceremony this time because Clara had made us unpopular. And Anita understood why the wedding dress intended for Martiro was so ample.

One of the houses in the courtyard became free. Lunes and Martirio moved into it and their first son was born there. Martirio never dared kiss him, but she cradled him endlessly in her dark arms and felt the need to have more, many more. She liked it when her belly was full, when life stirred in it. She offered herself without restraint to Lunes, her great devourer of shadows with his long feminine hands, who was never sated and gave her child after child. Death was fertile, she grew round and gave birth to joyful children who ran in all directions and yelled in the sun. They were given French names: Jean, Pierre, Françoise, Richard, Claire, Anne and Yvonne. They jostled one another in the little house, taking life between the teeth, and all lived off the cheeky glazier, who never ceased to be surprised at how many of them there were.

The blank page

The silence of the night has come to rest on my page.
Silence and nothing else.
I hear my sand-enclosed heart beating in the desert of
my life.

THE AVIARY

The storyteller has fallen silent, the stories now are mere memories encysted in my soul. They wander through my empty carcass and I dig them up one by one and put them down on paper.

But for several nights now, nothing has come out, not a word. The stories are hiding, voiceless, buried in my flesh, and my page remains blank. The murmurs have fallen silent. Only pain still shows me the way. I've kept the worst stories for last. They pretend to disappear, but I sense them, lurking, shrouded, in the shadows.

I dig my nails into my sick mind and the words come out, thick and yellow.

I've kept the aviary.

Memories and stories mixed together, drunk in with the milk and the tears, flowing in my blood.

I've kept Angela and the man who loved her voice too much.

Memories and stories, flung in the face of that distant woman, deaf to my entreaties, that great absent one who loved me so badly and abandoned me, alone, in a world where nothing awaits me but old sorrows that are not even mine!

May the ghosts that haunt me go back into their darkness, letting me savor the void inside me! May the echoes of bygone whispers fall silent!

And may I die at last like my sister Angela with her excessively round eyes, whose soul was cut to pieces by an idiot in order to chase away an imaginary devil. He silenced her to stop loving her, he forced her to die, then, realizing at last that his struggle was vain and that he was only a man, he threw himself into the dug-up earth and rolled on her corpse.

Since Salvador's mutilated face, Angela had not sung. She listened to the murmur of the multi-colored city, and heard the diversity of languages, the prayers of Jews, Muslims and Christians. She listened, but had not sung since a thorn had lodged in her throat on the other shore and all that blood had flowed through her mouth, flooding the streets of an unknown town, inflaming the souls of poor mute creatures suddenly thrown, thanks to her, into a battle that was bigger than them.

Her song here would have destroyed the city.

Her crow had led her one afternoon to a garden from which issued loud chirping. There were birds living beyond those walls.

As the gates of the property were open, she went in.

In a vast aviary, dozens of birds frolicked, releasing their long musical phrases.

Suddenly, the desire seized her to answer them, to sing too, in spite of the thorn.

Her voice rose, intact. Her crystal voice, flayer of souls.

She had not noticed the people having lunch in the grounds on the other side of the aviary.

The man was there, in that garden, gripped by doubts. It was the first time he had been invited to the table of these important people, and he was eating in silence, hoping that his decorum and good manners would make them forget the poverty of his parish.

They went into raptures over the beauty of the voice that seemed to be coming from the aviary and searched for its source.

Angela was brought before the great table laden with fine

food, crystal and porcelain. Who was she? What was she doing there? Who had let her in without permission? As a penalty, she must sing them a tune.

Disconcerted by the amused faces that contradicted her accusers' reprimands, Angela did as she was told, looking the only man who had said nothing full in the face. Troubled, he bowed his head and stared at his plate, which was decorated with painted birds. But the young singer with the unprepossessing face was there too, amid the carefully skinned chicken bones, she was still there, and singing of love, the jailer.

The guests applauded enthusiastically. A drunk woman, suddenly revolted by this collection of captive little creatures, decided that she absolutely had to open the aviary and release the birds. The master of the house, an elegant old man in a white suit, stopped her as she swayed across the flower beds, trampling them with her boots, and gently brought her back onto the path. There followed a long argument between the inebriated guests about the benefits of captivity, an argument in which the man who was still staring at his plate did not take part.

Putting an end to the quarrel, the crow came to rest on Angela's shoulder and everyone tried to touch it. The host with the silvery hair, a great bird lover, delighted at the thought of adding a new species to his collection, suggested that my sister come and work for him, taking care of this aviary and its musical inhabitants.

She was asked where she lived, in which quarter, and, when she had answered their questions, the host turned to that silent man who still had his nose in his plate. Hadn't she met Father André? A man of God and a great musician. He officiated at Our-Lady of A., in that same quarter, the quarter where so many Spanish immigrants lived. Those miserable wretches who had come in great numbers to this side of the Mediterranean to survive. Angela admitted she had not recognized him. What hypocrisy! How could one not recognize such a handsome man? cried the drunken lady in a burst of laughter.

"So you don't sing in church?" Monsieur D. went on. "It isn't charitable of you to keep such a voice to yourself and not use it to the advantage of God and men! Your tone would go well with the sound of an organ. Do you know any hymns? Never mind, Father André will teach you. On Sunday, we'll all come and hear you."

Angela felt light-hearted as she walked away, and paid no attention to the comments she had aroused, not even those of the lady in the boots who had no hesitation in remarking on the ugliness of their young visitor, her short, heavy figure, her snarl, her coarse features, her huge glassy eyes.

"Don't you think she looks like a hen? How could God choose to hide so much beauty in the throat of such a woman! Like a pearl trapped in a dirty gray oyster!"

"You're exaggerating," retorted Monsieur D. "She isn't ugly. Just a bit common."

"No, she's ugly and God's a practical joker, that's all! He likes to surprise his audience!" She approached the priest. "Isn't that so, father? To condemn a man like you to celibacy! What a waste! Could God be devilishly perverse?"

"Be quiet!" their host cut in. "You're going to scare my young guest away!"

So Angela found herself cast back into singing. And there did not seem to be anything grave or deadly in her voice. The city had not burst into flame.

A new life was beginning. She would spend her days in Monsieur D.'s aviary, taking care of its occupants, answering their trills and, since she was asked to, she would sing in church too, for men, as she used to do in Santavela, in Heredia's olive grove, when the *palmas flamencas* responded to her voice.

The next day, she plunged into the cool little church where the sunlight filtering through the stained glass windows joyfully splashed patches of colored light across the nave. There was nothing solemn about the place. In fact, the church was warmer than its priest. Although Angela had been familiar with it since her arrival on this side of the world, it seemed to her as if she was entering it for the first time.

The choir was rehearsing an *Ave María*. Without interrupting it, Father André motioned to my sister to approach. Unfortunately, he had a musical soul and himself conducted his choir, devoting a lot of time to it. When silence fell, he introduced Angela, whom the choristers all knew, at least by name, then asked her to sing something, so that they could hear how her voice sounded in the house of God. Anything, provided it was not sacrilegious.

The voice sprang up, loud and clear, and penetrated their bodies.

Father André, staring down at the flagstones, heard the thorn vibrating in Angela's throat, he heard that pain. That magnificent pain!

How could you not be fascinated by pain if you were a Christian, when the churches were built on the bones of martyrs, when the catechists took sacrificed children as their model, when the prayers of believers focused on the image of a mother mourning her son dead on the cross? How could you not admire suffering, when God set us an example by sacrificing his son, letting him weep tears of blood and display his stigmata? The crown of thorns, the cross, the redemption of saints: it was necessary to suffer so that the world could stay in balance, to pay so that others could continue to walk.

Yes, for Father André, pain was the spice of life! And now the voice of this little woman was pouring out into his church a pain that filled his body with unprecedented sweetness. His skin vibrated. Angela's singing flayed his flesh, penetrated it, excited his senses. He tried to defend himself, he tried to drown that voice among those of the other choristers, but it stood out so much that it broke the harmony of the choir. Only the organ could follow it.

"You'll sing as a soloist, that's all you're good for!" he concluded curtly before dismissing the gathering.

The following Sunday, Monsieur D., again dressed in a dazzling white suit, came with his friends to hear his young protégée sing.

On the square in front of the church, Clara was waiting, draped in sunlight. She saw the old man, white from head to foot, get out of his elegant carriage, she smiled at him and put her arm through his in the most natural way possible as if he was the very person she had been waiting for. If the old man was surprised, he did not show it and joined in the beautiful stranger's game. Together, they went in through the main door and walked side by side down the central nave. The rich shipowner's friends did not know what to think, they questioned each other in low voices, trying to find out who this new conquest was. Monsieur D. was not usually so secretive.

When they got halfway down the nave, he separated from my sister and let her take her seat on the side where the women sat. He threw her a brief glance, a young man's glance, and saw such great love in the straw-colored eyes staring back at him that he trembled at the thought that this splendid creature might get away from him. Then Angela began to sing and it was as if his feelings were multiplied tenfold. He sat down at the end of a pew, a long way from his friends, so that he could feast his eyes on Clara's exceptional beauty to his heart's content. Stunned by Angela's voice, the worshipers did not notice this burgeoning romance. Even the priest had to restrain his own emotions in order to celebrate mass.

After the blessing, the voice again swept through the church, pouring into everyone's soul a pain so sweet that nobody thought of leaving before it had fallen silent. Nobody, not even Clara, even though she was in a hurry to get back to the light and the man with the silver curls.

Once outside in the sun, Clara led Monsieur D. over to the Carascos, who were waiting on the square in front of the church to congratulate Angela.

Martirio was carrying her first-born in her arms, while, under her skirts, her belly was getting round again. Clara could do whatever she liked from now on, she did not care anymore, she kept her poisonous kisses for her husband. She was only surprised to see her sister becoming infatuated with an old man.

Monsieur D.'s entourage kept their distance, passing nasty comments in low voices.

Angela finally came out with the choristers and the old man was delighted to learn that Clara, who had so stirred his senses, was her sister. He kissed Clara's hand.

"Come and see my aviary whenever you wish," he said. "Your sister knows the way!"

He took his leave of the Carascos, went to congratulate Father André, got in the carriage that was waiting for him, and disappeared.

"Well," Lunes said with a laugh, "your little light has found herself a new beau and this time she hasn't chosen a glazier, but someone living in the lap of luxury! And you, my night, don't go paying anything in your sister's place!"

And we all set off back to our courtyard.

On the way, I held Clara's hand, on which the man in white had planted his kiss.

THE VOICE OF THE DEVIL

It is Sunday.

The church is crowded with mouths filled with a half-melted God. Angela walks slowly to the altar behind the other members of the choir.

From one rehearsal to the next, Father André has tamed her. She bends to his wishes now and takes notice of his criticisms. But her voice, however submissive, overwhelms him more every day. Senses are growing in him, old emotions coming back to the surface, tenderness, kisses . . . As he pulls the strings of this bird-woman, he can feel the knots that hold him tightening around his own neck. He orders, she obeys. And yet he feels possessed by the woman, by the voice, by the pain.

Father André presents the host to Angela. Mechanically, the choirboy holds his little gilded plate right under her chin, to prevent any divine crumb from falling to the ground.

But it is not a crumb that falls. It is God in his entirety who is falling. The priest has let go of Him. His hand has wandered for a moment and brushed against Angela's half-open lips. She has quivered at the touch and God has fallen. In spite of that, the priest's eyes remain fixed too long on the young woman's coarse features, and the congregation, jolted out of its prayer by the choirboy's cry, surprises the priest's lustful glance. For a few seconds the priest's hard mask has fallen, as if in a theatre, and everyone has seen a man in love bedecked in the clothes of the divine.

After the service, tongues loosen, they talk, they whisper,

they mock. She isn't even pretty! The Bible-thumpers are scandalized. Father André looked at that woman in a wholly indecent way!

They even talk of going to mass in another parish to avoid this sacrilegious priest. With great difficulty, Angela makes her way through the dense crowd of gossips, who refuse to move aside for her. The verdict has been announced: this girl has the voice of the devil!

But the very next day, these same gossips jostle one another in front of Father André's confessional. His presumed desire attracts some strange confessions. All these forbidden loves that have been silenced for fear of his judgement are now told in detail. It is the women above all who come to confess their indiscretions. The older women marvel at their old infidelities, their distant desires, and without false modestly, bring those caresses back to the surface. Hot palms wander over their lined skins, their flaccid bellies. A few young girls whisper to him of their lovemaking in the red desert, others even seize the opportunity to make eyes at him between the wooden bars. Behind the words, he notices certain hands playing in the shadows. He hears them all breathing on the other side of the grille. The air coming in and out of their half-open mouths he can see flowing over their moist, pulpy lips. He smells the heavy perfume of their bodies, the bars can no longer contain it . . .

In their stories, there is no trace of repentance. They are describing these contacts in the darkness of the little confessional in order to relive them, not to forget the taste of forbidden love.

Aghast, Father André discovers a whole amorous network in his respectable parish, a web of desire in which he feels caught. He prays in vain. His prayer dries up and the stained-glass virgins themselves smile at him.

"You must disappear behind the pain," the priest demands

curtly. "How dare you put yourself forward like that? What you are bearing is bigger than you. Will you ever be able to stop thinking about your wretched little voice? Will you ever be able to forget yourself?"

"Let me try again."

"Not today. You have wearied us enough with your crooning. I've told you a hundred times, the line, keep to the line."

The following Saturday, as he is getting ready to officiate, Father André notices the languid looks of the worshipers gathered in his church, he deciphers their gestures, loses count of their winks. His new found knowledge of the secrets of their hearts weighs on him.

Suddenly, Angela's voice splits the sky in two, and with slow steps, the sun advances down the central nave.

Clara, who is wearing her second wedding dress, a marvel spangled with silver and mother-of-pearl, approaches the altar on the arm of Anita's husband Juan, now potbellied in his everlasting formal suit. Then comes Monsieur D. As white as his young fiancée, he walks alone amid Angela's song.

Father André gazes at Clara, looking for the source of the light that seems to set her figure ablaze. He finally gives up and accepts his strange visions without looking for their cause. His church is filled with lovers, the sun has come to marry an unnatural old man, while the prettiest voice in the world, issuing from a woman without charm, pierces his senses. Well, let it be, if such is His will!

Angela does not come to take communion, he waits for her, looks for her in vain among the long line of grave faces approaching the altar. He misses the proximity of her lips! Why does she refuse the body of Christ? What sin is she concealing?

"May peace be with you!"

"And also with you!"
"Go in peace!"

If she did not sing, who would notice her? But she does sing! Is she not temptation? Behind that voice, there is the body of a woman who quivers when she succeeds in doing exactly what he asks of her. They communicate through the music. He demands, she obeys. But when you come down to it, who is pulling the strings?

He has learned with time to resist the beauty of women. But he was not wary of such a common face. Does she really have the voice of the devil, as the parishioners say?

It is whispered that her mother was a witch and that all her line is cursed. Soulless people! If the devil is behind this, he'll sniff him out!

"No, it's not working!" storms the priest. "Incapable, you're incapable of singing joy! The elation of the hymn escapes you. Your chest register is much too limited."

"Give this piece to someone else! I can't stand it any more!"

"Can you please stop playing the martyr? Start again. One more time"

Since Clara's wedding, the sun has been rising later and later. The light of the Gambetta courtyard has faded, its centre is empty. Nothing left but a little patch on the ground, the barely visible imprint of the vanished light. Clara is now in her husband's villa and the sky over the city is heavy with shadows.

It is some time now since Angela last saw her young sister in the grounds of the property. Obsessed by her singing, absorbed in her own sorrow, she is not worried and goes to the church to rehearse. The storm is approaching.

The nave is empty. Father André has sent away the other

choristers today, and is waiting for her in the confessionnal. To let her know that he is there, he taps on the skylight. A huge noise.

She kneels in the wooden cubicle. The priest's face is so close, she can hear him breathing. The church seems walled up, even the stained glass windows are mute. Their colors have fallen silent. Father André's own silence is like a question. He has probably lowered his eyes, as he does whenever he listens to her sing, he is probably looking down at his feet!

The crow, perched on a pew, is growing impatient.

What could she say to this man who is looking at his feet? Nothing.

But little by little their breaths mingle.

She would like to sing, but nothing comes, and it is her bird that does so in her place.

The world enters night. Outside, a violent rainshower chills bodies to the bone and the thick shadows drown all joy.

The cawing of the bird invades their privacy. Now they are separated.

"Why do you no longer take communion, my child?" the priest asks at last.

"I'm afraid of your hands."

"What's so terrible about them?"

"They're soft."

"Soft . . . " echoes Father André. "But my daughter, how could the hands of a priest frighten a pure soul?"

"Singing for you upsets me. Perhaps my soul is not so pure?"

"The others say that your voice is witchcraft."

"The others are probably right."

"What do you feel when you sing?"

"Both our presences. I sing only for you now. The rest of the world has collapsed. You listen to me and I know I exist."

"All you can do is pray to fight what is inside you."

"To fight my love?"

"To fight the creature who has made you his instrument!"

"I don't understand."

"You are the enemy! Don't you see that the creature inside you is trying to fool the two of us? His voice is worming its way into my faith, his voice is trying to bewitch me, to lead me from the light."

"But that voice is mine!"

"Have you noticed how dark the sky has suddenly become? The devil is singing through your mouth. He is trying to lead me astray. You must silence him, you must never sing again."

"Then I will cease to exist."

"And he will have lost! If you have no other sins to confess, make an act of contrition! Your penance will be this silence that God imposes on you."

My sister did as she was told, in a monotone voice.

"Be quiet now, my daughter, and take your bird out of here: it has no place in this house of prayer."

A few days later, Angela donned her wedding dress with its huge white armholes, the one our mother had made for her, went to the great aviary in the darkness of early morning, and hanged herself from one of the bars. Her black bird affectionately pecked her eyes out.

Swinging at the end of her rope, in a sky laden with motionless violence, she almost seemed to be flying.

THE LONG NIGHT

In the courtyard, the rumor spread that, some hours after Angela's body had been taken down, a woman in a wedding dress had taken her seat in Father André's confessional. A woman whose voice, it was said, he had immediately recognized. She had found the right words to express her love, then added that he no longer had anything to fear from her body, but that she was leaving him her voice to inhabit his solitude.

Deeply moved, the priest had been unable to pursue the apparition, which had faded in the light from outside. Already, Angela's song was rising in the church, that same sad song that had echoed in him since the first day and was now to haunt him forever.

I was the only one left. The only obstacle between the lovers.

I was as if I was lying across the bed of my eldest sister and her engine driver. The last sister to be married off before their desire for each other, endlessly kindled over the years, could at last satisfy itself with something other than words and stories.

Neither the sun nor Clara had reappeared and the tales in the courtyard became black and darkly humorous. Never before had we known such a winter!

At night, Anita would tell us terrible stories. She said that the Arab maids kept close to the walls every time she went to Monsieur D.'s villa to try to see Clara. She claimed to read a mute dread on their faces. The housekeeper always told her in a curt tone that her young mistress was in no fit state to receive her.

"They're forced to keep silent," she whispered to us in the thick darkness.

In her opinion, the order had been given, and Monsieur D.'s orders could not be questioned. Clara was sick, she needed shade and rest, no light from outside was to disturb her sleep.

The morning after the wedding, the old man apparently demanded that the sun not enter his young bride's room until he decided it could. Everything had been laid out with that purpose in mind and, incapable of enjoying our sister's exceptional beauty, he drew back the heavy curtains increasingly late in the morning, in order to keep her in his power for longer.

"Very soon, he only let weak winter sunlight come in once Clara's meal had been served," Anita's voice told us. "Then he did not wake her again until teatime, when the pale sun already starts to disappear behind the great aviary. Our little light would then rush onto the terrace overlooking the town while the sun, feeling her presence, would extricate itself with difficulty from its straitjacket of clouds and join her for a moment before sinking again."

In the end, the husband stopped waking her at all. Thus he could go about his daily business, smooth his features before his great mirror for hours, send for his tailor, his barber, his many friends without fearing that his wife might take advantage of his distraction to run away. The night seemed to him the most secure of prisons.

Driven mad with love and incapable of satisfying his hunger for her, he had chosen to keep her at his mercy in this way. To do so, it was enough for daylight not to interfere. The sun had turned its back on the city, and it had not been so difficult to guard against it.

Every morning, in the presence of that insomniac, suspicious husband, the maids changed the sheets and washed their unconscious young mistress's barely warm body by candle light. Little by little, they noticed the traces left by the nights. But the soiled sheets, the smell of sweat and semen, the bites and scratches on Clara's body did not alter her perfect smile. As the signs multiplied, they took fright and felt complicit in a horror that was bigger than them.

One night, one of them saw a long line of unknown men standing outside the young woman's bedroom, and they realized then that men were coming at night to take turns in the young bride's bed. Her impotent husband was using other men's sexual organs in an attempt to possess her. But the mystery remained, Clara's beauty was intact, and Monsieur D., unable to fully enjoy this young woman who was his, watched in horror as his own features withered and his body stooped. He tried to love her and each new failure weakened him, made him sicker, more powerless, more cruel. Increasingly large numbers of men had to wait their turn in the corridors to slip into that luminous body. And, as the little light was offered in this way, the sun outside lost its strength and the husband grew ever more somber.

At this point, Anita smiled slightly, and for a moment her audience held their breaths before she resumed the thread of her story.

It took only one shaft of light to revive Clara, who had been asleep for a week. A ray exhausted by its journey through the long dark corridors managed one day—thanks to the concerted blunders of the army of Arab chambermaids—to caress Clara's face. Several half-open doors had let it reach their mistress. It had sensed her presence and, tenderly, had lain down on her pale cheek. The ray revived the brightness of her complexion, tickled her eyelids. Then, without even noticing either her weakness or the disorder of her bed, Clara wrapped herself in a brightly colored blanket and, using the walls for support, dragged herself to the terrace, where the maids had left her a platter laden with honey cakes and hot milk.

As she ate slowly in the light of day, licking the honey that trickled down her fingers, the dying sun managed to send out a single ray over the streets of the city. It illumined the silver dagger a majestic Arab passer-by was carrying at his side. Clara leaned so far over to follow the doings of this man, selected by the sun, that she almost fell out. He was wearing the traditional costume of a young tribal chief, a heavy red woolen *burnous*. He finally looked up, and although, in accordance with Saharan custom, the bottom half of his face was covered in a white *cheche*, Clara could tell from his keen eyes that he was smiling at her. She immediately responded to this smile without restraint.

The man ordered one of his Sudanese servants to find out what he could about the *roumia* who lived in that house. Monsieur D.'s maids, knowing who his master was, told him the astonishing story of how the poor woman was being held captive and what her husband made her endure while she slept.

The young sheikh decided to abduct this child of the sun.

That very night, he was admitted to Monsieur D.'s villa. The whispering of the maids and the swish of their slippers on the marble guided him to my sister's apartments, where her husband was sitting in an armchair, looking down anxiously at the brown marks of time on his manicured hands.

The young man plunged his dagger into the love-weary husband's white suit, and all his old age was gone.

ANITA'S HONEYMOON

For some time after Clara's abduction, I harbored the secret hope of inheriting her third wedding dress. I even attempted to try it on surreptitiously. But, incapable of arranging that strange Mozabite-influenced garment and not knowing how to fix the openwork brooches on the peplum and the white woolen *ksa*, I had to give up.

A woman wrapped in a uniformly white *haouli* from which only a black eye emerged came one evening to demand that last nuptial adornment of us. Our little light, who now lived in the far south of the world, facing the immensity of the Sahara, was determined to wear it on the sixth day of her wedding celebrations.

After the messenger had left, I fell back on my black shawl, wrapped in my destiny.

In the courtyard, we were no longer to be associated with. Out of bravado, Lunes would mock the old women who had greeted him so badly that first evening, and his sons were the worst rascals who had ever trodden the earth, being suspected of throwing stones at the windows to give their father more work. But my nephews' behavior was doubtless the least of the reproaches they could make of us. The neighbors had associated us with the devil since a sudden sandstorm had saved Clara's strange beauty from the flames. Angela's suicide, Father André's madness and the deaths of our little light's first two husbands had merely confirmed their suspicions. The heirs of the dressmaker who had been unstitched by death were no longer loved, they were even feared.

The neighbors' children had to hide to hear the stories endlessly repeated and reinvented by Anita. Their mothers forbade them to enjoy what they called our tissue of lies.

It was autumn.

The sound of torn fabric marked the end of the stories.

My sister had heard me.

"Anita, I want to stay unmarried," I had whispered to her in the wash house. "You don't have to wait anymore for the last of your sisters to marry. Go, make your own children! My mother called me solitude, and I want to live up to the name. I free you from your promise. I will never marry."

That very night, just before my beauty faded, Martirio and her children waited in vain for Anita to tell her stories.

In the courtyard, in the night, only cries of pleasure echoed, the screams of an extraordinary love in which words no longer had a place.

Embarrassed, the neighbors all took their chairs inside. Even though it was a cool night, nobody come out to take the air.

In silence, Anita had stroked Juan's hand and drawn him into the absolute darkness of their bridal chamber, which had been deserted for fifteen years.

EPILOGUE

How long have I been retracing my steps, winding back the thread of time in order to find the traces left by my mother thirty years ago in the sand of this country?

I do not know where my legs will take me, and it seems to me that the box I am carrying is whispering to me in the dazzling solitude of the desert.

I stole nothing from my niece but a promised sorrow. The box will remain in the desert, I will not give it to her at Easter as tradition requires. It will no longer be passed from hand to hand. Its journey stops here, at my feet, in the absurd immensity of this white expanse. This incoherent book in which lie the dreamed fragments of our lives I am giving back, page by page, to the wind from which it came . . .

My pages fly away one by one . . .

I have nothing left to do now but waste the last of the prayers from the third night. Then the dead will rise for the last time before returning forever to oblivion, and the thread will be cut.

And now, through my prayer, the voice of mothers rises:

My name is Frasquita Carasco. My soul is a needle. Here are the sheets of paper you cast into the desert, bound together in a book that you will be able to close forever on my story.

Soledad, my daughter, feel this wind on your face.

It is my kiss.

The kiss I never gave you.

ABOUT THE AUTHOR

Carole Martinez teaches French at a middle school in Issy-les-Moulineaux. She began writing during her maternity leave in 2005. *The Threads of the Heart* is her debut novel.